OUR KIND OF GAME

OUR KIND OF GAME

A NOVEL

JOHANNA COPELAND

HARPER PERENNIAL

NEW YORK • LONDON • TORONTO • SYDNEY • NEW DELHI • AUCKLAND

HARPER ● PERENNIAL

This is a work of fiction. Names, characters, places, and incidents are products of the author's imagination or are used fictitiously and are not to be construed as real. Any resemblance to actual events, locales, organizations, or persons, living or dead, is entirely coincidental.

A hardcover edition of this book was published in 2024 by Harper, an imprint of HarperCollins Publishers.

OUR KIND OF GAME. Copyright © 2024 by Johanna Garth. All rights reserved. Printed in the United States of America. No part of this book may be used or reproduced in any manner whatsoever without written permission except in the case of brief quotations embodied in critical articles and reviews. For information, address HarperCollins Publishers, 195 Broadway, New York, NY 10007.

HarperCollins books may be purchased for educational, business, or sales promotional use. For information, please email the Special Markets Department at SPsales@harpercollins.com.

FIRST HARPER PERENNIAL EDITION PUBLISHED 2025.

Designed by Nancy Singer

Library of Congress Cataloging-in-Publication Data has been applied for.

ISBN 978-0-06-332972-0 (pbk.)

25 26 27 28 29 LBC 5 4 3 2 1

Praise for *Our Kind of Game*

"A rager of a psychological mystery about toxic men, murderous women, and the art of constructing fake realities . . . as audacious as it is intricately plotted."

—*New York Times*

"With expertly timed reveals and plenty of thorny insights into the causes and consequences of gender-based violence, this first-rate suspense novel thrills and provokes in equal measure. It's a must-read."

—*Publishers Weekly* (starred review)

"A riveting and suspenseful debut. Copeland's contemporary take on the balance of power in relationships, and the desire for control, is not to be missed."

—Karin Slaughter, *New York Times* and #1 international bestselling author

"With elaborate plotting, richly drawn characters, and razor-sharp social commentary with a fresh take on the perils of being a woman, *Our Kind of Game* is a wholly engrossing and darkly mesmerizing suspense! I couldn't put it down!"

—May Cobb, author of *A Likeable Woman*

"If the brains behind *Ginny & Georgia* and *The Feminine Mystique* had a baby, she would look a whole lot like Johanna Copeland's *Our Kind of Game*. Copeland explores the many ways marriage, motherhood, and generational trauma shape women via a wild vigilante fantasy that will keep readers guessing until the incredible, jaw-dropping end."

—Colleen McKeegan, author of *The Wild One*

"Johanna Copeland's *Our Kind of Game* is at the same time a dark, compelling thriller and a nuanced examination of the roots of female rage. Stella Parker's life may look perfect from the outside, but Copeland deftly reveals the hollowness of suburban privilege even as Stella faces how far she might have to go to save her family. Most of all, this novel is a daring and perceptive look at motherhood and caregiving: its anxiety, its loneliness, and its fierce and savage strength."
—Polly Stewart, author of *The Good Ones*

"*Our Kind of Game* is a twisted romp through the perils and pleasures of privilege. From the confines of a defanged suburbia, Stella Parker starts to see cracks in her lacquered life, hints of the childhood she outran. Getting to safety this time may require blowing the whole thing up. Because when the past comes calling, it isn't always neighborly."
—Jenny Milchman, *USA Today* bestselling author of *Cover of Snow* and *The Usual Silence*

For my father, who taught me the importance of a good story and inspired me to tell my own.

PART ONE

One

FALL

STELLA

Stella Parker loves hot summer nights. The warm embrace of them. The feel of the air against her body and the earthy smell of humidity. It's a visceral response, one that's almost embarrassing. Like a vice one doesn't mention in polite company.

When she first came to McLean, these languid nights were a revelation. She hadn't realized they existed outside the world of fiction. A night like this in early fall feels like an impossibility, much like her own privileged life.

Stella hugs her knees, still golden-brown from the summer sun, close to her chest. She makes herself small on the slate steps as though she could disappear into the night. Behind her, the house looms, sprawling up and out. It's always been too big for their family, but Tom rationalized the purchase based on the large backyard.

"The kids need to be able to play outside, Stella," he'd said.

She hadn't argued.

"Besides, look at this kitchen. It's perfect for entertaining." He'd smiled at their polished blonde real estate agent as he wrapped his arm around Stella's shoulders and squeezed.

The version of Stella that Tom saw, the one that can be easily swayed by a kitchen built for entertaining, doesn't quite match reality. The actual Stella doesn't like to throw dinner parties. Or any kind of parties, if she's being completely honest.

She doesn't mind that he got that wrong. She wants him to believe in that version of her. If Tom believes it, it means she's successfully excised the parts of her that aren't fit for public consumption. Stella tells herself that everyone has secrets.

If you tell the same story often enough, eventually it becomes the truth.

Except sometimes the past breaks into the present. Nights like these, when Tom and the kids are out and Stella is left to her own devices. These are the nights when she rejects the comfort of air-conditioning and television for sticky warmth and things that creep through the night. The heavy darkness draws out raccoons, blood-hungry mosquitos, the neighborhood fox that stares at her without fear, and, of course, Stella herself.

When her phone buzzes, Stella feels a flash of annoyance. She looks at it, all lit up on the flagstone. Her electronic monitor.

Does her deep-seated desire to, once in a while, be left completely alone make her a bad mother?

She sighs. A desperate sound, barely audible over the cicadas. It's already late September. There won't be many more nights like this. What she wants is to be uninterrupted.

Her phone buzzes again, and Stella does a quick calculation.

It's not Colin, because he's at his baseball tournament. Daisy is at a sleepover, but she's been there only an hour. It's too soon for the kind of drama Stella associates with Daisy sleepovers. That leaves Tom. He has a work dinner tonight, and Stella isn't expecting him home until late. She told Tom she was going out with friends from her book group. The women who think she's one of them.

They're all graduates of impressive universities. In theory, the conversation that takes place with her book group should be incisive and thoughtful. Instead, it focuses obsessively on SAT/ACT prep, college visits, recruiting for field hockey (which everyone refers to as fockey, a word that makes Stella cringe), and the purchase and subsequent renovation of second homes.

This is why Stella canceled at the last minute. She couldn't face two hours of that kind of conversation paired with half-eaten salads. They meet at a restaurant where it goes, almost, without saying that everyone will order a salad, then eat only half. Still, Stella is a member of this book club because Lorraine started it. Not everyone is invited to be part of Lorraine's book club.

Lorraine Loomis is Stella Parker's best friend. To be clear, by "best friend," Stella means Lorraine is the person she sees the most, apart from Tom and the kids. She does not mean Lorraine is the person with whom she shares her darkest secrets and fears.

Lorraine enjoys dividing people into baskets.

"There are two kinds of moms in McLean," she once told Stella while they were drinking white wine in Lorraine's backyard. "The gorgeous ones and the smart ones."

Stella, who had already been a stay-at-home mom for a decade, knew which basket Lorraine had placed her in, which is why she didn't take the bait. Instead, she'd smiled, smoothed her highlighted hair, and said, "You're too funny, Lorraine," in a way that implied exactly the opposite.

Despite Lorraine's proclamations, Stella knows there's only one word that describes the moms in this town.

Rich.

Her phone buzzes again, and Stella glares at it. Probably Daisy. She rolls her eyes in the dark. Whatever minor discomfort Daisy's texting her about is something she could solve on her own. It's important to learn problem-solving skills in childhood. And yet Stella always errs on the side of helping too much. Tom, well, somehow Tom is exempt from the twenty-four-hour child concierge service that Stella is supposed to provide.

She's not sure how that happened.

One minute, they were both lawyers, then Stella was not.

It made sense for Stella to stay home with the kids. Her last job before she stopped practicing law was with a boutique law firm that paid less than the cost of daycare or a full-time nanny. The childcare benefited them both, but as Tom pointed out, if Stella stayed home, they could funnel the money they would have spent on it into a college savings account. It was hard to argue with that logic.

"Kids need consistency," he'd said, cradling tiny Daisy in his arms with a tenderness that made her fall in love with him all over again. He'd just made partner and traveled constantly. The obvious choice for provider of consistency was her.

Besides, she liked the idea of being home with Colin and Daisy.

Though "like" is perhaps too strong a word.

She'd been exhausted by trying to balance work and motherhood. The option of doing just one job felt like an escape hatch. Like she'd been underwater breathing through a stir straw and someone had offered her an oxygen mask. The inequity of Tom not feeling similarly exhausted by trying to achieve his own balance hadn't occurred to her. Perhaps it was the oxygen deprivation, or the fact she hadn't slept in months.

She wasn't at her most rational.

When her phone starts to ring, Stella relents. She picks it up expecting to see Daisy's name, but Tom is the one calling. With a twinge of guilt, she sets the phone back down on the step. He'll assume she's in a crowded restaurant with her friends and didn't hear it.

She knows Tom is busy. She knows he can't always answer the phone when she or the kids call, but she also knows he gets to ignore his phone because Stella doesn't ignore hers. And the truth is, she doesn't resent the evenings when he's entertaining clients. Hours at a time when he never bothers to look at his phone. What she resents—no, covets—is his freedom. The knowledge that he doesn't *have* to look at his phone. If something urgent has happened, he knows Stella will handle it. Stella will be the fixer of problems, 100 percent of the time.

Last week, she'd had a biopsy. Nothing big, just a routine procedure after an abnormal Pap. When the school called, Stella was on the table. Feet up in those sock-covered metal stirrups, her ob-gyn probing her insides.

"We've been trying to reach someone all morning," the guidance counselor said, without asking whether this was a good time. "Daisy made a very concerning statement in her third block."

"You know—" Stella said, but the guidance counselor was on a roll.

Daisy had been overheard whispering "Kill me now," and given the rising rates of teen suicide, the third-block teacher wanted Daisy to speak to a counselor. Obviously they needed parental authorization to proceed.

"Yes, of course. And I'll talk with her tonight," Stella said, refusing to allow even a hint of pain into her voice as her doctor razored off a piece of her uterus.

The biopsy was fine, but Stella was not.

"They said they tried to call you. Multiple times," she told Tom when he got home. She was still seething with the indignity of it all.

"Look, you didn't have to take the call. Nothing would have happened if you hadn't picked up."

"It was the school. What if it had been an emergency?"

Tom shook his head and kissed her on the top of hers.

"They're teenagers, Stell. When we were teenagers, no one had constant access to our parents. Don't worry so much. They'll be fine."

She let it go. After nineteen years of marriage, she knows Tom truly believes this philosophy. He doesn't understand that sometimes things don't work out. He's never seen how quickly life can take a turn down a dark and narrow alley. When she met Tom, he reminded her of a glass of filtered water, pure and clean. She liked him that way. Even more, she liked that Tom thought of her the same way.

Stella spots a car moving slowly down their quiet street. A dark luxury SUV, almost indistinguishable from the one sitting in Stella's garage. It would be completely unremarkable in this neighborhood except its headlights are off.

The SUV slows, then pulls into Stella's driveway. Stella scrambles to her feet, phone in hand like a weapon. The driver's side door of the SUV flies open and a woman stumbles out. Instinct makes Stella press herself back into the darkness, but the next moment, she steps forward. She recognizes the woman.

It's her neighbor. Gwen Thompson.

Her first nonsensical thought is that Gwen has stopped by early to collect the auction basket Stella promised she'd drop off tomorrow.

"Gwen, hey," Stella says.

She feels ridiculous. Both about the blood pounding in her ears, an exaggerated reaction to non-danger, and about being caught skulking around outside in the dark.

"Stella?" Gwen stops, then looks around like she's confused. She's clutching a small Lilly Pulitzer bag embroidered with palm trees. The same kind that was on Daisy's birthday wish list two years ago, Stella notes.

Something's wrong. Stella feels it in her stomach. Once you acquire an instinct for danger, you can't shake it.

"Do you want to come in?"

They both glance at the front door.

"I'm..." Gwen lets the single word hang between them, which gives Stella time to notice that Gwen appears to be limping. That she's hiding one side of her face behind her hair.

"Are you..." Stella hesitates, then rewords the question. "Is everything okay?"

"Fine. I'm fine. It's okay." There's a slurred thickness to Gwen's words.

Stella takes a step closer, moving toward Gwen through the dark. The motion-sensor light that's supposed to illuminate the front walkway has gone out. She glances up at it, then back at Gwen.

"I'm fine," Gwen repeats, as though Stella is arguing with her. She sinks down on the stone step that Stella just vacated.

"I could make you some coffee," Stella offers.

Gwen laughs, but there's no amusement in the sound. "Funny how things come full circle."

The look she gives Stella is accusing, but Stella chalks it up to the alcohol, or whatever substance has thickened Gwen's speech. Still, something about the moment gives Stella an intense feeling of déjà vu.

"Let me drive you home," Stella says.

"Yeah." Gwen nods. "I probably shouldn't be driving."

She stands, and Stella follows Gwen to her car. It's a short drive. Three blocks.

"Leave it in the driveway," Gwen directs.

"Are you sure you're okay?" Stella asks, handing Gwen her keys.

Gwen nods. She's already getting out of the car, which means Stella has to follow suit.

"Love the pictures you post on Insta. You really have the perfect family," Gwen says.

"Thanks," Stella says, but before she can formulate another question, Gwen limps away toward her front door.

She's limping. There's no other word for it.

"Gwen," Stella calls, but Gwen either doesn't hear her or chooses to ignore her. She slams the front door, leaving Stella alone in the night.

Stella turns and walks the three blocks home to her too-big house. When she gets to the front walk, she spots something on the steps. Upon closer inspection, she recognizes it.

Gwen's Lilly Pulitzer bag.

She picks it up, then sits back down on the steps and pulls her phone out of her pocket. Scrolling through her contacts, she finds Gwen's number.

Hey, she writes. Just wanted to make sure you're okay. Btw, you forgot your bag. I can drop it off tomorrow.

She hits send, picks up the bag, and climbs the steps to the front door. Stella has had enough brooding darkness. As she opens the door, she hears the familiar buzz of a text. She glances at her phone, expecting a message from Gwen, but her phone is blank.

Stella sets down the bag, locks the front door, then jumps when she hears the buzz of another text. She glances at her phone again, but it's still blank.

Slowly, as though she already knows what she'll find, she picks up the Lilly Pulitzer bag. Inside, Gwen's phone is lit up with a text from Stella Parker.

But underneath that text, there's another one. The sender's name is a jumble of letters. SJIUYVP, like a bad hand of Scrabble.

Quick thinking! it reads.

But whatever Gwen was quick at thinking about is unclear, because the previous message has been deleted.

Two

SPRING 1987

JULIE

When the cheer coach tells us there's no funding for the freshman team, all the other eighth-grade girls look like dogs that got kicked real hard. I probably do too. This is a football town. Our high school's team goes to state every year. They've won three out of the last five years and are untouchable. Cheerleading is supposed to be part of that. But it turns out new football uniforms mean trading away freshman cheer.

Some of the girls leave, wiping away tears.

Others, like Ginny Schaeffer, the most popular girl in our class, take it better. Her eyes flick dismissively over to the girls who give up right away.

Losers.

You can almost hear her saying it in her head.

Cheer tryouts last a week. Every day after school, we cross the street from the middle school and meet in the high school gym. The girls on varsity teach us the routine. Today is the first day, and already our odds have narrowed. No freshman team means we have to compete for spots on JV against girls who already have a year of practice.

"It's not impossible," the coach tells us before she turns practice over to the captain of varsity.

Deanna McAdams has an infectious smile and wears her hair cut short so you notice her big eyes. You have to be confident to wear your hair like that. She's the kind of person everyone likes, including me.

What I don't like is Deanna's dance routine. It's long and complicated. After the ninth eight-count, even Ginny starts to mix up the moves.

More girls walk out, shoulders slumped in defeat.

Deanna teaches us another eight-count.

"This is impossible. I'm going to the bathroom," Ginny announces loudly.

As she walks by me, I see tears welling up in her eyes. Megan, her older sister, reaches out and squeezes Ginny's hand as she passes.

I already know Ginny is going to make the team. Megan knows the counts and will make sure her younger sister knows them too.

Re-creating the dance routine is key, but based on today's practice, I'm already failing.

You have to memorize the moves, then polish them at home until they shine. That's why they teach it on the first day. If you don't get the routine down, you don't make the team.

Instead of marking the counts with the other girls, I dig in my backpack for my notebook and a pencil and sit, sweaty back pressed against the concrete wall of the gym. As Deanna performs the routine again, I scribble down stick figures and notes.

After Deanna finishes, we break for water. I'm double-checking my notes when I feel someone standing over me. Megan is studying me with an unfriendly gaze. She and Ginny have the same blonde hair and wide blue-green eyes, but that's where the resemblance stops. Ginny is more petite. Not as small as me, but definitely smaller than Megan. Megan's probably got five inches on Ginny. Six on me.

"You should really show more spirit. Livingston cheerleaders don't sit around on the sidelines." Megan gives me a hard smile.

"I have cramps," I lie.

"You're an eighth grader, right? Do you know my sister, Ginny?"

"Yeah."

"That's weird. I don't remember her ever mentioning you. What's your name?"

"Julie."

She studies me, taking in my reddish-brown hair and hazel eyes. Body more like a kid's than a teenager's. Her eyes flick over my notes.

"Those won't help you." When she leans over me, I can smell the

Juicy Fruit gum on her breath. Her ample cleavage, encased in a lacy bra, is on full display.

"I don't know if you know this, Julie," she says, lowering her voice like she's telling me a secret, "but part of making the team is based on what they see in tryouts. So based on *this* whole thing"—she gestures at my notes like they're the strangest thing she's ever seen—"my guess is you're already a cut."

"Your sister went to the bathroom," I say.

"Not. The. Same." She rolls her eyes.

When she flounces back to her group of friends, they form a tight knot around her. The knot erupts with laughter after Megan glances back at me.

I wish Paula was still here. If Paula was here, those girls wouldn't mess with me. But Paula left two years ago, almost five years after Dad moved on. I miss Paula a lot.

Deanna claps her hands for everyone's attention, then we run through the routine four more times. I have every move in my notes. Megan doesn't have the second half of the routine down, and Ginny never comes back from the bathroom.

After practice, I wait outside for Kevin to pick me up. If I could, I'd avoid the looks Megan and her friends give me by hiding in the bathroom, but I can't. If Kevin comes and I'm not outside, he won't wait around. We live fifteen miles out of town, so it's not like I can walk.

Some of the varsity girls have cars and leave right away. Other girls have parents who pick them up on time. When Kevin finally pulls up in his old blue truck with the bed that's rusted out in places, I'm the only one left waiting. The back of his truck is filled with the tools he uses for his job as an HVAC tech. Best I can tell, he's a glorified handyman, although I know better than to say that. Mom and Kevin started dating in early spring, and he's lasted longer than I thought he would. Like Mom's other boyfriends, he comes from somewhere else and doesn't talk too much about his past.

He honks like he doesn't see me running toward the truck.

"Hey," I say as I get in. I put on my nicest smile so he won't accuse me of being sullen or having an attitude. Depending on Kevin's mood, I'm spoiled, ungrateful, or full of myself.

"Hey, Julie," he says and gives me a sour look.

I pretend not to notice. "How are you? How was your day?"

He grunts an unintelligible response, then speeds out of the high school parking lot, tires screeching.

"Your mom wants cigarettes," he says, pulling into a gas station on the way out of town.

"Okay."

"So go on in and get them. Jesus." Kevin rolls his eyes like I'm stupid.

"I don't—I don't have any money."

He sighs and makes a huge production out of giving me ten dollars. This is the highlight of the drive home for Kevin. He enjoys making me feel stupid. Also, he likes it when I have to ask him for things.

"You can get yourself a snack," he says, "but I expect the change."

"Thank you so much, Kevin."

I make my voice sweet and smile. This is another part of the game I have to play with Kevin. Manners, my facial expressions, whether I comport myself properly in the world according to him—all those things form the complicated chart he uses to evaluate and shame me. I try not to give him any ammunition, but sometimes I fail.

The first time Mom brought Kevin home, I thought he was good-looking. Tall, dark, and handsome with the kind of skin that tans easy in the summer. He has dark brown eyes and a grin that turns sharp and mean when he's provoked. Of course, it took a while before he showed us the mean grin. When I look at him now, I barely remember how I used to think he was handsome. All I see is the sneer at the corner of his mouth and the hardness that lurks under the surface of his eyes.

"One pack of Camel lights, please," I say to the gas station attendant.

As he pulls the cigarettes off the shelf, I glance out at the truck and the shiny pink of my notebook catches the sun. I didn't put it in my backpack, and now Kevin is paging through it. I should have known better. The grunt told me everything I need to know about his mood.

"And these too," I say, grabbing a package of Slim Jims.

The clerk rings them both up without comment and gives me my change.

"Took you long enough," Kevin says when I get back in the truck.

I don't say anything. At this point, it's like one of those cop shows on TV. Anything I say can be used against me.

"By the way, Julie. What the fuck is this?" He shoves my notebook across the seat of the truck like it's evidence of a crime.

"It's for the dance routine we have to learn."

Every part of me wants to grab my notebook and tuck it in my backpack, but I leave it open on the seat between us. The moment Kevin realizes I need those notes is the same moment he'll destroy them.

He doesn't say anything, so I keep talking. "They made us write it all down like we're too dumb to remember." I roll my eyes and give him a little half smile. "Hey, I wasn't hungry, so I got you something instead."

I slide the package of Slim Jims over to him, along with his change. It's like offering steak to an angry dog.

"That's sweet of you, Juliebell," he says, scooping up my offerings.

Juliebell, that's what he calls me when I've done everything right.

He starts the truck, and as we pull away, he becomes talkative.

"Back in my day, cheerleaders were dumb sluts who didn't know how to keep their legs closed. Bunch of stuck-up bitches who only talked to the guys on the football team. I heard they ain't gonna have a freshman cheer team this year, so you probably won't make it. Just as well. All those girls would be jealous of you. Still, who knows. Maybe you'll show 'em, right, Juliebell?"

This is Kevin's version of a pep talk, given between bites of his Slim Jim.

"You sure you're not hungry?" he asks, shoving the thin piece of meat in front of my face. "Go on, take a bite."

This is not an offer. It's an order.

The end of his Slim Jim is softly chewed and makes my stomach turn, but saying no thanks will be proof that I'm stuck-up and ungrateful. I open my mouth, and Kevin inserts the Slim Jim.

He watches as I attempt to bite off the smallest piece possible.

"You look just like your mom right now," he says with a chuckle. "I guess it's true what they say. Apple don't fall far from the tree."

Do I know what he's implying?

Absolutely.

Do I let on that I know?

I do not.

Instead, I smile sweetly and think about how happy I'll be when Mom decides it's time for Kevin to move on.

Three

FALL

STELLA

Tom's pitch for their too-big house was its history. How this house pre-existed the others. Before their neighborhood was filled with sprawling McMansions built on too-small lots, houses that squeeze against the edges of their space, reminding Stella of someone in pants two sizes too small, it was filled with modest brick split-levels. But sitting at the end of their street on a triple lot was an old house, spacious and welcoming with mature trees and a wide yard.

When they moved in, the backyard was a wasteland of weedy grass that sloped down to a stream that runs along the border of their property. After Colin and Daisy started to walk, Stella took on the garden. Working outside, weeding and pruning, allowed her to keep an eye on her toddlers while simultaneously giving them space to grow. She encouraged them to explore and create their own imaginary games, intervening only when necessary, with gentle words designed to shape them into the kind of thoughtful people she was determined they'd become.

Stella located her vegetable garden in the sunniest part of the backyard, which happens to be at the edge of the property line. It was from this vantage point that she first spied the window upstairs. Stella was weeding lettuces when she was interrupted by a phone call about volunteering for an upcoming field trip. As she talked, she gazed up and spotted an extra pane of glass. When she got off the call, she recounted the number of windows upstairs.

There was one too many.

Later, while the children were doing homework and before Tom came home from work, she counted again. Six windows on the second floor that looked out over the backyard. Outside, from her garden, there were seven. The seventh was visible only when she was kneeling at the very bottom of the yard. As she stood up, it disappeared behind the roofline.

In the week following that discovery, she spent her free time, tens of uninterrupted minutes, prowling the upstairs of her home. Pushing and knocking at the back of the deep hall cabinets and studying the floor plan they'd received when they bought the house. That mysterious seventh window was the kind of thing she should have mentioned to her family, but she didn't, because no one asked about her days.

Now Stella wonders if that first secret of omission was a step toward others. Like the way she's already preparing not to tell Tom about her strange encounter with Gwen.

"Stella? Honey?" Tom's voice carries from the kitchen to where Stella stands in the entryway.

"Hey, you're home."

She drops Gwen's Lilly Pulitzer bag into one of the bins in the entryway designed to hold shoes. Then she places her own shoes on top of it and joins her husband.

"How was the work dinner?" she asks as he rummages in the fridge for leftovers.

"Long. Boring. Mediocre food."

"Wow, too bad I couldn't be there."

He smiles at her. "If you'd been there, it would have been less long and less boring, and the food would have tasted better. How was your evening?"

"We actually talked about the book."

"At book club? Groundbreaking!"

He grins at her. Still the handsome lawyer she met when she was three years out of law school. His sandy blonde hair is now highlighted with gray and his face has more lines, but his eyes are the same warm brown. His long runs have helped him avoid the middle-age spread she's noticed on other dads.

Of course, it wouldn't matter if Tom gained weight. The only extra pounds frowned upon would be those gained by Stella.

"Daisy and Colin get off all right?"

"I haven't heard from either one of them."

"No news is good news," Tom says, eating enchiladas straight from the glass container where Stella has stored them. "I'm exhausted. Think I'll head upstairs."

"I'll be up in a minute. I'm just going to put the clothes in the dryer."

"It can't wait until morning?"

She makes a face. "They get musty if you leave them in the washing machine."

He nods, yawns, and turns toward the stairs, leaving the container of enchiladas open on the counter.

As Stella reseals the lid and puts the food back in the refrigerator, she wonders what would have happened if she'd told Tom she'd skipped book club and explained the unsettling encounter with Gwen, her limp and hunched-over posture. His brow would furrow with worry. She can almost hear him say, "I'll reach out to Dave and see if everything's okay. It's the least we can do."

Instinct, the kind learned in childhood and allowed to go dormant, resurfaces.

So instead, she waits until she hears Tom moving around upstairs, then returns to the entryway and retrieves Gwen's Lilly Pulitzer bag.

She'll keep the odd encounter with Gwen a secret, at least for now.

It took Stella months to solve the mystery of the seventh window, and even then it happened by chance. She was in the basement laundry room, the only part of the house that, other than the addition of new plumbing, has remained untouched since the house's construction.

There's a long, narrow closet next to the washing machine, designed for brooms, mops, and ironing boards. She rarely touches those items, which still catches her by surprise. In her current life, Stella has an efficient service that cleans her home. Her own efforts are sporadic. The sudden urge to empty and wipe out the snack drawer. Five minutes sweeping leaves off the front porch.

Sometimes Stella doesn't recognize herself.

She still does laundry, though. There's something meditative about bearing witness to the bounty that fills her children's closets. She was folding clothes when she accidentally knocked the seltzer water she likes to drink off the top of the dryer. Cursing at her own carelessness, she grabbed the mop. When she was done cleaning up her mess, she shoved the mop back in the closet at an odd angle. The door bounced back open and hit Stella on the knee, eliciting a word she would never use in front of her children.

When the throbbing faded, she tried to close the door again, but the back of the closet was broken. Then she realized what she was seeing, and her stomach filled with tingles of anticipation.

It wasn't broken.

A door had opened.

Beyond it was a narrow wooden stairwell. She crept up the stairs, a cat burglar in her own home, thinking of lions, witches, and wardrobes. Also wondering how this secret staircase had escaped discovery for so long.

At the top of the stairs, Stella found the window. Light flooded into a small room, approximately the same size as her walk-in closet. The room was furnished with a filing cabinet, a desk, and a chair. On the ceiling was a fluorescent light with a string. Stella tugged at it and found it still worked. As she wiped dust off the furniture, she decided this room would be her secret.

Now, Lilly Pulitzer bag in hand, Stella runs down to the basement. She transfers wet laundry to the dryer and turns it on. Then she unlatches the door to tiptoe up her secret staircase, emerging into the only space that is truly hers.

It's a space where she can read a book or stalk her children's social media accounts without the risk of being caught. It's also a space where she can think about the past. A place where her eyes can fill with tears without the need to reassure the rest of her family that she's fine. Better than fine. Her life contains more than she could have ever imagined. Even so, she still needs moments to herself.

The kids have their bedrooms.

Tom has an office, both here and in the city, where he can close the door. Everyone knocks before they come in, even Stella.

Technically, she has her own space: a built-in desk off the kitchen in the family room. Mostly, she uses it to pay bills. Or if she's feeling blue, she'll open up Colin and Daisy's swollen college savings accounts for reassurance that she's made the right choices. Still, no one would call her desk private. It's a space with no doors or walls. There's no way to immerse herself in any kind of project without the potential interruption of Colin, Daisy, or Tom. All three of whom take turns parking themselves on the chair nearby and venting about whatever is on their mind at any given moment.

Stella doesn't mind. In fact, she loves being the person they seek out, the person who exists at the heart of their family. But it hasn't escaped her attention how these conversations gobble up her spare time. Her family flows through her space as though she's a hoop, specifically designed for people to bounce their ideas through.

Another thing that has not escaped her attention: This is a one-way activity. They'll listen to her talk for a moment, then they'll disappear behind those doors they all have. The door she didn't have, until she discovered the one at the back of the laundry room closet.

At first, Stella thought the filing cabinet was empty, but upon careful inspection she discovered a single piece of paper that had slipped behind one drawer.

This page, formatted like a memo and labeled "Intelligence Information," with a brief preliminary summary of interactions using the code name of a well-known Russian defector, gave Stella a fairly good idea of how this room came to exist. Research, which is something she excels at, revealed that two owners ago, the house belonged to someone who listed their place of employment as "State Department."

Code for the CIA. Makes sense. CIA headquarters are less than a mile from their home. The room was installed with flawless design. Almost invisible, unless you happened to be kneeling at the edge of the yard and a glint of light from the window caught your eye.

In her secret room, truly alone, Stella sets the Lilly Pulitzer bag on the card table and inspects Gwen's forgotten phone.

Quick thinking.

Something about the message makes Stella's spine prickle. SJIUYVP is a saved contact, random letters clearly meant to hide their identity. Very cloak-and-dagger of Gwen, but what about her limp? The possible bruises on her face.

The obvious answer is that Dave is hitting his wife.

Stella comes back to the feeling of déjà vu. Something about Gwen's face in the dark felt . . . she searches for the word.

Familiar?

That expression of barely concealed contempt. Gwen wasn't here for Stella's help. Actually, as Stella parses their encounter, she's not sure why Gwen was here at all. Stella and Gwen are not close.

They're neighbors, but their children aren't the same ages, so their interactions are limited. No shared sports teams or carpools. Tom knows Dave because the boys were in the same Scout troop for a hot minute.

You really have the perfect family.

Gwen's tone felt almost mocking. Or was it just that her speech was slurred? Now that Stella's focused on it, she can't let it go. Did she hear something accusatory, or was it her imagination? All of Stella's childhood skills have grown rusty with disuse.

The phone buzzes in her hand, making Stella jump.

A text pops up. Banner across the lock screen.

It's from SJIUYVP. Really sorry. Let's reschedule.

The text makes her wonder if Gwen is having an affair. It's possible Stella misread the situation. Maybe Gwen pulled into Stella's driveway to collect her wits after a bad encounter with a secret lover. She wasn't expecting Stella to pop out of the dark.

What Stella needs is time to think, but as she mulls over the possibilities suggested by the messages from SJIUYVP, her own phone buzzes in her pocket. A series of texts from Daisy.

Mom? Are you awake?

Mom?

Mom? Hello????

Mom, are you there?

MOM???? I need you!!

The phone lights up with a FaceTime call.

Stella drops Gwen's phone on the desk and runs down the stairs. She hits Accept, and Daisy's disgruntled face fills her phone.

Daisy looks a lot like Stella.

Same shade of auburn hair, highlighted blonde by the sun (Daisy) and at the salon (Stella). Same hazel eyes. Her mouth is fuller than Stella's, though; that's from Tom. Daisy is also taller and more confident than Stella ever was; confidence being a quality Stella has carefully cultivated.

"Where are you?" Daisy asks. She sounds shaken in a way that grabs all of Stella's attention.

"Just turning off lights, then I was headed to bed. Everything okay?"

"No. Everyone's out in the hot tub, and my period just started." Tears of exclusion fill Daisy's eyes. "I feel like no one even cares about me."

"Oh, sweetie, I'm sure that's not true," Stella says and sits down at her kitchen island to coach Daisy through this imaginary crisis.

The thing about crises is, you never know when a real one will occur. What Stella *does* know is how to survive them. Practice makes perfect, which is why she's willing to give Daisy as much practice as she needs.

Four

SPRING 1987

JULIE

We live in an old farmhouse set back from the road. Mom inherited the house and the twenty-two acres it sits on from her parents. I don't remember her parents because they died before I was born. When I say "we," I mean me and Mom. "We" used to include Paula, until she took off. And when I was a whole lot younger, it included Dad.

Kevin lives with us, but I don't count him because it's temporary. Eventually, Mom will get tired of him and he'll move on. Of course, he doesn't understand that. He thinks he's here to stay. Mom's boyfriends always think they're here to stay, but the only kind of men Mom likes are the ones who move on.

Upstairs, I hear Mom walking around. She works at a retirement home, and her hours are always changing. Some weeks she gets home for dinner and sleeps at night. Some weeks she leaves after dinner and sleeps during the day. This is a sleep-during-the-day week, so when she comes downstairs, she's wearing her bathrobe.

"Hey, sweetheart. How was your day? How did the tryouts go? Did you say thank you to Kevin for giving you a ride home?"

She's all smiles and questions and long red hair that hangs down to her waist like a curtain. Before I can answer, Kevin cuts in.

"My day, in case anyone's wondering, was pretty shitty."

He sits down on the couch and thunks his dirty work boots up on the coffee table.

"Oh, baby, what happened?"

Mom arranges her face in a way that looks worried, but I can see behind the mask. She doesn't care about his day. Somehow, Kevin doesn't see that. He believes the mask. When she presses herself up against him, he puts one hand under her bathrobe. Her eyes meet mine and the mask slips away, but Kevin is too focused on what's under her bathrobe to notice.

"I'll tell you all about it upstairs," he says.

"Okay." She leans down and kisses him.

He pulls her closer, holding her tight until she squeals and squirms away.

"Julie, there's meatloaf in the oven. You go on ahead and eat," Mom calls as Kevin pulls her up the stairs.

Mom's tiny, and looks even smaller behind Kevin, who is tall and muscular. Her hair swings and swirls as she follows him. Mom's size and hair color are things that Kevin loves about her.

"My five-foot firecracker," he'll say, acting like her head is his armrest.

She pretends to find this amusing. For some reason, he never hears the way her laughter rings false.

I'm small like Mom. Hopefully, I'll grow a few more inches. Paula is five foot four. That seems like the perfect height. Tall enough not to be noticeably short, but short enough not to stick out. Paula has dark brown eyes and brown hair like Dad.

Mom and I have lighter eyes. Hazel, that's what Mom calls them. A mix of brown and green. Neither me or Paula got Mom's nose, which turns up at the tip. We also were lucky not to get her teeth. Ours are straight with no gaps. Mom's two front teeth have a big space between them, and the bottom ones are squished together. In pictures, she always smiles with her mouth closed. I don't think her teeth look bad, but she hates them.

In the kitchen, I take the meatloaf out of the oven, cut a slice, and put it on a plate. Somewhere between tryouts and the bite of Slim Jim, I lost my appetite. Mom won't make a big deal if I don't eat, but it's the kind of thing Kevin will notice. When she works nights and I'm alone with him, I have to make sure I do everything right. You never know what will set him off.

Mom is a good cook, but after the ride home with Kevin, my stomach hurts and I have to force down every bite. When I'm done, I carefully wash all my dishes, dry them, and put them away.

Things were easier when Paula still lived here. There were two of us and it's always easier when you're not alone. The best times were when Mom was between boyfriends and it was just me, Mom, and Paula. When Mom's days off fell on a weekend, we'd make pizza and stay up late watching TV. Sometimes we'd have dance parties and make ice cream sundaes with the kind of toppings you buy at the grocery store: whipped cream, pretzels, cherries, M&Ms, chocolate sauce.

After Paula got pregnant, everything changed. She dropped out of high school and moved to Hermiston, all the way on the other side of the state. Mom told me she lost the baby, but I guess she likes Hermiston pretty well because she hasn't come back. Mom says maybe we'll go see her this summer, if she can get the time off from work.

I used to write Paula a letter every week.

"When do you think you'll come home?" I would always ask.

She would always write back, but she never answered that question.

I wonder what Paula would have thought of Kevin. My gut tells me they wouldn't have seen eye to eye.

After I make sure the kitchen is spotless and the meatloaf is tightly covered, I grab my notebook with the eight-counts. For a minute, I let myself think about making the cheer team. Being part of something like that would be almost as good as having Paula back. The thought makes me smile, but then I wipe it off my face quick. Mom says not to count your chickens before they hatch. The only thing I should be counting is that dance routine.

In order to learn it, I need a mirror. I have a full-length mirror in my bedroom, but Kevin is weird about me overhearing him with Mom. Like he thinks I don't know what they're doing. Or that I haven't heard her with other men. So instead of going upstairs, I head outside where the air is damp and cold, and follow the path to the barn.

Our barn is old and tilts to one side like it's had too much to drink. For a while, we had sheep, but they got sick. Mom said those vet bills just about broke her, so now the barn sits empty unless Mom's in the mood to paint.

I slide open the metal door and tug the string that turns on the single light bulb hanging from the ceiling. The light gives me a fuzzy reflection of myself in the door. It's not perfect, but it works.

My notebook goes on top of the can where we used to keep the sheep food. I start working my way through those eight-counts. Committing each move to memory.

When the door opens, I freeze. But it's only Mom.

"I'm heading out soon," she says with a smile.

I nod.

"Let's see it."

She watches me perform what I've learned so far, her head tilted to one side. Her smile is genuine. No mask needed. One thing I never question is how much Mom loves me. And Paula; she loves Paula too. We're her whole world. That's what she tells us, and I believe her.

When Mom says something true, I recognize it, because I've seen all the masks she uses to tell her stories.

"The last part's still sloppy. Keep working. Another day and you'll have it down," she says when I finish. "Come on. Let's get you back to the house before I leave."

From the path to the house, I can see blue light flickering through the windows.

Kevin watching TV.

"He's in a better mood now," Mom says. She puts one arm around me, pulling me close. "Why don't you take a shower before I leave. Get to bed early. Rest up for tomorrow."

"Okay," I say.

What she's really telling me is how to avoid Kevin. He's like an undetonated bomb, and we have to tiptoe around him until he moves on.

A police drama blares from the TV.

"Looks like you'll have the TV all to yourself. Julie's tuckered out from that tryout," Mom says to Kevin.

"Night, Julie," he grunts.

"Kiss," Mom says, tapping her cheek.

I oblige, then I lean over and kiss Kevin's cheek too. I don't want to, but I'm careful not to let on. Mom's taught me how to pretend the water is calm and blue, so that no one can see what's churning down deep.

"Kevin says he'll pick you up again after tryouts tomorrow," Mom says as I turn toward the stairs.

"You sure it's not too much trouble? These tryouts go all week. I could try to get a ride with someone else if it's a problem."

Kevin scowls at me. "No way you're going to 'get a ride,'" he says, his voice going falsetto on the last three words. "Won't have you end up like your sister. Not on my watch."

He looks at Mom like he's expecting her to argue, but she nods and smiles. He doesn't notice the cold look in her eyes.

"I'll be there right at five thirty. You best be waiting outside for me."

"Thank you, Kevin. I really appreciate it."

The sweetness in my voice is cloying, but Kevin doesn't notice that either.

"It'll be good to see you do something besides stare at them books in your room," he calls as I climb the stairs.

In the shower, I imagine pointing out his inconsistencies. Cheerleaders are dumb sluts, but if I study too much, I'm a bookworm. Which is it, I think about asking, but I can't. A conversation like that wouldn't end well.

In the morning, I take the bus to school, same as always. Usually I sit by myself, but today Ginny Schaeffer sits next to me.

"Hey, Julie," she says.

I didn't think Ginny knew I existed, let alone knew my name.

"Hi," I say with a shy smile. So *this* is what it feels like to be part of something.

"I saw you at tryouts yesterday."

"Yeah." I look down at the sweatshirt and jeans I'm wearing. The sweatshirt used to be Paula's and the jeans are a little big because Mom got them secondhand, but she says I'll grow into them.

Next to me, in her pink button-down shirt and matching two-tone watch, Ginny looks bright and shiny, like she stepped out of *Seventeen* magazine.

"I like your watch," I say.

Ginny's mom is a teacher's aide and always picks her up after school. On Fridays, Ginny gets to bring friends home with her. Her dad is a detective on the Livingston police force. Every year at the Strawberry Festival Parade, Ginny rides with him on the police float. She's always bragging about how he has a perfect arrest record.

"It's a Swatch." Ginny shows it to me. "I have a collection." Smiling sweetly, she adds, "I can't decide whether I should go back to tryouts today. What are you going to do?"

I shrug. "Figured I'd finish what I started, you know?"

Ginny's voice turns conspiratorial. "That dance routine is so hard, right? Like, my sister was a cheerleader last year, and even she didn't have it completely memorized."

"Yeah, it's really hard," I say.

"The girls on varsity are saying it's unlikely any eighth graders will make JV. Like, it's not even personal. There just isn't enough space on the team. I don't know if it's worth going back today."

I nod, but I'm not thinking about tryouts.

I'm thinking about Kevin.

I already told him tryouts go all week. Even if Ginny's right and I don't stand a chance, I have to go. Quitting isn't an option. It would break one of the unwritten rules of the game I play with Kevin. If I quit and Kevin finds out, he'll use it against me over and over.

But then I realize why she's talking to me, and that this is a different game than the one I play with Kevin. "Are you going back?"

Ginny rolls her eyes. "I mean, obviously. My sister's trying out, so I have to ride home with her."

I nod. One thing I've learned from interacting with Mom's boyfriends is you don't need to say everything you know. Instead, I smile and make my voice sweet like I'm talking to Kevin. "My mom's boyfriend is picking me up, so I kinda have to go too."

"Bummer," Ginny says, blinking rapidly. She shrugs. "By the way, I hope you're not afraid of heights. We're working on lifts today. You and I are, like, the smallest of the eighth graders, so I could totally see us having to fly. It doesn't mean we'll make the team or anything. I just wouldn't want you to get hurt."

"I don't mind heights," I say.

Ginny looks disappointed.

The bus pulls into the parking lot and Ginny waves to the group of girls at the back where she usually sits.

I watch as they walk toward the entrance of the school, leaving me alone. It's not until they've gone inside that I think about how Ginny's taller than me. Probably weighs more too. If the choice is between me and Ginny, it's clear who will be easier to lift.

That's when I realize why Ginny doesn't want me to come to tryouts.

Which means I've got a shot at making the team.

Five

FALL

STELLA

Stella wakes to the smell of pancakes floating up to the bedroom.

"Morning." Tom looks up as she pads into the kitchen on bare feet.

He likes her this way. Eyes still sleepy, T-shirt that reveals her legs, toned from the workouts she squeezes in. A hint of underwear when she bends over.

"How'd you sleep?" he asks with a smile.

"Tossed and turned a little." She leans into him and gives him a hug.

He responds by kissing her on the top of her head. Before kids, this small amount of contact would have led to sex. Hot and urgent, right here in the kitchen.

"Worried about Daisy?" he asks.

She nods, but her mind is still on the sex they won't be having. "I just want her to be happy, you know. There's always so much drama."

"She's fifteen." He smiles. "I think drama *is* what makes her happy."

"When I was fifteen . . ." She pauses and doesn't finish.

Tom slides a spatula under each of the pancakes and flips them one by one. "No fifteen-year-old should have to deal with the death of a parent. This drama is normal. I promise. Daisy's going to be fine."

She leans in, finds the place on his neck that when she first discovered it, felt like it was made to fit her face. He kisses her in a brotherly-love kind of way. There's a creak upstairs followed by the sound of someone using the toilet.

Stella moves away and runs down to the basement to grab her Barre bag. She ties her bathrobe tighter to prevent shocking Colin with too much mom skin, but she's still thinking about sex. It's been four weeks since the last time. The realization makes her uncomfortable, like she's failing some secret exam.

When she comes back upstairs, Colin is sitting across from Tom, shoveling pancakes into his mouth with a singular focus.

"Good morning. You're up early," she says.

"Group history project. Langston chose the time." He doesn't look up from his phone. "By the way, I'm out of contact lens fluid."

"I think the phrase you're searching for is, 'Good morning, Mom.'" Stella softens the correction with a smile.

"Good morning, Mom. But seriously, I need more contact lens fluid. Can you get some today?"

"Yes, Colin. I will put it on my list."

"Thank you!"

This is said with more enthusiasm than contact lens fluid should generate, but she tells herself it's a testament to his good manners. Or the fact that he's grateful for all the contributions, small and large, Stella makes to his life. She glances at the griddle. It's empty. She looks back at the two plates where the only thing that remains is a smear of syrup.

"Did you want pancakes?" Tom asks.

"No, I'm fine," she says tightly. "I've got Barre class this morning anyway."

"Okay." Tom looks back down at his own phone.

Stella grabs a banana and pours herself a cup of coffee before going upstairs to change. She adds contact lens solution on her grocery app, and tells herself her irritation is an overreaction. Of course she will pick up contact lens solution. Of course she doesn't need a pancake. How could she maintain her perfect size two if she indulged in pancakes, she asks her reflection. Then she rolls her eyes.

Still, her life is filled with privilege. Privileges like Barre class and fancy workout clothes followed by the freedom to sit with Lorraine over coffee afterward. Who needs a paying job when she's paid in love?

She rolls her eyes again. Love hasn't gained a lot of traction as an official currency.

When she was paid in dollars, there were parameters and rewards. Meals to celebrate the end of transactions and bonuses to recognize extra effort. She works more hours now, but instead of receiving bonuses, she has to own the privilege of staying home. Own the privilege of providing free labor to her family.

Labor that currently includes, but is not limited to, coordinating travel for sports teams; buying endless amounts of snacks and setting up a snack table at each game; scheduling and attending all medical appointments from dermatological to orthodontic; driving the children to and from everything; planning vacations; filling the house with cheerful decor to celebrate each holiday; hiring, paying, and supervising the cleaning service and yard maintenance crew; purchasing groceries (different than snacks); running errands; attending PTO meetings designed to further her children's education; monitoring her children's grades; helping with homework and school projects; talking them through ethical dilemmas; spotting burgeoning mental health issues; planning and preparing meals that are simultaneously tasty, organic, and well-balanced; and attending functions with Tom dressed in a way that is attractive but not overtly sexy.

None of that, despite the amount of time and effort it requires, is considered work. Not real work, because if it were, she'd be paid in something besides love.

Of course, she shouldn't complain. Tom helps out when he can.

"You don't mind picking up Daisy?" she asks him as she fills her Hydro Flask in the kitchen.

He looks up from his newspaper. "Not at all. Have fun. Enjoy your girl time."

"Thanks," she says.

On the way to the front door, she detours toward the basement. In the laundry room, she opens the secret door and tiptoes up the stairs. Grabbing the Lilly Pulitzer bag, she shoves it inside her own bag. After Barre, she'll drop it at Gwen's.

Whatever blurriness possessed Stella last night is gone. She woke up with a clearheaded vision of how to handle the bag and phone. She and Gwen aren't close. Whatever's going on with Gwen is none of Stella's business.

When she arrives at the studio, she sees that Lorraine has already claimed their usual spot in the far corner.

"There she is!" Lorraine calls as Stella walks in. "Nice of you to finally show up," she hisses as Stella joins her. "I thought that woman over there was gonna knife me for your spot."

"Who? Which one?" Stella glances over her shoulder.

"Oh my God, don't look," Lorraine says.

The room is filled with women who all bear a passing resemblance to each other. Blonde, botoxed, and well-toned, with a few brunettes thrown in like accent pillows. If someone were to glance into the studio, Stella would be completely indistinguishable. That knowledge fills her with deep satisfaction. It was in high school that Stella first noted this form of visible invisibility. The way the popular girls, with their lip-gloss smiles and cookie-cutter clothing, were hard to tell apart. Later, in college, those same kinds of girls taught her the importance of counting calories. Being thin was a currency that would spit out rewards like a Las Vegas slot machine in permanent jackpot mode. It was a form of taking up less space while simultaneously claiming it. She was socialized, she supposes. A process that smoothed away her edges.

"Sorry I'm late." She makes an apologetic face. "I was on Daisy duty way too late last night."

Lorraine nods. "I had like, fourteen texts from Ainsley this morning. Something about getting cropped out of a photo on Instagram. She took it upon herself to Uber home at four a.m. Did Daisy make the photo cut?"

"I don't know." Parroting Tom, she adds, "I think drama is how they connect. No drama, no fun, you know?"

"So true. Poor Ains. Sucks to be the youngest. I spent an ungodly amount of time on teen drama when Mia was her age. Now I put my phone on Do Not Disturb."

"Really? But don't you—"

"No, not really." Lorraine grins. "I'm still a sucker. How do you think I know about the Insta-drama?"

Stella's laugh is interrupted by the buzz of an incoming text from the phone pocket of her leggings. She pulls out her phone, expecting a request for more items to be added to the shopping list, but the notification isn't from Daisy or Colin.

It's from Gwen.

Hey, I can't find my phone. Any chance you've seen it? Btw, was hoping to chat about something.

The text jogs Stella's memory, draining the color from her face.

"Stell, you okay?" Lorraine asks.

She nods and slips her phone back into its pocket. "Yeah. Just low blood sugar. I'm fine."

Lorraine looks unconvinced.

The instructor claps her hands for their attention as though she's a preschool teacher in a room full of unruly four-year-olds. "Okay, ladies, let's get started."

Stella, pink weights in hand, studies her reflection in the mirror. Her black tank is sweat-wicking with anti-stink technology and airflow zones. She paid sixty-two dollars for it. A price that struck her as exorbitant, but now the high-performance fabric is proving its worth soaking up the nervous sweat dampening her armpits as a result of Gwen's text.

The text itself isn't what's upset her. It could have easily come from Gwen's laptop.

What bothers Stella—no, "bothers" isn't the right word; what has Stella absolutely losing her shit—is a conversation she overheard last year.

Gwen, at the summer pool club, loudly explaining how she tracks all the devices in her family. How she keeps a file with the passwords used by everyone in her family.

Gwen has to know where her phone is, which means the text is really a pretext.

Stella's morning clarity vanishes, replaced by a creeping sense of unease. She forces herself to breathe, long and slow. The important thing is to consider all the angles, not jump to conclusions.

If you want to gain control of the narrative, you have to see the whole picture.

The last thought makes Stella blink at her reflection in the mirror. She's not supposed to have to do that anymore.

It's a sign of Stella's discipline that she does not lunge for her phone the moment class is over. Instead, she wipes her equipment and returns it to its place on the color-coordinated shelves. Blue Barre balls on the blue shelf. Hot-pink two- and three-pound weights on the pink shelf. And so on.

"Coffee?" Lorraine asks.

"Of course. Let me drop my bag in the car first."

They're about to enjoy the "girl time" Tom referenced. However, instead of leisurely drinking expensive lattes, they will devote most of the next hour to going over unfinished items for tonight's auction.

Stella opens her car, drops her bag, and finally (finally!) takes her phone out of her pocket, but as she's considering her response, Gwen's phone lights up with another message from SJIUYVP.

Hey, everything okay? Let's reschedule. Whenever you want.

Stella reads the message twice, then toggles Gwen's phone into airplane mode. Whatever Gwen is mixed up in feels messy and Stella would prefer not to be a confidante for Gwen's drama. With quick fingers, she types on her phone, Sorry, haven't seen it. Have you tried locating it?

As she tosses Gwen's phone in her bag, she's already thinking of ways to anonymously return it.

She heads to the coffee shop near the Barre studio, where she orders herself a six-dollar oat milk latte and she and Lorraine get to work.

Halfway through her coffee, Stella's phone buzzes.

"Sorry," she says.

Lorraine nods indulgently. As a mother of four, she understands.

It's another message from Gwen.

I'm dumb. Should have tried that first. Found it. Talk later?

Stella puts down her phone, careful to keep her face composed.

She sips her latte.

She focuses on Lorraine's list of to-do items.

She says "Yes" and "Oh my gosh" and "Of course" on cue, but the whole time, her mind is laser-focused on Gwen's phone in airplane mode at the bottom of her gym bag. And why Gwen would lie about finding it.

It's an inexpert attempt at manipulation that feels oddly familiar. Like a face glimpsed in a dream. For a moment, Stella is close. She almost identifies it.

Then, like every dream, it slips away.

Six

SPRING 1987

JULIE

I've got amazing balance.

When Paula was in middle school, we used to play this game she made up called Walk the Plank.

We played it with the neighbors who lived across the road before they moved away. They were boys, but Paula said they were better than nothing. Me and Paula, we were the best at Walk the Plank. Actually, Paula was the best. I was second best.

Walk the Plank is like Truth or Dare. Everyone rolls the dice. Highest roll means you're it. Lowest roll means you get to come up with a dare. Anything you want—no rules there. The person who goes first does the dare or has to walk the plank.

The plank is a maze of dead trees that washed down the river and created a logjam. If you walk the plank, you have to know which trees aren't rotten. Which trees are solid enough to hold your weight and get you to the other side of the river.

Winter is the best time to play Walk the Plank because the water is cold and moves fast. Plus, the moss on the trees is slippery from rain. There are only two bends in the river between our logjam and the waterfall farther downstream. That waterfall is about a thirty-foot drop. If it's winter and you're not sure about your balance, you should always take the dare. Chances are good that if you fall into the river, you won't make it out.

Unless you're me or Paula and know the tricks.

"You hold it all right here, Julie," Paula told me. She sucked in her gut so her belly button got long and narrow.

It's balance, but it's more than that. The best way to explain it is it's like holding your entire body in your stomach. Also, you keep your eyes up. If you do those two things, you won't fall.

Promise.

No matter what.

Not even if it's been raining for a week, the water is extra high, and the log is slippery and rotten in places, but the neighbor boy dared you to touch his dick with both hands. You'll walk across the plank just fine. Then, if you're like Paula, you'll dare him to swim across the river, even though it's January. He'll say he has to go home, but you'll know it's a lie.

You'll know you won.

After school at tryouts, I realize Ginny Schaeffer should always take the dare.

"Today is lift day," Deanna announces as we sit on the hard floor of the gym.

Ginny and I are both put in groups with JV girls. Megan Schaeffer, Ginny's older sister, is in mine.

Megan greets me with a cold smile, while the other girl, Bridget, explains where I should put my feet and how to time the counts.

"You're so tiny," Bridget says with an encouraging smile. "This is gonna be easy."

"It's not just about weight. It's about balance," Megan says without smiling. Then she spends the next thirty minutes trying to throw me off mine.

Bridget braces her thigh at a ninety-degree angle, but Megan's leg is a slope. When I step up to her shoulder, she moves, and I tumble down to the ground.

"You stepped on my hair," she snaps.

We try again and again, but Megan has a talent for sabotage. I can feel Bridget's frustration. She can't see Megan shifting and twisting out from under my weight and thinks the problem is me. I glance at Ginny, who hasn't managed to hit her lift yet either, despite a base who isn't actively working against her. She smirks. This is a competition, and she knows her sister isn't going to let me win.

"One more time," I say.

This time, I move fast and change the order of my climb. Right foot on Bridget's thigh, left foot on Megan's. Quickly, I step to Bridget's shoulder, but instead of putting the other foot on Megan's, where she can throw me off balance, I pull my left knee to my chest, hoping I'm not too heavy for Bridget.

Eyes fixed on the basketball hoop, I hear Bridget's sharp intake of breath at the same time that I catch a glimpse of Deanna moving our way. Slowly, left hand gripping left foot, I stretch my left leg straight above my head.

"Julie, wow, look at you," Deanna says. "You okay with her weight, Bridge? Can we get some more spotters over here?" She claps her hands. I'm aware of movement below, but my eyes never leave the hoop.

They bring me down, and Deanna is all smiles. "Let's try something new. Laura, you sub in for Megan. So, same thing, but instead of stepping on their shoulders, Julie, you'll step into their hands. Once you're up, they're going to count it out. It'll be up, down, throw. When you start to fall, pike your legs out in front of you. Can you do that?"

I nod.

When Laura replaces Megan, it's easy. Easier than walking the plank.

If Paula was watching, she'd say I was a little wobbly. *Hold it in your gut!* I can almost hear her yell. One, two and I'm flying up toward the ceiling of the gym.

"Pike!" Deanna yells, and I do.

"Nice job," she says once I've landed in the square of Laura and Bridget's arms. "How did that feel?"

"Fine. Good," I say, pretending my heart isn't pounding with adrenaline.

She nods, then glances from me to the varsity girls with a smile that makes me feel warm all over.

"Julie, hold on," Deanna calls as we leave tryouts. "I'm going to have you stunt with Laura and Bridget for tryouts. That means you'll be trying out with the other varsity girls, but the coaches will know you'll be a freshman next year. It's just a day early. Can you be ready?"

"Yeah," I say, recalculating the amount of time I have to prepare.

Today, Kevin comes roaring into the high school parking lot, tires screeching so everyone looks. The cab of his truck stinks of beer. Yesterday he was a coiled snake, waiting to strike. Today he's loose and happy, a cartoon bear.

"How was practice?" A drop of spit flies out of his mouth and lands on my cheek.

"Really good," I say, forcing a smile.

His saliva is hot on my face. I wait until he looks away to wipe it off with the sleeve of my sweatshirt.

"Yeah? Really good? Look who's so confident she's gonna make the team. You ain't nervous at all now?"

He takes one hand off the wheel, shaking it like he's afraid, then laughs.

"I'm still a little nervous," I say.

"Only a little? Gettin' pretty big for your britches, aren't ya?" He stares at me instead of the road. "Aren't ya?" he prompts as we blow through a stop sign.

"Yes. Yes I am."

Kevin nods, satisfied with my answer, and jerks the steering wheel at the last minute, barely avoiding the ditch.

"Thing is, Juliebell, I was talking to a few folks about that cheerleading team. They said it's spendy." He rubs his thumb against his fingers. "All kind of fees for your pom-poms and shit."

"I know how much it costs. I'll pay for it."

"Oh really?" he sneers. "And how do you plan to do that?"

"I'll get a job. Babysitting or something."

"And who do you think is gonna drive you to this babysitting job? Cause it sure as hell ain't me."

"You don't need to worry about it, Kevin," I say, but I forget to smile, and my voice is too hard. "If I make the team, it'll be my problem. I'll figure it out."

His hand snakes out so fast, I don't see it coming. My head bounces back against the seat. A thousand white stars float before my eyes, then disappear. Sharp pain spreads through my jaw, and my mouth fills with the taste of copper.

"You got anything else you'd like to say?" Kevin asks.

His face is bright red, and his hands are angry fists around the steering wheel. The cartoon bear is gone, replaced by a real one that's hungry for blood.

"No, sir," I say, blinking hard. "I'm sorry."

He nods, satisfied I know my place in the world. He likes reminding me of it because it solidifies his. We don't speak again until we turn onto the gravel driveway that leads to the house.

"You gonna go blubber to your mom now?"

He's looking straight ahead, and I can see the bloat setting in around his eyes. The shadow of who he'd become if he wasn't already destined to move on.

"No." I shake my head.

"Good. No one likes a little tattletale."

He gets out of the truck and goes inside.

When I come in, Mom is sitting next to Kevin on the couch.

"What happened to your face?" she asks.

"Stunt day at tryouts. I fell."

Mom nods and smiles her careful smile that doesn't reveal her teeth. If Kevin was looking at her, he would have seen the flash of anger in her eyes. Then again, even if he'd seen it, he wouldn't understand what it meant.

Over dinner, Mom dotes on Kevin, but he doesn't hear the saccharine tone in her voice. After dinner, I go back to the barn. I can cry over what happened or practice my dance routine. The memory of Deanna's warm smile makes it an easy choice. I want to be surrounded by a group of friends, laughing and happy like Ginny Schaeffer.

An hour passes before Mom slides open the corrugated metal door.

"Let's have a better look at that face," she says with her real smile.

I tilt my head toward the hanging light bulb so she can inspect the damage.

She takes me by the chin, turning my head this way and that. "It's not too bad. It'll cover up. No problem."

I nod. I know how to cover a bruise on my face.

"If I make the team, it costs money. A hundred and fifty for the uniforms and gear. There's also a weekend clinic that's another hundred dollars, but maybe I won't have to go."

Mom nods. "We've got it covered."

"Kevin knows how much it costs. He said some friends told him."

Mom raises one eyebrow. "Friends? Who?"

Mom is private. "I don't need anyone talking about my business," she'll say. Her boyfriends tend to be loners.

"Folks." I shrug. "He was at a bar, I think."

"Okay." Mom leans in and kisses me on the forehead. "I'll leave the foundation and powder in your room. Don't worry about the money, though. I'll take care of it. I think it's about time for Kevin to move on. Don't you?" Her voice is stern, but her eyes are warm.

I nod and smile. Her saying Kevin will be moving on is music to my ears.

When I come back to the house, Kevin and Mom are sitting at the kitchen table. He's eating vanilla ice cream topped with Mom's canned peaches. She's watching him eat with a dreamy look on her face.

"You don't want even one tiny bite?" Kevin asks Mom as I climb the stairs.

"Nope." Mom's voice is soft and sultry. "I'm saving my appetite for other things."

Kevin chuckles as his spoon scrapes the bowl. "I like the sound of that."

Upstairs, in my bedroom, I wonder how it will unfold this time, but I'm not worried. When Mom is in charge of the story, everything works out fine.

At least it does for us.

If Kevin knew how to read Mom, even a little bit, he'd be scared. He'd feel small and helpless the way he's made other people feel, but I'm not worried about what Kevin will do to anyone else.

Hopefully, by this weekend, no one will ever have to be afraid of Kevin again.

Seven

FALL

STELLA

Stella and Lorraine air-kiss goodbye in the parking lot, but Stella has no time to linger. She has a whole slate of errands to complete. Items to be checked off on a very long list, including purchasing contact lens solution for Colin. Tom's words echo in her ears.

Enjoy your girl time.

Girl time. Add the word "girl" before the word "time" and it's prima facie evidence that the time is without value.

To an observer—not that she's being observed—Stella is the picture of suburban domesticity. She wipes every glimmer of angst (suspicion, anxiety, desperate longing) from her face. She fills her grocery cart and exchanges greetings with the inevitable neighbors, while responding to the unrelenting onslaught of texts from her beloveds.

Daisy: Mom where are my white practice shorts
    Stella: Check the dryer.
Tom: What time is our thing tonight?
    Stella: 6:30. Invite with details on my desk. I sent you a calendar invite.
Daisy: Not there I checked
    Stella: Did you check your bag?
Colin: Can Jake and Ben come over tonight
    Stella: Dad and I won't be home.
Colin: Is that a no

Stella: Yes.
Colin: Yes they can come over
Stella: No, they cannot come over. Dad and I won't be home!
Colin: Ngl thought you said yes so I already texted them we're good
Stella: 🙄 I guess you'll have to text them again.
Stella: Tom, can you please tell Colin he can't have friends over tonight.
Colin: I asked dad too but he's not responding
Daisy: Ainsley has my shorts can we get them from her house before practice
Tom: Colin wants to have friends over tonight. What do you think?

She responds to the last three texts and glares at her phone. It's tempting to put it on silent, but she never does. The possibilities of what could go wrong haunt her.

Colin, her new driver, could get in a car accident. Tom could have a heart attack. Daisy could be kidnapped by sex traffickers at the mall. And while it's unlikely any of these things will happen, Stella knows firsthand how the balance of an entire life can shift in a single moment.

Her churning mind lands on Tom's comments about her childhood. He's right. No child should have to survive the death of first one parent, then another, which is the version of her childhood she told Tom. It was cleaner that way, even if it wasn't true. The truth wasn't something she could share with anyone, not even Tom. The important thing was that he understood she'd survived something difficult. By Stella's calculations, that's close enough to the truth to count as the real thing.

In the time it's taken her to think those thoughts, her phone has erupted with four more texts. She reads them, sighs heavily, then puts the phone back in her purse without responding. This soft, suburban life is what she wanted for her children. She and Tom worked hard for all the benefits it provides. And even though she worries about her children's softness, she finds reassurance in the smallest things.

Colin, who without a second thought corrected her after she misgendered one of his teammates.

"God, I'm so sorry," she said, flushing and uncomfortable.

"It's okay, Mom," Colin said, patting her on the back like she was the child. "You're learning."

And Daisy, who volunteer coaches Tulip field hockey. Tearing up and down the field with a pack of five-year-olds behind her.

"Who owns the ball?" Stella overheard her yell to the team.

"We do!" they screamed back as one.

"Who gets in our way?"

"No one!"

"Dais, you're amazing," she'd said later when they were in the car. "Is that something your coach taught you?"

"Um, no." Daisy had rolled her eyes. "You said that stuff to me, Mom. Don't you remember?"

Stella didn't, but she pretended she did.

Despite all the evidence that her children are turning into people she's proud to have in her life, sometimes she's filled with unease. What would happen if they were ejected from their suburban cocoon?

Could they survive the things she survived?

The idea sends a jolt to her stomach. Gwen Thompson lied for a reason, but Stella has no idea why. Her heart thuds in her ears and she's filled with a sudden irrational terror that everything she's created is about to implode. Her life thrives on order, and Gwen is an unknown variable.

You're overreacting, she tells herself as she swipes her credit card for their groceries. She clicks yes on the prompt asking her to round up for a donation to a local homeless shelter, trying to focus on the privilege of not having to worry about the cost of food. To be in the present moment, fully grateful for the bounties of her life.

Another part of her brain is sorting through what she knows. Drawing lines. Assembling motives. Gwen is clearly texting Stella from a laptop. But why is she pretending to have found her phone? Why did she show up in Stella's driveway in the first place? And then there are the texts from SJIUYVP.

An uncomfortable thought occurs to her, but Stella tells herself she's being ridiculous, overdramatic. And yet still, Stella shivers. Her stomach turns, and she knows this is instinct. There's something there. Something her conscious mind doesn't want to inspect too closely.

In the car, she exits the turnpike and navigates the series of streets that lead to her house. In sharp contrast to the explosion of messages on her phone, the house is silent. She mentally tracks everyone's schedule. Colin at Langston's, working on the AP History project. Tom and Daisy at Saturday practice. As she puts away the groceries, she wonders if Tom caved to Daisy's request to pick up the shorts. Or whether Daisy will come home complaining about the extra laps she had to run for being out of uniform.

When everything is tidy in the kitchen, including the mess of dishes left behind by Tom's pancake breakfast, she double-checks everyone's location on her phone, then runs down to the basement. Despite the house being empty, she tiptoes up the stairs to her retreat.

Alone, with no possibility for interruption, she plugs Gwen's phone into the charger she keeps in her secret room, checking to make sure its location services are still disabled. The phone case is pink and filled with glitter. What kind of adult has that?

The fabric of reality feels slippery. Stella wonders whether the sensation in her stomach is instinct or a longing for drama to break up the sameness of her days. The problem is, she knows intimately how fiction can turn to fact. Stories can be spun into truth and emerge immutable.

She leaves Gwen's phone on the desk to charge and turns to her filing cabinet.

Its top drawer is filled with old pictures. Tom has seen them, but they didn't inspire him to ask questions about the people from her past. Stella wrote his limited curiosity off as deference to a painful subject. It *is* a painful subject, which is why she keeps these photos here, boxed up in a drawer. Hidden from prying eyes and minds, not that anyone in her family is all that interested in faded photos of unfamiliar faces.

But she's not in the mood to reminisce. What she's after is under the photos in the false bottom of the box.

A penknife.

She takes it out now. Studies it, weighs it in her hand before putting it down on her desk. There's nothing special about it. She's seen ones with similarly carved handles at junky antique stores. Still, sometimes she likes to hold it. Remembering the person she once was is another thing she does up here in this secret space. It doesn't matter that that person is gone. Excised, as though Stella used this very knife to cut her out.

Next, she drags a chair to the corner of the room. Up under the eaves, her fingers connect with the key that's hidden there. It's encased in plastic for extra safekeeping and enclosed in a holder she attached to the beam with a Command strip. It's an insurance policy, because you never know.

Although people like the person she's become *do* know. There are mutual funds, portfolios, bonds, property deeds, wills, trusts, insurance, fancy cars, anniversary jewelry, and the ever-rising value of their already overpriced home to assure them they will always be safe.

Whatever disaster comes, there is certainty they will escape unscathed.

Despite that, it's this key, hidden in its secret spot in her secret room, that gives Stella certainty. It's a reminder that come what may, she'll be safe.

She leaves the key in its place and climbs down from the chair, feeling calmer.

It's time to put this (whatever this is) to rest.

Here's what's going to happen. She'll go downstairs and put together the auction basket. She's procrastinated preparing it because she's annoyed at having to organize the auction *and* donate a basket.

But still, she promised.

It's time to deliver.

She'll walk it over to the Thompsons' house along with that stupid Lilly Pulitzer bag. Knock on the door. If no one answers, she'll leave the basket on their porch. On her way over, she'll take Gwen's phone out of airplane mode and drop it, fully charged and ready to be found, in the ditch near Gwen's driveway where Stella won't be caught by a security camera.

Then she'll be done. It doesn't matter that someone is texting Gwen from a suspicious contact. It's none of Stella's business. She has more important things to worry about, like Colin and Daisy and the kind of people they are becoming, which sometimes gets lost amid the pressure to achieve good grades, perform well in sports, and get high scores on standardized tests all in service to the ever-looming shadow of college applications.

The process that made her the kind of woman who gives air-kisses also made her the kind of woman who keeps baskets and last-minute gifts in her basement wrapping center. Basement wrapping center; so ridiculous.

She knows this, but she also uses it regularly.

Stella finds a white wicker basket, sorts through the gift certificates she keeps on hand, and settles on one from a popular Italian restaurant. A fig-scented candle, dish towels covered with retro fruits, and two wooden spoons shaped like fruits. Food theme—perfect, she thinks as she encases the whole thing in cellophane.

Carrying the basket, with the Lilly Pulitzer bag tucked underneath her arm and Gwen's phone in her pocket, Stella heads toward the Thompsons'. At the corner of her street, she pauses to turn Gwen's phone on, then continues past well-tended yards. Green expanses of grass like her own with hydrangeas growing in the shade of large, seldom-used porches. This is her life, beautiful and perfect. She's low-key annoyed that she wasted eighteen hours of it going down this rabbit hole of worry. She has better things to do, and to worry about.

She's halfway to the Thompsons' when a car passes her, then stops and backs up.

The window rolls down to reveal Gwen's husband, Dave. "Bet I know where you're headed with that. Save you a trip?" he asks with a congenial smile.

"Oh . . . yeah. That would be great."

When Dave reaches out for the basket, he doesn't notice the bag. Or maybe he assumes it belongs to Stella. If he's as observant as Tom, this is probably the right answer.

"Thanks! You ladies have really outdone yourselves," Dave says.

In her pocket, Stella feels the unmistakable buzz of the phone she just turned on.

"Tonight should be great," Stella says, giving a wave and a bright smile to signal the end of the conversation.

"Our dining room is filled with baskets," Dave says, as though he's oblivious to her wave or its meaning. "It's going to be quite the shindig."

"Yeah, I really hope so." Stella smiles even wider. The only thing she's hoping for is the end of this conversation.

"Yep, your basket is one of the best of the bunch. Well done." He gives her an approving thumbs-up.

"Thank you," Stella says. "See you tonight."

"Okay, see you there."

Finally, she is dismissed. She turns back toward her house, waiting for his car to disappear before she pulls out the phone. On its face is the location finder. Someone, presumably Gwen, accessed its location.

Stella's heart pounds. What if Dave tells Gwen he ran into Stella on the street? He's definitely chatty. It seems like something he would do. Now that she's lied to Gwen, it would be embarrassing to be caught.

Worse, it would give Gwen an excuse to have that "chat" she suggested. On instinct, Stella switches the phone back into airplane mode and shoves it in her pocket.

The bag is small, designed to be worn cross-body. Instead, Stella tucks it into the waistband of her joggers in case Gwen decides to drive the neighborhood in search of her phone. Earlier, she swapped her sweat-wicking tank for one of Daisy's discarded T-shirts, big and boxy. Bag bulge disguised, Stella walks as fast as she can toward her house.

If someone stops her, she'll say she's power walking.

She'll say it's such a beautiful afternoon for a walk.

She'll say, A phone in the street that was recently spotted on location services? How strange, but no, she hasn't seen anything. Nothing at all.

She slows and tries to catch her breath. The phone isn't going to give her away. The only thing that's going to give her away is her own carelessness.

Give away what? a voice asks in the back of her head.

Stella nods, agreeing with that voice. She needs to calm the fuck down because she's done nothing wrong.

"Mom." Daisy's familiar voice makes her jump. "What are you doing?"

The late-model BMW that's pulled up alongside her is also familiar.

"Looking at the leaves," Stella says, giving a better response than she'd mentally rehearsed. "The colors are so beautiful right now."

"Wanna ride?" Tom asks.

"Sure, thanks." Stella fixes a smile on her face and climbs into the back seat.

"Guess what. Coach had me start today. I think I might be starting in the first game."

"Dais was on fire," Tom seconds.

"Wow," Stella says as Daisy begins to give her a blow-by-blow description of practice.

Tom pulls into the garage and is immediately sucked into the vortex of his own phone.

"Why are you wearing my old shirt?" Daisy asks as Stella gets out of the car. Her tone is disgusted, as though Stella is wearing a T-shirt smeared with dog poop or something equally distasteful.

"Oh, just the first thing I grabbed. I was chilly after Barre, I guess."

She smiles, shakes her head, as if to acknowledge that wearing her daughter's cast-off T-shirt is truly the height of ridiculousness.

"Oh God," Daisy says. "It's so middle school. I thought I put that in the donation bag."

"It's fine for around the house," Stella says. "Oh shoot. I need to fold the clothes in the dryer before they wrinkle."

Even though she normally enjoys hearing Daisy recap her triumphs at practice, today she has other things to take care of. Besides, she's fairly certain the conversation is headed toward a retrospective of other things that are "so middle school."

Downstairs, Stella opens the panel to the secret staircase and sets both bag and phone on the bottom step, where they'll be safe from prying eyes.

She pulls the door shut and leans against it. "This is ridiculous. You need to get a grip," she whispers under her breath as she reopens the door and grabs the phone.

No one will care about the purse. All it contained is the phone, but the phone is something else.

The phone is trouble.

The phone is trackable.

The phone should be easy to get rid of, which is why Stella will drop it at the auction tonight and finally be done.

PART TWO

Eight

SPRING 1987

JULIE

Paula, it's started again, I write.

Sometimes when I write in my diary, I pretend I'm talking to her. Seeing her name makes me feel like she's still here. Like she's still sharing the room that now belongs only to me.

When she first left, we wrote letters to each other all the time. Then they sort of died down. I don't know whose fault that was, but it was hard to keep the conversation going when she ignored half my questions. It's been six months since the last time she wrote. That letter made me feel as if she was even farther away. Like the person writing the letter might not even be Paula. When I talk to her like this, in my diary, I can imagine exactly how my Paula, the one I knew when she lived here, would respond.

She'd tell me exactly what to do.

I'm up early this morning because I need extra time to hide the bruise on my face. Paula's the one who showed me how to apply the special foundation. It's tinted green. When I'm done, you won't see the bruise. Sunset marks, that's what Paula used to call them when she was little, because they're all reds, purples, and streaks of blue.

"See? Magic," she said, the first time she used the foundation on me. In the mirror, the bruise had disappeared. "Real live invisibility powder."

She was right. The makeup always hides the damage, but that doesn't mean it's gone. No one will notice it, but I can feel it if I move my mouth the wrong way. Sometimes I feel bruised even if it's been months since it's happened. It sounds weird, but Paula would know what I mean.

After I finish putting on the makeup, I go back to my diary.

Kevin finally popped me real good. You'd be proud of how I did my makeup, though. Can't even tell, except maybe a little when I smile. Like you always say, guess that means I won't be smiling for a while. I don't think it'll happen again, though. Mom says it's time for Kevin to move on, so that's something else that started. I hope things are real good for you in Hermiston. If you'd had your baby, I would have been an aunt. I could come visit and play with him or her. That would have been fun, don't you think?

That last part about being an aunt is definitely not something I'd say to Paula. Paula's tough, and she has a temper. If I said this to Paula, she wouldn't speak to me for a week. Even Mom used to give Paula space when she was in a mood.

"Paula's bullheaded," Mom says.

I know that means she's stubborn, but also that Paula can be like a bull. If you provoke her, she'll charge. The thing about bulls is, you see them coming. That's one of the biggest differences between Mom and Paula. With Paula, you always know where you stand. With Mom, people never see her coming. I mean, Paula and I do, but her boyfriends don't. They think they've got her all figured out, but in the end, they're always wrong.

I've got one more day of practice for cheer tryouts. You said you thought the cheerleaders were full of themselves. Some of them are, but there are a few who aren't bad. If I make the team, I'll send you a picture.

That's all I write. Even though this is my diary and no one is supposed to see it, I'm still careful because you never know who might find it.

It's not hard to imagine Kevin waking up and prowling around my room while I'm at school, his greasy hands sliding under my mattress. He'd poke around in my shoebox filled with treasures. Pretty river rocks, a piece of wood shaped like a heart, trinkets from the vending machines outside the grocery store, and the collar from our cat who died. Come to think of it, he's probably already done that.

Fortunately, Kevin's not patient enough to test all the floorboards in my bedroom. Even if he happened on the loose board under my bed, I don't think he'd pull out the piece of insulation and reach deep into the dark to feel around. But if he did, he still wouldn't get the whole truth.

Heavy footsteps outside my door make me glad I've already hidden my diary away. The footsteps stop. Then there's a knock at my door.

"Come in," I say. It's not what I want to say, but there's no other option.

Kevin opens the door. "Hey, Julie." He stands in the entryway wearing dirty work jeans and a plaid shirt. "How you doing?" He looks down at the floor.

"I'm good." I force a tight smile even though it hurts my cheek.

"Look, I'm real sorry about yesterday." His eyes are still on the floor. "It's not right what I did. You hear me? I'm sorry. You didn't deserve that."

When he looks up, his face is a picture of remorse.

"It's okay," I say softly. For a split second, I feel sorry for him. Not because of the way he's looking at me, but because I know what happens next.

"No. I lost my temper and that's not okay." His mouth is pinched, and his skin is a sickly shade of white.

"I forgive you."

He smiles. "I'm gonna make it up to you, okay? When you make that team—and I know you will, Juliebell—I'm gonna take you and your mom out for surf and turf. You know what that is?"

"No," I say, because I know he wants to tell me.

"Lobster and steak. With a baked potato plus ice cream for dessert. How's that sound?"

"Sounds great." I smile again, but this time I'm more careful, so it doesn't hurt my cheek.

"Okay, it's a promise. We're gonna celebrate right."

"Okay," I say, even though I know he won't make good on the promise.

It's already too late. Kevin's future was set in motion last night. By the time I find out whether I've made the team, Kevin will have moved on.

When I come downstairs, he's gone. Mom is looking out at the gray drizzle that hangs over the pasture with a dreamy expression on her face.

"Morning, Julie." Her voice is like bells and sunshine. "What time does your practice end today?"

"Five thirty."

"Denise and I switched shifts, so I can pick you up. We'll get dinner at McDonald's. How's that sound?"

"What about Kevin?"

"He already left for some job up in Salem. Who knows when he'll get back."

She stands and puts her coffee mug in the sink, all the while humming a little tune under her breath. When she sees me standing where she left me, she feigns surprise.

"Julie, what are you doing? Make yourself some breakfast before you miss the bus."

I pour myself a bowl of Cheerios, but I'm not hungry. When I open the trash to throw them away, I'm greeted by the leftover peaches from last night. They glisten in a puddle of their own juice; slick, wet, and dangerous. I tip my soggy Cheerios on top of them and try to ignore the way my stomach churns.

All day, I'm on edge.

Jumpy.

In English, Ms. Swanson has to call my name three times before I respond.

"What's got into you today, Julie?" she asks, shaking her head like she's disappointed.

"I'm sorry. Cheer tryouts are this week."

"So I'll have your attention back on Monday?" she asks with a grin, like we're sharing a joke.

"Yes, ma'am," I say. I smile like I practiced in the mirror, so that the place where Kevin's hand connected with my cheek doesn't hurt. Cheer tryouts are a convenient excuse, but that's not why I'm distracted.

In the bathroom, I check my makeup to make sure the bruise is still hidden. On my way out, I pass Ginny Schaeffer and her group of friends. I smile, but she looks away, tossing her thick blonde hair like she doesn't see me.

"Trash," someone says after I walk by.

I tell myself they're talking about something on the floor, but my face burns all the same. It doesn't matter. If I make the team, they won't be able to say those things about me. Cheerleaders wear their uniforms, and a uniform means looking exactly like everyone else.

After school, I walk to the high school gym by myself. The eighth graders have dwindled to me, Ginny, and three girls from the other middle school that feeds into our high school. Somehow, Ginny has already become friends with them. They form a tight-knit group of four. I sit by myself at the back of the gym until we start.

Halfway through practice, Deanna pulls me aside. "Just a reminder that we need you here tomorrow instead of Friday. I already told the judges what to expect. Have you checked the varsity practice schedule? No guarantees about the tryout, but I'm just wondering if you'd be able to make those times."

I put on the careful smile I've used all day. "Yeah, sure."

"Okay, great. Again, no promises." But the way she grins at me says something else.

From behind Deanna, I catch a death stare from Ginny.

"I understand," I say and smile. This time, I forget to be careful, and it makes me wince.

Deanna tilts her head to one side. Then she leans closer, inspecting my cheek. "Did that happen yesterday when we were stunting?"

When I nod, she makes a face.

"Sorry about that. Sometimes it happens, but you did a good job covering it up. It's barely noticeable."

After tryouts, I walk outside. Mom is already waiting for me in the white Corolla she bought after her last boyfriend moved on. Mom smiles and waves like I might not see her.

"Hey, Mom," I say, tossing my backpack into the back seat as I get in.

"How did it go?" she asks as she pulls out of the parking lot.

"Great."

I tell her about how Deanna singled me out to do lifts with varsity, how I'm trying out early, and how Ginny Schaeffer gave me dirty looks at practice.

"She's just jealous," Mom says, dismissively. "People will always try to tear you down, but don't let them. You forge your own path, just the way I've taught you."

I nod even though her advice misses the point. I'm not looking for my own path. I want to be headed the same direction as everyone else.

We go to McDonald's, and Mom orders for us: cheeseburgers with extra pickles, French fries, and Diet Coke. Mom finds us a lonely table in the corner, then peels open her cheeseburger and lines it with French fries. When she's done, she fixes me with an expression I know well.

"So, are you ready?"

She's not asking about tryouts. A moment ago, I was starving, but her question turns the food to sawdust in my mouth. I take a long sip of Diet Coke so that I can swallow.

"Did it already happen?"

Mom smiles sweetly. "You know, it's not an exact science, but I'm guessing as soon as tonight or tomorrow." She glances around to make sure no one is within eavesdropping distance. "You want to practice? Just in case anyone asks questions."

I shake my head because I don't need to practice. "Same as with Chris, right?"

Mom nods. Her eyes glisten. "We write the story."

This is Mom's favorite part. She has a different kind of energy, like she's been sleeping but now she's fully awake.

I take another long drink of Diet Coke. "I think I just want to go home. You know, get in a few more hours of practice for my tryout."

"That's my girl. Eyes on the prize." Mom's laugh is a mix of amusement and pride. Then she leans in and grabs my hand across the table, squeezing it hard in her own. "You're going to make that team, Julie. I can feel it. How about we go home and make a recording of your routines? That way if anyone happens to stop by, we can show them exactly what we've been up to."

"Sure."

I give her my careful smile. The one that doesn't hurt. Mom might say we choose our story, but that doesn't mean I can choose not to be part of hers.

She glances down at my food. "You're not eating."

"Not real hungry."

"Probably better. Stay nice and light for your tryout tomorrow, right?"

"Right," I say.

She knows why I'm not hungry, but neither of us will acknowledge it. It's part of the game we play. Mom makes the rules, and I follow them. I'm the only one who knows what happens if you don't follow Mom's rules.

Actually, that's not true.

Paula knows the rules of this game too, but Paula got tired of playing.

Mom says Paula left because she was pregnant, but that's not the whole truth.

It's just the piece Mom chooses to tell.

Nine

FALL

STELLA

The bedroom Stella shares with Tom is the size of a living room. That's without taking into account the two walk-in closets, one for her, one for Tom, and the en suite bathroom with its oversize steam shower and soaking tub. One side of the room has large windows that look out over the backyard.

In front of the windows, Stella installed a comfy chair and a love seat upholstered in a cheerful mix of yellows and blues that simultaneously evokes Southern charm and a French country aesthetic. Instead of a coffee table, there is a rectangular ottoman in a nubby, darker blue that ties the sitting area to the upholstery on their king-size bed.

When she decorated this room, which is larger than her first apartment, she imagined it as a retreat. The sitting area would be the place she and Tom engaged in thoughtful discussions about the books they'd recently read, each with a glass of wine in hand. This conversation would be the foreplay to slipping under the organic cotton sheets of their marital bed.

Stella now enters the bedroom and takes in the armchair, loaded with Tom's not-quite-dirty but not-quite-clean clothes. The ottoman has become a dumping ground for his briefcase and gym bag. The love seat is aggressively empty. Stella's silent rebuke to the mess on his chair.

Tellingly, there are no in-progress books anywhere in this carefully curated spot. No wineglasses either. She doesn't remember that they've ever sat here together. It occurs to her that she decorated this spot for the fictional version of the life she thought she and Tom would lead.

Tom emerges from the bathroom aggressively toweling his hair. "What are we wearing to this thing?"

"I just picked up what you're wearing from the dry cleaner. Your blue-and-white-checked shirt and J. Crew chinos. I don't know about me. This"—she holds a dress up against her body—"or this?" She holds up another one.

"Looks good," Tom says.

"Which one? It was a choice." Stella hates the sharp tone of her voice.

"First one. Definitely," Tom says without looking.

She quells the urge to throw a shoe at his retreating back. She feels needy, like a small child calling "Look at me. Look at me." But he was supposed to be the counterbalance to her desired invisibility. *He* was supposed to always see her.

According to everyone she knows, this is the normal state of marriage. A state her friends have outlined in exquisite detail. The slow erosion that takes place. A timeline where lovers become teammates, then slowly drift into being roommates who sort of coexist. She never thought that would happen in her marriage, but somehow maybe it did. While she was being the perfect mom, maybe she forgot to play the part of perfect wife.

That loss of control fills Stella with panic and a flash of something cold, dark, and dangerous.

But *no*! She won't go there.

"No, what?" Tom asks.

Stella looks up, startled, as Tom pulls on the pants she picked out. "What?"

"You said no. You don't like that dress?"

"I do," she says, smiling. "No, I do like it."

She drops both dresses on the love seat and walks over to Tom, putting her hands on his bare chest. "I love you," she says, looking up at him.

Tom smiles down at her. "I love you too, Stell." He seals his words with a kiss on the top of her head. While he's still holding her close, he clears his throat. "By the way, I think I'm going to invest some of our savings into this company that's doing innovative work with the food supply chain."

Stella pulls away. She trusts Tom, but one legacy of growing up poor is her constant nagging fear that there will never be enough.

"How much of our savings?"

"Not that much. I think they said the initial investment is like ten thousand dollars. Besides, it's sustainable. Something we can feel good about."

"I don't know. Are you sure we can afford it?"

"Of course we can. Don't worry. Haven't I always taken care of you?"

She nods, but the sentiment bothers her. It ignores the team aspect of their marriage. She's on the verge of pointing out that she takes care of him too when Tom releases her from the warmth of his embrace.

"Okay, chop chop. We don't want to be late."

"Right," Stella says and shimmies into the dress he didn't really choose.

They used to discuss every financial move in detail, but at some point, Tom's expertise outpaced Stella's. He's becoming more and more like his father, who can talk about investments and taxes for hours. He's also started arriving ten to twenty minutes early for everything. When it comes to flights, he tacks on an extra thirty minutes to the recommended two hours even though they have Clear *and* TSA PreCheck.

As she chooses high-heeled sandals and puts on earrings, a necklace, and a bracelet, she wonders what similarities Tom would notice between Stella and her mother. It's an unanswerable question because he's never met her mother. And he never will. Stella erased her, as though she never existed. The version of her mother Stella told him about—long dead, obviously—is one of her own creation. If there is some legacy of her mother that Stella carries around, Tom would never spot it. Neither would she, because that's how long it's been.

At least that's what she likes to tell herself.

Tonight's event is at the community center, which is public in the same way the schools Colin and Daisy attend are public.

On Zillow, there is only one house in their school district with an asking price of less than a million dollars. That house, a modest two-bedroom, 1950s brick rambler, can be had for $945,000. The whole community, with its walking and jogging trails, parks, the community center where tonight's event will be held, prize-winning playgrounds, libraries, and high-performing schools with the latest technology including NASA-certified science labs, is, in theory, "public."

"Ready?" Tom asks impatiently.

"Yep," Stella says.

The community center was recently renovated with a swanky, modern aesthetic that pays homage to the traditional brick of Northern Virginia. Floor-to-ceiling windows look out over the park, and a sweeping terrace wraps around the front of the building.

As they walk hand in hand to the event, Stella reminds herself this is her life. She is not an imposter. She belongs here.

Even though they are early, other people are already milling about.

"Stella!" Lorraine waves energetically as they walk in.

With a parting squeeze of Tom's hand, Stella heads toward Lorraine.

Lorraine is flanked by two other members of the fundraising committee: Anna Duval, a former lobbyist, and Rachel Stewart, a former marketing exec.

As Stella greats them, she thinks about how they are all former somethings. Like Stella, they all *chose* to stay home. Even if "chose" isn't exactly the right word given the unappealing reality of balancing a paid job where salaries are often curtailed by never-ending mom labor.

Or, as Lorraine puts it, "The doctors don't tell you that active labor can last for twenty-one years."

"Someone should be circulating with drinks." Lorraine's eyes slice over to Anna, who is in charge of food and beverage.

"Fucking caterer," Anna growls, shaking her head. Her long earrings, delicate strands of silver that hang like miniature curtains, shimmer in the light. "I told them we needed at least five people on the floor. No one's offered you anything yet, right, Stella?"

Stella opens her mouth, but before she can speak, Anna is waving imperiously at a young man bearing a tray laden with glasses.

"Over here."

The man trots toward them like a well-trained puppy, and Anna presses a glass of pale, sparkling liquid into Stella's hand.

Now that Stella has a glass, Lorraine raises hers. "Here's to a recruitment season featuring all the Ivies."

As they obediently sip from their flutes, Lorraine adds, sotto voce,

"Thank God we can all stop pretending college is about academic merit."

They laugh, but in a muted way that won't draw too much attention.

As Stella glances around the room, she wonders how she slipped through the cracks into this life. It was a one-off. Those cracks are being shored up by women like these, whose children are like Stella's own. Adequately smart, moderately talented, with unlimited access to the best tutors and coaches money can buy.

That's what this auction is about.

That's what her life, and the lives of all these other women who left their jobs, is about. They're all in the business of preserving the status quo for their children. It's a thought that raises the specter, for the second time in a single evening, of her own mother. What legacy did she pass to Stella?

Stella quickly drains her glass as a way of avoiding the answer.

And yet there's her secret room. The hot burn of anger that (almost) compelled her to throw her shoe at Tom. That flash of imagining her spiky heel embedded in the back of her husband's skull. The weight of the penknife and her hidden key. That's who she is. Her mother's legacy is a snarling, teeth-bared creature that has nothing in common with the polished, pretty face Stella presents to the world.

Stella takes a deep breath, smiles, and forces her focus back to Lorraine.

"Okay, so we need to make sure people are bidding on baskets. We're not even going to talk about the fact that Rachel had to go pick them up from Gwen's house at the last minute. I'd like you all to work the room. Make sure everyone has a drink. Got it, ladies?" Lorraine smiles. She is an effortless leader who expects the best and gets it.

As they mix and mingle, a heretical thought occurs to Stella. What if she didn't follow orders? What if, instead, she slipped away? Escaped the small talk she dreads.

As though the thought has set her course of action, she makes her way to a side door like a fugitive. As she goes, she grabs another glass of sparkling wine. If someone asks where she's going, she'll say she's looking for the bathroom, or there's an issue with the caterers. Or she'll ask them why the fuck they need to know her every movement.

The idea of that retort makes her giggle.

What's wrong with her tonight?

It's the first of many questions emerging from somewhere deep within. Why, earlier, did Tom push her away instead of pushing her down on the bed and fucking her hard?

Again with the language. She rolls her eyes at her own potty mouth.

Why does Stella need a secret room? And why did Gwen leave her phone at Stella's house? Why didn't Stella return it immediately? And where should she drop it to make sure Gwen finds it and never, ever connects its temporary disappearance to Stella?

Something that's been hibernating inside her stirs. Or maybe this is some sort of anxiety attack? A midlife crisis? It's possible this is just too much Costco prosecco on an empty stomach.

The door opens behind her and Stella jumps, but it's only one of the caterers.

"Only," Stella whispers to herself.

How did she become this person who, in addition to air-kissing, looks through the people hired to make her life easier? Cleaning services, lawn maintenance crews, baristas, grocery store baggers, and caterers.

She needs air.

She needs space.

Nimbly, she slips away from the building, staying on the cement path so her heels won't sink into the ground. She pauses, looking back at the soft lighting that shines up through the trees near the community center, and feels grateful for the shroud of darkness. The path winds through the wooded part of the park. Stella walks into these woods without fear because in this community, the most dangerous thing she's likely to encounter is a mangy fox.

She finds a bench on the path and sits, slipping her feet halfway out of her heels. The home screen of her phone has zero notifications, a fact that is almost alarming. When she looks back up, she realizes she has a clear view of the festivities inside the community center. Lorraine, tall, blonde, and statuesque, nods, actively listening to a group of men dressed in outfits similar to what Stella selected for Tom. Stella squints; one of those men might actually be Tom, but she's not sure. Her vision isn't as good as it used to be. A wave of fatigue hits her. She wonders if this is what it feels like to grow old, then remembers she's had two glasses of prosecco.

She watches from the dark as the scene unfolds. Lorraine moves to another group. Stella spots Anna, then Rachel, and feels a flash of guilt. She should get back. She's being irresponsible, hiding out here in the dark like a child. The strange tide of emotions swept in by the combination of privilege-on-steroids and cheap prosecco is already waning. She is about to stand, to return to the party, where she will do Lorraine's bidding, when the sound of voices makes her freeze.

The reasonable, respectable thing to do would be to call out a cheerful hello.

Instead, Stella turns, on tiptoe, and flees toward the tennis courts.

"But we had an agreement." The voice is a woman's, her speech slurred as though she's had too much to drink. Or maybe that's just Stella.

The second voice is a man's, hushed. As much as she strains to hear, she can't make out his words.

"No. I'm done. I'm done with this bullshit," the woman protests.

It's the kind of conversation that shouldn't be overheard. Stella knows this by instinct. She peers through the dark, looking for an alternate route back to the community center off the sidewalk and through the trees, but she's hobbled by her heels.

The couple is still talking, but the woman's volume is more modulated now. The blue light of a phone illuminates them both, throwing them into relief so that the two figures are a black outline against the blacker darkness.

"Seriously?" the woman says. "I can't fucking believe you just did that."

"What?" says the man.

Stella's phone vibrates in her hand. She grits her teeth. Why now, at the worst possible time, has someone decided to text her? She can't look, though. Not when she's accidentally bearing witness to someone's secret drama. The light might give her away.

"You can't even focus on me for ten minutes? It's always about her. Everyone is always so fucking focused on her."

"What do you mean, 'everyone'? What are you talking about? I'm here, aren't I?" The man's voice is simultaneously strident and hushed. The voice of someone trying to win a fight without being overheard.

Stella feels the way his response is unsatisfactory. She's taking the woman's side without even seeing her. One of the figures breaks away, heading toward the light instead of deeper into the park. Stella draws a breath of relief, grateful she won't be discovered. The man steps out of the shadows too, but pauses to glance at his phone. In that brief moment, Stella squints at his receding back.

Is the man wearing a blue-and-white-checked shirt?

Like the one she picked for Tom?

Ten

SPRING 1987

JULIE

I was eight when Dad moved on. Paula was twelve. After he was gone, Mom taught me and Paula how to write our own story.

It's all about believing. Actors do it all the time. They slip into someone else's life like they're changing clothes. There's even a book that talks about it, sort of.

Ozma of Oz, by L. Frank Baum, who also wrote *The Wizard of Oz*. Ozma is a princess who always wears a white dress. She doesn't have lots of pretty dresses like other princesses because her closet is filled with different heads. She gets to be a different person whenever the mood strikes her. Instead of changing her dress, she changes her head and turns into someone else.

The tricky part is knowing how to become someone else without having a closet full of heads like Ozma.

"You decide who you're going to be, and that's that," Mom told me and Paula. She hadn't bothered to cover up the marks on her neck or arms, but her smile was so bright you barely noticed the blooms of purple and red.

"Whatever happened in the past, it happened the way you decide. And if you don't like the way it happened, you vanish it. Poof!" Mom snapped her fingers. "Just like that. It's gone."

Me and Paula were sitting next to each other on the couch.

"What if I want to be Princess Diana?" Paula asked, rolling her eyes. "I get to just make Paula disappear? Poof?"

The sparkle went out of Mom's smile. She pushed herself out of the rocking chair and crossed the living room so she was right in front of us. Then she crouched so she was eye level with Paula and waited, but Paula didn't understand that this was her chance to apologize. When Paula didn't say anything, Mom grabbed her by both shoulders. Her eyes got narrow in a way that meant business.

"Don't be stupid, Paula," she hissed. "This is important."

It might not sound like much, but Mom can be scary when she's mad. She scared Paula, anyway.

"I'm not the one that's stupid!" Paula yelled as she ran upstairs. Then the door to our bedroom slammed and the whole house shook.

Mom glared up at the ceiling like she had X-ray vision and could see Paula stretched out on her bed crying. "I don't know why your sister's so bullheaded," she said with a heavy sigh that made her shoulders slump.

She collapsed on the couch where Paula had been sitting. "I love you both so much," she whispered. "No matter what happens, we're going to survive. Everything I do is for you girls."

"I know, Mom," I said, because unlike Paula, I can read a cue.

"You know what I'm saying, don't you, Julie? Let's talk it through, okay?" She waited for me to nod, then said, "You miss your dad, right?"

I nodded again. Just thinking about him made my throat feel tight and like I couldn't catch my breath.

"I know, sweetheart. I miss him too." She rubbed my back. "But that's what happens after someone is gone. At first you feel so much pain you can barely stand it. After a while, though, you start to see the truth. And when you do, it makes you angry. You'll start to ask questions. How could he have been so careless? What kind of man behaves like that when he has a wife and two daughters who love him?"

"It wasn't his fault."

The words slipped out before I could stop them. I braced myself for Mom's anger, but it didn't come. Instead, she swiveled so she was facing me on the couch. Elbows on her knees, chin on her hands. Her eyes looked through me like she could see into my brain.

"But it *was* his fault, Julie. That's what you need to understand. Your dad made choice after choice. And each time, it took away *our* ability to choose. A person only gets to make so many decisions over the course of a lifetime. If things had continued, he would have used up all of mine."

I shifted my gaze down and she grabbed my chin, forcing me to look at her.

"You see what he did to me," she whispered. Her voice was soft, but her eyes were hard. "It couldn't go on like that. At some point, he would have gone too far. Then you and Paula would have been alone with him. I couldn't have that. Do you understand?"

She waited, her fingers digging into the flesh of my chin, until I nodded.

"Good," she said, smiling. "When he got liquored up that night and stumbled down to the river, he made a choice to move on, and now we're free."

"We get to write our own story," I said.

Mom nodded and gave me an encouraging smile. "That's exactly right, sweetheart. Now, there's one more thing that needs to happen in order for us to be safe. Can you help me retell the past so we can protect our future?"

I nodded again.

Mom made it sound glamorous. I couldn't be Princess Di—that was dumb—but I *could* be Princess Ozma. That's part of Mom's special skill. Whatever she's doing, she makes it feel magical. Like it's a special treat and you're the only one who gets to be part of it.

Mom grinned, then every trace of joy drained out of her face and her eyes went big. She had put on a different head. When Mom spoke, her voice was shaky.

"I never thought of your dad as someone with a drinking problem, but sometimes"—she took a deep breath and gently touched one of the marks on her neck—"he lost control. He wasn't himself, but he was a good father." Her eyes glistened with tears.

My eyes filled with tears too. It was like she said. I missed him so much it hurt.

"Your dad made some bad decisions," Mom said, shaking her head. "I worry those decisions could come back to haunt us."

"What kind of decisions?"

"It's a secret," she said, leaning close. "But I can tell you, Julie, because I trust you."

After she told me, I promised not to tell anyone. But that wasn't right either. This was the part where she needed my help. When your mom needs your help, you don't ask questions. You do what she needs. Especially when you know she'd do anything for you.

ON THURSDAY, I WEAR THE head that is Julie-who-minds-her-own-business. It's the version where I cover my bruises, keep Mom's secrets and my own. My secret isn't dangerous; it's just a cheer tryout. Technically, my early tryout isn't even a secret.

In science, I glance at Ginny and her friends. I wonder if Deanna invited Ginny to try out today too. Part of me wants to ask, but I'm afraid that the answer will be no. Mom says to never ask a question if you don't want to know the answer, so I don't. Instead, I imagine making the team and having a group of my own just like Ginny.

After my tryout, Deanna gives me a big hug.

"You looked great, Julie," she says.

"What about the dance routine? You think it was good enough?"

She grins at me. "You'll just have to wait for the list, along with everyone else." But she gives me a wink that answers my question.

For the first time in almost forever, my life feels absolutely perfect. I don't want anything to change.

Still, all day Friday, I'm shaky with nerves.

At lunchtime, even though I can't eat, I sit in the cafeteria with the girls who are the closest thing I have to friends. We share a lunch table and sit next to each other in classes. What we don't do is have sleepovers or socialize outside of school. We're not real friends. We're more like animals huddled together to survive a storm. In this case, the storm is middle school.

"Nervous?" Ginny Schaeffer stops at our table. Her face is tight, and her eyes are like twin blue lasers.

"Yeah," I say with an appropriately nervous smile.

This isn't a lie. I have a long list of things to be nervous about. Fortunately, getting through my tryout is at the bottom of that list.

"I don't even know why they're letting us try out." Ginny rolls her eyes. "Megan says none of the eighth graders are going to make it. At this point, it's honestly like a waste of time. I might not even go."

I nod along as she talks, but Ginny tilts her head to one side like a bird spotting a worm in the grass.

"If you want to just, like, skip it, we could go grab Slurpees at 7-Eleven. I mean, I *have* to try out. If I don't, Megan will know and I'll get in trouble, but we could go after I'm done."

I shrug. "Okay, sure."

"So you're not going to try out?"

Ginny's eyes light up with the same look Mom's boyfriends get when she asks if they want to go upstairs, a mixture of hope and anticipation.

"I'll definitely try out next year," I say, hoping Ginny doesn't notice the way I'm avoiding her question.

"Yeah, totally. I'll even help you. I mean, if I make it. And it's been such a good experience to go to tryout practice. It'll totally give you an advantage for next year." She's babbling, trying to hide her smile. "So, I'll do my tryout and we'll walk over to 7-Eleven afterward while we're waiting for them to post the list?"

"Yeah, sure."

"Great. You'll be my moral support!"

She bounces off to her table. When she sits down, her friends suck tight around her like a sea anemone after it's been touched.

"You're really not going to try out?" asks Erica Lempke.

Erica is pretty, with long, curly brown hair, but she's hit what Mom calls an awkward phase. She has curves but hasn't shed her baby fat yet. The boys in our class either make mooing noises when they pass her in the hallway or beg her to show them her tits.

"I already did," I tell her. "Yesterday, with varsity."

"Really?" Erica's eyes gleam. "How did it go?"

I allow myself a tiny smile. "I'll find out today."

Erica grins like I've given her a gift. "I hope you make it." Her eyes dart over to Ginny's table. "And I hope she doesn't."

After school, Ginny appears at my locker. "Let's walk over together," she says.

Her plan is as obvious as her unsubtle attempt to manipulate my nonexistent fear of heights. She's decided to babysit me so I won't have time to change my mind. I wonder if she understands how clearly this is written on her face.

The entry hall outside the auditorium where tryouts will take place is crowded with girls warming up.

"Megan! Hey, Megan!" Ginny calls. "Have you met Julie? She came to give me moral support."

"Are you trying out today too?" Megan asks.

Her face is blank, as though she's never seen me before. As though she didn't scold me when I sat on the sidelines or try to sabotage me on lift day.

"No," Ginny answers for me. "She's just keeping me company."

"Nice." Megan's smile sweeps over me and lands on Ginny with a look of understanding.

Ginny's tryout slot is fifteen out of forty-eight. "Wish me luck," she says, grabbing my hand before she goes in. Hers is slick with sweat.

"You'll do great," I say.

When she comes out of the auditorium, her face is grim.

"Let's go," she says, grabbing her wallet out of her backpack. As we walk to 7-Eleven, Ginny details all her mistakes.

"It's such tough competition, Julie," she tells me. "You should be so glad you didn't try out. I really don't think any eighth graders are going to make it."

We buy Slurpees. Coke flavor for Ginny, cherry for me. We drink them sitting on the metal bleachers that overlook the baseball field.

"Next year we'll be in high school." Ginny's tone is reverent as she looks out at the middle school kids. "It's like the official end of childhood."

"Yeah," I say, wondering what it must be like to be able to pinpoint that moment.

The list goes up at 6:00. We leave the bleachers at 5:55 and walk back to the gym.

"It's going to be okay," Ginny whispers under her breath. "Even if I don't make it, I can try out again next year. We'll try out together." She loops her arm through mine, and I feel like we're in this together. Today, we'll both make the team. Being cheerleaders will mark the start of our friendship. A real friendship, not the kind where you're just trying to survive.

"You're gonna make it," I say.

"You really think so?" Her voice quavers.

I nod. "I really do."

"Thanks, Julie," she says and smiles at me.

As we enter the high school, a girl passes us. She's walking fast in the opposite direction. There are tears in her eyes. Halfway down the hall, girls are crowded around the auditorium door. You can tell who made the team by who is jumping up and down and hugging.

Ginny grabs my hand and drags me toward the front of the knot. My heart hammers. My body floods with nerves. As I scan the list for JV, I realize how much I want this.

Ginny's on the list, right above her sister, Megan. They've both made the team.

I scan the entire list twice, but my name isn't there.

"Congratulations," I say softly, but Ginny has dropped my hand.

Her eyes are cold and angry.

"You fucking lied to me," she says.

I look back at the results. There are two lists. One for JV and one for varsity. I scan the varsity list and see my name.

Before I can explain to Ginny what happened, Deanna appears next to me.

"Here she is," she says, giving me a hug. Her smile is warm, and she drapes one arm around my shoulder, leading me over to the other girls who've made varsity. "Let me introduce our only varsity freshman."

The other girls welcome me with equal warmth. It's a feeling of perfect happiness. A wave sweeping over me and filling me with joy.

Then I make the mistake of looking back.

Ginny and Megan are in a huddle with the other girls who've made JV. When Ginny catches my gaze, her eyes narrow. Yesterday I didn't exist, but now she sees me. She's marked me in a way I recognize. I've seen that same expression on Mom's boyfriends' faces.

It tells me to watch out.

Be careful.

Never give them an excuse to attack.

Eleven

FALL

STELLA

Stella stumbles into the community center. She feels unsteady, as if she's had too many glasses of prosecco, but she hasn't. Instead, the ground has shifted beneath her.

The checked shirt the man was wearing only narrows her choices down to half the men attending tonight's event. Again, Stella replays what she overhead.

She'd recognize Tom's voice, wouldn't she? And there's no reason to think he would be sneaking off to argue with an unknown woman.

A warm hand presses against her back, and Stella starts as though she's guilty of something more than neglecting her auction duties.

"Hey," Tom says in her ear. "Where ya been? I was looking for you."

She studies him. He doesn't look like he was skulking around in the dark. There are no twigs in his hair or mud on his shoes. He seems normal, fine, like her Tom. The person she's known for almost two decades.

"I was in the bathroom."

"You okay?" He looks genuinely concerned.

Stella grasps at the first plausible excuse. "That prosecco." She makes a face. "I probably shouldn't have had it on an empty stomach."

He nods and hands her a small plate filled with appetizers. "Want me to get you anything else?"

"Ginger ale?" She says it like a question, and Tom smiles his approval.

"Come here." He pulls her in for a hug.

Setting the appetizers on a table, Stella allows Tom to hold her close, pressing her face into the blue-and-white check of his shirt. She breathes deep, searching the fabric for any hint of the outdoors, but all she smells is aftershave and the particular scent that is Tom. Familiar and comforting.

Stella has a theory that memories are contained not in the mind but in the body. Touch the right spot and your brain floods with buried images.

That's what happens when Tom pats her back. His hand travels to her bra strap area and he squeezes her side, just under her armpit. It's a small gesture, meant to be comforting, but Stella gasps and twists away.

"Stella, what's wrong?"

Her heart pounds. For a split second, he's someone else. Someone who can hurt her. Then the look on his face morphs. Whatever she remembered is already buried back in its proper place.

"Nothing," she says. "I'm ticklish."

Tom laughs. Not in a careful way designed to hide something, but in the way someone laughs when they've never had anything to hide. Then, making an exaggerated performance out of being careful, he pulls her close and kisses her like they're at a high school dance instead of a school fundraiser.

"Sorry to interrupt you two lovebirds," says Lorraine, looking slightly frazzled. "Tom, I need your gorgeous wife for like, an hour, tops."

"What if I'm not prepared to share her?" Tom asks.

"Aren't you funny," Lorraine says, although it's clear she's not amused.

She loops her arm through Stella's and steers her toward the silent auction table.

"Two things: Gwen Thompson totally flaked out on me, and people are being absolutely ruthless."

"What happened?" Stella asks.

"They're erasing bids. Like they don't think anyone will notice. I mean, come on, this is a fundraiser. They should be absolutely ashamed. That's why I need you on silent auction duty."

"No, I meant with Gwen."

"She said she had the whole thing under control, then disappeared.

I don't know where she went. Okay, stand here and pull the bid sheets in ten-minute increments."

"Got it," Stella says.

"Here." Lorraine presses a glass of something pale into Stella's hand. "White Burgundy. It's from my personal stash, not whatever shit Anna's caterer is pouring." She lands an extravagant smooch on Stella's cheek. "Thank you. You're a love."

Stella takes a sip of the Burgundy, then remembers she barely touched Tom's plate of appetizers. She sets the glass down and a little wine slops onto the silent auction table, earning her a disapproving look from a man wearing a shirt similar to Tom's.

"Hello and welcome to our annual boosters event," Lorraine says into a microphone on the dais near the windows. She pauses, and the room obediently grows quiet. "Langley is more than just our local high school. It's the reason many of us moved to this community. Consistently ranked in the top one hundred in the nation. We're fortunate to have access to such an amazing public school system. However, 'free' is a relative term, and public schools can always use our support, which brings me to the reason we've gathered here tonight. Why we've left our children at home, with strict instructions to not have more than two people over and definitely no one of the opposite sex."

This comment elicits both applause and laughter. Stella smiles from behind the table and scans the room, searching for Gwen. Instead, she spots Tom standing with three other men, looking politely up at the stage. He catches her glance and gives her a half smile and a raised eyebrow. She mimics his expression because, long ago, she learned that mimicry is the easiest way to signal agreement. Although she'd be hard-pressed to specify what exactly they're agreeing about. She tells herself the "what" isn't important. The important thing is that they agree.

What would have caused Gwen to flake, as Lorraine put it?

The only response is the growl of Stella's stomach. It's not a subtle sound.

A waiter hovers nearby with a tray of hors d'oeuvres. While Lorraine holds forth, Stella makes her way to the waiter and quickly devours two snack-size crab cakes. A nearby dad (clad in a green-and-white-checked shirt) observing this looks vaguely startled, as though the urgency of her hunger has caught him off guard.

"Such a busy day with the auction. I completely forgot to eat," she whispers, pairing the excuse with a smile.

He nods and grabs the waiter, who is moving away. "Another one for one of the fine ladies who put together tonight's event," he says.

Stella smiles and takes another crab cake.

"Thanks," she says, dutifully.

"No problem." He smiles like he's done more than provide her with a single bite of food.

Stella rolls her eyes. Tells herself to focus.

Where is Gwen?

Lorraine is still talking from the dais. Not droning, exactly, but it's clear she's only halfway through her speech. Stella makes a break for the bathroom.

As she leaves, she glances back at the auction table, because she doesn't want to be described as a flake.

That's when she sees her.

Gwen Thompson.

Her gaze is laser-focused on Stella. A look far more intense and calculated than any of their interactions warrant. Narrowed eyes and unsmiling mouth. It's actively aggressive. Women in McLean don't look at each other like that unless something is really and truly wrong.

Gwen must know Stella has her phone.

Even worse, she knows Stella has been lying and avoiding her.

Fortunately, Dave appears next to Gwen, commanding her attention. Stella uses the moment to slip Gwen's phone out of her clutch, turn it on, and kick it under the silent auction table. It's the thinnest veneer of plausible deniability, but it will have to do. She glances back at Gwen, who still has her back turned, and walks quickly toward the bathroom. Hopefully, in Stella's absence, Gwen will return to her assigned post at the silent auction table and discover her phone.

The bathroom is cool and semi-dark, with marble walls. Stella locks herself inside a stall and presses one cheek against the marble like she's feverish. As she puts a paper liner over the toilet seat, tugs her dress up over her hips, and pulls down her no-lines underwear, she tells herself another version of the story behind Gwen's glare.

She was upset that Stella took over the silent auction table.

People can be touchy about that kind of thing. That's what it is. She'll need to smooth things over. Find Gwen and compliment her on the baskets. Tell her she was happy to pinch-hit but doesn't want to steal her glory.

As Stella rehearses her words, she glances down. A spot of blood has stained her underwear.

"Fuck," she swears softly under her breath.

As she feels around in her clutch for a tampon, her hand makes contact with her phone. Somehow, an hour has passed without her checking it. Even worse, she forgot to read the text that came while she was in the park. The realization makes her feel panicky, like she's neglected something important. A litany of the things that could have gone wrong floods her mind.

A car crash.

A fall down the stairs.

Alcohol poisoning.

A freak accident like being hit while crossing the street or being shot by someone's father's gun or falling out of a second-story window or drowning or . . .

The possibilities leave her feeling dizzy with panic. She knows this is anxiety, but she also knows it's not unfounded, because the things she worries about have happened to people she knows (or knows about). Worry won't change the outcome, but somehow it really feels like it might. If she lists everything there is to worry about, she's somehow warding it off.

That's not how it works. She's aware. Although she's also aware that details are important. That you have to exercise caution, or you risk losing the thread that pulls you through the story you've chosen.

Her heart stops racing when she sees the text is from Tom.

Were are you

Tom's typo makes her smile and wonder if he's buzzed too. For a moment, she considers a flirtatious response. Something along the lines of *In the bathroom. Come find me.*

Stella starts to type it, but then remembers this text was sent earlier, while she was outside in the park. She swipes left to check the time. Yes, she's correct. He did say he was looking for her earlier.

She reads the text again. Something about it is off. It's not what Tom wrote that bothers her, but something else. Something she can't quite articulate.

She puts her phone down and picks up the tampon, then changes her mind. It's just a spot. She's wearing black. It'll be fine. So what if blood runs down her leg? Why can her husband rearrange his balls during polite conversation but her monthly cycle has to be invisible? She wipes, pulls down her dress, and leaves the toilet stall feeling like a rebel.

At the sinks, in the dim light that's designed to be flattering, she scrubs her hands. Reapplies her lipstick, smooths her hair, and reviews her plan: make nice to Gwen and claim complete and total innocence on every other front.

Lorraine is winding down as Stella reenters the room. She glances toward the place where she last saw Gwen, but she's not there. She's not at the silent auction table either. Stella heads back to her post with a vague sense of unease. Behind the table, she pastes on a smile and makes small talk with the people drifting over.

"Last bids for the Vail vacation house," she calls, one hand on the sheet of paper.

As she takes Vail off the table, it hits her.

Tom's text.

That typo plus the lack of question mark. Small things, barely noticeable. She *wouldn't* have noticed if the kids didn't tease him about his insistence on proofreading text messages and using correct punctuation. A list including, but not limited to, capital letters, commas, semicolons, periods, question marks, and definitely autocorrects. Two of his rules broken in a single text. Arguably, the question mark could have been a mistake. He could have hit send too soon, but there's no similar rationalization for a lawyer whose livelihood depends on word choice, to miss the autocorrect.

Unless he was in a rush.

Outside in the dark, trying to communicate with his wife while talking to another woman.

Gwen Thompson flaked on the silent auction.

Gwen and Tom are having an affair.

PART THREE

Twelve

APRIL 2015

PAULA

There are all kinds of smarts. It's something people talk about now, but they didn't talk about it when we were little. Nobody ever bothered to say to me, "Paula, you can't fly through a book the way your sister can, but that doesn't mean you're dumb."

Nope, they thought I was dumb.

I had a hard time in school. Reading was a struggle. By the time I'd get through a sentence, I couldn't remember the way it started. I'd have to go back and reread the whole thing. It took at least two times before I could get a sentence to take hold in my head. And math, well, it was kind of the same thing. I'd try to listen, but pretty soon I was staring out the window. The only subject I liked was science. It had rules that made sense to me. And there wasn't as much reading, so I could keep the meanings of the words straight without too much trouble.

I worked hard, but my grades were mostly Cs with a few Ds sprinkled in for variety. I usually managed a B for science, and let me tell you, that was something to celebrate. Mom didn't worry about my grades too much. It was always Julie, with her big books and fancy words, that Mom worried about most.

"Paula may be bullheaded, but she's got common sense," Mom would say when she was talking about us. "Julie, she's my little dreamer."

I was the practical one. Street-smart, is what they call it now. I could see what was going on around us, but Julie wasn't like that. She bought into Mom's vision, hook, line, and sinker.

Mom didn't like that I had my own thoughts about things. If she was in a bad mood, she'd turn it against me and say I wasn't good at writing my own story. That I'd never amount to anything in life.

She was wrong about that.

I knew who I was and where I was headed.

Another difference between me and Julie was that I didn't feel the need to dress the truth up in a fancy ballgown. Julie was good at putting lipstick on a pig.

As for me, I look at a pig and I see mud, shit, and the potential for bacon.

You ask Julie, and she'd have you believing Mom was some sort of fashion guru. You ask me, and I'd tell you the real reason Mom wore those long dresses with long sleeves, even in the summer. I'd also tell you why she hardly ever went out without makeup.

If you value your privacy the way Mom did, you can't walk around with bruises in every shade of the crayon box. Sunset marks, that's what I called them before I knew what they were. They moved around. Sometimes they were on her neck. Sometimes on her arms, and every so often on her face.

Dad never gave her black eyes, though. I don't know why. I never got to ask him about it.

I think about Dad most in April. That's when it happened.

In the morning, when we came downstairs, Mom was waiting for us. It was still cold outside and had rained hard the night before, so the river was swollen.

"Girls, your dad moved on," Mom said.

Her face was swollen too. She hadn't bothered with her makeup. Bruises climbed up her neck like some sort of disease.

"Are you sure?" I asked. I could feel the hot press of tears in my eyes.

Mom nodded.

Part of me wanted to ask questions about what happened the night before, but I didn't. I was stubborn that way. The more questions I asked, the more she'd swap her truth for mine. I didn't want to let that happen.

"Will he come back?" Julie asked.

"No," Mom said and pulled us both into a hug. "You don't need to worry. He's not ever coming back, and he can't hurt us anymore. I made sure of that. It's my job to keep you both safe. That's the only thing that matters."

"Dad never hurt me," I said.

It was the wrong thing to say. I could tell by the way her eyes burned. She looked like she was trying to set me on fire.

"And now he never will," Mom said in a way that shut me up.

I wanted to cry. Hell, I was twelve. I should have been allowed to cry, but Mom wanted me to be tougher than that. She wanted me to set a good example for Julie.

Sometimes I still think about how much I loved my dad. I knew what he was doing to Mom, but I loved him all the same. That knowledge has been real helpful to me in my line of work. If I'm on duty, they always send me on the DV calls. A lot of the men on the force don't understand that love isn't something you turn off and on like a switch. It's something that sticks around, even when your brain tells you you should know better.

Before Dad moved on, there was a routine to it.

As soon as it started up, I knew to grab Julie. We'd go upstairs and slide the boards across our bedroom door. Then we'd stay real quiet, like that would make us disappear. Julie would read her book. I'd lie on my bed and try not to hear what was happening on the other side of the door. No matter what, we had to keep the door locked until Mom gave us the signal to come out.

Mom built that special lock on our bedroom door herself. She did it while Dad was out so he wouldn't know what she was up to. Two large wooden brackets were mounted on either side of the door. Inside our closet, hidden behind our clothes, were two thick boards that slid through the brackets. Mom hung curtains around the door to hide the brackets and told Dad they were our princess curtains. He never thought to pull them back.

When it was over, she'd twist our doorknob twice to the right, once to the left. It was a silent signal that it was safe to come out. It had to be silent. Dad wouldn't have liked it if he'd known the three of us were keeping secrets.

That's the bad part.

That doesn't mean there weren't good parts.

Dad loved to roughhouse with me and Julie in the living room. We'd run at him and jump right on his back like puppies ready to tussle.

"Sharon, help. These wild animals have me outnumbered," he'd say, laughing and tossing us on the couch.

Mom would come to the kitchen door. She'd watch us with a little half smile. Like there was nothing better than what she saw in that living room.

"Look how pretty your mom is," Dad would say.

They'd share a look that contained a whole conversation that didn't involve me and Julie.

"Pretty" was the wrong word for Mom, but Dad was more like me when it came to words. "Pretty" makes Mom sound like the kind of mom you see in the Sears catalog, but she wasn't like that. There was something about her that made you want to keep looking. Fierce eyes that made you feel like she could see inside your head and long hair that floated down to her waist. One of her boyfriends, the one I was most intimately acquainted with, said she was a wild horse he intended to tame. I guess that was his way of saying she was always out of reach. Maybe that wildness is why people acted like they couldn't get enough of her.

As for me, I got plenty of her.

Sometimes more than I wanted.

When Dad was in a good mood, there wasn't anyone else like him. If Mom was working the evening shift at the nursing home and he had gas in his car, we'd drive into town for a fun run.

That's what he called it.

He'd take us to the grocery store and let us pick our favorite kind of candy.

At home, we'd have ice cream and microwave popcorn for dinner. Then we'd stay up late watching TV until we heard Mom's car in the driveway.

"Upstairs. Quick now. Don't make a sound," he'd say, shooing us out of the living room.

That was something they both agreed on. Neither of them wanted us to make a sound when we were in our room behind the door.

The problem was, there were too many things they didn't agree on. Things like Dad drinking or Mom working the night shift, which meant Dad had to fix us breakfast, or Dad growing weed out in the woods behind the house and selling it to make ends meet.

It was a big deal back then. A criminal offense. People went to jail for a long time for growing weed. It wasn't like now, when you can walk into a dispensary and buy it in the daylight.

"Paul, if you get caught, I could get fired. Or we could lose the girls," Mom would say.

"That's the problem right there. I don't know why you're working that goddamn job anyway. You should be home with the girls. I can't be looking after them all the time."

"My goddamn job is the only reason we could buy groceries last month."

A conversation like that was the signal for me and Julie to head upstairs and barricade the door. Sometimes I didn't lie on my bed. Sometimes I'd sit next to the door and listen. His fist made a particular sound when he hit her. Not loud like a slap, but a deep kind of thunk.

That sound made my stomach hurt like he'd hit me instead.

"It was a discussion, Paula. Sometimes adults disagree," Mom would say if I asked her about it later. Her face would be tight and her makeup freshly done.

"Your mom is one crazy bitch. That's what happened," Dad would say.

That's how I learned everyone has their own version of the truth.

Mom's version of the night Dad moved on is one where all the rough edges are smoothed away.

My version is a little different. The first thing I remember from that night is Mom shaking me out of bed.

"Paula. Paula," she whispered close to my ear so Julie wouldn't wake up. "I need your help."

Her voice sounded strange. Hoarse, like she'd been crying, but there was something else there too. Something that told me I needed to do whatever she said. Not ask questions.

She had me get dressed in the hallway outside our room. Downstairs, Dad was lying on the kitchen floor. He was kind of crumpled up like he'd had too much to drink and passed out. It wasn't the first time I'd seen him like that.

"We've gotta move him," Mom said.

"Where?" I reached for the kitchen light, but she slapped my hand away.

"No," she hissed. "We don't want to wake him up, Paula."

He was passed out drunk. Dead to the world. There was no way the kitchen light would have woken him up. It didn't make sense, but I knew better than to argue.

"Help me get him outside," Mom said. "I can't do it by myself."

"Outside?"

"Cold air. It'll be good for him."

That's when I noticed her hair was wet, like she'd already been out in the rain. She unfolded a blue plastic tarp that we kept in the barn, and I helped her roll him onto it. Underneath his head there was a dark pool of blood. His hair was matted at the back, all wet and sticky.

"Is Dad okay?"

"He's fine, honey," Mom whispered. "He had a little too much to drink and took a fall. He just needs to sleep it off."

Dad must have weighed two hundred pounds, but somehow the two of us managed to slide him down the front steps on that tarp.

"I've got his head," Mom told me as he bumped down the stairs. "He'll have a few sunset marks, but they'll heal."

I remember thinking Mom knew a lot about sunset marks. What I don't remember is whether I asked why we needed to take him so far. Mom said we had to go down to the river that runs along our property. That's why she needed my help. She couldn't move him that far by herself. He was heavy, that's for sure. Every time we stopped to rest, I was terrified he was going to wake up and tear into us both, but he never made a sound.

"Okay," Mom said when we got to the river.

By that time, it had started pouring. When she looked at me, I couldn't tell whether she was crying or her face was wet from the rain.

"This will sober him up. Teach him a lesson, right? Come on, Paula. Let's go."

We walked back to the house and she sat outside the bathroom door while I took a shower. When I came out, my clothes were gone, but Mom was there waiting.

"Let me see your hands," she said. Then she inspected each fingernail to make sure I'd gotten them real clean the way she told me to do. After that, she towel-dried my hair like I was a little kid. "You go on back to bed now, Paula. Everything's okay. It was just a bad dream. I'll be there in a minute to sleep with you. I'm gonna let Dad know what happened."

"You're going back down to the river?" I asked.

"It was just a bad dream, sweetheart. I'll be there in a minute, okay?"

She smiled at me, but the movement made her wince like her face hurt. That's when I saw the marks his hands had left around her neck.

"Go on now," she said, kissing me on the top of my head.

I did like I was told and went back to bed.

"Where were you?" Julie asked when I came back.

"I had a bad dream. I went to find Mom," I said, and I remember how much I wanted that to be the truth.

Thirteen

FALL

STELLA

The booster fundraiser is an unqualified success. Lorraine calls her helpers up to the stage. Anna, Rachel, Stella, and Gwen.

But Gwen has ghosted.

"Literally, I could not have put tonight's event together without these magnificent women," Lorraine says. Her words are a tiny bit slurred, but no one notices. Or no one cares. Almost everyone has had one too many. Some have had two or three too many.

From the vantage point of the stage, Stella searches for Gwen. She doesn't see her, but she spots Tom. He smiles and waves. This is not the behavior of someone who was whispering with another woman in the park. This is crazy. She's acting crazy. All the man did is send her a text with a typo and improper punctuation.

Lorraine is still talking. "Please give yourself a hand. Tonight we raised $131,000 for our amazing athletes. Sixteen thousand more than last year!"

The room erupts in cheers. Again, Stella looks at Tom. The shiny look on his face tells her he's among the people who've overdone it. It means he'll snore loudly tonight. She sighs and tries to remember where she left her earplugs.

"Thank you, ladies," Lorraine says, drawing them all close. "I owe you lunch!"

As one, they demur.

They tell Lorraine that actually *they* are the ones who owe *her* lunch.

It's been the best booster auction ever. Far better than last year's. They use all the appropriate words. They are modest and humble. They give credit but don't accept it.

"No, you guys are the reason this happened. It was a team effort," Lorraine assures them.

For a moment, Stella imagines a different scenario. One where Lorraine takes all the credit. Spikes the metaphorical football and does a victory dance. As she should.

They disperse, each of them searching the crowd for their respective husbands.

Stella heads toward Tom, then she remembers Gwen's phone and changes course. It's right where she left it. Gwen has not tracked it down. No one has outed themselves as a master criminal of the suburbs.

In an instant, her whole night is recast as one dramatic overreaction after another. She's a teenage forty-something.

She should leave it and be done with it. Even as the thought is forming, Stella reaches under the table with one sandal-clad toe and nudges the phone. She took it out of airplane mode before dropping it. When it lights up, there are no new notifications.

Tom, however, has located her. His face has the distinct look of someone who wants to go home. Stella feels the same way. She's tired. Literally, because it's late, and also figuratively, because she's really ready to be done with her own drama.

Tonight, she learned Gwen is a flake. This would explain most of what's taken place. The forgotten purse. The haphazardness about location services.

"Ready to go, my auction queen?" Tom asks.

His silvering hair is mussed, and he smiles at her like she's the love of his life. He's adorable. She is beautiful. Their children are happy and well-adjusted. Their home is enviable.

This is your life, Stella Parker, she thinks as she returns his smile.

"Lorraine is the true auction queen," she says. "If anything, I'm a princess, or maybe a duchess. Lady-in-waiting?"

Tom shakes his head, amused.

"Almost ready," she says and shuffles the silent auction papers into a pile. Then she deposits them in a Redwell with *BOOSTERS* written on it in black Sharpie.

"Don't want to forget this." Tom scoops up Gwen's phone and drops it into the Redwell as though he doesn't realize his wife is not the type of woman to encase her phone in sparkly pink glitter.

"Oh, right," Stella says.

"Ready?" Tom is clearly impatient.

The room is almost empty. It's like someone snapped their fingers. Poof! Suburbanites have dispersed in their SUVs.

They return to their too-big house, which is empty tonight.

Daisy is at a sleepover with Ainsley, supervised by Lorraine's mother.

Colin is "crashing at Max's house," which means he will be out long past his curfew. Max is the fourth child and his parents long ago abandoned curfews, although this is more of a guess on Stella's part than actual knowledge.

She and Tom are alone.

They could have sex in any room in the house. Or loudly in their marital bed.

The fact that Stella still wants sex somehow feels tacky, like a breach of etiquette she didn't realize existed. The first time she heard her friends complain about sex was during preschool playgroups while the children were occupied. The consensus was they'd all been over-touched during the course of the day. At night, all they wanted to do was sleep. Stella nodded along and didn't discuss her own desires. She worried they were something that would out her as the one thing not like the other.

This is the lens through which she views all her behavior. If it falls outside the narrowly prescribed norm for suburban motherhood, it could be the thing that gives her away. The tell that will, finally, be her undoing. She'd excise her desire like a tumor if she could, but she can't. Instead, she tries to pretend it into nonexistence.

"You looked beautiful up there tonight," Tom whispers, even though there's no reason to be quiet.

"I did?"

She knows she did. She's not supposed to admit this, but it would be dishonest to pretend she's not physically blessed. It's not about the compliment. Her need is more basic. It's about knowing Tom still believes in this version of her. That she's still in control and her marriage is solid. It's about being safe.

Safe from what? asks that voice in her head.

Stella doesn't bother to answer the question because Tom is fumbling with the zipper of her dress. He loses patience with it and tugs the dress over her head. He kisses her, deep and hard, the way he kissed her when they were first dating.

His clothes come off like an afterthought. A crumpled mess at the bottom of the bed. He presses inside her. They are fucking. No other word for it. Both of them temporarily reduced to a state where their only purpose is carnal satisfaction. The here and now. No room for questions or second guesses.

As Tom moves on top of her, Stella thinks of him out in the dark with Gwen. Mercifully, that thought is cast out by his last thrust, which sends her over the edge. A moan catches in her throat as waves of pleasure crest through her body.

Afterward, they lie in each other's arms, covered in a light sheen of sweat.

Stella lifts one hand and trails it across his chest.

He traps it, holding her tight. So tight it makes her want to pull away. "I love you, Stella," he says. "It's perfect, almost . . ."

There is a deep pause, interrupted by a rattling snore.

Almost what? she wonders as she extricates her hand.

The movement wakes him a little. Instead of finishing his thought, he pulls her close like she's a treasured stuffed animal. He strokes her hair and runs one hand down her back, stopping at her naked thighs. His breathing is rhythmic.

Stella forces her body to go limp. She breathes in, then out, mimicking sleep.

Here's what she'd like to do.

She'd like to roll away from the furnace of Tom's body. She needs to pee. She should put in a tampon; otherwise, she'll wake up with her thighs covered in blood, which will mean changing the sheets.

Tom's breathing grows noisier.

Stella studies him.

What she wants is to be alone. After sex like that, she needs a moment to get a handle on the part of herself she keeps hidden.

Stella waits until Tom's snoring hits a regular rhythm. Then she does exactly what she imagined. Slips away to pee and insert a tampon. Wraps herself in the big fluffy bathrobe her mother-in-law sent her for Christmas last year. Phone in pocket, she tiptoes down the stairs.

It's not until she spots her abandoned auction Redwell on the kitchen island that she realizes her mistake.

She snatches up the Redwell.

Gwen's phone is right where Tom dropped it.

And it's not in airplane mode.

"Too late now, Stella." She scolds herself in the same tone she uses with her children when she is extremely displeased.

Age has made her sloppy. She's lost the thread.

The face of the phone is already lit up as she pulls it out of the Redwell.

Slowly, Stella forces herself to look down. There is a text message from an unsaved number.

I saw you.

The message went to Gwen's phone.

It was intended for Gwen.

This is what Stella tells herself, but it doesn't ring true. The message arrived after the phone had been at her house, announcing its location to the ether. The animal part of Stella knows this message was intended for her. Her finger caresses the phone's Off button. She needs to end this. Cut the signal this phone is sending to whoever is out there, watching.

Instead, she rereads the message.

Sweat makes a cold trail down Stella's spine. She fights the urge to respond.

Her fingers act on their own. A quick swipe up. Last time she checked—although she doesn't remember checking, now that she thinks of it—Gwen's phone was locked.

Now it's not.

Someone has changed the privacy settings. Stella doesn't know if that can be done remotely.

What she does know is she made a mistake. The phone should not have come home with her. She needs to get rid of it.

Right now.

Somehow, her willpower has vanished. It's a familiar sensation. Similar to the moment when she decides to indulge in a handful of Tostitos and somehow, it turns into five followed by a cookie, or two cookies, or three.

Her willpower is extraordinary, except when it's not.

It's okay, she reassures herself in those moments. Eat as much as you want. Eat them all. Eat like you've known hunger, because you have.

And she does. Stuffing herself with whatever she craves. Ice cream, chips, cookies, leftover pasta. She eats until she feels sick to her stomach. Does it go without saying that she never does this in front of Tom or the kids? If not, it should.

She always pays for it the next day, starving her body back into submission. But that moment when her walls come down is almost better than the sex she just had with Tom.

This time is different. There's no diet or workout or walk that will undo the damage that's about to occur, but she can't stop herself. She opens Gwen's texts, eyes scanning the messages. The ones she sent Gwen yesterday and the texts from the mysterious SJIUYVP that Stella has already read.

Then there's this new one, from an unsaved number.

It arrived an hour ago while Stella was upstairs in bed with Tom.

Using her own phone, she snaps a picture of the number. This small, pointless act makes her feel like she's taking control. Then she closes out of Gwen's contacts, and her moment of control vanishes.

In the box below the last message sent by the unsaved number, there are the three blue dots that indicate someone is writing.

As though someone, somewhere, knows that Stella read the last message. Someone is monitoring Gwen's phone. Stella reaches for the Off button so she can put an end to whatever is happening, but she's too late.

Another message appears on Gwen's phone.

I know what you did.

Fourteen

SPRING 1987

JULIE

Everyone is leaving. I let myself be swept toward the door with the varsity girls but stop when I see Ginny and Megan Schaeffer standing outside. My eyes sweep the parking lot; Mom isn't there yet. If I go outside, I'll have to wait with them. Instead, I turn toward the bathroom, hoping they'll be gone by the time I come back out.

I pick a stall and look at my watch. Five minutes is how long I'll give it. It doesn't sound like long, but it's a long time to sit in a bathroom stall. If Mom comes while I'm in here, at least I know she'll wait for me.

Someone else comes into the bathroom. They flush and wash their hands. I wait until I hear them leave, then I open the door of my stall.

Megan is waiting for me.

"Are you hiding?" she asks.

Megan moves closer, and I tense.

"I know about your family. Your sister, Paula." She emphasizes my sister's name like it's a curse word. "She was just giving it away. No one was surprised to hear she got knocked up. And your mom. Everyone knows about her. Town pump."

She's so close that the "p" in "pump" makes a puff of air against my cheek.

"You know what they say, right?" Megan's eyes meet mine in the mirror. "The slutty apple doesn't fall far from the slutty tree." She smiles, but it feels like a slap. Then she leaves. Mission accomplished while I'm still running my hands under the water.

I take a deep breath, but it doesn't help. It's only a matter of time before Megan gets the varsity girls to turn on me. I imagine the warmth on Deanna's and Laura's faces replaced by disgust. They won't want anything to do with me. Tears fill my eyes, but I blink them back.

"She's a liar," I say to the mirror.

The fluorescent light makes my skin sallow. My hair looks like an off-brand shade of brownish red. Even without this harsh light, no one ever mistakes me for someone else. I wish I looked like Ginny and Megan. Pretty and blonde in a way that is both recognizable and forgettable. It must be a little like invisibility, but the kind where everyone sees you and smiles.

That's when I understand my mistake. The only freshman on varsity is the opposite of invisible.

When I come out of the bathroom, Ginny and Megan are gone. Through the windows, I see Mom's car. When I get in, the air feels thick and tight in a way that tells me something is wrong. Mom puts the car in reverse without saying a word.

When Mom gets like this, it's important to be quiet and give her all the time she needs. I wait for her to speak, both hands balled into fists in my lap. My fingernails dig deep into the flesh of my palms.

She pulls over at the last strip mall on the edge of town. There's a pay phone outside the drugstore. Mom picks up the receiver, thumbs a quarter into the slot, and punches in a number. I watch her carefully, but her lips don't move.

When she gets back in the car, the air feels different.

"No one's home," she says, smiling.

"What do you think happened?" I ask.

She takes a deep breath. "I worry about the way Kevin's been stopping off at that bar after work. Seems like he's been drinking more and more. Have you noticed that?"

I nod and wait. Sometimes it takes her a few tries to create a story. She has to weave in details. A thousand tiny threads that, when braided together, make up the whole picture. It's like a long rope she uses to climb up out of a dark well.

"Kevin"—she pauses, thinking—"said he wasn't feeling well this morning before he left. Said he was . . . off." Her eyes cut over to me to make sure I understand.

"But he wasn't sick or anything."

I say this even though I saw the sickly pallor of his skin and the remorse in his eyes. I say this despite what I already know.

"Of course he wasn't," she snaps. "It was a hangover. That's all." Her voice has turned hard. "I ended things between us. You should know that, Julie. I didn't like all the drinking. Did you ever notice that bottle of Jack Daniel's in his truck?"

"Behind his seat?"

I've never noticed a bottle of Jack Daniel's in Kevin's truck. Is that what he drinks? Mom would know. She's careful about details like that. What I do know is that if he were going to stash a bottle of something in his truck, that's where it would have gone.

She smiles in a way that's both fond and forlorn. Danger crackles in the air between us. Mom breathes it in deep like it's her drug of choice.

"He likes to take one for the road. I've been telling him that's a bad habit. I wonder . . ." She pauses. "He never came back for his things after I told him we were through."

This is a cue. "Do you think something happened to him?"

"I sure hope not. Things might not have worked out between the two of us, but I still care about him." The tears in her eyes are real. "After I ended it, he was so down. Looked like someone's dog that had been kicked. I'm guessing he stayed over with friends in Salem. He probably packed his things while we were gone today so he wouldn't have to face us. We shouldn't worry too much about it, Julie. This is for the best."

"So it's just us?"

She smiles and grabs my hand. "That's the way it always ends. You and me against the world, kiddo."

I smile, then lean my head against the passenger's side window. The glass is cold and clean. As the car picks up speed, I close my eyes and imagine a different ending. Our car is in a head-on collision. Glass shatters and cuts me open. My blood seeps all over the front seat. The end. A clean, simple storyline with facts that cannot be rearranged.

When we get home, the driveway is empty. I notice the way Mom's shoulders slump, ever so slightly, with relief. Inside the house, there's no sign of Kevin. His clothes are gone, and so are the things he moved into the upstairs bathroom we all shared. She must have got rid of his things while I was at school.

"It's okay, Julie," Mom says after I've double-checked all the places he used to assert his domain. "Kevin's not coming back. He moved on."

I let her hug me.

I don't ask about the tension I can feel in her arms.

There are things I want to say to her, but I can't. Mom thinks her boyfriends are a secret, but people know.

They may not know everything. Obviously, they don't know the most important thing, but people like Megan know enough to call Mom names. They know Paula was pregnant. Mom said it was Paula's boyfriend, but that's only because she didn't like the truth. It was a boyfriend all right, but he was never Paula's. He was the one who claimed he was going to tame Mom. When he failed, he looked around for an easier target and found Paula.

"Julie," Mom says as I head toward the stairs, "you didn't tell me about your tryout. How did it go?" There's a note of reproach in her voice.

"I made it. Only freshman on varsity."

"Figured you would," she says with the smile that shows the gap in her teeth. "Hold on a minute." She digs in her purse. "Here you go. This should be enough to cover it."

The envelope she holds out is thick and white.

"Thanks, Mom," I say, and I'm careful not to let her see that my smile is forced.

Upstairs in my room, I open the envelope and count out twenty-five twenties. Five hundred dollars. It's more than enough.

I take the lock boards out of my closet and slide them through the brackets hidden behind the princess curtains. When I was little, Paula told me the lock was to keep us safe. It was only for when the grown-up voices got too loud. You can't stay in one room forever, though, which is why it didn't protect Paula.

After Paula left, I added other times to use the lock. Like when I'm asleep or moments like right now. Moments when I don't want anyone to be able to open my door.

Not even Mom.

Especially not Mom.

I don't want to memorize the details we talked about in the car. I don't want to need the contents of this envelope. Most of all, I don't want to think about what happened to Kevin.

Under my bed, I pull up the loose board, push the insulation to one side, and put the envelope under my diary. Not even Mom will be able to find it now.

I take off the makeup Mom gave me to hide the damage Kevin did to my face. The marks are purple with a faint yellow cast. It doesn't matter whether you call it a bruise or a sunset mark, it's still an ugly stain. I touch my face, gently at first. Then I push down hard so it hurts.

"He had a choice," I say to my reflection in the mirror. "He didn't have to hit you, but he did." I push harder, and my eyes fill with tears. "He took away your choice to not be hurt. He made his own bed."

This is what I tell myself, over and over, until it becomes the only truth in my head. Then I cover the marks with makeup again. Once everything is hidden, I put the boards away, arrange the princess curtains over the brackets, and go downstairs to join Mom.

The kitchen table is set with the special china and silverware we use on holidays. They used to belong to my grandma and came with the house when she died. Mom says that Grandma outliving Grandpa was pure luck. She also says that's how she learned luck isn't something to rely on.

The table is loaded with my favorite foods, also like on a holiday. Chicken fingers, Tater Tots, peas, and sliced-up bananas. In front of my plate is a crystal glass filled with orange juice. Mom has the same glass, but hers is filled with wine.

The meal is both apology and bribe. If anyone asked, Mom would say we're celebrating the fact that I made the cheerleading team.

What we're really celebrating is our survival.

"It's been a big week," Mom says.

"It has."

"It'll be nice to have a quiet weekend."

Almost before Mom finishes the sentence, there's the sound of a car out on the road. Her body stiffens and she cocks her head to one side, listening. My stomach churns. The lights of the kitchen feel too bright, like we're on display for anyone lurking outside. Then the car passes and Mom takes a breath.

"You know what I heard, Julie?" she asks as she scoops food onto my plate.

I shake my head.

"I heard they opened an indoor water park up in Portland. How'd you like it if we went up there for the weekend?"

"For the weekend?"

She smiles. "We'll stay in a hotel. It'll be nice to get away for a few days."

"That sounds like fun," I say, because I don't have a choice.

"We'll leave right after dinner." She glances at the window, but the only thing it reveals is our reflection.

This is new.

We've never gone away after one of Mom boyfriends moved on.

It tells me she's not as confident as she's acting. That maybe something didn't go according to her plan.

Fifteen

APRIL 2015

PAULA

Julie was always better at Mom's games. I couldn't keep all the details straight in my head the way she could. It was like she slipped inside a story and it became real. For her, the truth was something she created. For me, the truth was what it was. I couldn't escape it. I got weighed down with pesky details. If I wasn't telling the truth, my words came out like bread that didn't rise right.

It rained the whole week after Dad moved on. Not a heavy downpour, but a drizzle. The kind of rain that enters your bones and chills your whole body. April showers bring May flowers. That's what they say, anyway. You ask me, that's just what people tell themselves so they can pretend the rain isn't so bad.

The day the police came, we had been canning peaches. I remember that because it was April.

"Got us some Florida peaches, girls," Mom said. There was real triumph in her voice.

Back then, food was more seasonal. You didn't get strawberries in January, and you sure as heck didn't get peaches in April. Still, Mom had found herself three big boxes of fuzzy yellow fruit. Something about a truck that got its wires crossed and needed to dump its load before it went bad.

"Julie's going to peel. Paula, you'll slice," Mom said as she sterilized the jars and laid them out on clean dish towels.

We were not excited.

Canning peaches is hot, sticky work. If you're peeling, the juice runs down your arms and turns the sleeves of your shirt stiff and itchy. If you're slicing, the juice eats at your fingers until they're bright red.

"Come on, girls. Let's get to it. These peaches won't last," Mom said as we slurped the last of our cereal.

We went to work. Trapped in the kitchen with Mom, who talked the whole time. Her voice slipped into our heads. Her words were filled with syrup, every bit as slippery as the peaches I was slicing.

"We all make choices in life, girls. That's what it means to live in America. This country is the greatest place on earth."

She turned to us. Her eyes scanned the kitchen like she was underwater and trying to swim to the surface.

"In this country, we get to choose how things unfold. It's like a movie, except it's real life. If you don't like the way your life is going, you move things around. Shake them up so they work better. No sense picking something that doesn't make you happy, right? Who wants a tragedy when you can have a fairy tale? A big castle, pretty dresses, and a ballroom where you dance all night long, if that's what you want. Everyone loves a good story."

She twirled around, holding up the hem of her dress like she was Cinderella. This time I didn't mention Princess Diana. I'd learned my lesson about being a smart aleck.

"Do you understand what I'm saying, girls?" Her smile felt like an invitation to that ballroom dance.

"We pick a story that makes us happy," Julie said.

Julie had a way of boiling things down to their essential elements.

"Exactly. That's exactly right."

Mom seized on Julie's words like they were the air she needed. Then she got real quiet. It was like her mind was working while her hands were busy with the peaches. She stirred them into the sugar syrup bubbling on the stovetop. Then she methodically ladled the mixture into the waiting jars. Pressed on the lids and tightened the rings to keep them in place. The jars went into the canner, where they processed until it was time to take them out with long metal tongs.

When they were done, she laid out fresh dish towels. Then, one by one, she set the jars carefully on the towels until they lined the counter like slices of sunshine distilled under glass.

"I'm worried about your dad," she said, turning away from the jars. "It's been a few days since he's been home."

"You mean after we—"

"No, Paula." Her voice was sharper than the knife I'd used to slice the peaches. "Last time he was home was Friday. You girls went to bed about what time? Do you remember?"

"Ten," said Julie. "Right after *The Love Boat*."

"That's right. It was a fun episode."

Mom said this like she'd been sitting on the couch watching it with us. Then she rubbed her shoulder with one hand. I figured her arms and back were sore like mine. The image of Dad, still and silent on that tarp as we dragged him down to the river, flashed into my head. I tensed and glanced at the door like the thought was enough to call him home.

Of course, Mom had already told us he'd moved on. She'd told us she was worried he'd had too much to drink. That he wasn't coming back.

With news like that, sometimes you don't hear what's being said until someone else says it.

"What's wrong, Paula?" Mom asked. Her voice was light. Her smile was a ray of sunshine on that rainy day.

"Nothing," I said, but the memory of Dad on that tarp must have shown on my face.

"Oh, sweetie." She crossed the kitchen, taking my face in her hands. "Is that nightmare you had still bothering you? I don't think I've ever seen you so scared."

"What?"

She laughed like I'd said something funny. "I wonder if it was something you saw on *The Love Boat* that triggered it. I slept in that little bed of yours all night long."

I nodded. Mom's stories were something you got caught in. They wrapped you up like a spiderweb around a fly. Only thing to do was give in.

She reached up and massaged her shoulder again with a little laugh. "I'm still sore from sleeping pressed up against that wall."

"You really don't remember, Paula?" Julie asked, looking up from the peaches she was peeling. Her surprise was genuine. "You were screaming so loud you woke me up too."

Have you ever been certain of something, then suddenly that certainty slips away?

In my memory, Mom and I dragged Dad down to the river. We left him out in the rain to sober up, but he never came back. When Julie remembered my nightmare, it made me feel like I was going crazy.

What if it really *was* just a bad dream? It was impossible to know the truth.

Mom was nodding. "Scared the living daylights out of me. You were all sweaty. I was worried you were running a fever. You remember taking a shower, don't you, sweetheart?"

I nodded. I remembered the shower.

"I got you back to bed and you asked me to stay with you."

It made more sense if the memory was a nightmare. The pool of blood under his head. Mom and I dragging him down to the river. Why would she have taken him out in the rain if he was bleeding? Besides, the river had to be at least half a mile away.

"I guess it was a bad dream," I said.

Mom nodded. "Nothing scarier than your own imagination. That's what they say at least."

I looked up at her, but her face gave nothing away. That's when my hand slipped and the knife grazed my finger.

"Paula, sweetie, oh my goodness. Julie, run upstairs and get the Band-Aids."

Julie pounded up the stairs while Mom pressed a dishcloth down on my finger. A string of comforting words slipped out of her mouth, but her eyes were hard. Those eyes told me there was only one version of what had happened that night. If I got it wrong, there would be consequences. It felt a little like she'd taken that knife and cut me herself as punishment for questioning her.

While she bandaged my finger, she talked real soft about the peaches we were canning.

"I was so happy when I saw those peaches. They're your dad's favorite thing. We were just about out, and now he can have a fresh supply. He'll be so thrilled when he gets home."

This was confusing. She'd told us he'd moved on. That he wasn't coming home.

When the timer went off again, Mom turned back to her canner and removed the next batch of steaming-hot jars.

"Paula, dump that water in the sink," Mom told me, as though she'd forgotten all about the cut on my finger. "I'm going to wash the canner again before I do the next batch."

Mom was meticulous about everything.

"Canning is a dangerous business," she was quick to remind us. "If you're not careful, poison will grow inside those jars. It's invisible. You can't see, taste, or smell it, but if it's there, it'll kill you."

We canned peaches all morning.

That afternoon, I went back into the kitchen for a glass of water and found Mom. She was tapping on the jars to see if they were sealed. There are always a few that don't seal right. Usually, she tossed the contents of those in the garbage right away. This time, something unfurled on her face. A seedling of an idea, poking its head aboveground. She put the unsealed jars in the pantry. Not with the rest of the canned fruit, but down low. On the floor, behind her cleaning supplies.

I think about that moment a lot.

Maybe things would have worked out different if I'd gone back later and thrown those jars away. Or maybe the seedling would have unfurled and bloomed all the same.

When the police came, Julie and I were eating popcorn in front of the TV.

"Let's go upstairs," I said.

"Why?" Julie's eyes were big and wide like she had no idea what was going to happen.

I left her there. Ran up to the top step of the stairs. From there I could hear the whole conversation without being seen.

"Ma'am." The police officer spoke gently, as though Mom was fragile. "Could we go somewhere else?"

"What's wrong? Did something happen? Is it Paul?" The worry in Mom's voice filled the whole house.

They went to the kitchen. I came back downstairs and sat next to Julie. When she looked at me, her eyes didn't look innocent anymore. They were emptied out, like she'd gone somewhere else altogether. We could hear the low rumble of voices in the next room, then the unmistakable sound of Mom's grief.

When the police officers came back into the living room, they gave us a sad smile. Mom's face was red and puffy.

The older officer paused in the doorway. His eyes rested on me and

Julie. For a moment, I thought he was going to ask us questions, but instead, he looked back at Mom.

"Don't hesitate to call if you need anything," he said.

That was the moment I decided to be a police officer. I remember my surprise at the way he missed the truth at the edges of Mom's grief. I knew that if I was the officer, I'd have caught that truth.

Also, I could see Mom was right.

Everyone loves a good story, including the officers who investigated Dad's death.

Officially, it was an accident. Plenty of people saw him leave the bar on Friday night. He was weaving, barely able to stand. For some reason, no one thought to take his keys. They found his truck down by the river. Blood on the steering wheel like he'd banged his head. He had a head injury when they pulled him out of the water. It didn't match the steering wheel, but they figured it must have happened earlier on his drive.

The police report, which I've read, states he suffered a concussion. It surmises that the concussion, on top of the alcohol, caused him to become confused. Somehow, he stumbled into the river.

Here's what didn't make it into the report: any mention of the blue tarp Mom and I used to drag Dad to the river. When I found it in the barn after the police left, there was still blood on it. The next day, when I went looking for that tarp, it was gone.

Sixteen

FALL

STELLA

Stella has done nothing wrong.

Nothing at all, and yet she feels like she's dissolving. Five words on a phone that doesn't belong to her are acting like some form of sulfuric acid. Delivered through the ether, to turn her bones to liquid.

It's a message meant for Gwen.

That knowledge does nothing to pull Stella's body out of fight-or-flight mode.

Heart pounding, she makes her way down the stairs, up the stairs, and into her secret room. She sits on the floor, clutching Gwen's phone.

Her knees are pulled tight to her chest. A small moan erupts from her throat.

She pushes herself to her feet, but she feels like an animal caught in a trap.

I know what you did.

Saliva pools in Stella's mouth. She forces herself to swallow.

"That's not who I am," she whispers to the room. Then she whispers a litany of her credentials. Offering them up like a prayer.

"Mom to Colin and Daisy. Tom's wife. Member of the PTO and the boosters auction board. Social coordinator for Daisy's field hockey team. Former lawyer. Best friends with Lorraine."

Her mind catalogs her other friends. So many friends—although can she really call them that?

"Acquaintances" is perhaps the better word. There's a plethora of them. All those people running around with knowledge about the boring minutia of her life. The minutia she's chosen to share, that is, because there are parts of her no one knows about.

Everyone has their secrets, though.

It's allowed.

Her secrets don't change who she's become.

Stella snarls. An actual animal sound she didn't realize she was capable of making. She thought being invisible meant she was safe. It was the price she was willing to pay.

But what if she isn't?

What if someone saw beneath the shell she created? Discovered her secrets.

"Deep breaths," she says out loud. "Count to ten." It's what she would say to the kids when they were little.

This is good advice, and she manages to follow it. Her heart rate slows. Mind sharpens. Eyes go back to the phone.

Obviously, she's put it back in airplane mode. Unfortunately, the last location it recorded is Stella's house.

A plan hatches. Whoever is tracking her, messaging her through Gwen's phone, needs to be thrown off the trail. The phone can't appear anywhere in the neighborhood. She has to take it somewhere else, as though Stella's house was only a stop before its final destination. She tiptoes back down the stairs, holding the phone between two fingers like it's something rotten pulled from the bottom of the veggie bin.

Stella is not religious, but in the laundry room, she offers up a quick prayer of thanks to the powers that be. She loves it when the kids congregate with their friends in the basement, but tonight she's thankful to not have to contend with the additional obstacle of tiptoeing around them.

Two floors below her husband, who is in the deep, postcoital sleep particular to forty-something men, she drops her bathrobe on the floor and grabs a set of Daisy's workout clothes from the pile waiting to be put away.

She has a fleeting sense of pride that they fit her middle-aged body. As though a flat stomach offers up some sort of protection, even though, rationally, she knows that line of thinking is some Stockholm syndrome bullshit and she'd do anything to protect Daisy from feeling the same way.

"Focus," she whispers to herself.

Keys.

She squeezes her eyes shut, retracing her entry into the house with Tom. Did she leave her keys in her purse? Are they upstairs? She's not sure.

With a deep sigh of relief, she remembers the extra keys to each car that Tom leaves in the kitchen drawer. Unlike Stella, who carries an enormous key ring filled with all the keys to their life, Tom prefers to be unencumbered. He never carries anything more than a car key and house key.

"When would you ever need all those?" he asks, teasingly, whenever she pulls out her tumble of metal.

"I like to be prepared. Like a Girl Scout," Stella responds.

She says this ironically, with a half smile or a raised eyebrow to indicate she's owning her ridiculousness. In truth, the giant ring was originally designed to hide one key in particular, the one that's now tucked away in its hiding spot.

"But I'm okay," she says out loud to Daisy and Colin's teetering piles of folded laundry that they have neglected to carry up to their bedrooms despite repeated reminders. "I don't need to escape. Everything's fine."

In the kitchen, she grabs the spare key, a sandwich bag, garden gloves, and the trowel she uses to transplant the herbs that thrive in her kitchen garden. It's a space right outside the back door, separate from the larger garden down by the stream. Protected from the frost, it allows her to clip sprigs of rosemary, sage, basil, chives, or parsley.

Plus, as Stella has said too many times, to too many people, "It smells so delightful when you come in the house. A little like vacationing in the south of France."

It's a pretentious thing to say. She knows that, but a certain amount of pretentiousness is expected by her group of friends.

Outside, the night air is warm like a blanket that is precisely the right weight. A month ago, it was heavy. A comforter soaked in hot water and draped over a feverish body. In another month, she'll need leggings and a sweater, but right now, it's perfect. Stella inhales and imagines her yoga instructor's approving nod at this demonstrated ability to embrace small amounts of joy in the present moment.

In her car, she drops Gwen's phone into one of the cup holders by the dashboard. In a few, oddly specific ways, McLean is exactly like where she grew up. It's safe here. She has no fear of going out into the night. No one is waiting to do all the things women are taught to fear. There are no muggers, carjackers, rapists, or serial killers with a mommy fetish. Of course, all those violent scenarios she's been warned about happen with much less frequency than the daily slights. Things so small she never considered them violent until she stopped to consider what they steal.

The interrupting while she's speaking, the assumptions about her intelligence, the shrinking options to make choices about her body, the underrepresentation in every decision-making sphere, the free-for-all on guns that has given her a constant case of low-grade anxiety, and the consistent commoditization of the female body, to name the first things that come to mind. It all amounts to a flashing sign with the message that women are not so much unique individuals as vessels for other people's fixations and desires.

She backs out, thankful her car was moved to the driveway when Colin took his bike out of the garage so Tom will not be woken by the rumble of the garage door. Grateful she can escape without explanation.

Worst-case scenario, she might be seen by teenagers out past their curfew. If any of her neighbors, up in the middle of the night and peering out their windows during a bout of perimenopause-induced insomnia, should happen to spot her, they'll assume she's on Mom Duty. Headed to pick up Daisy or Colin, both of whom have standing instructions to call her, no questions asked, if they can't get home safely.

The real question is, where does she go now?

It's not so easy in this age of scrutiny. Hidden cameras on front doors silently monitor the activities of McLean's nocturnal residents. Stella herself has often clicked on emails sent to her neighborhood's Nextdoor feed. Videos of raccoons, coyotes, and foxes in the middle of the night, along with the random drunk driver mowing down a mailbox.

Stella bites the inside of her bottom lip until it bleeds. The taste of iron floods her brain with memories she's worked hard to suppress. Somehow, she autopilots herself to the park where Colin used to play soccer. A park that sits on the border of McLean and North Arlington.

She parks the car and looks past the manicured fields to the woods beyond. There's a bottle of hand sanitizer in the other cup holder. Stella squirts a generous amount on her hands, then smears it on Gwen's phone, not caring what the alcohol does to the screen. She dons the garden gloves, then uses the bottom of Daisy's T-shirt to wipe all traces of her own DNA off the phone. Once she's done, she places the phone in the sandwich bag.

As she shuts and locks her car, she practices what she'll say if she's spotted and questioned. She couldn't sleep. She decided to take a midnight walk. She misses those days when the kids were little.

To be clear, the questions won't be about why she's carrying a trowel and a phone in a bag. They'll be about why a petite forty-something white woman is roaming solo through a park in the middle of the night.

Her response will need to be appropriately rueful.

"I know." She'll shake her head. "My husband would be upset too, but . . ." She'll pause here and blink like she's trying not to cry. "There were some things that happened earlier this evening. I just . . ." Again a pause, followed by a sniffle. "My son used to play soccer here. I don't know where the time went. It slips away. I can't believe they're already in high school. You know?"

She might even say the word "menopause," which feels like the mid-life equivalent of using your period to get out of gym. It's an age-old tactic, this use of squeamishness about the biological functions of the female body. After menopause, that's it. No more body cards left to play, but maybe by then she won't need them.

Stella understands that if she's stopped, she will be scolded about personal safety and promptly escorted back to her car. Possibly even her house.

This is privilege.

She knows this.

Based on her latest understanding of privilege, she's pretty sure it's okay to use it, so long as you own it. Or maybe that's wrong. Maybe she's only supposed to use it for other people?

Honestly, she can't remember. And yes, she has all the privileges of a white woman, which means it's unlikely she'll be shot or injured by the police but does not mean she is free of the requirement to provide a satisfying account of her actions to any interested party.

Stella follows the path that leads through the trees and down to the stream. If she remembers correctly, there is a series of wooden bridges that crisscross over the water. She has one particular bridge in mind. It lies off the curving blacktop path, in the deepest part of the park where invasive species are doing their best to overtake the natives. Ivy, winding up tree trunks. Kudzu and Japanese knotweed, choking out the eastern redbud and wild sorrel like stand-ins for the paranoid ramblings of every anti-immigration nutjob.

Stella carefully navigates down the muddy bank that leads to the water. She takes one hand out of the baggie to toggle Gwen's phone out of airplane mode, turns on its flashlight, then wipes it clean.

The space underneath the bridge is overgrown and abandoned. Most important, it's unmonitored. Stella props the phone against a rock and, using its light, digs a shallow hole with her trowel.

Is it habit or phone addiction that makes her glance at the lock screen one last time?

She's not sure, but there it is.

Another message, as though the sender is watching her in real time.

Stella reads it and adrenaline kicks in like a very high-quality drug. Her heart races. Her five senses become superpowers. She hears a car accelerate from somewhere far away. Close by, there is the unmistakable night rustle of tiny park rodents, moles or voles or mice. Her mouth fills with the bitter flavor of anxiety mixed with blood, still seeping from the inside of her bottom lip.

It was a mistake not to monitor the phone while she dug the hole. She has no idea if the message was written earlier or if it just arrived. She wipes the plastic bag meticulously (compulsively) with Daisy's T-shirt, then places the phone in the hole and covers it with dirt. Her finishing touch is a rock to hide the place where she's disturbed the earth.

Stella takes off her gloves and winds her way back through the park. Gwen's phone is gone. Buried. She wishes she could also bury the memory of that last text, but too late for that. It's seared into her brain.

You made a choice.

Stella thinks about her ungainly set of keys and the talismans she keeps in her secret room. All this time, she's been thinking of them like charms used to ward off the evil eye attracted by her good fortune. As long as they're with her, close at hand, she'll never need to use them. This, she realizes, was extremely naive. There's no escape, not even with the doors her key might open. She no longer inhabits the world where she grew up. Anonymity is a distant dream of the nineties.

In this world, you can always be found.

The thought makes her want to give up. Give in to whoever is hunting her. Check into a nice mental institution, the way women did during the Victorian age, and never check out. If she were truly the person she has trained the world to see, that's what she would do. The problem is, she's been pretending, playing out a long con that's been so successful she even conned herself.

She gets into her SUV and locks it like she's suddenly afraid of whatever creeps through the night.

"You are Stella fucking Parker," she whispers, gripping the steering wheel hard. "And you haven't done anything wrong."

And that's true. Or at least, truth adjacent. She hasn't done anything wrong in a very long time.

Fuck it, she hasn't done anything wrong.

Whoever this is, texting and tracking her, hasn't said anything solid. It's a case built out of innuendo. They're fishing. Picking at an old scar that is sealed and healed. Stella doesn't understand who is doing this or why, but she's done with this game. Whoever is taking aim at Stella is also taking aim at her family. She won't have that. Despite having half her genetic code and a lifetime of positive experiences, her children are fragile, prone to scrutinizing every aspect of their personalities through the filter of trending topics.

She thinks of Colin two weeks ago when he parked himself on the chair across from her kitchen desk, his face a storm that dropped the barometric pressure in the room.

"Another B on a history test," he said, as though he was announcing a terminal disease. "What am I gonna do?"

"That's not so bad."

"Are you kidding, Mom? It's a B. I can't get a B in this class. It's not even honors. I might as well forget about college."

This was said at a volume far too loud to be considered an inside voice. He was screaming. Having a total breakdown, complete with tears.

She calmed him down. His world has nothing in common with her own teenage world, but it's a troubling example of his fragility. Her children don't understand that they can and will survive something like a B. Also survivable? Not getting into their first-choice college, or being fired from a job. These detours on the road to adulthood were speed bumps for Stella. To her children, life's inevitabilities are more like hairpin turns with the potential to send them careening over a sharp cliff.

"It's the environment," Tom said when she brought it up.

"Was it like that for you?" she asked.

He'd looked surprised by the question. "I mean, yeah. It's a rite of passage, but they'll figure things out. They're good kids."

She let the subject drop because she could tell they were talking past each other. Stella's rites of passage were escaping danger. Learning to survive on her own. Creating a shell of adulthood to protect her from ever having to undergo another rite of passage again.

Although, to be fair, stress over college acceptance is probably a more typical use of the phrase "rite of passage."

And wasn't that one of the things that drew her to Tom? His childhood, and the way it unfolded in a similarly privileged cocoon. His understanding of rites of passage underscores the life she chose for her children. The meaning of that choice is clear. The life she made for her children means Stella can't disappear.

They need her. As long as they need her, she'll be there.

Nothing in her life before children prepared her for the fierce way she would love them. A love so deep she'd die for them.

Kill for them?

She doesn't answer that question.

Instead, she glances in the rearview mirror and meets her own eyes. Whoever's coming for her will not succeed.

Seventeen

SPRING 1987

JULIE

"It was a good weekend, right?" Mom asks as we drive home late on Sunday night.

"Yeah." I try not to let her hear my lack of enthusiasm.

It was the first time I've stayed in a hotel. There was a breakfast buffet and little soaps encased in floral paper next to the sink. We visited an indoor waterslide park that crinkled our fingers and left us smelling like chlorine. Mom went down all the slides with me while the other mothers sat, bored, at the side of the pool. We ate pizza at a restaurant with organ music and shopped at a mall with a big ice-skating rink at its center. Mom bought frothy drinks from Orange Julius for us and summer clothes for me. Shorts, T-shirts, and a pair of sandals.

All weekend, I tried not to worry. I didn't ask the questions running through my head. What happened to Kevin?

Why did Mom make us leave the house?

I think about her hands clutching the steering wheel as we drove home from school on Friday. The way she froze at the sound of a car on the road while we ate our dinner.

Had Kevin moved on?

I didn't ask how Mom could afford the things we bought, but I silently tallied their cost. It was a lot. More than we spend on groceries in a month. She paid for everything in cash. Twenty-dollar bills like the ones stuffed in the envelope under the floorboard of my bedroom.

The house is cold when we get home. I check on my envelope of money. When I find it untouched, it feels like safety.

In the morning, all Mom can talk about is my first practice. "So exciting. Are you excited, Julie? You're going to be a freshman on varsity! I'll pick you up after school and you can tell me all about it."

"Sure," I say as I pack my practice things into a bag.

Ginny and I are the only eighth graders who made the team, but she avoids me all day. After school, when I get to the gym, she's already talking with the JV girls.

As I walk toward the varsity group, I hear someone from JV say "Slut" under her breath.

I don't look over because looking lets them know it bothers me. Still, the whisper makes my stomach hurt. I thought making the team would magically fix everything that was wrong with my life, but here I am. Same as before.

Focus, Julie, I tell myself, and that's what I do.

I learn the chants and cheers. I smile and talk to the girls on varsity. They treat me like their favorite little sister. When practice is over, Laura gives me a hug.

"You've got a ride?" Deanna asks with her big smile.

"My mom," I say, returning her smile.

"Good practice today," she says and gives me a thumbs-up.

The varsity girls disperse in their cars. The JV girls wait outside in a tight knot. None of them look at me. They are not-looking at me in a way that feels purposeful. Like I don't exist. Like they've never heard of me and wouldn't say hello if we passed each other on the street.

I wrap my arms around myself and look down, hoping Mom doesn't take too long. I don't see the truck until the horn honks. I look up, along with everyone else.

That's when I recognize the truck and its driver.

Kevin.

He's still here.

"Juliebell," he calls.

His voice is thick, and the smell of Camels floats through his open window. He grins, running one hand through his dark curls.

"Your mom asked me to pick you up," he says when I don't move.

The JV girls are watching. Eyes sharp like two dozen tiny knives.

Kevin, appearing here in the parking lot, is a gift to them. Something else for them to whisper about while I pretend not to hear.

"You want a ride home or not?" he asks, slapping the side of his truck.

When I run to his truck, it's not because Mom sent him. It's because I need to escape. I need to disappear from the collective gaze of Livingston High's JV cheerleading squad.

"Heard you made varsity," Kevin says as he pulls out of the parking lot.

"You did?"

I feel like I'm caught in a story that's gone sideways. Kevin isn't supposed to hear anything. He's supposed to be lying dead in a ditch somewhere. How is he driving around? What happened? Why isn't he gone?

"I did. Remember, I told you we'd celebrate?"

When I don't immediately respond, he reaches out for my chin.

I flinch, and a shadow of anger crosses his face. His fingers grip hard as he turns my head toward him.

"Remember?" he asks.

"Yes, I remember." I force a smile.

He tightens his grip, turning my head to the light like he's searching for the mark he left behind.

"I still feel bad about popping you like that."

I know better than to respond. Anything I say will be an opening for questions I don't want to answer. A conversation about using makeup to cover the damage he did to my face is a trapdoor to questions about where his money went. Five hundred dollars in an envelope plus the cash that paid for our hotel room, entry to the water park, pizza, new clothes, and those sticky-sweet Orange Juliuses.

Things that have been devoured. Things we can't give back.

"Looks like it healed up okay," he says.

"It's fine," I say. All I know is I need to keep whatever is happening in neutral until I understand more.

Is it possible Mom changed her mind?

A memory comes to me. Paula is still at home. The two of us are in the kitchen listening to Mom talk while she makes jam.

"Men are like summer berries," Mom told us.

I can see her stirring the pot and smell the sweetness of blackberries as they fill the air. Mom's hair is in a ponytail at the nape of her neck. Curls have escaped to frame her face.

"You pick them when they're ripe and juicy, but you can only hold on to them for so long. After a while, they get moldy."

She plucked a moldy, discarded berry out of the sink to underscore her point.

"When they're this far gone, it's over." She tossed the berry back in the sink and ran her fingers under the water. "You gotta get rid of them or else they ruin the flavor of everything else."

"Men aren't like berries," Paula said, drawing a straight line when Mom would have preferred an elegant curve. "You can't just throw them away."

"Oh, you'd be surprised, Paula." Mom laughed. "If you don't, you're in for some trouble. You have no idea the way one bad berry can ruin a whole batch of jam."

"Are we talking about jam or men?" Paula asked.

"Both," Mom said.

Sunlight shines through the window of Kevin's truck. He smiles at me, but his smile is rotten. He's a bad berry. There's no way Mom changed her mind.

I know what she took.

And I know what happens after she's told me someone's moved on.

Clouds pass over the sun and the sky becomes a slate of gray. As if this is the signal he was waiting for, Kevin reaches out and rests his hand on my thigh.

"Anyone ever tell you how much you look like your mom?"

His voice is soft, but it sends adrenaline up my spine.

"No." It's a response to his hand, not the question.

"Yep, same hair and fair skin. Just a little bitty thing, aren't ya? Look"—his fingers dig into my flesh—"I can almost wrap my hand around your leg."

"That hurts."

"I'm not gonna hurt you, Juliebell," he says in that same soft voice. "What kind of celebration would that be?"

His grip loosens. His fingers slide up toward the edge of my shorts. Hot and grainy against my skin, like his hands are dirty.

Megan's words reverberate in my head.

Town pump

Slutty apple
Slutty tree

My hands clench into fists. I take a breath and force them to open. Somehow, Megan got the most important piece right. I *am* like Mom, but not in the way Megan meant. I know how this story goes. I've learned it by watching Mom.

I know what comes next.

What I have to do.

And how this will end.

"Kevin," I say with a smile that doesn't reach my eyes, "I think we should celebrate with ice cream."

He laughs. "You do? Do you, Juliebell?" He tugs me closer, sliding my body across the bench seat so my left leg is pressed against the right side of his.

I force a giggle. "Yeah, of course. We have some at home. You like it with peaches, right?"

If Kevin understood he was no longer in control, he'd hear the false note in my voice. But he doesn't and he won't. He never noticed the coldness in Mom's eyes or the calculation on her face. He doesn't understand he's expendable. Something to be tossed out before he ruins the flavor of our lives.

"I do like my peaches," he chuckles.

His hand travels up the leg of my shorts, dirty fingers brushing at my underpants. As he gropes underneath the elastic, pressing on private places, I imagine slicing off his fingers, one by one.

I'd debone them. Dice the flesh and sauté it in a pan. Then I'd scrape it into a bowl. Add mayonnaise, pickles, apples, and celery. Feed Kevin a sandwich made from his own dirty fingers. I wouldn't tell him what he was eating until he finished it. Then I'd explain exactly what I'd done and watch him choke on his own filthy flesh.

This is how I distract myself from what he's doing with his fingers. I breathe a sigh of relief when he removes his hand. It's a short-lived reprieve because he takes my hand and places it on the hard bulge in his lap.

"You're a cheerleader now, Juliebell," he says. "Time to start acting like one."

Dumb sluts, that's what he said cheerleaders were, but that's not what he's saying now. He's telling me I don't have a choice.

So I do it. I squeeze the lump in his pants. In my head, I add that repulsive piece of flesh, its dampness seeping through his jeans, to my finger salad recipe.

Kevin parks his truck in the driveway. I know where this is going. I remind myself I'm in control of the story, even if it's not the story I want to write.

I hadn't given up hope that Mom would be home, that she'd swoop in to save me. But her car is nowhere to be seen. Maybe she parked it behind the barn. She could be lying in wait, ready to strike. Maybe she's waiting inside with a river of words that will swirl around Kevin, holding him still until she can administer the final dose of poison. I stare at the front door, willing Mom to appear, but she doesn't.

Silence descends over the truck. Kevin reaches for me. In one respect, he and Ginny are the same. Both of them have faces that broadcast their plans.

"Wait," I say, giving him my sweetest smile. "Let's go inside."

The sound of blood whooshes in my ears. It's so loud I'm certain Kevin's going to hear it. It's going to tip him off.

Instead, he smiles. "Sure, Juliebell. If that's what you want, we'll go inside."

Mom has taught me that sometimes you get a story that's stubborn. It might have facts you don't like or things you can't change, but you have to work with the raw material you're given.

"Okay," I say and put one hand on his chest. I leave it there, the way I've seen Mom do with Kevin and all the boyfriends who came before him. "But can we have ice cream first?" My voice is babyish, like I'm even younger than thirteen.

Kevin smiles like I'm the cutest thing he's ever seen. An adorable little kitten he picked up at the animal shelter.

And I let him think that.

It's the only way I can make sure Kevin moves on.

Eighteen

APRIL 2015

PAULA

Julie got Mom's looks, no doubt about it. If you set two pictures of them at the same age side by side, you'd be hard-pressed to tell them apart. It's not so much about hair and eye color. It's something else. They both have something in their faces that looks soft. Vulnerable, I guess you'd say. It draws people in. Most folks don't understand that people can look like one thing on the outside but be entirely different within.

When people meet Mom, they assume I wish I looked like her. The fact is, I'm happy not to see her face when I look in the mirror. To me, Mom's pretty face and hair are like window dressing that hides hard surfaces and dangerous corners. You want to avoid bumping into what's hidden underneath.

Same goes for Julie. There was nothing or no one that was going to take either of them down.

It sounds scary for a kid to have a mom like that, but I was never afraid. I knew the minute me or Julie were hurt, Mom would attack. The only thing I was afraid of was becoming like her. It's funny how you can love someone with your whole heart and still not want to be anything like them.

Truth be told, I don't have that streak of ruthlessness in me. It doesn't take a fancy psychiatrist to tell me I joined the police force to try to make up for my past. I suppose I also wanted to be the kind of person I wished we'd had in our lives when we were growing up.

Someone should have stepped in, protected us. And I don't just mean me and Julie. All three of us deserved better. Much as I'd like to blame Mom for what happened, the blame isn't hers alone.

It rests just as much on the people who suspected that Mom was getting roughed up but turned a blind eye to it. You could even take it back a whole generation earlier and blame the violence her father did to her mother. When Mom told us stories about her childhood, she always ended them by reminding us that "you can cry and lick your wounds or you can do something about it." The point I'm trying to make is that I don't blame Mom any more than I'd blame a cat for hunting mice. Still, doesn't mean I want to be the cat.

That day, after the police came to tell Mom what she already knew about Dad, Julie and I went up to our room. Each of us laid down on our bed like that was the plan.

"You okay?" I asked her.

She looked over at the door, which was hanging open. Instead of answering, she rolled over so she was facing the wall.

"You think we still need the board lock?"

Her voice was sad, but I could hear relief there too. We loved him, but we both felt safer now that we knew he couldn't come back. Before I could answer her question, Mom appeared at our door. She'd climbed the stairs on silent feet. Her eyes flicked from me to Julie, like she could hear the thoughts churning inside our heads.

"Girls," she said.

We both sat up on our beds like we'd done something wrong.

"I need to go to town to make arrangements for your father. Julie, you'll come with me. Paula, you need to stay here. If anyone comes to the door, you tell them I went to town, but I'll be back soon because the police are coming to check a few things. Otherwise, I want you to stay inside. You understand?"

"What are the police checking?"

It was the wrong question. I could tell by the way her lips pressed tight together.

Julie got up off her bed. "It's just what you'd say if someone comes to the door, Paula," she whispered. "No one expects you to know. No one expects girls to know much of anything."

"That's right," Mom said with a smile. "When I come back, we'll take care of a few little chores."

"Few little chores like the other night?"

The words came out of my mouth so quick I didn't have time to think about the consequences. It's possible I resented the way she made me feel like I never quite measured up. Or maybe, it's what I'd been wanting to say for some time.

Mom was in front of me in an instant. Like an animal going in for the kill. She crouched down so we were eye to eye, and her voice got real soft.

"It's important to be smart about life. To understand which side of the bread is buttered and make sure that side never touches the floor. Do you understand what I'm saying to you, Paula?"

These words were a concession. A gift, because they acknowledged a reality Mom hadn't created. I should have accepted it, but I wanted more.

"You pushed him in, didn't you? You let him drown."

Her hand snaked out so fast I didn't see it coming. The slap across my face didn't hurt, but the sound of it, sharp and cracking, made me catch my breath.

"I'm sorry," Mom said and gripped me hard, one hand on each shoulder. "You're in shock, Paula. You're saying crazy things. Imagining things that never happened. That's why I slapped you. That's what you do when someone is in shock."

I shook my head to protest, but Mom was still talking in that same voice, low and dangerous.

"I know you lost your father today, but I lost my husband. You have no idea what that means."

She blinked, and the tears in her eyes spilled out and ran down her cheeks.

"Whatever you think or imagine, I loved him. Now that he's gone, I suppose it's natural to want to make me into something bad, but I'm not. As much as I loved your father, I love the two of you more. You girls are the most important things in my world."

I was crying too. I remember that clearly.

Crying because Dad was gone and he could never come back. And also because some part of me understood that was a good thing.

I knew where Mom's bruises came from. I didn't want to admit it, but I knew that eventually he'd come for us too. Other memories came boiling out with my tears. Like the time I tracked mud into the living room and he pulled me up the stairs by my hair. Or the time I sassed him and he twisted my arm until I thought it would break.

My tears were the acknowledgment that at some point, the lock on our bedroom door wouldn't be enough to protect us.

Mom sat down next to me and let me cry. Julie squeezed in on the other side. We stayed like that for a long time. We could take all the time we wanted. No need to lock the bedroom door because there was nothing left to fear.

Mom had Dad cremated.

She changed her mind and took both of us with her to the funeral home. It's possible she decided I shouldn't be left alone after losing Dad. Equally possible, she weighed the odds of people coming to the house while she was gone against the odds of me getting the details right and decided it was better to take me with her.

The funeral home was a big brick building with pillars like a mansion. The funeral director brought Mom a cup of tea and powdered hot chocolate for me and Julie. He was a small man in a tidy dark suit who bustled around us like someone's grandmother.

"You'll do it as soon as possible?" Mom asked. "I want it over. I can't bear to think of him—" She broke off like she couldn't finish the sentence.

"Of course," he said, handing her a tissue.

Sometimes the real story slips out, unprotected. That's what happened with the funeral director.

Mom told him the truth. She couldn't bear to think of Dad. Full stop.

After his body was reduced to ash, she'd never have to think about him again.

When we got back in the car, Mom's face was puffy from crying, but the soft, liquid way she'd looked at the funeral director was gone. Her eyes were as hard as a blue sky in January.

We drove straight home and Mom outlined the chores she had planned. For Julie, it was cleaning. She had to start with the kitchen, then dust and vacuum.

"Paula and I have to do some things outside. You stay in the house," Mom told her.

We walked down to the barn together and Mom handed me a hammer. "We have to pull up these floorboards," she told me, "but carefully, so no one can tell we took them up. They're going right back down when we're through."

"What's under there?"

"Our future."

"What do you mean?"

"Let's get to it, Paula," she said, her eyes narrowing in a way that told me I'd asked enough questions.

It was hard work, pulling all those nails out of the floorboards. I told myself that's why Mom chose me to help her. She understood words and imagination were never going to be enough for me. Sometimes the only way I could escape my thoughts was through hard work. I've carried that idea around with me ever since. Whenever my thoughts keep me up at night, I push my body to exhaustion. Works every time to calm my mind.

Under the floorboards, there were plastic bags from our local grocery store. The bags were tripled up and shoved under there, all haphazard. No order to it at all. It didn't take much to imagine Dad stumbling out to the barn at night with those bags. It would have been like him to pull up the boards at random, without stopping to think about which floorboard he'd pulled up last.

Mom was the opposite. Systematic.

She gathered the bags one by one and piled them in a corner of the barn. I knew I wasn't allowed to ask what was in them, but I didn't need to. There was no mistaking the stacks of cash, rubber-banded together.

"Be careful, Paula," Mom scolded when I bent a nail pulling it out of a board. "We have to put all these boards back down with the same nails. Can't have any shiny new nails giving us away. If it's worth doing, it's worth doing right."

After we'd checked under every floorboard and nailed them back down, Mom hopped down into the mud where the sheep came in to eat and shoveled muck up onto the barn floor.

"Spread it around. Stomp it into the cracks between the boards," she told me.

When she was satisfied, we swept the rest of the muck back down to the ground, but she was careful not to leave the barn floor looking too clean.

While we worked, I wondered what else she'd hidden. The barn broom was wide with bristles that looked like they'd been used in the mud. It wasn't hard to imagine her out in the rain, using this same broom to disguise the path left after we dragged Dad down to the river.

Something about the calculation on her face made me wonder what was accidental and what was planned. Had she picked a night when it was raining because she knew it would help wash away our trail? I thought about retracing our path to the river, but I knew it was gone. Smoothed away, same way she smoothed away my memories. If I happened to remember something different, it was only a dream.

It was almost dark when we finished with the floor.

"What did we do this afternoon, Paula?" Mom asked, dusting off her hands.

"We made arrangements for Dad."

My voice came out flat and robotic. I wasn't like Julie. I was never any good at creating the life I wanted by retelling it.

"Anything else?" Mom prompted.

I glanced at the tripled-up bags in the corner. Mom shook her head, warning me not to give that answer.

"We . . . cleaned the house?"

"Yes, we did," Mom said, putting one arm around me and ushering me out of the barn. "Let's go take a look to see exactly what we cleaned.

"It's been a hard few days," she said as we walked back to the house. "The rough part's not quite over, but it will be soon. What you need to remember is what happened today. We visited the funeral home. We cleaned the house. Afterward, the three of us watched TV. You wanted popcorn, so I made some. Do you remember what we watched?"

"I'll look at the *TV Guide*."

Mom nodded and hugged me tight. "That's right. The difference between a good job and a bad one is all in the details. You've got to get every detail right. You go check the *TV Guide*. Memorize what was on today. Then I want you to make some popcorn for you and Julie. Leave the pan in the sink. You girls pick something you like to watch, but I want you in bed by ten. Both of you need to shower and put your clothes in the washing machine. I'll do a load when I come in."

"You're not coming in now?"

"I'll be there in a bit." Her eyes flicked back toward the barn.

I did everything she told me.

When I went inside, Julie had finished her chores and was reading a book on the couch. I checked the *TV Guide*, made the popcorn, and picked out a show to watch with Julie, then we took turns showering before bed.

But before I did any of that, I went upstairs to our bedroom.

Without turning on the lights, I went straight to the window that looked out toward the barn and cupped my hands around my face. Mom was headed into the barn. When she came out, she was carrying as many bags as she could hold in one hand and a shovel in the other. I watched until she disappeared into the forest on the hill.

Did I know what she was going to do with those bags?

The shovel pretty much gave it away.

Did I have questions?

Sure I did, but I wasn't about to ask them. I'd seen the hardness in her eyes and the pool of blood under Dad's head. I knew better than to push too hard.

It makes it sound like I was afraid of her, but that's not exactly right. I was pretty sure she'd hit Dad on the head and rolled him into the river, so I had a healthy respect for her, but I didn't fear her. No more than a lion cub fears its mother when she drags a carcass back for them to feed on. The cub knows its mother is a killer, but it also knows she killed so it could survive.

Doesn't matter if you're twelve or twenty. Survival is not a complicated concept.

The next day, Mom started her painting on the back of the barn wall.

When Julie and I asked about it, at first she told us it was a memory of Dad. Later that week, she changed her mind. Brought a book home from the library and made us learn all about a system that numbers every star in the constellation. It wasn't complicated, not even for me. You could look at a chart and match the numbers to the stars she'd painted.

Neither of us thought to ask why she chose numbered stars for her painting.

She lost interest in that painting a few weeks later and didn't go back to it until Brett moved on. He was the first boyfriend she had after Dad.

"I don't like the bruises," I told her after he was gone.

"Remember how you used to call them sunset marks?" Mom asked, tracing the marks with one finger while I watched. "At first, they're dark. Then they start to change. Finally they fade away to nothing. Same pattern the colors in the sky follow when the sun goes to bed. Before you know it, they're gone until the next time."

"I don't want there to be a next time," I said.

She smiled and hugged me tight. "It's okay, sweetheart. Eventually, they're the ones who run out of next times."

"Look," she said, gesturing with her paintbrush at the wall. "You know what this is?"

"Canis Major," I said, feeling proud that I was able to recognize one of the constellations.

She shrugged like she didn't like that answer. "Yes, but it's more than that. This"—she tapped the barn wall with one finger, her eyes burning brighter than any star, painted or real—"is the map to your future. See how the prime number stars are bigger? That's where you look for treasure. Never forget that, Paula."

Nineteen

FALL

STELLA

First, Stella showers. This is important. Crucial, even.

The importance of this ritual was drilled into her long ago. So long ago, it feels like she was someone else.

Arguably, she was. She wasn't Stella Parker yet. She was a different person, in the way that everyone is someone else before they solidify as an adult. Stella tells herself this as she cleans under her fingernails and vigorously scrubs her scalp in the basement bathroom. She's washing away every trace of evidence. Not that she's done anything wrong. It's just . . . good to be clean.

If it's worth doing, it's worth doing right.

The voice is so clear that, for a moment, Stella thinks someone is in the bathroom with her. But no, it's only her memory mixed with an overly active imagination. That feeling from childhood washes over her. The liminal space between what is real and what your mind has created to present to the world.

With her body clean, she feels calm again. In control. She throws Daisy's shorts and T-shirt in the washing machine along with the other laundry that's accumulated in the eight hours since she last did a load and turns it on.

If Tom has noticed her absence, she'll blame the wine.

"I thought a shower would help my headache. I didn't want to wake you up, so I used the basement bathroom," she'll tell him.

He'll tell her to try to get some more sleep. Bring her a glass of water and insist that she take an Advil. He's the kind of man who believes this is what it means to be in a relationship. He's a good person. Even if he's having an affair with her neighbor, he wouldn't hurt anyone. The situation isn't black or white but one of the myriad shades between. Stella knows the ways Tom could be worse. Not that she's excusing infidelity, but it's somewhere on the spectrum between good and evil.

Tom isn't perfect, but neither is she.

Tom is solid. That's what counts. It's why she picked him.

According to her phone, it's 3:07 a.m. Tom, with his middle-aged bladder, is likely to wake up soon to use the bathroom. Stella climbs the stairs and slips under the covers next to her husband. His body radiates heat like a stove. Stella lets his deep inhales and whistling exhales calm her. Focuses on them like a mantra, allowing them to push away all her spinning thoughts.

I'm safe, she tells herself as Tom breathes in.

I'm safe, she tells herself as Tom breathes out. Over and over until her muscles uncoil. And finally, she sleeps.

Stella wakes to light filtering through the shades of their bedroom. Tom is opening drawers and shutting them. Making absolutely no effort to silence any of the rattling noise. She rolls over, stifling her flash of annoyance.

"You awake?" he asks, because clearly he thinks she should be.

"Yep," she mumbles into the pillow.

"It's almost eight."

Stella feels like a child being chastised for sleeping in.

"I used the last coffee pod. If you happen to go to the store today, could you grab some more? I'm meeting Ed for golf."

"Mmmkay," she says without opening her eyes.

Later, she'll tell him she had too much wine. Remind him that even when they met, she couldn't drink more than two glasses with dinner. She turns over and does her best imitation of going back to sleep while Tom slams a few more drawers, then spends an ungodly amount of time opening something that makes a loud crinkling noise.

Stella stays motionless as he gallops down the stairs. Resentment creeps over her. Why does she have to explain her every impulse? Why can't she drive to the park in the middle of the night or sleep in on a Sunday while Tom spends the next five hours playing golf? When did her life dwindle down to this narrow path?

The front door slams.

Seven minutes. That's how long she'll stay in bed in case Tom realizes he's forgotten something and comes back.

Sure enough, two minutes later the door opens. Something clatters to the floor in the kitchen. There are curse words followed by the door slamming again.

Stella waits five more minutes, then scrambles out of bed.

She throws on workout clothes, the kind you wear when you're not working out. Then brushes her teeth, washes her face, and adds a touch of color: lipstick, blush. Piles her hair into a messy bun. Superficial things that are important because they make her look pleasant, pleasing, and perfectly invisible.

In her car, she reviews her plan. It's not until she pulls into the empty parking lot of the Westover branch library that she remembers it's Sunday. The library is closed.

"Fuck," Stella says in a low, harsh voice that she never uses around her family.

"Okay, okay," she says. "Plan B."

But there is no plan B. She has to make one. Sometimes you get a story that's tricky. It doesn't want to be told the way you want to tell it. Sometimes you have to work extra hard to control the plot.

A private search on her phone reveals a nearby Hilton Garden Inn with a "business center."

The buzz of an incoming text makes her jump, but it's only spam. A sale at Uniqlo. She closes her eyes and remembers the texts from last night.

I saw you.

I know what you did.

You made a choice.

Stella runs through the alternatives again. Again, she reaches the same conclusion. She needs to know more about Gwen.

It's possible those messages were meant for Gwen and Stella is simply being overdramatic. A bored housewife running around in the middle of the night burying other people's cell phones. Her reaction to an accidentally forgotten cell phone might be completely overblown. Low-key crazy. A little drama for the mama.

Equally possible, her entire life is at stake.

There's no way to know which version of the truth is correct until she knows everything she can about who Gwen Thompson is.

Stella opens the browser again and studies the map. Arlington is a complicated maze of streets, roads, and highways. Normally, she relies on GPS, but today she needs to trust her memory. She doesn't want an electronic trail of breadcrumbs to reveal her morning activities.

The Hilton Garden Inn is the kind of place frequented by budget business travelers. A simple lobby with a room dedicated to a breakfast buffet. As Stella walks past the reception desk unnoticed, she remembers when a hotel like this would have felt fancy. When was it, exactly, that she stopped taking the hotel toiletries to use later?

The business center is situated off a long hallway that ends at a small, overchlorinated pool. Stella stops in front of the business center door and peers through the window into the small room on the other side. An ancient computer sits on a desk next to an equally ancient fax machine. She pushes the door handle down, but it doesn't budge.

It's locked. Of course it is. She needs a key card.

As she's considering her options, a man appears behind her.

"Excuse me," Stella calls.

He pauses and gives her a friendly smile.

"I'm so sorry. I was in the gym and lost my key card." Stella makes a scrunchy face to show the ridiculousness of the situation. "My boss's assistant texted me. I have to pick up a fax."

The man laughs. "A fax?"

"I know!" Stella shakes her head. Rolls her eyes.

She is a petite, attractive white woman. Adorable and harmless in her privilege. He's happy to help.

"It's important that they keep the valuables locked up," he says, pulling a white plastic rectangle out of his pocket. "You never know when someone might walk off with that fax machine."

"I think it's the desktop computer they're worried about. It's vintage. A collector's item."

He laughs as the door clicks open.

"Thank you so much!" Stella enthuses. Her smile is both rueful and grateful. They're both playing familiar, comfortable roles. She's the damsel in distress. He's the hero.

"My pleasure," he says. Then he continues toward the elevator, leaving Stella to the windowless room with its geriatric computer.

She taps at it and it wheezes like an old man. Stella sits down when the screen lights up and opens Google in private search mode.

It's a small detail, but Stella knows the importance of careful research. It's funny how people think of details as something to be delegated to others. Also funny (not-funny) how many of those people are men.

She remembers a statement made by the partner at her law firm who took her under his wing.

"I'm a big-picture guy," he said, his hands moving apart as if to indicate a lofty frame for his singular vision. "I leave the details to other people. You think you could be that person?"

"I'm very thorough," Stella said, and he smiled his approval.

She'd wanted that approval. It never occurred to her to correct him, or even add an alternative point of view, but still, she'd known precision was at the heart of everything. The smallest detail could push you over the top. Or drag you under water.

Later, after she left the firm, that partner was embroiled in some sort of mess involving client confidentiality. A mere detail that cost him his partnership.

She scowls at the computer and types "Gwen Thompson" into the search engine.

What can she learn about Gwen?

What clue has this soft suburban life caused Stella to overlook?

She peruses the holy trinity of Instagram, Facebook, and Twitter. Gwen's Instagram is a public display of curated photos. Matching pajamas for the family on Christmas morning and mother/daughter outfits for Easter. Stella double clicks. She remembers Gwen's hunched-over walk and scans the photos for the telltale signs.

But if that sort of damage occurs regularly, Gwen has hidden it well.

Gwen doesn't have a Twitter account, and her Facebook is private. Her LinkedIn profile displays a two-year-old résumé that lists Gwen as CEO of the Thompson residence and a sales representative for a popular multilevel marketing candle company. Her places of residence are listed as Okinawa, San Diego, Manila, and McLean.

Stella searches her memory bank for what she already knows about Gwen Thompson. Her husband, Dave, used to work at the Pentagon, but

Stella has a vague recollection that he retired and now works somewhere else. As a defense contractor, or something like that. The Thompsons' house is slightly run-down, with the kind of lack of maintenance that would make sense for a rental. The Northern Virginia suburbs are filled with military families. Wives who have followed their husband from one base to another. Typically, they keep to themselves, forming a tight-knit community with other people who understand government acronyms and know what it's like to have to start their lives over in a new place every three years.

Interesting that Gwen has actively stepped outside that community. Of course, it's possible Dave is retiring here. It's not uncommon for people to come to the DC area for work and stay for the schools.

Stella digs deeper and discovers she and Gwen are the same age. There are no recent updates to Gwen's LinkedIn profile, but at least she has a profile. That's more than Stella can say for herself. It's as though the career Stella worked so hard for has disappeared. She and every one of her friends have allowed the achievements of their children to stand in for their own. As though despite the promise of female advancement, mothers are still represented by the fruit of their collective womb.

Stella switches tactics and decides to focus on Dave Thompson.

Dave displays his entire life on the internet. He rose through the ranks of the Marine Corps, then retired. Dave's Facebook posts are a compilation of pictures of men in uniform saluting the flag with the caption "Semper Fidelis," his kids, college reunions, parents, siblings, friends, and vacations.

Nothing out of the ordinary, Stella thinks.

She moves to close out of his profile, but an anniversary post stops her. It details the many ways his life has changed over the last twenty-five years since meeting his beautiful wife and uses the word "blessed" no less than five times. It's the last blessed that catches Stella's attention.

"Blessed to be married to a Strawberry Queen." This, followed by a strawberry emoji and a picture of a tiara.

Stella's heart beats a little faster as she types "strawberry festival" into the search engine. It turns out there are a number of strawberry festivals across the country.

Next to her, her phone erupts.

Daisy: Were r u

Stella: Gym. Why?

Daisy: Were out of bagels

Stella: I just bought some. Check the freezer.

Daisy: Nothing there can u get some

Stella considers asking Daisy to dig deeper inside the freezer but weighs the possibility of a FaceTime call where an indignant Daisy will *show* her the inside of the freezer and decides against it.

Sure, she types on her phone.

Daisy responds with a giant swelling heart emoji.

Stella sighs. She feels defeated. Along with her career, she's lost her knack for research. She glances back at the giant heart for consolation. A symbol of her daughter's love that reassures her she's made the right choices. As if prompted by Daisy's giant heart, a thought pops into her head.

Stella opens TikTok on her phone and types in Daisy's handle: DizzeDais123.

Stella isn't supposed to know about this account, but she overheard Daisy give it to a friend and tucked it away in her mother brain.

Now she monitors it semi-regularly. Not because she's worried about the booty-shaking or the "fockey" group dance that racked up thousands of likes. It's the videos of Daisy in tears confessing her insecurities to the world that Stella tracks. She uses this account as a way to check in on her daughter's mental health. It's a fragile thing, the mental health of a teenage girl. Stella is well aware of the ways in which teenage girls are under attack, so she tries to play defense whenever and wherever she can. The trick is in identifying the problem, then finding a subtle way to incorporate a message of strength and resilience into a casual conversation.

This time, however, she's not here to monitor Daisy. Instead, she scrolls through Daisy's followers, clicking on each of them.

She hits pay dirt at *ThirteenReasonsWhyCharDances*. Otherwise known as Charlotte Thompson.

Gwen's oldest daughter, who is between Colin and Daisy in age.

Stella scrolls, then stops with a little gasp.

She plays the video again. Squints. Hits Stop. But she can't get the timing right. Each time, the thing she wants to see has passed by the time she freezes the video. It takes her four tries and even when she's staring at it, she's still not sure.

Is it something? Or is she losing her mind?

The TikTok itself isn't the problem. It's like every other teenage girl's TikTok Stella has seen. Charlotte, hair in a ponytail, face without makeup, wearing an oversize T-shirt paired with sweats. She snaps her fingers and *BAM* she transforms into a teenage sexpot. Blown-out hair, lips pouting into the camera, tight dress.

It would be more horrifying if Stella hadn't already seen videos like this that Daisy has posted. For better or worse, she's grown used to it.

No, what causes Stella to wipe her search history, turn off the computer, close the app on her phone, and exit the business center of the Hilton Garden Inn at a very businesslike clip is something in the background of Charlotte's pre-transformation look.

A pennant in American flag colors. Red, white, and blue like fireworks. The color combination prized by small towns all across the country. The same small towns that celebrate the humble strawberry and select queens and princesses with strawberry-colored cheeks to represent that fruit in a local parade.

Stella has more than a passing familiarity with those kinds of towns. She knows all about pennants with the name of the local high school written on them in fancy script. In fact, Stella used to own a pennant exactly like the one tacked to Charlotte Thompsons's wall. Not Stella, precisely, but the Stella before Stella existed. She left that pennant behind along with everything else, but the bulldog mascot lives on in her memory.

The problem with fancy script is that it's hard to read. It's especially hard to read glimpsed in the background of a frozen TikTok frame. She could watch the clip on an endless loop, but it's not going to bring the pennant into tighter focus. Could it be another high school that starts with an L and has a grinning bulldog mascot?

Stella slides into her car with a frown and focuses on the threshold question.

Where did Charlotte get that pennant?

Once she knows that, she'll know whether this has been a long and pointless exercise in overactive imagination or whether she's in trouble.

In other words, she'll know whether her secret is safe.

Twenty

SPRING 1987

JULIE

The house is cold. This makes sense because Mom turns off the heat when no one's home. Still, it tells me she's not here. She's not hiding somewhere with a plan to save me.

I make the mistake of shivering, and Kevin takes it as an invitation.

"Don't worry, Juliebell. I'll keep you warm."

He sits down on the couch and pulls me onto his lap.

"I thought we were going to have ice cream," I say, trying to ignore his hands.

"You take care of me, then I'll take care of you."

Part of me knew this was inevitable, but I was still hoping for an escape. A last-minute miracle. I think about Paula and wonder if this is how she felt the first time Mom's boyfriend cornered her outside while Mom was at work.

When Kevin mashes his lips against mine, I don't resist. His mouth tastes like cigarettes and the way the vegetable drawer in the refrigerator smells when something is rotting. He pulls off my shorts and underpants, and I think about other unpleasant things I've survived. Going to the doctor or dentist, where they probe your body in a way that's uncomfortable. You get through it by putting your mind somewhere else. Before you know it, it's over.

"This your first time?"

Kevin asks the question like this is something we've agreed to do. Like it doesn't matter that he's my mom's boyfriend.

"Yes."

My voice is a weak little whimper. I hate that. I don't want him to know I'm afraid.

"I'll be gentle," he says. Then he shoves my legs apart with his knee.

I turn my head to the side so I don't have to smell his vegetable-rot breath. There's a stab of pain, but I focus on the wallpaper that borders the top of the living room. It's a dark pattern with different kinds of flowers. I bite down on the inside of my cheek as I count them. The small pink ones, the trailing roses, and what looks like sprinkles of daisies. When I get to twenty-seven, Kevin grunts loudly like a pig in the barn. Instead of thinking about the searing pain between my legs, I think about what happens to pigs.

Death.

Slaughter.

They eat at the trough, never knowing they're destined to be turned into cuts and sold at the grocery store. Bacon. Ribs. Ham.

"This'll be our secret, Juliebell," Kevin whispers.

He pets my hair like I'm soft and sweet, his adorable little kitten. He doesn't understand that nothing about me belongs to him.

"Something between you and old Kevin. You won't tell no one."

"No one," I echo.

He nods, satisfied.

I sit up, and the pain feels like something alive. It burns and makes me afraid to move too quickly. A noise slips out of my mouth.

Kevin glances at me. "It gets better after the first time."

He reaches under my shirt and rubs my back. Like he's trying to comfort me, even though he's the reason everything is bad.

My stomach churns, but I have to keep that a secret. I hold it inside me along with the pain between my legs. I know how this ends, but Kevin doesn't.

Not yet, anyway.

"How about you fix us a couple bowls of ice cream," Kevin says.

One need satisfied, he's moved on to the next.

"With peaches?" I ask.

"Wouldn't have it any other way."

"Me neither," I say. This time, my smile is genuine.

As I walk into the kitchen, he turns on the TV. Flicks through channels and settles on sports. Something wet trickles down the inside of my thigh. I wipe it away with a dish towel, but I can't look. Not yet, because what I see might break me. My bladder feels swollen, but I'm afraid to pee. If I stop moving and think about what just happened, I'll lose control.

I'll fall apart, and so will my story.

Our house is old with a deep kitchen pantry designed to hold a winter's worth of food. Most people don't live like that anymore, but we do. Between Mom's garden and the overgrown orchard, we store summer in jars that carry us to spring. Jam, cherries, plums, pickles, tomatoes, green beans, beets, and, of course, the peaches Mom spooned onto Kevin's ice cream Thursday night.

Canning is a precise science. Dangerous business, that's what Mom calls it. If you do it right, you can preserve everything you grow. You can eat from your garden all winter.

If you don't do it right, poison can grow in those jars.

The upper shelves of the pantry are filled with the jars Mom knows are safe. She's tested them. The other ones, the jars that didn't seal properly, are stored in the space below the bottom shelf.

I bend down, and there's a stab of pain. Another wet trickle down my leg. I force myself to take deep breaths. In and out until the throbbing subsides.

Behind the Comet scrubbing powder, Lysol, a generic bottle of bleach, hydrogen peroxide, and the apple cider vinegar that Mom buys cheap and mixes with water to make a cleaning solution sits a neat row of canned fruit.

One jar in the row is gone. That jar contained Thursday's peaches. It's clean now, sitting on the counter. Maybe the poison inside it didn't grow right, or maybe Kevin's just tough. Mom must have suspected something. She wasn't certain he'd moved on. That's why she was so jumpy on Friday. Why we made that impromptu trip to Portland. She should be here, but she's not. I don't know where she is, but I know what I have to do.

One of the jars in the row is darker than the others. Cherries, suspended in cloudy amber. That's the one I pick.

The problem with Mom's method is that it's not guaranteed. The poison that grows inside these jars is natural. You can't smell it or taste it. It keeps its secrets hidden, and its most important secret is whether it exists at all. Sometimes you need only one jar. Sometimes it takes two, even three jars before you find one that will do the trick.

I grab a second jar of cherries from an upper shelf and close the pantry door.

It's a risk to make a last-minute change—cherries, when he was expecting peaches—but I know Kevin loves cherry pie. And I need a guarantee. The cloudy liquid in the jar of cherries feels like a sure thing.

I take out one large bowl and one small one.

The large one is for Kevin. Four enormous scoops of ice cream. I unscrew the ring on the cloudy cherries, then using a bottle opener, I pry off the lid. It releases without a sound, which in another situation would be a sign to throw it away.

The cherries are dark pink and sticky like an open wound. Like the wreckage he left between my legs. I don't know how much it takes, but I err on the side of too much. Spoonful after dripping spoonful to top his ice cream. The canning liquid isn't thick and goopy like the syrup in store-bought cherries. The syrup Mom makes tastes like cinnamon ambrosia. Good enough to make you want to lick the bowl, which I hope he does.

Working quickly, I fix myself a smaller bowl, but not too small. I don't want him to decide I don't have enough and give me some of his. This is unlikely. He warns Mom about getting fat whenever she eats something sweet. The problem with Kevin is he can be unpredictable.

Details are important. I need to be prepared for every possibility.

My jar doesn't look empty enough, so I dump a few spoonfuls of cherries into the garbage can and hide them under a wadded-up paper towel. Then I take Kevin's jar and tuck it behind the trash can just in case he comes into the kitchen.

I carry his bowl out first.

"I remembered how much you like cherry pie, so . . . I hope this is okay?"

Sweet smile, soft gaze through my eyelashes. This is how you approach men like Kevin. Men who need to believe they're in control. If I changed the plan, it's only because I'm trying to make him happy.

"Quite a memory you got there, Juliebell."

He smiles his approval and takes the bowl from me. Then he scoops a big spoonful of ice cream into his mouth. It's only after he swallows and takes another bite that my breath starts to circulate in my body again. The pain between my legs pulses to the rhythm of my heart.

I turn to go back to the kitchen, but he stops me.

"Hold on, sweetheart." He dips the spoon back into the bowl and holds it out to me. Vanilla ice cream glistening with dark pink juice. A toxic cherry poised off-center. At least, I hope it's toxic.

"It's okay. I have my own bowl in the kitchen."

His hand clamps around my wrist. He grins like we're playing a game.

"Open wide, Juliebell. That's what we gotta practice next."

If I pull away, the game will shift. Playfulness will become force. I do what he asks. I open wide and let him spoon poison into my mouth.

"Mmm," I say and smile with my mouth closed. The ice cream melts, pooling under my tongue.

Kevin studies me.

I look down, hoping he can't feel my racing pulse.

Then his fingers loosen. He glances back at the TV and takes another bite of ice cream.

I walk quickly, but not too quickly, to the kitchen. Leaning over the sink, I spit. Then I rinse with water and spit again. I do this twice more, but it's not enough. I need to make sure I've destroyed all the poison he put inside me.

Back on my hands and knees, I grab the hydrogen peroxide and swish it around in my mouth. It fizzes and burns. I hold it there, count to twenty, and spit. Rinse with water. Repeat. All the while, I'm glancing at the door to the living room. I don't want Kevin to come looking for me.

The bowl of ice cream I made for myself is starting to melt. The thought of eating it makes me sick, but not half as sick as Kevin's going to feel. I tip some of it into the sink and rinse it down the drain. Then I carry the rest back to the living room and sit next to Kevin on the couch. By the time I force down two bites, he's scraping the bottom of his bowl.

He reaches his spoon toward mine, but I twist away.

"C'mon now. Don't be a pig. They won't let you be a cheerleader if you get fat."

"Okay, fine," I say. I feed him a bite the way I've watched Mom feed other boyfriends who've moved on.

"There's a little bit more. I could fix you another bowl."

My voice is teasing, playful, also like Mom's.

I wonder if her body ever throbbed with pain while she fed them her special concoction. Then I think about all the times I've watched her smooth makeup over bruised skin. It's a dumb question with an obvious answer.

Kevin leans back and rubs his stomach with a groan. Then he grins. "Okay, twist my arm."

I take both bowls back to the kitchen. Mine goes in the sink, his gets refilled. Ice cream, topped with what's left of the cherries from the cloudy jar. I fill the jar with soap and hot water. Then I carry Kevin's bowl back to him. This time, when I hand it to him, his eyes barely flick away from the TV.

I'm invisible, in the best possible way.

"I should start my homework," I say.

He nods but doesn't look at me.

Upstairs, I grab clean clothes from my bedroom. In the bathroom, I lock the door. Then I push a chair under the handle for an extra layer of protection.

My clothes land in a pile on the floor. I can't look at them. I don't want to see the stains, reminders of what Kevin did to my body. When I sit on the toilet, the seat is cold against my thighs. My teeth chatter like I'm feverish. The stream of urine I've been holding comes out with a searing pain. So intense that I squeeze hard, stopping it, but that hurts even worse.

It feels like knives, or teeth or a hungry mouth intent on devouring the person I used to be. It spreads through body parts I'm not supposed to name. Or touch. Private parts. You're not supposed to talk about them. You're not supposed to talk about the things that happen to them, whether you wanted those things to happen or not.

I dig my fingernails deep into my thighs because that's a pain I can control. My stomach twists. Then I'm vomiting, over and over, until there's nothing left.

I'm emptied out.

Purified.

I get in the shower and the water cocoons me.

For the moment, I'm safe.

Twenty-One

APRIL 2015

PAULA

The men who came to our house wore jeans, flannel shirts, and heavy work boots like Dad. They banged on the door. When Mom didn't answer fast enough, they kicked it. Hard enough to make it splinter.

Before Dad moved on, I was scared of the cops. Dad would always slow way down when he saw their cars.

"Don't want any trouble," he'd say under his breath. "Never give the pigs a reason to pull you over, Paula."

When the cops came to tell Mom they'd found Dad in the river, at first I was scared. Then I was disappointed when they didn't realize the truth about what had happened. It wasn't until later that I realized they'd done their best to be kind and make us feel safe. After those men came to our house, I decided who I wanted to be. Not the kind of person who kicked down doors but the kind of person who made other people feel safe.

Of course, we knew the men would come. Mom had already rehearsed it with us.

"Girls, do you understand what happened to Dad?" she asked us the day after I helped her pull up the barn floorboards.

"He drank too much and fell in the river. He drowned." Julie's voice broke, and she was blinking away real tears.

"That's not what happened," I said, real low and tight.

"It's okay, Paula." Mom put one hand on mine. "It's normal to feel angry. It's part of the grieving process. I know you don't want to believe it, but that's the truth." Mom was blinking back her own tears. "You know what? I blame myself. I was sound asleep with you when it happened. I wonder if he came looking for me. Maybe things would have been different . . ." Her voice trailed off as she choked back sobs.

It's a strange sensation to know something but not know it at the same time. It makes you doubt everything. Especially if you're a kid.

"Come here," Mom said and pulled me into a tight hug. "Now tell me what happened."

So I told her. Just the way she wanted me to say it. I wanted to believe her version because it didn't have the ugly moments mine did.

"Good," she said when she was satisfied with the way I told it. She reached for Julie and pulled her close, and I remember thinking we were a solid triangle. No one could pull us apart.

The men came to our house two days later.

"Come on in," Mom said, real friendly.

She smiled like they hadn't splintered our front door. Like she couldn't see the threat in their eyes. But she knew. I could tell by the way her hands fluttered for a moment, like two little birds.

"Girls, this is Joe and Marty. They were friends of your dad's." She threaded her fingers together, caging those birds up tight.

Joe and Marty didn't look like anyone's friends. Joe's hair was dark and greasy, slicked back from his forehead. His skin was pockmarked like he'd had bad acne when he was a kid. Marty was shorter, balding, but with a long beard, like the hair on his head had migrated downward. On his forearm, he had a tattoo of a clenched fist. Half of it disappeared up under his sleeve.

"Let's talk in there." Marty gestured at the kitchen with his head.

It was stupid to listen at the door, but I did it anyway. I was scared. We'd lost Dad, and I wasn't about to lose Mom too.

"He owed us money, Sharon," Marty said. His voice was cold.

"You know I didn't ever get involved with Paul's dealings."

"You're involved now."

"If I had the money, I'd give it to you. It isn't like he had an insurance policy or anything. He left us dead broke."

Mom's voice was sad. She sounded hopeless. Not at all like the kind of woman who would pull up a barn floor and bury plastic grocery bags filled with cash.

There was a long silence like they were waiting for her to say more.

"Hundred K." Joe's voice was deep and filled with gravel. "That kind of money doesn't just disappear."

"Paul never talked to me about his business. You know I work out at the nursing home. Maybe you could put me on a payment plan?"

The sound that followed that question was familiar. I'd heard it plenty of times. It was the sound a man's hand makes when it hits a woman's face. Mom gasped, then I heard a sound that was less familiar. It was the soft sound of her tears.

"Don't get smart, Sharon. You got two little girls out there who need you," said Joe.

"What do you want from me?"

The fear in Mom's voice was unfamiliar, but there was an undertone that comforted me. Of course, Joe and Marty missed it. Same way, later on, her boyfriends never caught that look in her eyes that told me they were in trouble. The undertone told me the same thing. Despite all appearances to the contrary, Mom was in control of the situation.

"We want the money," said Marty.

"I don't know where it is. I didn't even know he borrowed it. Take what you want from the house. There's nothing in the bank. My statements are all upstairs on the desk. Take his truck, if you think it's worth something."

"How much you think you could fetch for this little farm?" Joe asked.

My heart started beating real fast. The house kept us safe.

"You'd have to ask the landlord," Mom said. "I got the lease somewhere if you want to look at it."

That gave me the same feeling I had when she told us how Dad died. I wasn't sure where her story ended and the truth began. It was like being on a merry-go-round that spins so fast the world turns into a blur. Nothing feels real.

I tiptoed over to Julie, who was sitting on the couch staring at the TV.

"This house used to be Grandma and Grandpa's, didn't it?" I whispered.

Her eyes cut over to me, but she didn't answer.

Marty pushed open the kitchen door with a bang. He walked through the living room and headed up the stairs. I could see the gun shoved in his back pocket. When I looked at Julie, I could tell she'd seen it too. Her breathing was shallow and fast, the way it got when she was scared but trying not to let on. I reached over and threaded my fingers through hers.

Marty clomped around upstairs in Mom's room. We could hear him moving things and the sound of something heavy hitting the floor.

Julie and I didn't move. We stared at the TV like we were playing statues.

Mom came out of the kitchen with Joe.

"Girls, put your shoes on. We're gonna go for a drive." She smiled like everything was fine.

"Where are we going?" Julie asked.

"If you're a real good girl, I'll take you to McDonald's," Joe said.

His voice sent a shiver down my spine.

"Just get in the car," Mom said.

So that's what we did.

The minute Joe got in the car, he lit a cigarette. When he finished, he started another one. He kept on that way until the air inside the car turned thick and hazy.

"Sure was sorry to hear about your dad," Joe said as the car climbed into the mountains behind our farm. "Trouble is, he borrowed something from me and I need it back."

"What did he borrow?" Julie's voice was all sweetness and light, like she had no idea what Joe meant.

"They don't know anything." Mom's voice was taut.

"Kids are always snooping." Joe glanced in the rearview mirror and his cold eyes met mine. "Ain't that right?"

"Not these two." Mom was dismissive. "They just stare at the TV all day."

I looked at Julie, but she was looking out the window.

We turned off the main road onto one that was narrow and twisty. The car climbed and climbed without passing any other cars. Finally, Joe stopped.

"End of the line, ladies."

"This isn't McDonald's," Julie said.

Joe laughed like she'd said something funny. "Well, sweetheart, you ain't been a good girl yet."

"Come on, girls. Out of the car," Mom said.

The air smelled clean and pure after being trapped in all that smoke.

I breathed it deep into my lungs, then I looked around. We were on a road cut into the mountain. One side was a steep ravine. Above us, the deep green of Douglas firs stretched up and out as far as I could see.

Joe gestured at Mom with his gun. "Sharon, you get back in the car."

"You can't leave them here. They're just kids. Little girls. They don't know anything."

This time, the fear in her voice sounded real. That scared me more than anything because until that moment, I'd trusted Mom was in control.

"I'm gonna talk to them. That's all. Only person that's gonna get hurt is you, if you don't get back in that car."

Mom's eyes settled on me with a silent message. The only version of the truth was the one we'd practiced.

Joe waited until Mom was in the car, then he turned back to us with a grin.

"Bet you two are ready for a couple of hamburgers right about now."

Julie nodded eagerly. And if you knew anything about Julie, that would have made you suspicious. Julie wasn't like other little kids. Mom was lying when she said we watched TV all the time. Julie read books. Also, Julie didn't like hamburgers. Her favorite thing at McDonald's was Chicken McNuggets.

Of course, Joe didn't know a thing about Julie.

"Remember how I said your daddy borrowed something from me?" Joe asked. I could tell he was trying to make his voice sound sweet.

Julie nodded. Her eyes were big and innocent, like she had no idea what was at stake.

"He didn't ever tell you about a secret hiding place, did he? We all got 'em. Places we hide things when we don't want no one to find them. Betcha got a secret hiding spot yourself, right?" He smiled, but his eyes were hard.

I looked at the gun that he'd moved to his jacket pocket, but he didn't notice because he was focused on Julie.

"My mom hides her chocolate in the cookie jar."

"That's right, sweetheart." Joe squatted down so he and Julie were eye to eye. "What about your daddy? Did he have a cookie jar?"

Julie nodded, then shrugged. "Not really a cookie jar."

"No? But something like a cookie jar. A place where he hid things?"

My heart was pounding hard. All I could think about was Mom with the plastic bags and the shovel. I wanted to shake Julie, tell her to stop talking. But the gun in Joe's pocket turned my tongue into something thick and heavy.

"It's a drawer. He puts special things in it."

"Oh yeah? Where is this drawer?" Joe asked, leaning close.

If she could smell his cigarette breath, she didn't let on. Instead, she lowered her voice. "It's a secret. I'm not supposed to tell."

Joe's eyes flicked toward the car. "Is that what your mom told you?"

Julie shook her head vehemently. "No. Mom doesn't know about it. Paula doesn't know either," she added quickly. "I'm the only one who knows."

"You're the only one he told?" I could hear the note of disbelief in Joe's voice.

"He, well, he . . ." Her eyes flicked up, then back down at the gravel on the side of the road. "He didn't actually tell me. I—I saw him."

"You was spying on him?" Joe sounded pleased, as though Julie had done something to make him proud.

"I wasn't," Julie protested, looking back up at him. "I was in the barn and I just happened to see."

"How about this. You whisper his hiding place in my ear. It'll be a secret just between us."

Julie hesitated, glancing at the car.

"Don't worry," Joe said. "I won't even tell your mom."

A ghost of a smile flickered across her face. Then she leaned close and whispered.

Joe left us there in the mountains. Drove away with a promise that he'd be back. That's how things worked back then. No cell phones. No way to call and ask someone to check a secret drawer for you.

After Joe's car disappeared, Mom hugged us both tight. Then she bent down to Julie, same way Joe had.

"You told him what we talked about?"

Julie nodded.

"He'll go find it and come back for us," Mom said with a smile. "Just like I planned."

We walked right down the middle of that empty road, one of us on each side of Mom, listening as she talked.

"Think about it, girls. It's not much of a story if all you manage to do is survive. No way I was going to let those men take what your dad left behind. It's a guarantee we'll have the freedom to do whatever we damn please. You know what that requires, right?"

She waited, but neither one of us knew the answer.

"Cold, hard cash. Nothing else like it. It means you don't have to answer to anyone else. You get to make all the decisions. Live any kind of life you choose."

We walked for a long time while Mom talked. At least that's how I remember it. In the end, she was right. Joe came back for us. There are other things she was right about too, but I'll get to those things later.

What I remember most clearly about the moment Joe's car reappeared is Mom's face. It transformed from looking certain to looking scared.

He stopped and motioned for us to get in the car.

"Turns out Paul kept a little stash," he said, grinning at Mom.

"I don't know anything about a stash," Mom said.

"Let's just say we'll take his truck and call it even."

Mom sighed, and her shoulders slumped. She looked defeated, but as we got in the car, I could see the glint of triumph in her eyes.

There was no doubt in my mind she put cash in that drawer and told Julie about it. Despite what she said, she must have known more about Dad's side business than she let on. Enough to know how much it would take to pay off a couple of small-town loan sharks. She also understood people are more likely to believe something is true if they think they coaxed it out of a child.

Joe kept his promise. Took us to McDonald's and didn't even notice when Julie ordered Chicken McNuggets instead of a hamburger. After we got home, Mom watched the two of them drive away. Joe in his car, Marty in Dad's truck. When they were gone, she turned to us and smiled.

"They won't come back. We're safe."

To most people, "safe" means out of harm's way, but safety meant something else to Mom. To her, it was cash hidden away.

Truth is, we were never safe.

Twenty-Two

FALL

STELLA

As Stella waits in line at the bagel store, she catalogs what she knows. Three accusatory texts, a blurry pennant, and a reference to a Strawberry Queen. An overheard rendezvous in the park between a woman and a man wearing a shirt similar to Tom's.

Honestly, she knows nothing. Still, she can't erase that litany of texts from her thoughts.

I saw you.
I know what you did.
You made a choice.

Does it add up to something? Or maybe it's nothing. Quite possibly, the messages were intended for Gwen. Should she continue down this path of reactionary research or wait for whoever's on the path to find her?

What if there is no path?
What if this is a long exercise in self-titillation?
What if she's been enjoying this excitement a little too much?

She'll admit it's been a distraction from the endless rounds of laundry, meals, appointment scheduling, grocery shopping, homework supervision, sports practices, and squeezing in her own workouts. One day bleeds into the next until she can't tell Tuesday from Thursday.

Yes, she knows she's supposed to be so fucking thankful for this life. But what if she's just incredibly exhausted by the overwhelming amount of repetitive labor that has been repackaged and branded as

"Motherhood"? She's probably experiencing some form of Mom Brain, but isn't that the same thing? A dismissive phrase for the cognitive failures of women doing the labor of three jobs while being paid for none.

Or is she trying to talk herself down from the ledge. Dismiss what she feels in her bones. Deny her truth.

If the pennant on Charlotte's wall is from Livingston High School, that's a direct link to Stella's past. A past she severed long ago. Does it mean someone has found her? That Gwen's phone left on Stella's steps was no accident?

Gwen.

It all leads back to Gwen, Dave's Strawberry Queen.

I saw you.

I know what you did.

You made a choice.

If the messages are coming from Gwen, does she know what Stella did?

Is Gwen texting her own phone from a burner in order to . . . ?

Stella sets the bag of bagels on the passenger seat and starts her car.

Three decades have passed, but the sight of that pennant still speaks to her. She was so close. She worked so hard, then it all fell apart. She promised herself she'd work hard for other things she wanted, but she'd be more careful. She wouldn't allow herself to become a target. Once she had those things, she'd never give them up. There would be no more need to hide and scurry away from what was rightfully hers. She'd be free to do whatever she wanted. Enjoy the fruits of her labor. She wrote a story with a big paycheck, a guarantee of safety in the form of financial freedom.

Then Colin was born and she gave it up. Tom's suggestion to stay home and invest the money they saved in the kids' college accounts felt like a chance to do one job, and do it really well. She couldn't give up the job of motherhood, so she gave up the other one. Practicing law would have meant a constant scaling back of job opportunities and money, while the work at home scaled infinitely upward. And she loves her children, she really does. The idea of a life without them makes her heart break in two.

She pulls into the parking lot of McDonald's and puts her phone's browser in private mode, even though she's fairly certain that does nothing to hide her search. Then she pulls up the website of Livingston High School. The mascot is still the same. A grinning bulldog.

"Bulldogs are a common mascot," she whispers like a crazy person.

Instead of attempting to freeze-frame Charlotte's TikTok again, Stella squeezes her eyes shut, trying to re-create the night Gwen left her phone behind.

Funny how things come full circle.

Those words paired with Gwen's smile like frosting, designed to cover up something ugly. What else was it that she felt that night? That sense of déjà vu. Familiarity as though her brain was dangling knowledge just out of Stella's reach.

The obvious conclusion makes Stella's eyes pop open.

Her first suspicion was correct.

Gwen and Tom are having an affair.

"An affair," Stella whispers to her car. Then she giggles. What she feels is . . . relief? An affair is so easily managed. The possibilities for a new narrative are already swirling in her brain. The knowledge feels delicious. Delightful, like learning about a life hack that gives you an extra hour every single day.

"An affair," Stella says. She hears the glee in her voice and wonders if she still loves her husband.

It all makes sense. She and Tom have grown increasingly distant. Some days it feels less like a marriage and more like a stage-managed production of what marriage is supposed to look like. Family dinner, weekly sex (monthly, if she's being honest), a partnership that is serviceable but not intimate.

That's why Gwen was at her house. It's why Tom was home suspiciously early. It's the source of Gwen's knowing mean-girl smile that evoked feelings of déjà vu.

SJIUYVP has to be Tom. Stella checks the picture she took of Gwen's contact, but she doesn't recognize the number.

This has to be the conversation Gwen wants to have with her. In the time it's taken Stella to recognize the truth, the prospect of that conversation has gone from root canal to tired trope. Whatever Gwen is going to trot forth is definitely a conversation Stella would prefer to avoid.

A thought emerges before she can squash it. Her mother had it right. The female of the species should never mate for life. It presses her into a smaller, weaker form. Made invisible by the task of caring for offspring without support or acknowledgment, aside from the condescension of Mother's Day.

Stella takes a deep breath and pulls into the drive-thru lane, where she orders a cheeseburger and a vanilla milkshake. She waits in the line of cars until it's her turn to receive a bag spotted with grease. As she pulls away, she reaches into the bag. Brings the cheeseburger to her lips, then stops.

"Eat the fucking cheeseburger, Stella," she says, but she's already putting it down.

There was a time when she could have become anyone, done anything, but now she's constrained by all the choices she's already made. She can't eat the cheeseburger any more than she can abandon her children.

Besides, she never liked cheeseburgers.

At home, she dumps the McDonald's bag in the outside trash, then goes in through the front door and trips over Daisy's field hockey gear. Five hundred dollars' worth of equipment, abandoned like an uneaten bag of food from McDonald's.

"Daisy," she calls, cupping her hands around her mouth.

The only response is the *thump ba-da thump* of rap music from the basement, where Colin is lifting weights.

"Daisy," she calls, louder this time.

When there is still no response, Stella screams out her daughter's name. "DAISY!"

Daisy appears at the top of the stairs. "Oh my God, Mom! What? I'm doing homework."

Headphones dangle around her daughter's neck. They might as well be a sign that Daisy was watching Netflix, but Stella isn't in the mood for an argument that will veer quickly into semantics.

"Pick up your shit."

"What?" Daisy looks confused.

"Pick. Up. Your. Shit."

Stella stares at her daughter. She wonders if Daisy has any notion of what lies inside her mother.

"Fine." Daisy sighs heavily and stomps down the stairs. "You don't have to be so passive-aggressive."

Stella considers correcting her, but she's not in the mood for a long conversation about the difference between aggression and passive aggression. Instead, she asks, "Is Dad home?"

"No." Daisy's face could be titled *Portrait of a Sullen Teenage Girl*.

"Do you know where he went?"

"He had to run into his office. I guess he forgot something."

Stella nods and waits until Daisy puts everything away. When her daughter disappears back behind her bedroom door, Stella goes to her own bedroom and turns the lock.

If someone asks....

She rolls her eyes. If someone asks, she'll say she deserves five minutes to herself.

She surveys the room, trying to come up with an attack plan. Sitting area, closet, dresser, bed, and nightstand. In Tom's closet, she studies his clothes. Dips her hand into a few pockets. What does she expect to find? Receipts? Lipstick on the collar?

All she finds are business cards that don't arouse any suspicions, a few mints, and a field hockey permission slip that was due last week. She takes the permission slip with a heavy sigh and continues her search. She is thorough, but there is no hidden shoebox full of love notes. No matchbox from a romantic restaurant or phone number scrawled on a piece of paper.

All of those items are outdated. In this technological age, the only trail that matters is electronic.

Even so, she gives it her best shot, rifling through his underwear drawer and feeling underneath his piles of T-shirts that she puts away herself. The nightstand seems too obvious, but Tom isn't particularly creative. The drawer of his nightstand is a clutter of spare change, old wallet-size school pictures of the kids, a sock, a paperback he started to read last year while they were on vacation. She picks up the book. It's one of those female thrillers. Tom said he couldn't get into it.

Underneath the book lies a small phone.

Not an iPhone or an Android. Something off-brand. She's never seen a burner phone before, but she has no doubt that's what this is. She picks it up and gently opens it.

It takes a minute to figure out how to work the text messaging function, but it's empty. Too empty. She remembers the deletion of whatever message preceded Quick thinking. Clearly, they are being cautious.

She switches to saved contacts, and here she is met with an immediate reward. The deep satisfaction of being right.

There is only one saved contact: GT.

It's not a leap to assume the initials stand for Gwen Thompson.

Stella puts the phone back. Replaces the book (irrelevant to Tom's life because why would he be interested in the inner lives of a bunch of women), shuts the drawer, and tiptoes down the stairs so as not to be waylaid by either Daisy or Colin.

She needs time to think.

Time to create a plan.

Outside, she pulls on her gardening gloves and grabs the wicker basket she uses to carry vegetables back to the kitchen. Her garden is messy and exuberant in a way that makes Stella envious. Cucumbers stretch out to take up as much room as they can claim. They would have eaten the cheeseburger. Stella's sure of it.

She starts to pick them but realizes there are far too many to eat. For a moment, she considers pickling them. Putting them up in jars so her family can have a taste of summer even when there's snow on the ground. Filling jars with salty brine, then adding the carefully sliced cucumbers. Tightening the lids before loading them into a home canner. Tucking away the ones that didn't seal. She'd need somewhere secret to store those jars. Somewhere no one would mess with them. A secret room, perhaps?

Stella shudders.

"Too much work," she says under her breath and tries to convince herself it is the thought of the work involved that's making her shudder.

Movement from inside the house catches her attention.

It's Tom.

Home from the office, or wherever he was.

She watches him, framed by the large windows. He fills a glass of water, takes it to the kitchen island, then glances over his shoulder like he's looking for something.

Or someone.

Is he looking for her?

Tom picks up his phone. His fingers move over its surface. He's typing. This takes a while because he's not fleet of finger like their children. Every so often, he pauses, head cocked to one side like he's listening for something.

Is he listening for her?

Stella moves deeper into the shadows, where she can observe him, undetected.

She waits until he finishes with his phone. Then she empties her basket of cucumbers back onto the soil of her garden. Circling around to the front yard, she comes in through the front door.

"Hey," Tom calls. "Where you been?"

"Over at Ellen's. I dropped off some cukes. My garden's out of control. Ellen said the Vaughns might be putting their house on the market."

Tom's eyes light up. Real estate gossip is his favorite kind. "What do you think they'll ask for it?"

"Ellen said 2.3."

"Wow! Do you think it'll sell?" The number makes Tom gleeful.

Stella shrugs. "I mean, I guess we'll see."

"True." He stretches and yawns. "Colin and I are gonna watch the game."

"Okay," she says.

He leaves the room and she waits motionless like a rabbit freezing to escape the notice of a hawk. When the sound of the television floats into the kitchen, she takes a deep breath, as though she's escaped.

But of course, that's backward.

If there's a predator in the house, it's not Tom.

It's Stella.

Twenty-Three

SPRING 1987

JULIE

While I'm in the shower, I realize Mom's not coming home. If she was here, she wouldn't have let Kevin do what he did to me on the couch. After Mom found out Paula was pregnant, she blamed herself. She promised she'd never let anything like that happen to me, but it did. That's how I know she lost control of the story. The moment you lose control, you start to disappear. Slide into nothingness like everyone who's moved on. I'm worried that's what happened to Mom.

My face is pale in the mirror as I comb tangles out of my wet hair. I pull on the heavy sweatpants and oversize sweatshirt I brought into the bathroom with me. Even so, I shiver like there's something cold inside of me.

Slowly, I open the bathroom door and listen. The TV is on, but there are no other voices. Some part of me is still hoping Mom will come home and fix everything. I tiptoe into her bedroom and peer out the window. Weeds poke up through the gravel driveway and brambles cover the muddy ditches, but there's no sign of Mom's car.

It's starting to get dark. She's not working the night shift this week, so she should be home.

It occurs to me Kevin hasn't mentioned Mom, other than to say she asked him to pick me up. He didn't say when she'd be home or why her plans changed or even complain about the way her work schedule inconvenienced him. That last piece is particularly strange because it's one of his favorite topics. He never misses a chance to point out how much he does for us.

There's a dark smudge on the wall next to the door of Mom's bedroom. Actually, it's more of a smear.

I move closer to inspect it.

It looks like blood. When I touch it, it's dry.

My heart pounds a little harder. The coldness inside me spreads to my limbs. This mark wasn't here when I left for school this morning. I can't prove it, but I know Mom is meticulous. She scrubs and cleans our house until every surface is pristine. She laughs at herself, says it's a compulsion. If she didn't get the house clean enough when she was a kid, she had to answer to her dad's belt. After someone moves on, there's not a trace of dirt or a smudge anywhere. If there was a mark on the wall, Mom would have noticed immediately. She would have put on her yellow plastic gloves and used Comet to scrub it off the wall.

When Kevin wipes the kitchen counter, he leaves a trail of crumbs behind. He doesn't notice the mud he tracks in on his shoes or the splatter he leaves on the mirror after he shaves. Kevin wouldn't have noticed a smear on the wall.

I glance around Mom's bedroom, looking for anything else out of place, and a glint of metal catches my eye.

On the dresser, blade out, is Kevin's penknife. The handle is carved from bone and engraved with a pattern of stars. Based on that alone, you'd think he would have paid more attention to the stars Mom paints on the barn wall. A guy like Kevin would enjoy pointing out what she got wrong. How some stars are bigger than they should be. When he looks at that painting, all he sees is a pointless activity. Mom's boyfriends miss the true purpose of her painting. Same way they miss the true nature of their relationship with her. The men who pass through our lives think they're writing the story. All the while, she's writing their last chapter.

I close my fingers around the bone handle and study the dark substance on the blade. It's the same color as the smear on the wall.

Blood.

It's Mom's blood. I'm certain. It's something I feel in my stomach, the same way I knew what Kevin had planned for me from the moment I got in his truck. Carefully, I fold the blade so it's tucked back into the bone handle and slip the knife into the pocket of my sweatpants.

It's okay, I tell myself as I walk toward the door. The worst is over.

Then I realize that's not necessarily true. There are worse things that could happen. As those things play through my mind, I open Kevin's knife. Then I hold it tightly in my hand as I walk down the stairs.

He's on the couch. Right where I left him. Even though I need to talk to him, I'm still disappointed to find him upright.

"Hey, Kevin." I force my lips into a smile and hold the knife so he won't see it. "Did my mom say when she would be home?"

"Nope." He smiles up at me.

"But she's at work, right?"

Do his eyes look glassy, or is that just wishful thinking?

"Nope."

His smile gets bigger. He loves this game—any game, really, that forces me to beg for information.

"So, where is she?"

"At the hospital."

"What do you mean?" My mouth goes dry.

"I had to take her there earlier. She had a little accident today. Tumbled down the stairs. She was drinking. I think that's how it happened."

"Mom fell down the stairs?" My voice sounds like it's coming from far away.

Kevin nods like he's pleased with himself. He likes this story.

"Hit her head against the wall pretty hard. Happened right after I figured out she took something from me."

A chill runs down my spine. I grip the knife tighter.

"Is she . . . okay?"

Kevin shrugs. "Broke her arm. Got banged up pretty bad when she fell. Might have a concussion, but she'll live. One thing's for sure, she won't be stealing from me no more."

Visions of the fat envelope stuffed with money dance in my head. My palms go slick with sweat.

"What did she steal?"

I have to ask. If I don't, he'll know I know.

Kevin shifts on the couch like he's uncomfortable. "It don't matter. Important thing is she learned her lesson. By the time she comes home, she'll be ready to give it back."

"She's coming home, though, right?"

He tilts his head to one side and smiles. "She sure is. Don't you worry, Juliebell. When I dropped her off at the hospital, she told me to take care of her baby. That's what I intend to do."

His eyes run over me like he can see through the bulky clothes I'm wearing. His lips curve into a small smile, and that's when I understand. His plan is to repeat what he did on the couch. Repeat it over and over, punishing Mom and rewarding himself.

The worst is definitely not over.

Then Kevin's stomach gurgles. He shifts again and grimaces.

"Are you hungry?" I ask, and this time my smile is real. "I could make us some dinner."

"Sure."

He grimaces and burps loudly.

Here's what I know. Men like Kevin want more. More money, more food, more bodies to control. Whatever I offer him, he'll take on principle. He'll devour it because he thinks the act of taking is what makes him strong.

In the kitchen, I set the knife under a dish towel and make dinner. Pasta, because it's cheap and easy. As I fill a pot with water, I think about the poison inside those jars.

It's not a guarantee. With other boyfriends, it took two jars. Sometimes even three before they ate enough toxin to move them on. It happens slowly. At first they feel off, then their throats get sticky. They can't swallow. Then their words disappear. After that, they stop breathing.

At least that's what Mom told me. We've never watched it happen. When Mom gives them one of her special desserts, she waits for the initial signs. Then she manages to send them somewhere else. A weekend of camping or a long drive or a fishing trip. Anything to get them out of the house. Their deaths are accidents, like Dad's, or from natural causes. Heart attack, stroke, drunk driving, that kind of thing.

I try not to imagine the scene that took place between Mom and Kevin while I was at school, but I can't help it. Kevin's fist as it hits her face. His knife cutting into her flesh. The smudge on a bedroom wall left by a hand that has wiped away blood. He pushes her down the stairs and she tumbles. He must have caught her by surprise. If she'd returned that fat envelope stuffed with cash, he might have settled for a black eye or broken nose.

It was my fault she couldn't give it back.

If she'd had the money to give him, she could have controlled the story. She took that money for me. The realization is a different kind of poison inside my stomach.

The water is boiling.

It splashes my hand and I jerk away.

Here's another story. I carry the pot of boiling water into the living room. Sneak up behind Kevin on silent feet. Pour it over his head and watch while he writhes in pain. Except what if it's not enough? I picture him, burned and screaming. His hand fastens around my wrist like it did earlier. His other hand connects with my jaw.

No, that's not a sure thing. I open the box of pasta and dump it in the pot. I have to be patient, trust the cherries will work their magic. Soon, he'll be out of our life forever. Or as Mom would say, Kevin is about to move on.

I'm opening a jar of tomatoes from last summer when Kevin stumbles into the kitchen.

"I'm not feeling so good." He burps and collapses on one of the metal chairs at the Formica table in the corner.

"Do you want a glass of water or something?" I ask with feigned concern. I grab a glass, fill it, and set it on the table. Then with my body between Kevin and his penknife, I close it and slip it in my pocket.

"You got any . . ." He tilts his head to one side and massages his neck like it's stiff.

"Any?"

"What?" He looks back at me, confused. "Pink stuff. You know, for stomachache."

"Pepto-Bismol?"

"Yeah. Maybe too much ice cream." He gives me a weak smile. His eyes are unfocused, and there's a bubble of saliva at the corner of his mouth.

"Sure. It's upstairs. I'll be right back." I turn the water down. The pasta will be ruined, but that's okay. It's not like anyone's going to eat it.

Botulism isn't like regular food poisoning. It's unpredictable. Sometimes the toxins take a while before they go to work on the body.

Sometimes it happens fast. When Mom decides she's had enough of a boyfriend, she has to be organized and anticipate every detail. Timing is important when it comes to cooking, canning, and planning for someone to move on.

Mom's boyfriend Scott was the one who got Paula pregnant. When Mom figured out what he'd done, she fixed him a big bowl of ice cream and peaches. He was leaving for a hunting trip that afternoon. That time it took only one try. Scott's buddies woke up the next day, but he didn't. They called it a stroke.

Brett was around longer. At first he was just mean, then he got mean with his fists. He stole from Mom too. That was the clincher. Gambled one of her paychecks at the casino out by the coast and won big. He come back saying he was going to take us out to dinner.

"I sure wish we could go," Mom said as she spooned strawberries into a dish, just the way he liked. "Julie and I are headed out to visit Paula this weekend. You want some more of those, honey?"

It took two days of strawberries and ice cream to move him on. Mom waited until his eyes got glassy, then we went on a camping trip and read about his drunk-driving accident in the paper.

"Damn shame he didn't get to enjoy the money he won. Seems like there's a lesson there," Mom said when she showed me the article.

Men fall for her because she's pretty, but it's more than that. She feeds them and coddles them. Lets them believe they are in control. She laughs at their jokes, even the dumb ones. When they speak, she tells them how smart they are, how truly remarkable. They believe her. They mistake the glisten in her eyes for love. They get tangled up in her web of words. Don't even know they're stuck until it's too late. By the time they realize what's happened, if they ever realize it at all, there's no room for a rewrite.

That part's always the same. Little by little, the animal that lives inside those men shows its teeth. Mom waits for it. She's never in a rush.

"Patience is a deadly virtue," she'll say with a smile and glance up at the picture of her parents that still hangs in the living room. Her eyes get narrow and hard when they land on her dad.

Sometimes she even gives her boyfriends a couple of chances. It's part of the game she plays that makes her eyes gleam like she's in love. There's some threshold inside her, though. Once she's been hit hard enough or they hurt us, she's done.

She puts the animal out of its misery.

I sit on Mom's bed and remind myself that's what's happening right now. Kevin is an animal that is being put down. He's rabid. A danger to everyone he meets. It was me or him. That all makes sense, but what I don't understand is how he caught Mom off guard. The answer comes to me in a rush of guilt.

Me, that's the difference. I needed the money for cheerleading. She couldn't be patient and wait, because she had a deadline. It's my fault that Mom's in the hospital. What happened on the couch and what's happening to Kevin, those things are my fault too.

Suddenly, I realize what I've neglected. The realization makes me jump up and run to my bedroom. Using Kevin's knife, I rip open the inside seam of my school backpack. I take twenty dollars out of the fat envelope and shove the rest between the canvas and the lining. After that, I pack a change of clothes, my toothbrush, and the picture of Mom, Dad, me, and Paula that's taped to my mirror.

Then I grab the Pepto-Bismol and head back downstairs.

"Sorry. It was hard to find," I say, holding up the pink bottle as I come into the kitchen.

Kevin squints like he's having trouble seeing me.

"I'm tired." His words are slurred.

"Maybe you should lie down on the couch."

He stands. Knocks over the glass of water I put in front of him, but he doesn't notice. He stumbles toward the living room and collapses on the couch.

"Do you want a blanket?" I ask, but he doesn't answer.

Slowly, I back away. Kevin shouldn't be here. I should have gotten him out of the house, but now it's too late.

The problem, and it's a big one, is this isn't Mom's story anymore.

It's not Kevin's either.

It's mine.

And I wasn't careful about the way I wrote it.

When Kevin turns into something cold, hard, and lifeless on the living room couch, I'll be the only one who was here when it happened. It'll be obvious that I'm the reason Kevin moved on. When the police come, which they will, they'll take me to jail. Worse, they might decide to look into all the other men who haven't survived their relationship with Mom. She could end up in jail too.

I turn off the stove, grab my backpack, and lock the door on my way out. The key goes in my pocket with the knife. It's a long walk to town, but I can do it. As long as I'm moving, I'm not thinking about Kevin.

Or the raw feeling between my legs.

Or the weight of his body on top of me.

Or the way he was struggling to breathe when I shut the door.

Twenty-Four

APRIL 2015

PAULA

We all have moments etched in our memory. Days preserved like butterflies under glass. For me, it was the day Julie showed up at my house. I'd been living on my own like an adult since I was sixteen. Far as anyone knew, I *was* an adult and had been ever since I moved to Hermiston. That was the magic of the fake ID Mom got me when I left.

More than just a driver's license; a whole set of documents that changed my age and last name. Mom always said I was bullheaded, and maybe I am, because I wouldn't change my first name. I'd already given up my whole life in Livingston. I told Mom there are plenty of Paulas in this world. One more wouldn't make much of a difference.

Those fake documents made me eighteen overnight, which meant I was legally an adult. It also meant I could check groceries at the Albertsons without anyone's permission. Mom didn't need to worry about me anymore.

According to those papers, I was grown and she was done.

The day Julie showed up, I almost tripped on her. Stepped out my front door and found her on my porch like some sort of stray. Her hair hung around her face, all stringy like she hadn't washed it in a while. She was hugging her knees tight to her chest.

"Julie? Is that you?" I asked, because to be honest, I wasn't completely sure.

"Paula?"

She had the same hesitation I did. That's how long it had been.

Later, she told me she'd been sitting there for an hour trying to work up the nerve to knock on my door.

"Come in off the porch," I said.

I figured I knew what she was running from.

It turns out, I didn't know the half of it. I sent Julie to take a shower and called my manager at Albertsons to tell her I was going to be late. Then I scrambled up a big mess of eggs with toast on the side.

"How'd you find me?" I asked after Julie got herself cleaned up.

She kind of shrugged, but I already knew. Mom is an expert at building all kinds of life rafts. That's what she was doing when she arranged for me to live in Hermiston. This house was one more form of survival. It kept a roof over my head and doubled as a place for Julie to land, if she ever needed it.

"Things went bad at home?"

"Not all bad. I made varsity cheer," she said with a little smile. Then she started to cry.

I hugged her real tight. What else could I do?

Mom is a like a storm. The kind that causes flash floods where the rain pours down so hard you can't catch your breath. Julie and me, we were the sofa cushions left out in that storm. Soaked through. Even after they dry, they're never the same.

When Julie told me what happened, I did nothing but listen.

Some officers on the police force don't understand how to get a confession. The secret is simple. You let the person say what they need to say. Less you interrupt, more likely you are to get the whole story.

That's how it went with Julie. She told me what Kevin did, which I was expecting. Then she told me what she did back. I wasn't expecting that, but I didn't blame her. I'd lived through my own version of Kevin.

You know what happens to men like Kevin when a girl like Julie reports him?

Not much, that's what.

You ask me, Kevin got what he deserved. Some might call what Julie did murder, but I was proud of her. I wish I'd done the same, although in the end Mom did it for me.

Since I made detective, I've investigated my fair share of murders. They fall into two categories.

Men who get murdered taking risks.

And women and children who are murdered trying to survive.

Sometimes I tell myself Mom is some kind of karma for all those women and children. I'm not saying she was the best mom, but she did a whole lot more than just survive. She made sure other people wouldn't have to fight for their survival against certain predators.

Julie explained how she'd left Kevin at the house. We talked through all the details. I was still just a checker at Albertsons, but I loved those true crime shows on TV. I'd watched enough of them to know she and Mom would both need an alibi.

First thing I did was call the Livingston hospital to make sure Mom was still there. Her voice was weak when she picked up the phone.

"It's Paula," I said.

"She with you?" Mom's voice went hard in a way that told me she'd be just fine.

"Yeah."

"Good," Mom said.

"She's going to stay here," I said.

Mom was quiet for a second and I could hear the wheels turning in her head. "Fine," she said. Then she hung up the phone.

These days, it's harder to make someone disappear. You've got the internet, cell phones, social media, credit card trails, and cameras everywhere you go. People still manage to do it, but there's more of a fuss when it's a girl like Julie. White and pretty, a girl who just made varsity cheer. A girl like that disappears today and it's all over the internet, but this was before the internet. All it took for Julie to start a whole new life was an eight-hour trip across the state.

It was summer, which made it easier. No school to wonder what happened to her right away. Julie researched what we needed to do. She spent whole afternoons at the library figuring out how she could enroll in the local school without anyone asking questions.

Her attention to detail reminded me of Mom.

"You have to be my guardian, Paula," she explained. "I want to go to high school, but without a guardian, the state can take me away."

Mom had a post office box two towns over from Livingston. That's where I sent letters explaining what we needed. New documents for Julie. A whole new name, first and last so it would match mine. Everything buttoned up so no one would ask questions.

"Do I get to choose?" Julie asked.

She was reading the letter I was writing over my shoulder.

"Choose what?"

"My new first name?"

"Sure," I told her.

She nodded and thought about it a bit.

"I don't want to be Julie anymore. Bad things happened to her. I want to start over. This time, I'm going to choose everything that happens in my life."

The first letter we got from Mom was a big envelope filled with family photos. Other than that, it was careful. You might even call it clean. The same way she cleaned those canning jars after they'd served their purpose. Scrubbed them until not a trace of evidence was left behind.

Hello Paula,

You probably heard I was in the hospital. I had a fall. Busted up my arm, but I'm okay now. That's not why I'm writing. There's some sad news about my friend Kevin. He took ill while I was in the hospital. Police suspect it was a real bad case of food poisoning, or something like that. It was the dehydration that got him in the end. I tell myself he's in a better place, but it sure is sad. They told me it's real common to die at home.

Some other sad news is that your sister ran off. One of the police officers is working hard to find her. He stops by a couple times a week, says he's got a perfect record when it comes to solving cases, but no leads yet. If you want to add your prayers for her safety to mine, they'd be welcome.

I'm glad you're doing well. I was digging through some old albums and thought you might like these pictures. They made me smile.

Otherwise, I've been keeping busy working on my painting. Thought you'd like to see the updated version, so I sent a picture of it along with the rest of the photos.

All my love,
Mom

Julie spread out the photos Mom sent across our kitchen table. They were mostly photos of us when we were little. Me, Julie, Mom, and Dad, smiling at the camera like a normal family.

"Can I keep some of these?" she asked.

"Of course you can," I said.

She stopped when she came to the photo of the barn wall. "You remember what the stars mean?"

I nodded.

"I don't want anything to do with those stars," she whispered in a voice so quiet I had to lean in to hear. "I'm going to live a different kind of life. One where I don't ever need them."

In some ways, living with Julie was a little like living with Mom again. Only this time around, there were no boyfriends, just me and Julie with a whole house to ourselves. We told people we were sisters, which was true. We said our parents had died in a fire. That made people sad. Then we told them we were lucky because I was Julie's guardian and we got to live together. That made them happy again.

"At least you have each other," they'd say and we'd smile and nod.

After we got Mom's letter, Julie started reading the Livingston newspaper at the library. It was stored on these tiny rolls of film called microfiche. You had to load it onto a special machine and scroll through, page by page. We read everything we could find about Kevin's death, but there wasn't much. We followed the search for Julie too. The local paper called her a runaway and printed her eighth-grade picture with a number to call if you'd seen her.

"Let's go home, Paula," she said after she saw her own face staring out at her.

When we got home, she made me chop off her hair so she wouldn't look like those photos in the paper.

After that, we stopped going to the library to read the Livingston paper.

Mom wrote me one more time that summer with instructions on how to get the documents we needed to enroll Julie in school. She said she'd send us money, but Julie didn't want to wait.

"I've got money," she told me and handed me an envelope stuffed with twenties.

I didn't ask where she got it. Sometimes the kindest thing you can do is know which questions not to ask.

We drove to Idaho to get her new birth certificate and social security card. On our way home, she opened the envelope and studied the birth certificate for a long time.

"I'm someone else now," she said.

I nodded. Outside, along the interstate, dry grass stretched out as far as the eye could see. Inside the car we were protected, safe. Not because we had a backup plan, but because no one could hurt us. It was a different kind of safety than we'd ever known. When we lived with Mom, the idea of safety was tangled so deeply with cash being hidden away it was hard to separate one from the other. And yet somehow, we'd made it to this place. Here we were, untangled and free.

"Where'd you come up with that name?" I asked, nodding at Julie's new birth certificate.

"From a play."

"What play?"

"Something I read on my own. Why do you even care, Paula? It's not like you're going to read it." She rolled her eyes and looked out the window.

It was no secret she was the smarter one, but it hurt my feelings all the same. She must have sensed she stepped over a line because she grabbed my hand.

"It's about sisters," she said, real soft. "But it's also a reminder."

"Reminder of what?"

"A reminder to not be like Mom," she said, then she laughed. "Actually, it's a reminder to be like her, but better. My life is going to be something she couldn't even imagine."

"That sounds good to me," I said.

When we got home, I asked her what she wanted for dinner.

"Paula," she said, all serious, "you can't call me Julie anymore. From now on, you have to use my new name."

"You still look like the same Julie to me," I said, sinking down onto the living room couch. I'd found it at a garage sale and was real proud of it. It was purple velvet and felt fancy. It smelled musty when I brought it home, but a couple boxes of baking soda and a few passes with a vacuum cleaner and you couldn't even tell it was used.

"But I'm not."

She sat down next to me and rubbed her hand back and forth on the couch cushion like she was trying to put a hole in it.

"Julie's gone. And everything that happened to her is gone too. It's like it never happened at all."

"Good riddance," I said.

"What about Mom?" she asked.

"What do you mean?"

"Did she happen?"

It was getting dark and the shadows had turned everything soft. You couldn't see that the floors were dirty or the dust that hung in the summer air. We sat there on my velvet couch. Two girls, safe in a house paid for with money Mom had taken from all those boyfriends.

They hit her.

Then, when they weren't expecting it, she hit them back.

Hit them back hard.

"She happened. If she hadn't happened the way she did, we wouldn't have happened into all this."

Julie looked around at our cocoon and smiled, but I could see her brain going to work. Filing away what I'd said and using it to create a story of her own, one that would put her safely out of Mom's reach.

Twenty-Five

FALL

STELLA

Stella has questions.

The answers to her questions reside with Gwen.

Gwen Thompson with her Lilly Pulitzer bag, slurred speech, hunched walk of someone in pain, and bruise she tried to hide beneath her hair.

Stella's no longer willing to lie to herself about these things. She recognized them right away, even though she wanted to pretend she didn't. She's supposed to be the kind of person who doesn't know how to interpret those signs. One who has no firsthand experience with the bad things men do to women. The fist balled up next to a leg, like hackles on a dog. The smile that is actually a warning. The smears of blood left behind on a wall.

Stella Parker shouldn't know about these things, but she does.

She knows enough to tread cautiously. It would be easy to ask Tom. Lay out her accusations as though they are merely concerns, but the bruises on Gwen's face stop her.

Is Tom behind those marks?

It's an unpleasant thought, but not in the usual way. Stella was careful. Selective. Did she somehow misstep? Take a road lined with apples and trees and daughters following in their mother's footsteps?

The sidelines erupt in cheers, and Stella realizes she hasn't been watching Daisy's game. She claps loudly and yells out encouraging words to cover her inattention.

"Hey, you," Lorraine says, arriving late.

She's wearing a variation of Stella's outfit. Yoga pants paired with a fleece, topped with a vest. Blonde-highlighted hair in a messy bun.

"Hey." Stella pastes a welcoming smile on her face.

Something about the way Lorraine is studying her makes Stella uncomfortable. She looks out at the field, searching for a safe topic, and lands on Lorraine's daughter.

"Ainsley looks good out there!"

"Thanks. Daisy too."

It's an automatic response that means nothing at all.

Stella feels a deep well of longing. She wishes she could confess. Confide all her worries; but it's too much. Telling Lorraine will provide Stella with a fleeting moment of release followed by too much vulnerability. She'll be seen, when the most important thing is to remain invisible.

Lorraine's eyes flick over to Stella. She looks worried. Stella opens her mouth to ask if something is wrong, but before she can form the words, Lorraine nudges her down the field like a dog herding sheep.

"Look, Anna told me something. I don't know how to say this, so I'm just going to say it, okay?"

"Yeah, of course. What's wrong?"

"Nothing, I mean. It's . . . deep breath, okay?" Lorraine says.

Stella nods.

"Anna told me she had to take Morgan, her youngest, to a special psychologist to have her ADHD diagnosed. She wants Morgan to have more time for her tests and SATs. Anna thinks it will be good for her self-esteem."

Stella nods along to this litany of mind-numbing details.

"So anyway." Lorraine sighs heavily. "The office is right next to the Fairmont Hotel, and while she was waiting for Morgan to be evaluated, she saw Tom go in."

Stella feels her fingers clench into fists. She suspects she knows where this is headed.

"Then, like ten minutes later, Anna spots Gwen Thompson go in too."

Stella returns to the question she asked yesterday. Is she still in love with Tom? As Lorraine continues, Stella tries to define the precise nature of her feelings for her husband. He's definitely a distant third to

Colin and Daisy, but he's not horrible. Nothing like the men she knew long ago.

That comparison, and what it implies, makes her shudder.

"Are you okay?" Lorraine asks, misinterpreting Stella's shudder. She puts one hand on Stella's arm and gives it a supportive squeeze.

"I'm fine. What did Anna see?"

"I mean nothing, really. She saw Tom leave after about an hour, then Gwen left too."

Stella swallows the saliva that has pooled in her mouth. She already suspected the affair. But hearing about it from Lorraine feels different. Some small part of her had been clinging to the hope that she would be proven wrong. That this would all be a misunderstanding.

Lorraine sighs. "Anna told me, but we haven't told anyone else. Not that we would. Just, you know, if you were worried. No one's gossiping."

Their team scores another goal. Even though Lorraine and Stella missed it, they still make a show of smiling and clapping. Lorraine's eyes cut back to Stella.

"Is that all? Anything else?" Stella's voice is harsher than normal.

"I'm so sorry. Maybe I shouldn't have said anything. You know, I never . . ." She hesitates in a way that is very un-Lorraine.

"Never what?"

"I don't know. This probably sounds too after-the-fact, but I never liked her."

"Gwen?"

Lorraine nods. It's a miserable gesture, like she's admitting to a personal failing. "It's not even that I'm blaming her totally. I mean it takes two, right? Right after they moved here, years ago, she kept asking me all these questions about you. It gave me such a weird vibe. I should have told you, but that felt weird too, you know?"

The hairs on the back of Stella's neck prickle like a dog catching a wayward scent. "What kind of questions?"

Lorraine shrugs. "I don't remember. Stuff like how long we had been friends. If we knew each other from college. It was too much. Too personal, you know? I remember thinking she had some sort of mom crush on you, or something."

Stella nods and looks at the scoreboard. There is less than a minute left in the game and their girls are ahead. She is deeply thankful, because if they win, it means Daisy won't need to be consoled in the car on the way home. She will chatter or look at her phone, giving Stella time to process this new information.

"I'm so sorry. Are you okay?" Lorraine asks.

"Yes," Stella says, then reaches out and squeezes Lorraine's hand. "Thank you."

In the car, Daisy talks and Stella nods along, but her mind is on Gwen Thompson.

Why was she asking questions about Stella, presumably long before she was fucking Tom?

Again, Stella sees the sneer on Gwen's face.

Funny how things come full circle.

"Mom? Mom, are you listening?"

"Yes," Stella says quickly. "Face paint for the next game is a great idea."

"Not just face paint," Daisy says with an exasperated sigh. "I feel like you weren't listening."

"You have all my attention, Daisy," Stella says, and somehow, improbably, the smile on her face is real. She focuses on Daisy's plan to outfit the team in matching hair bows and face paint, possibly sourced from Amazon.

"Or Target?" Daisy asks.

"Let's check Amazon first. Might be easier to get it all in one place," Stella says.

She's definitely listening, because she is a Good Mom. Her job is motherhood, and she has put her entire heart and soul into it. She is not the kind of mother who puts her own needs first—not that there's anything wrong with that. Definitely not the kind of mother who invites danger into their home. Tom isn't dangerous. He wouldn't hurt anything. She's personally witnessed him rescue spiders. He wouldn't hurt Stella or the kids and especially wouldn't hurt his side piece.

"I love how close you and Dad are," Stella says, like her words are an incantation that will turn Tom into the person she believed him to be.

"What?" Daisy makes a face.

"Your relationship with Dad. It's special. I mean, I never really knew my dad."

Daisy shrugs. "Whatever. I mean, I'm way closer with you. Oh look, we could get hair bows in bulk from the Trading Company."

Stella sighs, but if Daisy hears it, she doesn't let on.

At home, in the kitchen, Stella watches Tom do normal, non-suspicious things. He toasts a bagel and smears it with cream cheese. He cracks a dad joke that makes Colin and Daisy roll their eyes. He leaves crumbs on the counter. He scrolls through sports scores on his phone.

Stella studies him. Who is this man she married? She watches his hand on his phone and tries to imagine it curled into a fist. The sound that fist would make when it hit Gwen's face.

He might be cheating on me, but he's not capable of causing harm, Stella tells herself as he laughs and talks with Daisy and Colin.

He wouldn't hurt Gwen Thompson or Stella. Most certainly, he wouldn't hurt Daisy or Colin.

He's kind. One hundred percent not someone who could do damage to another human being.

Tom looks up from his phone. "Shoot," he says, making a face.

"What?" Stella asks.

"I was going to take the cars in to have them inspected this weekend, but I completely forgot."

Stella nods and makes a noncommittal sound.

"Unless . . . what are you doing tomorrow? It wouldn't take long, if you want to do it."

"Tomorrow is kind of busy," she says.

He makes another face. "Really? You can't squeeze it in?"

The questions are loaded with innuendo. Stella can't possibly be busy, because she doesn't really work.

"No, I can't," she says.

In her head, she prepares her oral argument. Tomorrow she has to attend the college seminar at the high school auditorium that, inexplicably, is being held at 9:30 a.m. It will run for two hours, probably longer with the Q and A. After that, she needs to pick up Tom's dry cleaning. This is a task he has mentioned at least three times in as many days. They're out of milk, orange juice, and cereal bars, so she will need to restock at the grocery store. Also, Daisy has a physical therapy appointment during her free period, which means Stella will need to be back at the high school at 1:15. If she gets Daisy back to school by 2:15, she'll have an hour to respond to emails and the text messages that pile up during the day before the kids get home. Colin has a game at 4:00, and even though Colin is in high school, there is still a snack sign-up, and participation in the "mom cheering section" is strongly encouraged. She mentally adds snacks to her grocery list. Hopefully, they'll be home from the game by 6:30 and maybe she can multitask, prepping dinner in that free hour while she's responding to emails and texts.

This is the landscape of all her days.

Tom should know this because she's outlined it for him before, but he chooses to think of her time as free.

"Maybe you can get to it later this week?" he asks.

It's phrased like a question, but that's not how it's meant.

Darkness oozes in from the corners of Stella's vision. "This whole week is kind of crazy."

"Yep," Tom says. He's looking back down at his phone. "One of my deals is closing this week. Unless you can squeeze it in, it probably won't happen."

"There's always Uber, I guess," she says flippantly. What the fuck does he think she does all day?

"Seriously, Stella?" He sighs.

"Fine." She mentally rearranges her schedule for Thursday. "I'll fit it in. Sometime this week."

"Thank you." He reaches out to squeeze her arm, but she moves before his hand can make contact with her skin. "I really appreciate it. I'm so overwhelmed right now."

"Sure." Her tone is clipped.

She's thinking of Tom and Gwen in a hotel room while she completes an endless list of mindless tasks. Tom entertaining clients at dinner while she cooks responsible meals for their children. Tom at his office, where he has the luxury of uninterrupted focus.

Car inspection settled, Tom flops down on the sofa in the family room. One hand on the remote, he turns the television up to a volume that precludes conversation. Stella wipes up the bagel crumbs, puts his dishes in the dishwasher, and returns the cream cheese to the refrigerator.

She studies the back of his head, retracing the path that led her here. Tom's life unfolded while Stella's grew smaller. A tiny world that revolved around the even tinier humans she and Tom created. A world so narrow, sometimes it feels like there's not even room for Stella.

All the same, it's a world of privilege and good fortune. Stella chose a fairy tale, and that's what it's been.

Big house, two kids, fancy car—everything she could have possibly imagined.

The thing about fairy tales is, they actually skew pretty dark. Maybe that's why Stella likes them. She knows all about deals gone bad, secret games of retribution, and punishments meted out to those who fail a test. Webs spun, things that hide, risks, rewards, and blood drawn by an errant sword.

Isn't there some adage about stories?

Write what you know.

If that's the case, Stella is in her comfort zone.

Twenty-Six

APRIL 2015

PAULA

In high school, Julie disappeared into her books. I'd wake up in the middle of the night and see a line of light underneath her door. She hadn't gone to bed yet. Up studying until two or three in the morning.

"It's like living with a mad scientist," I'd say, teasing her.

She'd roll her eyes. I knew she didn't think that was funny, but I was trying to make conversation. Even then, I could feel her slipping away.

It was Julie's idea for me to get my GED.

"You'll need it, Paula," she said. "If you ever want to do anything besides check groceries."

"I'm doing just fine," I told her.

She didn't say anything. That was her way of saying she didn't agree. Later, when she was at school, I looked into the requirements for the police academy. Julie was right. I needed a high school diploma. She looked like the cat that ate the canary when I told her I'd signed up for a GED program.

"I'll help you," she said. "We'll study together."

When I tell people my sister lived with me during high school, they make a fuss about it. Tell me what a good thing I did by taking her in and raising her. The truth is more like she raised me.

Every day, we'd both head to work. My job was at Albertsons. Her job was school. At home, we'd make meals and study together. I hadn't been to school in four years. Those GED classes were hard. I was out of the habit of reading. Had never been in the habit of studying. Julie could tell whenever I was on the verge of giving up.

"You want to get into the police academy, don't you, Paula?" she'd ask. She found a picture of a female cop in a magazine. Cut it out and taped it to our fridge for inspiration.

She was just a kid, but also like an adult. One eye on the horizon and the other eye on both of our futures. If Mom had been there, she would have put it different. She would have said the way Julie managed was proof that she'd raised her right.

We worked real hard at school during those years. The other thing we did was try to make sense of our childhood. Those years were a lot like Mom's painting on the barn wall. On the surface, they looked like one thing. The closer you looked, the more you realized things weren't what they should have been.

Starting with Dad, we'd go through Mom's boyfriends, one by one. All told, there were six we could name. We were both pretty sure Dad was her first. Victim, not boyfriend, although he was probably that too. They were together when she was fifteen years old, and he was the blueprint for everything that came after.

Although maybe the real blueprint was her dad. Mom loved to tell us stories about the early games of revenge she played after he took his belt to her. Small things like letting an egg go bad and pouring some of it in the floorboard of his car.

"He never did get rid of that smell," she'd say with a giggle.

Her father had died in a car accident, and Mom made no secret out of her belief that he got what he deserved. Whether she had a hand in that car accident is still a mystery, but one thing is clear: At some point during her childhood, violence and the joy of retribution were permanently fused in her brain.

Julie and I got to know the sound of that violence while we were locked away behind our bedroom door. After it was safe to come out, we saw evidence of it everywhere. The holes Dad's fists made in the walls. The dark blue of fingerprints on Mom's neck, a cut lip or a broken rib that made it so she couldn't laugh for a week or two. Instead of shorts, she wore those long flowy dresses. Sometimes she'd cross her legs and you'd see sickly yellow marks spreading up her thighs like some kind of disease.

Despite what I know about Mom's love for games of revenge, I think what happened with Dad was an accident. He hit her, and she hit him back a little too hard.

With respect to that initial hit, there's a solid argument for self-defense, but that argument falls apart somewhere between the tarp and the river.

"She was protecting herself and us," Julie would say. "It's not like she's a serial killer or anything."

Julie needed that to be true because of Kevin. I understood that. What's more, I agreed with her.

"People think it's childbirth that kills women," Mom told us, "but they forget how that always starts with a man."

In my time on the police force, I've learned criminals are usually sloppy, but Mom was the opposite. Careful as they come.

The last person who called her Sharon was Dad. After that, it was a series of fake names. Chris, Jen, Tina. If someone was going to brag about his girlfriend, she wanted to make sure he wasn't using a name that led back to her. They might have met at a bar, but before long she would claim to hate crowds. Food didn't taste right when other people cooked it. What she liked best was staying home. If there's a man out there who doesn't like to stay home and have his girlfriend cook for him, I haven't met him yet.

"How about I make us steak and baked potatoes. Then we'll go upstairs."

I can still remember her saying that, along with the smile that made sure her boyfriends understood exactly what "upstairs" meant. If they were the kind of man who'd turn down that offer, she didn't bring them home.

What I struggled most to understand was Mom's definition of safety. Even more hazy than that, how she managed it all. It wasn't until I joined the police force that I realized how much Mom relied on her own invisibility as a woman.

She knew if the police found a smashed-up car with an open bottle of JD, their investigation would be cursory. Same for a stroke or liver failure. Why look for the underlying disease if you can pin the result on the symptoms?

During Julie's junior year, she returned to the library. Dug out the microfiche again and went through all the newspapers from Livingston.

She made copies of every obituary for a man who'd died an untimely or unfortunate death and put them in a folder.

"Handsome," I can remember her saying, showing me one of the obituaries.

"Liver failure," I read. "He was young too."

"If he's one of hers, I'm sure he deserved it. The world's better off without him."

The way she said it sent a chill down my spine.

By that time, it was clear Julie was going to college. She was making straight As. I figured it would be junior college for two years, then she'd finish up her degree somewhere close. I don't know why I thought I could predict her future like that. She told me right from the start it was going to be something I couldn't imagine.

Her senior year was when the fat yellow envelopes started showing up. Most of the time, she'd open them and put them aside. Then one came from UCLA in California.

"It's a full ride. Scholarship, the kind that pays for everything," she said, spreading the paperwork out on the kitchen table.

"California." The thought of it made something catch in my throat. "You're really gonna go off to California?"

"I really am."

The thing I remember most is the light in her eyes. She was doing exactly what Mom taught us to do.

Julie had a plan for her life, and it wasn't just any old plan. Like she said, it was something bigger than either me or Mom could have ever imagined.

No way was I going to hold her back.

She didn't need to tell me what would happen when she got to Los Angeles. It was written all over her face. There would be no limitations on that girl. She'd turn her life into the sparkling diamond I could see in her eyes.

I hugged her tight before she got on the bus to L.A. Didn't matter that my friends were telling me she'd be back soon. That she'd get homesick and come looking for me. I knew this was goodbye. Those friends of mine didn't know the first thing about Julie. They didn't even know her real name.

"I'll write to you," she said.

And she did. Three times.

First time was a postcard picture of the beach. On the back, she wrote, *I made it, Paula!* Words circled with a great big heart.

The second time, she wrote me a long letter describing the campus. It was filled with all kinds of words I didn't know how to pronounce.

After that, I didn't hear from her for a long while. I knew I should write to her after I got accepted to the police academy, but I kept putting it off. I was waiting so I could tell her I'd graduated. As soon as that happened, I wrote and sent a picture. I told her I was going to be a member of the Livingston PD.

She wrote me back right away.

I knew you could do it, Paula! I'm so proud of you. I'm sorry I don't write more, but you're on my mind every day.

You're the reason I made it this far. You are my sister and my best friend. There is no one else who will ever understand what we share. It's why I understand your decision. The past is hard to leave behind. There's no replacement for family. I'm sure that's part of the reason you're going back to Livingston.

I'm not ready to go back, though. I'm not sure I'll ever be ready. I've been writing my story, the way Mom taught us to do. That's why I have to let go of the person I used to be. You're the last connection I have to Julie, but it's time for her to move on.

Just know this: Above all else, I love you.

She wrote in the language we'd spoken since childhood. After I read that letter, I broke down and cried. I knew what she was saying and that I had to let go.

And for a while, that's what I managed to do.

PART FOUR

Twenty-Seven

FALL

STELLA

Weekdays are the calm before the storm. The storm is, obviously, evenings, mornings before the kids leave for school and Tom leaves for work, weekends, and anything deemed as a "family vacation." The storm is her children and husband taking up too much space in their too-big house, demanding to know where she's been and where she's going, calling her name.

Hon? Stell?
Mom? Mom? Mom?
Sweetie?
Mom?
Stella?
Mooooom!

It's a storm that sweeps her off her feet, which isn't to say she doesn't love the people who cause it. Somehow, improbably, the storm and her love for the people who create it coexist. There's no word for that disconnect. Her children are one of her great joys, even if they have no idea what she does all day.

She doesn't hold this against them. It's developmentally appropriate for teenagers to be self-involved.

Tom is another matter. He *should* know better. He should *be* better.

She thinks back, longingly, to the time when she was paid for her work. It had seemed like an astronomical amount of money. So much, she had to convince herself it wasn't a mistake. For the first time in her life, she allowed herself to go shopping and not look at the prices of the things she purchased. A pair of shoes, a box of rainbow-colored macarons packaged like art, or a drugstore lipstick that she'd toss in her purse.

The point was never the item.

It was the freedom.

Stella is tired of explaining her every movement and decision.

She takes her coffee and slumps into the chair at her family-room desk. The one thing she doesn't have to explain or justify is the amount of money she and Tom put away for the kids' college. Stella traded her career for the cost of childcare, and she'd do it again. Each time she takes stock of her children's stocks, ha ha, it's a reminder that she created this future security for her children. What's more, those ever-growing numbers, buoyed by the stock market, act like a security blanket for Stella. Something to wrap around herself when she's feeling anxious.

It takes only two clicks to open the college accounts, but she waits because the gratification is better if it's slightly delayed.

First, she goes to the checking account. As she schedules the payment of bills, a calm descends over her. Next up, retirement accounts. Tom must have updated the password, because she can't get in. She lets out a noisy exhale. This is annoying, but probably not worth texting him about while he's at work.

College accounts next. Or, as Stella thinks of them, the crown jewels of the Parker family portfolio. Stella's careful investment of this money has swollen these two accounts to an amount that guarantees her children will be free from debt and financial insecurity.

Colin and Daisy have no idea how lucky they are.

And Stella wouldn't want it any other way.

She opens Colin's account first. Clicking, she studies the balance, but it's not right. There should be more. Much, much more. Her heart starts to pound as she clicks on the most recent transactions.

What she sees makes her mouth go dry.

Someone (it has to be Tom) has transferred out a sum that is equal to two-thirds of the account. A wire transfer to an unfamiliar bank account.

Stunned, she opens Daisy's account and discovers a similar transfer.

Her immediate reaction is panic. With these two transfers, her children's college accounts have been decimated.

What did Tom do?

She calls him, but her call goes to voicemail. She calls him again, and again it goes to voicemail. The third time, he picks up.

"What is it?" He sounds impatient.

"What's going on with the kids' college accounts?"

"Don't you remember? We talked about it."

"What? No we didn't."

"We did. Remember I said I was going to invest in a sustainable food company?"

"From the savings account. Not the kids' college funds."

He sighs, long and weary. "They needed a larger buy-in amount than I realized. I did all the research and it's an incredible opportunity. The company is called Regenerative and they're dominating the sustainably prepared food supply market. You seemed fine with it when we talked the other night. Look, I've got to hop on another call, but research it for yourself. We'll talk more tonight."

"Tom," she says, but he's already gone.

Stella stares at her phone to make sure. Yes, he ended the call. She tries not to be annoyed at this dismissal but falls short.

"He had a call," she says out loud. Instead of calming her, this only makes her seethe. Vaguely, she remembers the conversation on the night of the auction. He definitely said he was going to use their personal savings. She would have asked more questions if he'd mentioned the college savings accounts. Now she wonders if that earlier acquiescence somehow made her complicit.

Still, Tom should have known better. That money was *hers*. Money she saved, managed, and grew for the kids.

Feeling like a low-level employee who's been given a research assignment, she types "Regenerative Foods" into her laptop. Like Tom said, it's a large supplier of sustainable food to high-end national chains. The problem is, they are privately owned, but there are rumors of an IPO on the horizon.

For the first five years that Stella practiced law, before she moved to the small boutique firm, she regularly handled IPOs. Taking a company public is like walking a tightrope. She knows the amount of preparation and strategy that takes place before the IPO filing hits the Securities and Exchange Commission. Billions of dollars ride on keeping a potential filing quiet while details are shored up.

Billions of dollars, plus half a million that Tom unilaterally transferred out of their kids' college savings accounts. Primal rage rises up in her.

The only explanation she can think of is that he has some inside information, which would be illegal, but at least it would explain why he was being so cagey. She navigates to Regenerative's "About Us" page to see if any of the faces in the bio headshots are familiar from Tom's high school or college reunions, but she doesn't recognize anyone. The bios read like the ones on generic corporate websites everywhere. She rubs her eyes and realizes her head is throbbing.

Why didn't Tom talk to her first?

Haven't I always taken care of you?

His words from the night of the auction return to her. It bothered her then. Too late, she understands why. It's a sentiment that dismisses Stella. They're supposed to be equals in this marriage, each of them doing their agreed part. But with those seven words, Tom reduced her to a 1950s housewife, forced to rely on her husband's "better" judgment.

What will they do if this risky investment doesn't work out?

The thought makes her stomach lurch. She runs for the powder room that she redecorated three years ago and vomits. When she's finished, she collapses on the floor.

She needs a plan.

Specifically, a backup plan.

A rainy day fund.

The kind she was never supposed to need.

She stands and, despite the buzzy feeling in her head, navigates the stairs down to the laundry room. Pauses to switch the clothes from washer to dryer, then slides open the secret panel and climbs the stairs to the only place that is hers alone.

She goes straight to the drawer in her desk with its photo box and false bottom. It's not like she's going to knife Tom, although if he were here, all bets would be off. No, she needs the knife because it's a symbol. A reminder of what she's survived. She'll survive this too.

We all come from our past, and that's what Stella needs now. Proof that the person she left behind still exists.

She takes the photos out of the box, noticing how light it feels. With shaking hands, she removes the false bottom.

The knife is not there.

Impossible. This is her secret space. A private tree house, where no one else is admitted.

"No, no, no," she whispers, reaching toward the back of the drawer. Did she forget to put the knife back in the box? Hide it somewhere else? She yanks the drawer out and dumps its contents on the floor.

Still no knife.

All these years, she's thought of the knife as proof of her strength and resilience. What now, belatedly, occurs to her is the knife could be a different kind of proof.

Stella doesn't know much about DNA evidence. She wasn't that kind of lawyer, but she knows enough to imagine old DNA still clings to the crevices of the stars carved into bone. A hint of blood or flake of skin that could unwind Stella's entire life. It doesn't matter that it's hers, not his. It would be enough to establish motive. It would connect Stella to her past. Destroy the life she's created, reveal the one she hid, and put her at the scene of the crime. And even though she's not that kind of lawyer, she remembers from her criminal law class that murder has no statute of limitations.

I know what you did.

The message on Gwen's phone flashes in her memory.

A warning.

Her heart pounds with adrenaline.

The most likely answer is Stella moved the knife.

She's done that kind of thing in the past. Hidden it so well, she's hidden it from herself. There was the time she thought she'd lost it, only to find it zipped into the inner lining of an old fleece jacket. She tries to walk her memory back to the last time she held the knife, but the memory that emerges is one where her hands are smaller, younger. Still shaking as she closed the door behind her.

A different drawer, then?

She opens them all. Dumps all their contents on the floor.

The knife is not there.

"No," Stella says. The single syllable comes out like a plaintive whimper.

Quickly, she tosses everything back into the drawers, then runs back downstairs. In the kitchen, she checks her phone for texts. No one has missed her. She forces herself to drink a glass of water. Take deep breaths.

You're in control, she coaches herself. You decide what happens next.

Back in the basement, she digs through boxes of junk. Toys she's boxed up. Baby clothes, art projects and supplies in the form of dried-up markers and a bundle of pencils held together with a rubber band. Here's a box of Polly Pockets, four DS handheld game consoles, the Skylanders plastic figurines that her children delighted in collecting, and a notebook full of Pokémon cards. Board books with charming art, exorbitantly priced wooden pull toys, and, at last, there it is.

A teddy bear with a camera hidden inside its stomach. A baby shower gift, if she remembers correctly. She grabs the bear and runs back upstairs to find batteries.

Then Stella carries it up to her perhaps not-so-secret room. She sets the teddy bear on the desk with a pile of index cards in its lap. If Tom is the one who's breached her private space, he won't remember this bear is equipped with a camera. Tom can't even remember the words to *The Cat in the Hat*, which was Colin's favorite book and is forever imprinted on Stella's brain.

If the culprit is Daisy or Colin . . . she pauses. What are the odds her children would discover a secret room and not mention it?

Honestly, her odds of winning the lottery are better.

That leaves Gwen, who is probably the most likely option. Although how would Gwen know about her secret room?

Why would Gwen be in her house?

At least that question has a clear answer.

Stella grabs her purse, glancing at her phone again to make sure she's still not needed. Then, without hesitation (okay, with a moment's hesitation), she turns it off. If Tom can do it, so can I, she tells herself as she backs her car out of the garage.

She drives, too fast, to the park on the edge of Arlington. As she runs through the parking lot toward the bridge, she practices her story. If anyone stops her, she's going for a run. *Getting some exercise.*

Out here enjoying this gorgeous day!

She heads for the trail, then down under the bridge. Clambering through the underbrush like a wild thing, she mentally adjusts what she'll say.

Looking for water plants for my son's science project. Such a helicopter parent! Ha ha!

It's crazy. Ridiculous.

People told her she'd become public property with that first appearance of a baby bump. They warned her about the unsolicited advice and hands reaching out to pat her stomach like it wasn't actually part of her body. She was less prepared for the group of residents who gathered in her delivery room to watch her give birth. Legs splayed open, reduced to a naked screaming animal on the hospital bed.

Somehow, though, she assumed the transformation to public property was temporary. No one told her it was a permanent condition of motherhood. No one warned her how her every move would need to be explained. Every snack scrutinized. Every choice from organic cotton baby clothing to socially responsible test prep would invite public comment. Stella thinks of nineteenth-century women sent to sanitariums for their use of "abusive language" and knows, with chilling certainty, they were women who went fucking crazy at having to justify their every move.

"Privilege." The word grinds. It's not that she doesn't enjoy privilege. It's that her privilege is so conditional, so dependent on others. It's not worthless, but it's definitely not bankable.

The rock she used to mark her hiding place has tumbled over.

Has a dog been down here?

Maybe a raccoon?

A cold bead of sweat makes its way down her back.

Stella crouches and digs with her bare hands. It should be easy to find the plastic bag with its hidden prize—she didn't bury it that deep. She digs deeper, but hits nothing. She digs around the general area like a crazy woman, but still nothing.

The phone is gone.

Anyone could have taken it, she tells herself.

A homeless person. A kid. One of those old men with metal detectors and too much time on their hands.

But her body knows the truth. The corners of her vision are dark and swirling, as though she might pass out. She runs to the shallow water and rinses mud from her hands.

Her head is filled with recriminations.

Why did she bury the phone in the first place? It seemed like a good idea in the middle of the night, but now she sees it from a different perspective.

She is literally losing her mind.

It's a realization that calls all her other decisions into question. Her whole life, revealed as a fraud. A woman playing a game that is pretending to be someone she's not. At least her mother created a backup plan. Stella hasn't even done that. Instead, she relied on Tom and the myth of domestic bliss. She let go of her own narrative. Allowed herself to become a secondary character, unimportant to the plot. Trusted in her husband so blindly that he felt fully empowered to make a risky investment with the money she saved for their children without even mentioning it to her.

Crouched by the side of the stream, Stella places her wet hands over her face and weeps softly.

"Hello. Hello down there."

An older woman, walking a standard poodle, peers down at her from the bridge.

"Everything okay? Do you need help?"

"I'm fine," Stella says. "Sorry." She stands and wipes at her tears. "I was on a walk. My kids used to play here. Hormones, I guess."

Blaming one's body is an acceptable practice first learned in middle school gym class.

The older woman nods. "It'll get worse before it gets better," she says cheerfully. Then she continues on her walk. As Stella watches her go, she considers the alternatives and decides to call this a win.

Back in her car, she realizes the day has disappeared. She turns on her phone and watches the text messages roll in. Dentist appointments to be confirmed. Volunteer hours for Daisy and Colin to be verified. Colin sent her a draft of his college essay to read. Tom texted an hour ago.

I've got a few minutes if you want to talk.

She rolls her eyes.

What she has to say won't fit into a few minutes.

Colin's physics tutor will be at the house in forty-five minutes. The tutor insists Stella be present. Being alone with any of his students opens him up to liability, he explained. And, of course, Stella understands. Also of course, even though Tom insisted Colin needs this tutor, she is the default parent who must be home to babysit him.

As she drives home, she thinks about Daisy and Colin. She loves them more than she knew it was possible to love. Her body built them from nothingness, and she'll use that same body to protect them. Spend (expend) her whole life on their behalf.

Everything I do is for you girls.

Stella is many things, but she is not her mother. Despite the fact that she looks like her mother. Or the way her own voice sometimes catches her off guard with its remembered similarity to that of her mother.

Her plan was to be better than her mother, but she ceded control of her life to Tom.

And, of course, this is why Stella's thoughts are on her mother. She thought she'd left Julie behind. She thought she'd reached a place of safety where she could let down her guard, but that place doesn't exist. If you don't write the story, there are no guarantees.

That was the primary lesson of her childhood, but somehow she forgot it.

Now she has to remember all those things she worked so hard to forget.

She has to reclaim her story.

Twenty-Eight

APRIL 2015

PAULA

Moving back to Livingston wasn't a complicated decision. They had an opening on the force, and I applied. When I got the job, it felt like fate was calling me home. My sister was gone for good. The job offer felt like a sign that it was time to reconnect with Mom.

For my training, the chief paired me with a guy named Adam Schaeffer. Schaeffer had had a long career with the LPD, but apparently he'd run into some trouble before my time. No one talked about it, but it was the kind of trouble that gets you on permanent desk duty and stuck training the first female hire. Although according to Schaeffer, he'd told the LPD brass it was high time they had a woman on the force.

Schaeffer's past didn't much matter to me because we took to each other like a house on fire. I was a young woman on the force of a medium-small conservative town in the early nineties. Schaeffer was a desk jockey. The two of us were a perfect pair of misfits. I liked Schaeffer, and he felt the same about me. More important, I respected him. He was a smart guy who taught me everything I know about how to work a case.

Research, step back, circle around. Don't make assumptions. Give a case enough attention and eventually everything clicks.

Schaeffer was an early adopter of the internet. Understood how it worked before most people knew it existed. Before the internet, the world felt bigger. A place you could get lost, lose yourself, or some combination of both those things.

When Schaeffer showed me the possibilities for research, I couldn't wrap my mind around it.

"But where's it located?" I kept asking, imagining some sort of headquarters.

"Nowhere. Everywhere," he'd say with a grin.

At that time, the concept of something existing in a place you couldn't touch was completely foreign.

I'd sold my house in Hermiston, which meant I had enough to buy a little house in Livingston. The first few months after I moved back, I was jumpy. Always on edge.

I was living in the same town as Mom, but I hadn't reached out. After all that time, I wasn't sure how to go about it.

Turned out, I didn't need to worry. Mom was just biding her time. One afternoon, I picked up the phone and her voice was on the other end.

"Thought I'd let you get settled in a bit," she said.

No preamble. Not even hello.

"How'd you know I was back?"

"Read it in the paper. Livingston PD's newest recruit. I'm real proud of you, Paula."

It had been ten years since I'd lived at home. A whole decade. I was closer to thirty than twenty. Felt old and wise, even though I wasn't. That praise was like sunshine in the spring. It melted away the questions I should have asked.

Those questions had started a long time ago, but the police academy helped me put them into specific words.

How does a woman who, dripping wet, doesn't weigh more than a buck ten drag a grown man half a mile without leaving a trace behind? Even if she had the help of a twelve-year-old girl. Seems like there would be some evidence left behind.

How did that same woman manipulate loan sharks armed with guns? Doesn't it make more sense that she gave them back the money? Then again, how did she pay for my house in Hermiston?

And the biggest question of all—what had happened to all those boyfriends I remembered? The losers and drifters who ran after her like dogs chasing a fox.

Wasn't it more likely they just left? Got bored with her?

Otherwise, you'd think someone would have noticed. Someone

would have connected the dots. Followed the trail that led from her front door to multiple disappearances.

Time and distance made me doubt what I knew and softened my memories of Mom.

I told myself it had to be one of two things: bad police work or my own bad memory. By the time I joined the LPD, I'd convinced myself it was the second option. That's why I didn't hesitate when she suggested we meet at the diner in town.

The day after Mom phoned me, Schaeffer waved me over to where he was tapping away on the computer. Back then there was only one for our whole squad.

"Look at this, Paula," he said. "Magic of the internet. You can buy real Eye-talian pasta. They ship it all the way from Italy. Don't even have to leave your house."

"Won't be fresh by the time it gets here," I told him.

"Paid extra for expedited shipping," he said with a grin. "I got a lady friend who likes to cook. Maybe you'll have dinner with us one of these days."

After he got up from the computer, I couldn't resist doing some research of my own. Schaeffer was right about being able to find the whole world with a keyboard. Everything from Italian pasta to people who'd gone missing. I'd been committed to letting Julie live her life, but seeing how easy it was to gather information made me waver. Couldn't imagine there'd be much harm to finding out where she ended up.

The day I was supposed to meet Mom, I got to the diner early and waited. My hands were so clammy I had to keep wiping them on my jeans. There I was, a grown woman with a career. I had no business being so nervous. I reminded myself everything was different now. She didn't have the same power she did when I was a little girl.

Then I caught a glimpse of her walking through the parking lot and understood that I'd gotten it all wrong.

Mom walked into that diner like a strong gust of wind. Heads turned to look at her, but all she focused on was me. She'd barely changed. Same long hair hanging down like Ariel the Mermaid's. Same smile that lit up her eyes. Made me think about those fancy bottles of wine you hear about. The kind that get better with age.

"Paula," she said, sliding onto the red vinyl banquette across from me.

Her lips turned up at the corners, and I saw the answers to all my questions in her face. It wasn't bad police work or a bad memory. I'd allowed time and distance to diminish her. Now that she was staring at me, I could feel the force of her personality. The way she wove words into something that felt a little like magic.

"You look good."

"I *am* good." My own words came out defensive.

"Sorry your marriage didn't work out," she said, sliding an envelope across the table to me.

Inside was a divorce decree.

"Now that you're an officer of the law, I figured you'd want everything buttoned up." When I didn't respond, she continued. "I should have guessed you'd be drawn to law enforcement. For you, it was always about control."

"What do you mean?"

She leaned forward, and her hair made a curtain around her face. Suddenly, I was six years old again. I had to force myself not to reach out and wind those strands around my fingers the way I'd done when she tucked us in at bedtime.

"You always held something back because you thought it helped you control the narrative. That's why it didn't work for you. You have to trust the process of creation. Throw yourself into the stream. Let it wash you down the river."

"Like Dad?" I hissed.

If I was hoping to catch her off guard, it was only because I'd forgotten who she was.

"Is that a happy time in your memory?"

"Yeah, we were happy. Mostly happy."

I watched as she turned my words over in her head.

"That happiness you felt, Paula, that was something I created. I took misery and created joy for you and Julie. The things that would have made you"—she paused to consider her word choice—"unhappy. I swallowed them whole so you wouldn't have to feel them. The world wants us to believe that women find their happiness with a man, but there's a better form. Do you remember when we discovered it?"

The waitress arrived, and Mom turned her smile on that poor unsuspecting woman. They had a long conversation about the merits of the pie versus the crumb cake while I watched and listened. We learned the crumb cake was homemade with blueberries.

"It'll go quick," the waitress warned.

She was charmed by Mom. You could see it on her face.

"Put us down for two pieces," Mom said. "With whipped cream."

"I'll have to check. We might be out of whipped cream," the waitress said.

Mom smiled. "Doesn't take much to make some more, does it? Especially not if one of your customers has a hankering."

The waitress seemed almost hypnotized as she smiled back. Like she couldn't quite control what was coming out of her mouth. "A hankering?" she said. "You know, I could probably whip it up myself."

"I believe you could," Mom said.

Then the waitress left, and Mom's focus was back on me.

"Do you remember the men who visited after your dad moved on?"

When I nodded, she smiled like she'd won a prize.

"After those men left, we found a better kind of happiness. People tell little girls that happiness is found in wearing a white dress and being given away like someone else's property, but you, me, and Julie, we know better. Remember how it felt to be free from your dad and the things he'd done? It was better than happiness. It was pure joy. No filter needed."

That's the funny thing about memory. Moments can burrow down into your brain so deep you don't know they're there. Then, without warning, they pop up so clear you don't understand how you forgot them in the first place.

I'd forgotten what happened after the men left, but Mom's words brought it back. I remembered the big dinner Mom fixed us. All our favorite foods: hash browns from the freezer, a big bowl of raspberries for Julie, and pickles for me. Scrambled eggs with extra cheese, plus toast cut into triangles and spread with butter because it felt fancy to eat it that way.

When we couldn't eat another bite, Mom told us to put on our boots. The three of us walked out to the barn. Mom in the middle, holding hands with both of us.

"Do you girls recognize this?" she asked after she turned on the light.

We stared at the dark blue on the wall, the initial incarnation of her painting. Both of us shook our heads, waiting for her to explain.

"It's the night sky. You see, this will be the Big Dipper and the little one," she said, her finger tracing a line. "And over here, that's going to be Orion."

"Are you going to do the entire sky?" Julie asked, studying the wall.

Mom laughed and bent down to kiss Julie, once on each of her cheeks.

"I don't think it will come to that. No, what you girls need to understand is this painting is a map to your future."

After that, she led us out of the barn and up the hill onto the forest path. We walked the path outlined by the painting until she was certain we understood.

When we were deep in the forest, she pulled us both tight to her. One under each arm. "You see, no matter what happens, you girls will always be safe. This is your backup plan. Do you understand?"

I'd like to say we didn't.

I'd like to say Mom was wrong, but that would be a lie. From the moment I understood what that painting represented, it filled me with something clean and pure. The knowledge that come what may, we had something we could rely on.

There's no kind of happiness more perfect than that.

Mom saw the change in my face and smiled. "You remember."

It wasn't a question, but I nodded anyway.

She reached across the table, taking my hand in hers. "It's still there for you. It's yours. Everything I've done. It's all to make sure you and Julie will always be safe."

I could have reminded her I was a police officer. Told her what she'd done was illegal and that I would have no part of the map or anything else. The only problem is, I was already part of it. That's what I mean about Mom's stories. It's easy to get tangled in her threads, caught so you can't get out.

It's also possible I didn't want to get out.

It's hard to give up that kind of safety.

The waitress came with our coffee and crumb cake topped with whipped cream. Mom let go of my hand and applied the full force of her attention to the waitress. How kind she was to whip that cream just for us. How the crumb cake wouldn't have been right without it. How the color, shade, and texture were perfect.

After the waitress left, we ate in silence.

"When your grandfather hit your grandmother, she never fought back."

Mom said this like she was making light conversation.

"She told me all kinds of stories about how it wasn't so bad. He beat us both black and blue, but she'd talk about how we had a roof over our heads, clothes on our backs, and food on the table. Other people had it worse. It's a funny thing people do, always looking around to see who has it worse."

Mom dipped her finger in the whipped cream and licked it off.

"After your grandfather died, things got a whole lot better. It taught me we'd been placing too much value on the things we had. Not enough value on what was missing. The problem with getting married is it only takes one day. You gotta focus on all the other days. You might think I didn't make the best choices about men, but that's because I had my eye on all the other days."

I took her speech for an apology.

It wasn't until later I realized it was a justification.

"Wouldn't it have been easier if you'd just picked different men?" I asked.

"That's what I've been working on lately, Paula. A different kind of man. In fact, I think you're already acquainted with the man in my life." Mom leaned back against the banquette with a sly smile.

I froze like a mouse when a hawk flies overhead.

"What do you mean?"

"Adam says the nicest things about you. He comes over real regular for dinner, and let me tell you, that man can eat half a pie." Her smile was fond.

"Schaeffer's lady friend," I said, following the trail of breadcrumbs they'd sprinkled for me. "The one who likes to cook?"

"Guilty as charged," Mom said as her smile turned into the grin of someone who has just played their winning card.

Twenty-Nine

FALL

STELLA

"Mom? You home?" Daisy calls, slamming the door as she comes in.

Stella tiptoes toward the foyer, snack in hand. She smiles at Daisy, then puts one finger over her lips. "Tutor," she whispers, gesturing with her head.

"Aw, thank you," Daisy whispers, taking the small plate of cucumbers and hummus. "You're the best." She gives Stella a quick side hug, then tiptoes up the stairs.

As her daughter disappears, Tom's decision to ransack their children's college savings accounts crystallizes into something hard in Stella's heart.

She takes a deep breath and pushes those thoughts aside. Not because she's decided to let it go, but because her children will soon be hungry and she needs to make dinner.

Stella has read that children who eat dinner with their families more than three times a week are more successful and stable than those who don't. In addition, family dinners are correlated with better long-term health. Because of this, she aims for four sit-down dinners per week. She tallies up the dinners this week. Sunday, Monday, Tuesday, and Thursday, which means they're on track. It means Colin and Daisy will be successful, stable, and healthy. Also, they have more than eighty books in their home, a factor shown to improve children's literacy and numeracy.

One more ridiculous statistic touted like proof of future results when the only underlying factor is money.

Money.

Money to buy books.

Money enough to allow one parent to stay home and prepare those family dinners cooked from organic ingredients. Money for tutors to improve grades and standardized test scores. Money for sports that will improve health and look good on college applications. Money for college tuition.

That was the plan, until Tom put an enormous chunk of that money at risk.

Stella's jaw clenches. She considers worst-case scenarios while chopping onions and garlic. It'll be okay, she tells herself. After all, she managed to get a good education without a college fund.

The problem is, Colin and Daisy have never had to fight for their survival. Stella's pretty sure her children wouldn't have the faintest idea of what that kind of fight entails. Compounding the problem, the world has changed dramatically. Her children are coming of age in a world where there is less of everything. Less opportunity and upward mobility. Fewer scholarships, more applicants. Everyone fighting to hold on to whatever ground they've gained.

The investment could still work out, Stella thinks as she pays the tutor. More money out the door. Another kind of investment that *Tom* insisted they make.

When she hears the rumble of the garage door signaling Tom's arrival, it takes every ounce of her willpower not to confront him immediately. She refrains because she has a feeling it will be an unpleasant discussion. The kind that will ruin the dinner she just made. Instead, she takes a deep breath, the deepest breath of all.

"Dinner," she calls up the stairs to where the kids hibernate behind their closed doors.

Daisy arrives in the kitchen first. "Ugh, carrots," she says.

"You like carrots," Stella says, placing a dish of them on the table.

This is not true, but she pretends it is, as though that will change Daisy's mind. Colin arrives next, then Tom. When he kisses Stella on one cheek, she forces a smile through gritted teeth.

"Wallace Wins are literally the stupidest thing ever," Daisy says, pushing the carrots Stella placed on her plate to one side.

"What are Wallace Wins?" Tom asks.

The sound of Tom's voice grates on Stella's ears. She avoids looking at him. She tries not to hear him. If she interacts with him even a little bit, she'll explode, which will counteract the benefits of a family dinner.

"Our principal makes these weekly announcements about 'wins.'" Daisy makes air quotes around the word while rolling her eyes. "But it's stuff like, 'The group of sophomores picking up garbage in the cafeteria was a Wallace Win.'"

Stella nods, half listening. She's preoccupied by the memory of an old painting on the back of an older barn. Of buried treasure saved for a rainy day.

The life Stella created wasn't supposed to have rainy days.

"Last year someone made a Wallace Wins T-shirt and Ms. Wallace announced it," Colin says, smirking. "It sold out in, like, five minutes, then after the school saw what was on it, it got banned. Like, literally, people got detention for wearing it to school."

"Oh my God, Sophie's older sister has that shirt. I can't believe they got her to announce it. Mom, you okay? Your face looks so weird."

"What? Yes, I was just . . . wondering what the T-shirt said," Stella says, forcing her lips into a smile.

Both her children dissolve into laughter.

"What?"

"Nothing, Mom. It was, you know, inappropriate." Colin shakes his head. "I mean, it got banned, so . . ."

Stella shrugs. "How bad could it have been?"

This sends Daisy and Colin into another paroxysm of laughter.

"I guess we're just not cool enough, Stell," Tom says, but his smile argues the opposite.

Stella gives him a cold look. A literal ice bath of a look, but Tom doesn't notice.

"By the way, did you have time to get the cars inspected?" he asks.

Stella nods.

Despite the curtness of her nod, Tom remains oblivious. He pushes his chair back from the table.

"Thanks for that. Great dinner, honey. Anyone want dessert?"

"Ice cream." Daisy jumps up.

Stella watches her daughter rummage through the refrigerator in search of chocolate sauce. The toppings Stella stocks in her fridge are prepackaged. Despite her own fondness for canned summer fruits, she's never gone to the trouble of preserving the raspberries or strawberries that fill her garden. It's so much work. Besides, if you don't do it right, it can be dangerous.

Her gaze falls on Tom.

Maybe this summer, she'll reconsider.

"Mom, have you seen my Lilly Pulitzer bag?" Daisy asks.

It's an innocuous question that startles Stella more than it should. "Um, your Lilly Pulitzer bag?" she repeats, stalling.

"It's pink with turqoise palm trees. You know what I'm talking about, right?"

Stella nods. "I saw it somewhere."

"Where? I need it for Y2K day." Daisy is on her feet in a way that foretells drama if the bag is not located.

"I can't remember, but I'll look for it after I clean up the dinner dishes."

"But you know the one? You gave it to me for my birthday, like a hundred years ago."

Stella nods. "I think Gwen Thompson has one just like it."

"That's weird," Daisy says.

Stella looks at Tom. Is it her imagination, or did he flinch?

"That *is* weird," he says. "I didn't realize you were close with Gwen Thompson."

"We're not, but we worked on the auction together. Daisy has the same one, so of course I noticed," Stella says.

"I heard the Thompsons might be moving," Daisy says.

Tom looks down at his phone.

"Since when do you hang out with Charlotte Thompson? Isn't she a freshman?" Colin asks.

"It was during fockey tryouts. She was a cut, but I heard her talking to some other girls in the locker room." Daisy lowers her voice. "Her parents are getting a divorce."

"Probably want to keep that kind of gossip to yourself, Daisy." Tom's voice is stern.

"It's not like I'm gossiping." Daisy's voice immediately trends toward strident. "I mean, you act like I'm posting it online, but I'm supposed to be able to talk about things with my family, right?"

"Your dad's just saying Charlotte's probably going through a hard time right now. She wouldn't want people talking about her," Stella says, automatically supporting Tom because it's healthy for children to have parents who present a united front.

"Seriously? Is that really what you think of me? Like I'm some insensitive, horrible person who would say something hurtful like that? Fine! I'll just keep my mouth shut and never tell anyone in this family anything ever again."

Daisy's voice has climbed the scales and landed firmly on shrill. She stands up from the kitchen table, slams her bowl into the sink, then turns and glares at them.

"May I be excused? I have homework to do, and obviously no one in this family wants to hear anything from my point of view."

"Go ahead," Stella says.

Daisy stomps up the stairs and slams her bedroom door. Then she opens it and slams it again, in case the first time wasn't loud enough.

Colin slips out of the dining room without a word.

"Nice family dinner," Tom says.

His grin is rueful. Not at all the expression of someone who has endured the discussion of his affair partner at the dinner table. Or of someone who has hit that same woman hard enough to crack a rib or bruise a face. Or of someone who has transferred a large portion of his children's college savings accounts into an extremely questionable investment without fully disclosing it to his spouse.

"Tom." Stella's hands shake with barely controlled fury.

"What?" He looks up, and she catches something furtive in his gaze.

"I looked into Regenerative Foods. They're not publicly traded."

"Not yet." He smiles and raises his eyebrows.

"Why didn't you talk to me first?"

"We *did* talk and you said it was fine."

"We talked about a small investment. You took five hundred thousand dollars out of the kids' accounts," she hisses, careful to keep her voice low so as not to be overheard.

"Like I said earlier, it was a bigger initial buy-in than I realized."

"How can you say we discussed it? You put Daisy and Colin's money in a high-risk investment. You know I used to run IPOs."

Tom makes a sound. Something between a laugh and a cough. There's a word for it, but it's not coming to her.

"Yes, I remember you were involved in a few IPOs, but that was what, eighteen years ago? The market is a different place now. Look"—his tone shifts to placating—"I brought home my whole file on Regenerative. You can read through it."

The word for the sound he made comes to her. "Scoff." He's scoffing at the expertise she gained through the career she abandoned at his suggestion. The career she gave up so he would never have to worry about who was taking care of his kids. Her head pounds as anger steals her words.

Tom puts one hand on her shoulder. "Stella, we did talk about this investment. You said it was fine. This is no different than half a dozen other investments I've made. You had no issue with any of those."

She shrugs off the weight of his hand. "I agreed to an investment out of our savings account."

"Look, money is money. I'm not going to argue semantics with you. You're always telling me how busy you are, but now you've suddenly decided to second-guess my decisions."

Blood pounds in Stella's temples. She forces her voice into a lower register, as though that will force him to take her seriously. "Tom, we could lose that money. When is the option date? What if Regenerative doesn't ever go public? What do we do then?" Her tone is withering. Her hands press hard against the table. She imagines what it would feel like to wrap both of them around his neck. "I want to look at the contract."

"Of course. It's in the file I brought home."

His tone is downright patronizing, like she's some little housewife who can't wrap her little housewife brain around complicated facts and figures.

"You can read all the terms. Obviously, I did my research, like I've done on every other investment I've made for our family. Take a look at the file. You'll see. Worst-case scenario, Regenerative doesn't make their IPO date and we borrow against my 401(k) for the first couple years Colin's in college. We have options."

Instead of making her feel better, Tom's words make her feel like she can't breathe. Tears fill her eyes.

Tom notices and sighs loudly. "It's going to be fine. I'm just talking worst-case scenario, which is not going to happen. Remember, I usually get one hundred and fifty percent of my bonus. Try to have a little faith in me and not overreact. Like, do you think you might actually give me the benefit of doubt for a change?"

He stomps out of the kitchen toward his office. A moment later, he returns and tosses a file folder on the table, next to his uncleared plate.

Then he walks back to his office. Stella hears his door open, then shut, louder than necessary.

She looks around at the dinner mess. Rather than cleaning it up, she pushes the dishes to one side and opens Tom's research file. The contract brings her a little peace of mind. Its terms are better than she feared. The research on Regenerative is promising, but it's not like she can conduct due diligence. She doesn't have access to their internal files. The thought of internal files makes her pause and look back at the file in front of her.

There's no correspondence in this file.

No printed-out emails or letters.

Where's the cover letter that should accompany the contract?

There's no paper trail detailing any communication with anyone. In fact, as she pages through Tom's file, she sees there's no proof that any of these documents weren't simply printed out at his office.

"Mom." Daisy appears in the kitchen. "Did you have time to look for my Lilly bag yet?"

"Oh, right," Stella says, quickly closing Tom's file. "I think I saw it in the basement."

Daisy turns toward the basement.

"Hold on, it might be . . ." Stella pauses like she can't remember. "You know what, let me look for it. It'll probably be faster."

Daisy nods. "Okay. I can clean up the kitchen if you want."

"Thanks, Dais. That would be really nice."

Stella gives Daisy a quick hug. She gets that this is Daisy's way of apologizing for the scene during dinner.

Downstairs, she glances over her shoulder to make sure Daisy hasn't followed her before she slides open the secret panel door. Gwen's abandoned Lilly Pulitzer bag is on the first step, where Stella left it. She opens it and searches for the label sewn inside.

A cutesy tag that invites the owner to inscribe their name.

I belong to the Lilly Girl named _____.

There, just as Stella suspected, she finds Daisy's name written in Sharpie, in Stella's own handwriting.

The forgotten Lilly Pulitzer bag never belonged to Gwen.

It was Daisy's all along.

Thirty

APRIL 2015

PAULA

You might be wondering why I never hooked up with anyone. For a long time, I told myself relationships weren't worth the time and effort. Truth is, I don't like to let people get close. Once you let them in, you open yourself up to getting hurt. I learned that with Mom and Julie. Some bonds are so strong you can't break them without breaking yourself.

Perfect example is the realization I had after Mom and I left that diner.

When she told me she was dating Schaeffer, I took some time to think about it, then I tried to warn her off. "You can't underestimate him," I told her. "Schaeffer's not like ordinary officers on the force. He's real smart."

"You know, he says the same thing about you, Paula," she told me. "Smartest new recruit he's seen in a while. Of course, I reminded him that's not much of a compliment. I know for a fact the LPD had to fire three of their last recruits."

"Mom, with everything in your past—"

She cut me off quick.

"About that. You might want to take advantage of your position at the LPD to do some reading. I'm sure there are old files tucked away that would catch you up on the past real fast. But for the moment, we don't have a thing to worry about. Schaeffer is . . . well, let's say he's very content."

Somehow, I knew better than to roll my eyes.

Most people would have taken the bait and headed straight for the LPD records room. Me, I like to take my time with things. I sat on that velvet sofa that Julie liked so much when she was in high school and replayed my conversations with Mom from start to finish. Forward and backward. Finally, it hit me.

It wasn't that *she* didn't have a thing to worry about. What she'd said was *we* didn't have a thing to worry about.

The stories Mom created meant I was stuck. It wasn't just about being an accessory to what she'd done to Dad. It was a whole lot more than that. I'd changed my age and last name and taken an oath to protect and serve using that false identity. Now I had divorce papers to memorialize a union that had never taken place. If I didn't go along with Mom's version of events, both our lives would be pretty much ruined. I'd lose my job, or worse. She'd definitely end up in prison.

That was all bad, but it wasn't the worst of it. The worst was that I'd doubted my own memory. I'd told myself Mom couldn't be what I remembered.

If I'd substituted my memories of Mom for a more palatable version, there was a chance Julie would do the same. And if she came back, Mom would figure out a way to trap her too.

Right then and there, I made a decision.

Julie was vulnerable in all the same ways I was. It was up to me to protect her from repeating my mistakes.

But in order to do that, I had to find her. I took the investigative techniques Schaeffer taught me and put them to work looking for my sister. Let me tell you, when I *did* find her, it was like discovering a part of me that had been amputated.

Julie graduated from UCLA in 1995 summa cum laude.

According to the internet, that means with highest honors. After she graduated, her online trail went cold. I called the folks down at UCLA, and after some prodding, including sending them my badge number, they told me she'd requested transcripts be sent to five different law schools. I tracked her down to the one she enrolled in.

The Georgetown University Law Center in Washington, DC.

The pictures of Georgetown online showed redbrick buildings with tall spires and wide grassy lawns. All of it set high up over a river. It was so pretty it looked fake. It was hard to believe the people who lived there would have anything in common with someone like me.

Julie and I had something in common, though.

We were both drawn to the law.

I found an article she wrote for the *Georgetown Law Journal*. It was about abortion, filled with footnotes and citations. If I'm being honest, I read only half of it. I thought it would be like reading one of her letters, but there was no trace of my sister in that article.

Julie had moved on. She disappeared herself into a life neither Mom or I could have imagined, just the way she always said she would.

Now there was only Stella.

When I first located her, she was working for a law firm in New York City. It gave me a lot of reassurance to see what she'd done with her life. She was free from her past. As far as I was concerned, she was going to stay that way.

I had to do my research on Julie in bits and pieces. Sneak it in while I was working late because my dial-up at home was too slow. The internet was still new. People used it along with the things they'd always used. Case in point: When I emailed to request that article Julie wrote for the *Georgetown Law Journal*, it showed up three months later in my mailbox. It doesn't take long to retell it, but locating my sister took me the better part of a year.

By the time I showed up in Livingston, Mom had been Schaeffer's "lady friend" for over two years. Three since I'd tracked Julie to New York City. Despite the fact that Mom had practically invited me to dig into Schaeffer's background, I didn't do it.

There are a couple reasons for that.

One, I was still new at the LPD. I thought it was likely that the woman in charge of records might take it upon herself to inform Schaeffer I was putting my nose where it didn't belong. Mom thought she had a leash on Schaeffer, but he was smart and determined. Maybe not as smart as Mom, but smart enough for me to be careful about digging into his past.

Two, I needed to be sure Julie was safe. Out of harm's way and Mom's reach, which, come to think of it, felt like the same thing.

Three—and this was the most powerful reason of all—I didn't much want to see what was in Schaeffer's file. I liked him. Respected him. It felt good to work with someone who respected me too.

I had a hunch that whatever was in that file would change how I felt about Schaeffer. Of course, by then I'd heard whispers about some sort of dustup earlier in his career. Folks said that's why Schaeffer was on desk duty, but I figured his age was another reason. Desk duty was a common last stop before people retired. That's what I told myself, anyway.

That's all a long way of saying life was good. I liked my work at the LPD and had settled in. Reconnected with old friends and ate dinner out at the farm with Mom and Schaeffer most Sundays. Once you've weathered a few storms, you understand the value of blue sky. I suppose that's why I avoided Schaeffer's file for the better part of five years.

In the end, it was Schaeffer himself who motivated me to do some research. Not on purpose, or maybe it was. Hard to say.

We were both staying late to file a report. He got sidetracked talking about some sort of argument between his two girls. When he finished, he shook his head.

"I guess they never grow out of being sisters," he said with a wry sort of laugh.

I shrugged like I wouldn't know.

"Sorry, Paula," he said, looking like he put his foot somewhere he shouldn't have.

"What do you mean?"

"Nothing." He let the subject drop.

That's all it took for me to understand he knew about Julie. The next day, I went down to the records room.

In the spring of 1987, Schaeffer was assigned to investigate the death of Kevin Mulroney, age thirty-six. That investigation led to a second one. The disappearance of Julie Waits, age thirteen.

Schaeffer's report starts off with a detailed description of the stench in the house. No obvious signs of struggle on the victim's body, but blood on the bedroom wall upstairs. The blood type on the wall matched the type found on the deceased's shirt, which turned out to be a match with that of the house's owner, Sharon Waits.

An autopsy attributed Mulroney's death to heart failure. The underlying cause was thought to be food poisoning. The pertinent section of Mulroney's autopsy that I reread multiple times is as follows:

> Summary of Clinical History: The main pathological features were acute nonspecific gastroenteritis and fatty degeneration of the heart and liver. *Bacillus cereus* was isolated and

identified from the peritoneal exudate and intestinal contents. Type A *Clostridium botulinum* was demonstrated from the stools and the toxin from the blood serum. The infection source of *botulinus bacilli*, however, was not clarified. The cause of death is identified as heart failure resulting from myocardial fatty degeneration.

That's one paragraph in a medical report that goes on for five pages. In case you're not a doctor or a coroner, that paragraph is technical speak for food poisoning. No one was around to take care of Mulroney after he ate something bad. Without hydration, the heart stops.

Most officers would call that an open-and-shut case, but there was also a missing girl.

Sometimes you work a case that gets to you. Maybe you have a theory in your head you can't shake. It eats at you. Makes you think up is down and bad choices are good.

That's what this investigation did to Schaeffer.

In his lengthy file, he comes back again and again to the three different blood types found at the scene of the crime.

There was Kevin Mulroney's.

Mom's.

And a third, taken from dried blood found on the couch along with traces of semen.

Schaeffer was certain the third blood type belonged to Julie Waits, now listed as a runaway, but he couldn't prove it. If it was the girl's, then odds were good something bad had happened to get it there. At the time of the girl's disappearance and the boyfriend's death, the mom was laid up in the hospital saying she slipped on the stairs. In the scenario where something bad had happened to the girl, it was probable to think the mom had a motive for revenge. The problem was, there was no way to prove that theory. The girl was gone, the mom had a rock-solid alibi, and there was no sign of a murder weapon. But Schaeffer couldn't let it go.

At some point, he stumbled on the file written up after Dad's body was pulled out of the river. That's when Schaeffer realized Mom didn't have one missing teenage daughter; she had two. The coroner's report on Dad makes up another section of Schaeffer's file. One sentence in that report is underlined with heavy black ink.

> The deceased suffered a head injury prior to drowning.

Two accidental deaths and two missing daughters were too many coincidences.

Like I said, Schaeffer's a smart guy.

But he didn't have a murder weapon.

If you have a dark sense of humor, you might find that funny, given how the murder weapon was spelled out in Mulroney's autopsy. It was probably sitting at the bottom of Mom's pantry the whole time Schaeffer was running down leads.

Clostridium botulinum.

If Schaeffer had focused on those two words in the autopsy, he might have researched the symptoms and onset of botulism. He would have discovered it's caused by a toxin that dissolves after death. Almost impossible to trace, but a common source is canned food. All it would have taken was a toxicology report on a few of those jars in Mom's pantry and Schaeffer would have had enough evidence to justify his hunch. It still would have been tricky to prove Mom intended to kill him, but it would have allowed Schaeffer to put more resources into the investigation and keep the respect of his colleagues at LPD.

But that's not the way it played out.

He never could piece it all together.

Mom was in the hospital when Mulroney died. That was a fact verified by multiple nurses and doctors, and there were photos and a report of the damage done to her when Mulroney dropped her off. That hospital file would have been enough for most folks, but Schaeffer doubled down. Staked his whole reputation on the investigation.

Based on his case notes, which I read from cover to cover the way other people might read a novel, Schaeffer suspected Mom had a hand in both Dad's death and Mulroney's. He felt certain that if he could find Julie, dead or alive, she would tie it all together. I don't know why he didn't look for me. Maybe he did, but he didn't find me until I showed up at the LPD.

After two years of listening to Schaeffer's theories, the LPD brass ran out of patience. They told Schaeffer to put the case to bed. He was wasting time and money on it, but he couldn't let go. It was in his bloodstream, a different kind of toxin that caused its own type of damage.

Based on the disciplinary notes in his file, that toxin took the form of an obsession with Mom. He talked to everyone at the nursing home where she worked. Followed her around town when he was off duty. Kept a record of her daily comings and goings and analyzed the letters of complaint Mom wrote to LPD.

The first letter she sent has two photos attached, time and date marked on the back. In the first picture, you can see Schaeffer in his car at the end of Mom's driveway. The second photo shows him sitting outside the nursing home.

While I appreciate the police escort, it's hard to believe this is the best use of Livingston's tax dollars, Mom wrote.

The letters Mom wrote after that one have more photos attached. Images of Schaeffer sitting in his car while she's at the diner in town. Schaeffer, looking furtive, while she shops at the mall two towns over. Schaeffer loitering outside while Mom is at the beauty salon.

Mom's letters tell a story of an unhinged man abusing his power. A man who won't leave her alone as she goes about the quiet business of her life. She understood the power of suggestion. How to seed an idea and let it grow.

I suppose that's another way of saying Schaeffer was out of his league.

Schaeffer and his wife split the winter of 1990. If you're keeping track, that's three and a half years after the date on Kevin Mulroney's death certificate. It's hard to say what happens in any marriage, but if I were to hazard a guess, I'd say Mrs. Schaeffer didn't much like her husband's obsession with Sharon Waits. The multiple warnings he received from LPD, including a one-month suspension without pay, couldn't have helped.

About a year after Schaeffer split with his wife, the letters from Mom stop. The best I can tell, he got his act together after that, but it wasn't enough to change the chief's opinion of him. Schaeffer was a wild card. He hadn't done anything crazy enough to be fired, but they didn't trust him not to go rogue out in the field.

When I was done reading his file, I was left with multiple questions. Schaeffer knew exactly who I was, so why hadn't he asked me about my past? Where I'd gone and why? The lack of questions made me nervous.

Also, how had Schaeffer gone from suspecting my mother of murder to sleeping in her bed? It took a while, but eventually I realized those two things were not mutually exclusive.

My last questions were for Mom, and they were by far the most worrisome.

What was her plan for Schaeffer, and did she envision it having a final chapter?

Thirty-One

FALL

STELLA

Stella wakes as Tom leaves their bedroom. Last night she barely slept.

Before bed, they had another heated discussion about Tom's investment.

"Where are the cover letters and correspondence?" she asked.

He rolled his eyes and promised to bring them home. "What about the other investments I've made over the last ten years. Do you want the correspondence for those too?"

She refused to be sidetracked. "I don't understand why it wasn't in the file in the first place."

"I don't know. I guess I put it in a separate file. You know, it feels an awful lot like you don't trust me."

She didn't respond.

It took everything she had not to reveal the reasons for her lack of trust. Somehow, she managed to hold back accusations of infidelity and the smoking gun in the shape of a Lilly Pulitzer bag. Before she accuses him of anything, she needs to understand all the details that make up the big picture. Those unknown details kept her awake most of the night.

When Stella hears the garage door open, she slips on her yoga pants and heads downstairs. Colin and Daisy appear moments later, but they are sullen, as though their parents' mood is a dark cloud, infecting the entire household.

Once they've left for school, the calm that descends over the house allows Stella to consider her options. Option, actually. There's only one, and she's been putting it off for too long. It's time to pay a visit to Gwen.

Gwen Thompson, whose daughter has a pennant on her bedroom wall that looks a lot like it came from Livingston High School.

Gwen Thompson, the former Strawberry Queen, which is a Livingston tradition, who pumped Lorraine for information about Stella.

Gwen Thompson, who is apparently fucking Stella's husband. Stella imagines Gwen prowling through her too-big house. Waiting until Tom left the room or used the bathroom to pilfer items; a Lilly Pulitzer bag and a knife tucked away in a secret room. The why and how are details that give rise to more questions.

Stella needs answers, and they all lie with Gwen.

Even though it's an easy walk, Stella drives the three blocks to Gwen's house. She wants to be able to make a quick getaway. She puts the car in park, her heart racing as she studies the Thompsons' house.

It's not as big as the Parkers'. The location is significantly less desirable. Too close to a main road. It looks run-down and needs a coat of paint. It's definitely a rental.

On the heels of that observation comes the self-observation that she's stalling. Slowly, Stella gets out of her car and approaches Gwen's front door. She knocks, feeling ridiculous. What is she going to say? She's a terrible Girl Scout, completely unprepared.

When no one answers, Stella presses the doorbell.

"Gwen," she calls, knocking lightly.

It occurs to her Gwen might not be home. The realization feels like a reprieve. Stella takes a step back, ready to retrace her steps, but a sound on the other side of the door stops her.

The door swings open, and Stella freezes. Caught in the act of sneaking away.

"Took you long enough," Gwen says.

Stella knows she should respond, but instead, she studies Gwen in silence. The moment stretches into something uncomfortable. A unit of time long enough for Stella to notice the particular beige of Gwen's skin, a color she associates with middle age. The way Gwen's hair is unbrushed. When Gwen sighs noisily, it's clear her teeth are unbrushed too.

"You want some coffee?" Gwen asks, opening the door a little wider.

Stella, forgetting everything she learned from horror movies, steps inside. She lets Gwen lead her into the kitchen.

Unlike Stella's kitchen, carefully designed and magazine-spread fancy, Gwen's kitchen is pure developer's special. Mass-produced to fool the casual observer into thinking it's high quality when it's not. There is an island and a pot filler, a holdover feature from the early 2000s, but the cabinets are thin. The doors hang slightly askew. The range is a Frigidaire, not a Wolf. The refrigerator is freestanding, not built-in.

Details, but the truth is always found in the details.

Gwen pours a cup of coffee. "Black?"

"With oat milk, if you have it."

Gwen nods, and pulls a carton from her refrigerator. It's a store brand, which doesn't mean the Thompsons are poor. Still, in this community of excess, middle class masquerades as poverty.

Stella adds milk to her coffee. She's unsure how to proceed. Is Gwen expecting her to scream and demand answers? Play the role of aggrieved wife?

Gwen's eyes are narrowed, her body tense as though she's prepared to defend herself.

For this reason, Stella decides to take a calm approach. She sips her coffee, then sets it down hard enough for some to slop a bit over the edge of the cup. The coffee spreads across Gwen's white faux-marble countertops with their tacky gold swirls.

"Oops. Sorry."

Stella smiles sweetly as Gwen grabs a dish towel and mops up the spill.

"These countertops stain," Gwen says.

It occurs to Stella that despite their differences, in this way they are alike. Two women conditioned to clean up other people's messes.

When Gwen turns to dump her dish towel in the sink, Stella stages a semi-escape. Clutching her coffee, she heads toward the adjacent sitting room. She looks around, searching, not sure what she's hoping to find.

A Livingston High School pennant?

A trail of emails?

As a Supreme Court Justice once wrote about pornography, she'll know it when she sees it.

"I got your texts," Stella says, turning around abruptly.

"What texts?"

Gwen has followed Stella into the sitting room and now looks genuinely confused. Like Stella has gone off script in a way Gwen was not expecting.

Stella pauses midway between a pristine white couch and an equally pristine pale yellow accent chair. Fuck, she curses silently. That was a misstep that gave too much away. As she's reassured herself over and over, the accusatory texts might have actually been intended for Gwen. Stella's imagination might be the only thing giving those texts power.

Also—fuck again—how does Gwen keep her furniture so clean?

Gwen smooths her hair away from her face and weaves it into a braid. Something about the gesture is familiar, as though Stella has seen it before.

Everything about this situation is off, starting with the confusion on Gwen's face. As though Stella is missing something obvious. She quickly retraces the one-sided narrative she's created. Gwen leaving her phone for Stella to find, then sending threatening messages from a burner to her own phone, with the knowledge that Stella would see them. It's far-fetched, with too many plot holes. Stella sees it clearly now. The kind of story a guilty person makes up in their guilty brain.

What's really happening is more straightforward. A narrative as old as time. Cheating husband. Wife betrayed.

"You texted me about your phone," Stella says, attempting to recast her first statement. "It was missing."

Gwen rolls her eyes. "Did you really barge into my house to talk about my phone?"

Again, Stella is hit with an overpowering sensation of déjà vu. Is it something about this house? The weirdly clean furniture?

No, she realizes, it's Gwen. Her tone is somehow familiar. Stella's heard it before, paired with the same dismissive eye roll.

"You really don't know?"

Gwen's smile is both gloating and also weirdly familiar. Stella feels she really *should* know whatever Gwen is going to reveal.

"No memory at all?" The smile fades, and Gwen sinks down onto her pristine couch, wincing slightly as though the act of sitting causes her pain. "Honestly, I thought this would be more satisfying. I didn't think you were this slow."

Stella takes a step closer to Gwen.

The blonde braid, the wide blue-green eyes, the way Gwen's smile turns down at the corners. It's all familiar.

Suddenly, Stella is in fourth-grade history.

Gwen, short for Guinevere, easily shortened to the cute-as-a-button Ginny, is explaining the provenance of her name to their teacher. Ginny, dressed in the kind of clothing Julie could never afford, commands the attention of the entire class as she tells them how she's named after the legendary wife of King Arthur.

"I'm practically a queen," she giggles.

"Queen for the day," their teacher agrees and lets Ginny sit at his desk.

Stella stares at Gwen as she does the math. Twenty-five years. It's enough time to turn yourself into another person. She knows firsthand how easy it is to become someone else.

But really?

The most popular girl in her middle school lives three blocks away? And is having an affair with her husband? What are the odds? Also, if this is karma, it's a particularly harsh form.

Except this isn't about odds or karma. Gwen is here for a reason. She's tracked Stella down. Even as comprehension dawns, the fact pattern doesn't make sense. They are both adults with families. Who would do that? And why?

Gwen nods as though she can read Stella's mind.

"Seems like the perfect payback, don't you think?" Gwen's smile is smug.

"Payback for what?" It's Stella's turn for genuine confusion.

"Don't give me that innocent act," Gwen snarls. "Your family, your slutty sister, and your whore of a mother. Don't pretend you don't know what I'm talking about. You took everything that was supposed to be mine. You think you can hide the past and become fancy Stella Parker who everyone adores, along with her perfect kids. Like I said, things come full circle. You were never better than me and you still aren't. I know who you *really* are."

The gloves are off, along with Stella's armor. She's back in the Livingston High School gym. Alone and unprotected, nothing but trash, which is obviously how she managed to disappear.

And simultaneously, she's confused.

This is . . . well, it's really weird.

A forty-something woman with a family of her own has tracked Stella down to avenge herself over a high school cheerleading grudge?

What in the actual fuck?

The only logical conclusion is that Gwen is insane. Stella should never have come here. Now, somehow, she has to get out.

"I don't know what you're talking about," Stella says, because she knows the best defense is a good offense. "But you need to stay out of my house and away from my family. Especially my kids. You see them coming and you turn around and go the other way."

"What will you do if I don't?" Gwen is on her feet. Her eyes flash with the same vindictive anger Stella remembers from middle school. "Have me murdered too?"

Stella's body flushes with sudden heat. Her stomach twists. Gwen's walls, painted early 2000s beige, close in on her. She takes a step back, but Gwen's not done.

"It's like my sister always said. Apple." Gwen reaches out and pokes Stella hard in the chest. "And tree."

Stella turns, fleeing toward the entryway of Gwen's house. In the oversize mirror that leans against a wall, she sees her own face, also lined with middle age.

Behind her, Gwen smiles.

Stella runs. Out the front door, away from everything. Past and present. Her hands grip the steering wheel hard. Her tires screech as she pulls out of the driveway. All this time, she thought she'd performed a magic trick. She disappeared.

But somehow, Gwen found her.

Somehow, Gwen knows what Stella did and wants to make her pay.

Thirty-Two

APRIL 2015

PAULA

If you're a cop, you've got to be able to read people. Bodies tell a story in their own language. The best cops get fluent in that language real fast. Bulging veins, a telltale flush of fear, tension along the jawline, or a certain type of stare. The kind that tells you someone is working overtime to hold your eye contact. You gotta be able to look at the woman who tells you she's fine and notice she's afraid to look at the man sitting next to her on the couch.

You gotta hear what she doesn't say.

What she's afraid to say.

You miss that message and maybe she winds up in the hospital. Maybe the morgue.

In Schaeffer's file on Mom, there were two reports of domestic disturbance. First house visit happened in 1979. The next one was two years later.

In both cases, the parties declined to file charges.

Those parts of Schaeffer's file read like a cautionary tale about cops who didn't know how to read body language. Whatever signals Mom was giving, and I guarantee she was giving some, they missed them. The only thing that makes her case unique is that Dad is the one who ended up in the morgue.

Before I returned Schaeffer's file to the records room, I made a copy of it. I knew I'd want to reread it, and I was right. Over the next ten years, I read and reread that file until it was dog-eared and ringed with coffee stains.

It's an odd fact about life, but a person can get used to almost anything.

Case in point: I spent the next ten years telling myself I had things under control. Whatever game Mom and Schaeffer were playing had nothing to do with me. If I'd been paying attention to my own body language, I would have noted the number of times I returned to that file.

Instead, I tried to reassure myself that everything was just fine. Despite my efforts, there were things I couldn't ignore. Like the way Schaeffer's favorite drug was Mom. Just like any other addict, he never could get his fill. All she had to do was sigh, and his eyes would slide over to her. If she smiled, he'd be in her thrall. If she narrowed her eyes, he couldn't rest until he fixed what was wrong. In fact, I've dealt with junkies who exhibited more willpower than Schaeffer did around my mother. What I still didn't know was whether it was her he couldn't resist, or what she represented.

Was it love or a long game?

Maybe they're one and the same.

Mom's an addict too, but at least she knows it.

Danger is her drug of choice. She got hooked as a kid, then figured out how to feed that addiction with all those boyfriends. It's what draws her to Schaeffer too, although he's not a physical threat. It's like she got bored with that kind of danger and went looking for something to spice things up.

Of course, I've never asked her about any of that. There's no point. Mom doesn't have conversations where things are laid out plain and simple. My best guess, based on ten years of observation, is it went something like this:

Mom knew Schaeffer was keeping an eye on her. As long as she was the focus of his attention, she couldn't bring any new men into her life. Instead of satisfying her addiction with losers and drifters who had some cash, she changed the game and got cozy with Schaeffer. She's always liked a challenge.

From what I know of Schaeffer, he likes one too.

In that way, they're a perfect match.

At some point, I managed to stop worrying about what they had planned for each other. I figured I could go about the business of my life and leave them to theirs.

Then Mom introduced a new wrinkle.

It was after one of her Sunday dinners. Schaeffer and I had both overindulged. As I was getting ready to leave, Mom offered to walk me to my car.

"Adam and I have so much in common," she said, leaning in through my open window. Up close, she smelled like violets and danger.

"Yeah? How's that?" My eyes were focused on the length of the driveway like I already had an inkling of what was coming and was preparing an escape route.

"We both have two girls. Had, I mean." Mom glanced back at the house, making sure Schaeffer couldn't overhear our conversation. "He told me his younger daughter lives in Washington, DC."

"That's quite some distance." I kept my voice calm, even though this news was like a shot of adrenaline. Of course, I knew exactly where Stella was living. How else could I protect her if I wasn't keeping tabs on her?

Mom's smile got wide, putting the gap in her teeth on full display. "Wonder what took his girl out there?"

I shrugged. "Almost anything, I suppose."

Her eyes narrowed in a way that told me she didn't appreciate that response.

"I'll see what I can find out," I said in a voice just above a whisper.

Her face softened into a smile. "You do that, Paula," she said and kissed me on the cheek.

As I drove home, I realized my hands were shaking. Mom never talked about Julie. She was careful to abide by the version of truth told by the newspapers and police files.

The way that story goes is Julie Waits is a runaway who disappeared.

Cold case.

Unsolved.

It happens all the time. Girls, boys, even adults. They don't disappear by the handful; they vanish by the truckload. Hundreds of thousands of them, like the population of small towns all across America. The vast majority of kids who disappear are never found. Girls vanish at the highest rate.

In his file, Schaeffer returns again and again to the traces of blood and semen on the couch where Kevin Mulroney's body was found. He suspected that blood belonged to Julie. The ownership of the other bodily fluids was obvious. Julie's disappearance was a mystery, but not the kind that's hard to solve.

In Schaeffer's opinion, it also supplied motive.

"The Lord will judge his people" is how one of the responding officers put it, which is another way of saying few tears were shed on behalf of Kevin Mulroney.

But Schaeffer wasn't content to let the Lord judge. In his notes, he questions whether Mulroney's death was revenge for Julie's disappearance. Not divine interference, but the kind enacted by flesh and blood. He was certain that Julie Waits was the key to unraveling the full story of Mulroney's death.

After a kid has been missing for forty-eight hours, the assumption is they aren't coming back. Schaeffer refused to buy that. He ran Julie's picture in the paper and tracked down every lead, no matter how crazy, but eventually the leads dried up. He couldn't find her.

As soon as I drove away from Mom, I understood what I needed to do. I went to work right away, using every angle, the way Schaeffer taught me.

Megan Little is Schaeffer's older daughter. Born and raised in Livingston. She's got three kids, a husband who works for the state, and a nice little house about two miles outside of town. Four days a week, Megan cuts hair at the Dolce Vita Salon on Ash Street. Even if you don't know Megan Little, you know someone like her.

After I found out where Megan worked, I made an appointment at the Dolce Vita under the name Susan Waits.

The day of my appointment, I sat in the pink waiting area pretending to thumb through magazines while I studied Megan. She wears her hair short and spiky like some kind of exotic bird. Add in the sweatsuits in bright colors, you got yourself a regular parrot.

Like any other parrot, Megan likes to repeat what she's heard.

"There was a girl who went missing back when I was in high school," she said as she fastened the cape around my neck, "Same last name as you. No one ever found out whether she was a runaway or something happened to her. Real sad."

"Julie Waits?" I asked and made a face like I was troubled.

"Oh God, I wondered when I saw your last name in the appointment book. Is she your family? I'm so sorry. Really, I am."

"Second cousin," I said with a regretful nod.

"Oh, Susan, I'm so sorry." Unlike me, Megan had tears in her eyes. "I'm such an idiot, but gosh, you know, I met her a few times. She was such a tiny little thing. Real cute too."

I looked at her in the mirror. Tried not to be distracted by the pink flamingos painted on the frame.

"I wasn't around when it happened," I said.

"If it brings you any peace of mind, my father was part of that investigation. They spent weeks looking for her." Megan lowered her voice.

"I'm sure they did what they could."

Megan gave me a quick hug like we were already best friends. Then she started rearranging my hair, moving it from one side to the other in that way hairdressers do. "What are we thinking today? Layers? A trim? You want to keep it in a bob?"

"Just a trim," I said. "How about you, you got family here in town?"

That was all I had to say. Megan liked to talk, and family was one of her favorite subjects. After that first visit, I put myself on a clockwork schedule at the Dolce Vita. Every six weeks, whether I needed it or not. I even let her put in highlights, against my better judgment.

What I learned while sitting in Megan's beauty salon chair was that her younger sister, Ginny, was always her father's favorite and had everything handed to her. Ginny was a junior in high school the year her parents split up. According to Megan, Ginny took the news hard.

Two summers after high school, Ginny married her high school sweetheart, Dave Thompson. Dave was a second-string quarterback, which meant he wasn't talented enough to get a scholarship at a four-year university and had to settle for community college. That's where he discovered the Marine Corps. He signed up for the NROTC and was shipped out for training two weeks after their honeymoon.

"He was deployed to San Diego. Ginny went with him. From there on out, it was all pictures of beaches and sunshine," Megan said. "Just between you and me, my sister isn't one to let anyone forget how well she's done for herself."

The Marine Corps paid for the rest of Dave's college education, and Ginny's too through a scholarship program for spouses. They were stationed overseas for a long time, but eventually they wound up in Washington, DC.

It took quite a few visits to the Dolce Vita for me to get all that out of

Megan. We had to establish a rapport and get through the awkwardness of my connection to Mom.

"Second cousin by marriage through our dads," I told her when she asked.

The plan was to distance myself as much as I could. I had a complicated story of family connection all ready to go. One that I was fairly confident Megan wouldn't be able to follow, but she took my proclamation on faith. The only thing she asked was whether our families were close.

"Not particularly. Julie's mom and mine didn't see eye to eye on much of anything."

Megan nodded, then leaned close so no one else could hear, not that it was likely over the sound of the blow-dryers.

"Your cousin, the one who went missing? Her mom and my dad have a thing." She rolled her eyes to let me know exactly what she thought of this "thing."

"You ever meet her?" I asked.

"Once. That's why I asked. I didn't want to talk out of turn, but she's a real piece of work." Megan shook her head. "Talk about not seeing eye to eye, I truly do not understand what my father sees in that woman. Don't mind saying, that relationship has put a bit of a wedge between me and my dad. I hardly ever see him."

I nodded and didn't push for more. That's a trick I learned from Mom.

Megan liked to dole out a new piece of information each time I was sitting in her chair. As long as I kept coming back, she kept talking.

"How's that sister of yours?" I asked at my next visit. "Ginny, right?"

"Too big for her britches." Megan rolled her eyes while her scissors did a little dance around my face. "She goes by Gwen now, but she's still Ginny to me. You want some layers this time, Susan?" She tilted her head to study me. "I think it would highlight your cheekbones."

We both studied my face in the mirror.

"Why not," I said, even though my cheekbones didn't seem worth highlighting. If layers were the price I had to pay to listen to Megan talk about Ginny, then I was game.

"My sister," Megan said as she went to work, "acts like a college degree means something special, but all she does is stay home with her kids. It's not like she even has a job."

"Some people say motherhood is the most important job," I said.

"Oh, of course it is," Megan added quickly, like she hadn't just said the opposite. "But it doesn't take a college degree, that's for sure. Anyhow, Ginny likes to think of herself as the 'successful one'"—Megan paused to make air quotes with her fingers—"even though I'm the one who just got promoted to manager. Now she's too good to stay with her own family. They're coming to visit the second week in July. She told my mom she's going to rent a house nearby so they won't have to 'crowd in.' You ask me, she just wanted a pool."

Megan made a face to let me know what she thought of that. "Can you imagine? My mom barely gets to see her grandchildren as it is. My guess is she wants her own place so she and my dad can talk about their little schemes."

"'Schemes'?" I laughed like that word wasn't a red flag.

Megan rolled her eyes. "Whenever Gwen is in town she's always off cooking up ridiculous ideas with our dad. I try not to play favorites with my kids because I know how it feels to always be second fiddle."

The layers Megan gave me that day were not my best look, but they were more than worth that single piece of information. Given that there aren't a lot of houses with pools in Livingston, it was easy to track down the house Gwen was renting. It was a Vrbo. When I told Vrbo about the drug ring I was working, which happened to be true, they had no problem giving me access to their rental agreements.

In police work, there are coincidences and there are *coincidences*.

I could buy the coincidence of Gwen living in Washington, DC. After all, it's a big city with a lot of folks from the military. What I couldn't ignore was the renter's home address listed in that Vrbo rental agreement.

McLean, Virginia.

Gwen living in the same town as Julie. You can't tell me that happened by accident. That, combined with the knowledge that Gwen and Schaeffer enjoyed cooking up "little schemes," told me it was time to take a closer look.

Thirty-Three

FALL

STELLA

Stella is halfway home before she remembers Gwen's wince as she sat down. That tracks with her appearance the first night she arrived at Stella's house. The fall of her hair over her face and the awkward hunched-over limp.

The night everything started.

In retrospect, Stella sees it for what it was. That night is the key to everything, which is why she can't ignore any part of it. Even though she'd really like to ignore this one piece. It would be so much more comfortable to heap blame solely on Gwen, write her wince off to overdoing it in her HIIT class, but Stella knows what she saw. Exercise isn't what caused Gwen to make that face.

Whatever had Gwen hunched over and wincing hasn't healed yet. Stella is familiar with how long it takes certain kinds of injuries to heal.

She searches for other clues and finds one in the cast of Gwen's skin. It wasn't the lackluster pigment of middle age that caught her eye, but a thick coat of foundation. Stella pulls down her vanity mirror and studies her own skin for comparison. When she realizes she's been sidetracked by the way her upper eyelids are beginning to sag, she slams it shut.

What if she could just age into a crone? Go shapeless, wrinkled, and gray. A form of invisibility that is completely terrifying. It's one thing to be indistinguishable in a way that still draws smiles; there's a small amount of power there.

It's another thing to not be seen at all.

A vanishing. A nothingness, as though she has ceased to exist.

Who needs a prison when the prisoners happily build their own cells?

"Focus," she whispers and pinches the inside of her arm as hard as she can. The pain does the trick, bringing her mind to heel.

She should have asked Gwen about the marks on her face, but she missed the opportunity. So dumb—it would have been an easy way to push Gwen off-kilter. Instead, Stella let herself be ambushed. She's completely lost her touch. Although, to be fair, who would have expected a confrontation from a stalker clinging to a middle school grudge?

A stalker with knowledge of her past.

She thinks about the Ginny she once knew and the way Julie believed it was cheer that would seal their friendship. So naive! She didn't understand that Ginny was the kind of person who assigned people a fixed place in the world. Us or Them. Deserving or Not. Ginny and Julie were never going to be friends.

Gorgeous or Smart.

Lorraine's words echo in Stella's head, along with the rock-solid security of Lorraine's friendship. Proof that Stella learned to shine, but in a way that doesn't threaten anyone else.

None of this changes the past, or the fact that Gwen was limping. Hiding marks on her face, which means she's hiding how she got them.

Tom.

Gwen's words ring in Stella's ears. *Apple . . . tree.* Only this time, they take on a different meaning.

What if . . . ?

The thought that follows the "what if" makes Stella hit the brakes hard and pull over in front of Ellen Meisner's house. Her stomach churns. A low moan emits from somewhere within her body.

It sounded like a taunt, but what if it was a warning?

Could it have actually been Tom?

No, because above all else, that's the thing she promised herself would never happen again.

No violence.

Zero tolerance policy.

Stella selected Tom carefully. She knew all the signs and made sure he didn't raise any red flags. An affair, well, that's unpleasant. The fact that he used the kids' college funds for a high-risk investment makes her want to lock him out of the house. But if Tom caused that limp, it's unforgivable. If his hand is the one that left a mark on Gwen's face, it's a crime.

In the world where Stella grew up, that crime is punishable by death.

Her body fizzes with rage. "Breathe," she whispers through gritted teeth. Outside, she catches movement.

It's Ellen, walking briskly toward Stella's car. She waves, and Stella rolls down the window.

"I saw your car and thought I'd come out and say hello."

"Ellen, hi, sorry." Stella puts on her blandest smile. "I just . . . um . . . dropped my phone and I didn't want it sliding around under my feet while I was driving."

"Oh my gosh, I'm always doing that." Ellen shakes her head as though admitting to a personal failing. "When you're on an airplane, they tell you to ask for assistance if you drop your phone in the seat. Something about the battery. I think it's kind of dangerous."

"Yeah," Stella says, then holds up her phone like a talisman. "Figured, better safe than sorry."

"Oh, for sure."

Ellen smiles.

Stella smiles.

Ellen looks like she's on the cusp of saying something real. Something meaningful and true. A howl that will harmonize with the cacophony of howls inside Stella.

"Oh, I almost forgot," Ellen says. "I still have your basket from the cucumbers you dropped off. Let me run in and get it."

"Actually, I have to go."

Stella suspects that if she's forced to wait for her garden basket, she might actually explode. "Daisy called. She forgot her lunch, so I was just running out and . . ."

"Of course. I completely understand."

This is said conspiratorially, as though they are both in on the secret of semi-indentured servitude to their families.

"Good to see you," Stella says with a cheerful smile.

As soon as Stella gets home, she collapses with her forehead resting on her kitchen island. She's disgusted to realize that as she's slowing her breath, she's also comparing her marble favorably to Gwen's. The life she once chased takes on a new sinister cast. It's a competition with no end in sight. Instead of setting her free, it's imprisoned her in a constant quest for more. Taking another deep breath, she focuses on her priorities.

Really, they are quite simple.

She has two.

Colin and Daisy.

She'd do anything for them.

That thought unwinds a spool of other thoughts.

Anything?

Would she kill for them? Not in a metaphorical sense, but literally. And if she were going to kill, who would go first? The possibly violent husband who sunk their children's college fund into a risky investment or the middle school bully hinting at past transgressions that Stella has gone to great lengths to hide?

The problem with murder is that the world has changed. Now there's DNA evidence. Technology to record likes, dislikes, searches on the internet, proclivities, and whereabouts at every given moment.

Stella's pretty sure no one gets away with murder anymore.

Unless they're the CEO of a drug company or someone like that.

An image of Kevin flashes before her eyes. Yellow foam staining his lips. Eyes vacant as she closes the door.

Actually, people do get away with murder. It happens all the time.

Stella blinks, but there are no tears in her eyes. A coldness descends over her, as though the marble of her countertops has entered her bloodstream.

She catalogs Tom's faults in her head.

The big things are somehow less grating than the little things.

Tom has nothing but respect for women, except he can't help but notice how the mothers in his office are always playing the mommy card to leave early. *He* couldn't get away with that. Ha ha!

What goes unacknowledged is that *he* doesn't have to make child-related excuses because he has Stella.

His jokey devaluation of all her daily tasks.

"I'd love to stay home with these two peanuts every day," after a weekend "babysitting" so Stella could focus on running a school fundraiser.

No credit given for the hours she spent prepping the meals and arranging the playdates that ensured the weekend would be "relaxing." No comprehension that her planning was made necessary by his refusal to correctly perform any of the tasks she does.

As Tom has pointed out, what she does isn't hard. Cooking, laundry, scheduling, and juggling all the moving parts of their family. Like electricity, Stella is the constant hum that no one notices until she cuts out.

But what if she wasn't the thing that got cut out?

What if it was Tom, who makes her feel like she's living in a *Gaslight* reboot. Does his behavior require a Kevin-level solution?

Of course the answer is no. He's the father of her children. A good man who loves his family. What is it he keeps saying to her? Oh yes: *Haven't I always taken care of you?* The phrase rankles because Stella has provided too.

Her thoughts return to Gwen. Who hit her? Who made her limp?

Stella is certain Gwen didn't slip on the stairs. She didn't walk into a wall. She didn't bump into a counter. Someone made those marks on her skin. Technically, it's not Stella's responsibility to solve the mystery of those marks, but she knows the consequences of ignoring that kind of violence.

Could it be Tom?

How could it be Tom?

He's never threatened the children, not even in the smallest of ways. Despite the faults she's cataloged, he's never made her feel physically threatened. Never raised his hand in violence against any of them. She knows that if something were to happen to her, Daisy and Colin would be safe. It's not like she is her mother lying in a hospital bed. He is not a predator. If she has to leave for a while, her children will be okay.

She stands and heads to the basement. As she climbs the steps to her secret space, she thinks of blood smeared on a wall. It's one of her forbidden memories. She told herself if she didn't acknowledge it, it couldn't follow her. And yet, somehow, it bridged the distance between past and present. Snuck through cracks in the foundation of the house she built and found her.

Upstairs, the nanny cam bear is undisturbed. No motion to trigger any footage.

In her mind, she sees the text messages on Gwen's phone.

I saw you.

I know what you did.

You made a choice.

Ambiguous enough to spark anxiety in any secret-keeper, but Stella isn't the only one in this town with secrets.

Gwen has secrets too. It's impossible to know who sent those messages, but what she knows for sure is Gwen was in her house. Gwen took Daisy's Lilly Pulitzer bag. And the knife Stella has kept with her all these years is missing.

No ambiguity there.

Also, no ambiguity to Gwen's accusation.

What if that accusation were combined with proof? DNA evidence on an ancient knife. It has the power to drag Stella back to the past. Tie her to an unsolved murder. It might be enough to unravel a whole series of suspicious deaths.

Think of the media storm if her story became part of the public domain.

"Storm" is the wrong word. It would be a tornado, flattening them all. She could accept those consequences for herself, but she won't accept them for Colin and Daisy. A day ago, she could have reassured herself that she and Tom had the financial means to protect their children. Send them to boarding school in Europe or something like that until the storm passed. But Tom has left them vulnerable.

Regenerative Foods. Two innocent words that make her blood boil.

Stella needs to safeguard her children's future against whatever is coming for her.

She needs an insurance policy.

A backup plan.

There's no time to waste. She has to act now while she's still anonymous. She reaches under the rafters. When her fingers make contact with cold, hard metal, she sighs with relief. Whoever violated her private space didn't get everything. It's a thought that resurrects images of Kevin. His body on hers. Her body something to be used. He didn't get everything either, she thinks as she tucks the key into her pocket.

People are always underestimating her.

As Stella leaves her secret room, it occurs to her that people who need secret hideouts aren't really free. Same goes for people with secret identities.

From the main floor of her house, she hears a muffled chime. She chalks it up to one of the many bells and whistles that go off in her home, demanding her attention. The beep of the dishwasher or the chirp of the dryer. The alarm system that chimes each time the door opens. The sound the wireless speakers make when one happens to disconnect, requiring a reboot of the system. A new download of the app used to control it, a reset of the password, and a group text with the new information to her family, who invariably ignore the message, only to text her frantically for the new password while she's doing something like handling raw chicken. Something that requires her to stop what she was doing for them, thoroughly wash and dry her hands in order to avoid spreading salmonella, and turn her attention to a thing she has already done for them but now needs to do again.

The chime sounds again. She needs to grab her keys, drive to the bank where, long ago, she and Paula rented that lockbox. The lockbox Stella claimed she'd never need. She rented it in part to humor her sister, and in part as an apology for leaving her behind. She wanted Paula to know they would always be connected. If not in the typical way, at least in this small way.

The chime sounds a third time as Stella climbs the stairs toward the main floor. She lets out a sigh of frustration. She's done being responsive to everything in her life in a way that leaves no room for herself, except there's that chime again.

It's the doorbell.

Probably UPS or FedEx needing a signature, she thinks as it sounds again. Maybe Tom's beer of the month delivery, also requiring a signature, or Ellen Meisner getting really insistent about returning that garden basket. It's too early for her children, accidentally locked out and too lazy to access the hidden key.

It sounds again.

Whoever is pressing on the doorbell stops, then starts again. A series of staccato bleats followed by a loud knock. The equivalent of someone calling out, "Move your ass."

Which Stella does, tiptoeing to the foyer to look through the side window.

What she sees makes her inhale sharply and blink.

A wish so fleeting and private she dared not put it in words has come to life. Flesh and blood, standing on Stella's front porch, looking low-key annoyed. It's another moment from the forbidden parts of her memory, played out in reverse. Once, she was the one waiting on the porch.

Now she's on the inside.

Stella opens the door a crack as though she still doesn't trust her eyes.

It's her sister.

"Paula?" she whispers and opens the door wider. "You're here."

PART FIVE

Thirty-Four

APRIL 2015 INTO FALL 2019

PAULA

Dulles Airport is located right outside Washington, DC.

I'm not much of a traveler, but Dulles is one airport I know.

It was October 2002 when Mom called and asked me to come visit her at the farm. When I got there, it was just the two of us.

We walked out to the barn together and she said, "Paula, I want you to take as many photos as you need of that painting. This barn is getting old. You never know what might happen to it."

This was before you could take a picture with as much thought as wiping your nose. Back then, people had cameras, not cell phones. Instead of posting things on social media, we printed pictures out from negatives and left them in a drawer.

I did what she asked. Of course, we still had the pictures of the painting she'd sent us right after Julie came to live with me, but there'd been some additions since that time. As I snapped photos from every angle, the new constellations weren't lost on me. I knew what they meant, but I tried not to think about it too much.

About a month later, the barn caught fire and burned down.

After it burned, I realized I was the only one in possession of what was essentially a treasure map.

What if something happened to me? My line of work is not without risk.

I figured Mom had her own copies stashed away somewhere, but that meant Julie would have to ask for them. Come back and beg for the thing she swore she'd left behind. Mom had told us time and again that everything she'd done was for us. To me, that meant Julie should have access to the map. That painting, and what it represented, belonged to Julie just as much as it did to me. We'd paid for it in every possible way.

My first time through Dulles Airport was to take those pictures to Julie.

I thought she might ask how I'd found her, but instead, she asked me to meet her for coffee. Not at her house, but at a fancy coffee shop where they had expensive lattes topped with hearts made out of foam. At first, I felt awkward. Here I was talking about the past with this woman who was barely recognizable.

She'd transformed. Sanded away all her edges so all you could see was the smooth skin, fancy hair, big house, and perfect family.

"It's so good to see you, Paula," she said. "I was trying to think of a way you could meet the kids. My husband is working late tonight. Maybe you could stop by the house for dinner?"

Even her voice sounded different. It made me think of that day we bought Julie's new identity papers. She told me the name she'd picked was from a play. "Julie's gone," she said. I didn't believe it then, but I believed it now. The look of fierce ambition that was particular to my sister had faded. Without it, she was almost unrecognizable.

"What are their names?" I asked.

"Colin and Daisy." She slid pictures of them across the table to me.

I looked at those pictures for quite some time. Daisy, my niece, could have been Julie at six years old.

"Don't worry," I told her, swallowing the lump in my throat. "I'm not here to interrupt your life. Now that you're a lawyer, I'm sure you've got all kinds of important business."

She laughed like I'd made a joke.

"I don't practice anymore. It was too hard to balance. Besides, the kids need me at home, so, you know." She shrugged like she was saying something obvious.

I nodded, even though I *didn't* know. Plenty of women go to work and have kids, but I didn't yet fully understand my sister's world. Also, not having children myself, I didn't have firsthand knowledge of what it meant to balance job and family. This was before anyone was writing articles about working mothers doing the equivalent of three jobs. I stared at her, searching for that girl who'd pushed me to get my GED, then packed up and moved to California all by herself. I couldn't understand why she'd given up on her dreams.

"Here." I pushed my own set of pictures across the table to her in an envelope.

"The barn painting," she said after she opened it.

"Those pictures are yours to keep. I took them right before the barn burned down."

"The barn burned down?"

Her eyes snapped to life. There she was. The sister I remembered. I nodded.

"But everything else is okay?" It was her way of asking about Mom.

"Everything else is pretty much the same as it always was," I said.

She nodded, and a little smile appeared at the corners of her mouth.

"If you're not working, you should put those pictures somewhere safe."

"What do you mean?"

"You know what they say. A man is not a financial plan."

She laughed at that. "Seems to contradict everything about our entire childhood, including these pictures." Then her eyes went dark and flat. "I know what you're saying, Paula. I should go back to work, but nobody warns you."

"Warns you about what?"

"Things were supposed to be equal for us. When people told me the playing field was level, I believed them, but the game is rigged. Maybe that's why Mom broke the rules. She saw the truth and decided that was the only way she could win."

Her eyes were wide in a way that reminded me of Mom right before she decided it was time for someone to move on. It was a worrisome resemblance.

"Things okay with you and your husband?" I asked.

"Yes, we're fine. It's not that." She shook her head like she was saying the opposite. "All I'm asking is if Mom somehow knew."

"Knew what?"

"That you can do everything right and it's still not enough. When a woman plays by the rules, she loses."

"What did you lose, Julie?" I asked.

"Stella," she said quickly.

With that one word, it was like a wall went up around her.

"It was good to see you, Paula," she said, standing up, "but I have to run. School pickup in fifteen minutes."

The light in her eyes was gone. Whatever window I'd been peering through had slammed closed. When she hugged me goodbye, she seemed like a stranger.

All the way home, I thought about what Stella was trying to say. What had she lost?

The answer occurred to me a few weeks later, after I'd interviewed a rape victim. That particular duty was one the male officers in the LPD were happy to give to me. Later that day, I overheard two of my colleagues talking about the report I'd written.

"Since when are we in the business of policing what happens in a marriage?"

One overheard question was all it took for things to click in my head.

What Stella had been trying to say is that violence isn't always physical. It sneaks up on you. Takes you by surprise in places you thought were safe, like a marriage or the moment a colleague questions your definition of violence. It's found in the lies women are told about their worth and the way those lies harden into truth. Violence is telling women the path is clear when, in fact, it's filled with land mines in the shape of no childcare and unequal pay.

Like Megan Little put it, being a mother is the most important job, but no one really believes that.

Not even the mothers.

That brings me to the second time I flew into Dulles, which was shortly after I discovered Gwen Thompson's home address.

I took three days' vacation and posted up in an airport hotel. Rented a budget four-door and drove straight to the address I'd found on the rental agreement. My plan was to park that white rental and fade into the background while I watched Gwen come and go. Figured a car like that wouldn't stick out, but that's where I miscalculated. You don't know how much money exists in this world until you see it all massed together in one town. The first time I came to McLean, I'd been focused on my sister.

That second time, I was focused on where my sister lived.

Her town was one enormous home after another, but the Thompsons' house didn't fit that mold. They lived on the edge of McLean. The house looked plenty big to me, but it was smaller than most of the others. When I looked up the tax records, I found it was a rental. A little more digging and I discovered Dave Thompson had retired from the Marine Corps and already bounced through two jobs. His military pension didn't amount to much, or at least not much in a town where the average house goes for more than a million.

At first, it didn't add up. What were the Thompsons doing in a town they couldn't begin to afford?

The more I researched it, the more I started to understand about folks in fancy suburbs. The games they play are different, and I'm not talking about golf and tennis. Parenting is a competitive sport. People treat their kids like they're prize ponies running in the Kentucky Derby. That's why the Thompsons were in McLean.

They were there for the excellent public schools that regularly sent kids to the Ivies.

And they weren't alone. When I started looking, I found multiple ex-military families living in overpriced rentals within that school district. That's when I started to think my instincts were off.

What I'd worried was a *coincidence* was something driven by an outside factor I hadn't fully understood. I decided Gwen Thompson was trying to give her kids their best shot at life. Same as my sister.

It took the full three days to come to that conclusion.

Did I see Julie during those three days?

I did, although she didn't see me. I drove by her house more than once. Followed her to the grocery store and sat through one inning of my nephew's baseball game. Of course, I wanted to reach out, but I was afraid that Julie would see straight through whatever excuse I offered up. She looked happy. If she figured out why I was there, her happiness would vanish.

I couldn't do that to her.

Instead, I convinced myself there was nothing to worry about. Wishful thinking at its best. I might as well have stuck my fingers in my ears and hummed a tune. I shouldn't have been surprised when all that hoping and wishing came crashing down.

And that's exactly what happened two days ago.

I was at the office, working on a report. Standard paperwork, nothing memorable, which is possibly why I happened to look over at Schaeffer's desk at the same moment a notification popped up on his screen.

Most of the time, I would have ignored something like that, but the name caught my attention.

G. Thompson.

Knowing what I do, you can see why I reached over to his desk, jiggled his mouse, and clicked on that notification.

It was footage from a front door security camera. A short clip, but I recognized all the participants. There was Tom Parker looking straight into the camera, his face tight with nerves. The door swung open, and Gwen invited him in.

That's all it took. Funny how instinct kicks in. Five seconds was all I needed to assess the situation and understand I was watching something that was supposed to be a secret. The security feed delivered to Schaeffer's computer reminded me of Megan's statement about the secret schemes cooked up between father and daughter. Also, I know my sister. I knew that whatever she was going to do next, I wanted to be there to help.

Sixteen hours later, I'd completed my third trip to Dulles Airport. An hour after I landed, I was standing on Julie's front porch.

THE MINUTE SHE OPENS HER door, I see the difference. The smoothed-out version that goes by the name Stella is gone. The person I'm looking at now is the grown-up version of the sister I once knew.

"Paula? You're here," she whispers, and a smile lights up her face.

"I am indeed."

"You must have known I needed you."

I step inside and tell her what I saw.

Her smile fades. Eyes harden. "Tom's having an affair. He's not the person I thought he was, Paula. That woman—there were marks on her face. She was hurt."

Her eyes go liquid like she's about to cry, then she blinks back her tears.

"I made a mistake. I thought I was safe. That going to school, getting a law degree, everything I'd done would protect me." She swallows hard. "He took most of the money we saved for the kids and invested it in something risky. I haven't gotten to the bottom of it yet, but I don't trust it. I don't think I can trust him anymore."

"Good thing you have a backup plan."

She starts as though I've slapped her, then her face grows calm. Julie taking over where Stella left off.

"That's right. I do," she says.

"Your kids will be okay?"

"He won't hurt them."

I tilt my head to one side, raise an eyebrow.

"I'm sure," she says, because she knows what I'm asking. Then she pulls out her phone. Types a text, takes a deep breath, and hits send. Even before she sets the phone down, it lights up with text messages.

Daisy: Where are you going

Colin: Imma hang with the boys tomorrow night and Dad said you were chill

Daisy: Will you back in time for my game tomorrow morning

She reaches for the phone. For a moment, I think the person she's become will win, but instead of picking it up, she turns it face down.

"They'll be okay." The look she gives me tells me she's certain.

I wait until we're on the plane before I tell her what I know about Gwen Thompson. I summarize Schaeffer's suspicions about Mom and his search for Julie. How it was the case that ended his perfect record, ruined his career, and broke up his marriage. As I talk, Stella's eyes start to burn with an intensity that makes me shift in my seat.

"Funny how things come full circle. That's what Gwen said to me. She was so angry, Paula. It was like I'd stolen something from her. Like she wanted to destroy me."

We're both silent for a moment.

I don't know where Stella's thoughts go, but mine return to the Dolce Vita Salon where Megan Little told me Gwen isn't one to let people forget how well she's done for herself. I haven't forgotten high school, and how girls like Megan and Ginny talked about girls like me and Julie. I'd say an affair with Stella's husband offered Gwen a way to right a perceived imbalance. It let her tell herself she was still better. The successful one, even if her house wasn't as fancy and her husband couldn't hold down a job outside of the military.

Still, there's one piece that doesn't fit, and that's Tom. I'm a frequent visitor to Stella's Instagram account. The way Tom smiles at Stella is hard to fake. I've seen a lot, and it's a stretch to imagine him with Gwen. All those thoughts lead me back to my threshold question about Schaeffer's relationship with my mother.

Is he playing a long game, or is he in love?

Thirty-Five

FALL

STELLA

The plane banks, slips down through the clouds, and Portland spreads out beneath them. Gray and gritty, Mount Hood in the distance has a pallor that reflects Stella's own mental state.

It's been over two decades since she's been home.

Home.

The word catches her by surprise. How can this still be home? She wants to take a quick picture of this place that was once so familiar, but when she reaches for her phone, it's not in her purse. A moment of panic, then she remembers she left it behind. Without it, she feels untethered, but also free.

In the long-term parking lot, Paula unlocks a white Dodge pickup.

As Stella gets into the cab, something catches inside of her. Memories flood back. Other trucks. Another life. She pushes it all away. It's in the past. She made it here, to the future. Whatever comes next, she and Paula are a unit built to survive. They did it before, and they can do it again. This is what she tells herself, but another part of her is less certain. They're older now. It shouldn't mean anything, but somehow it does.

Before they left Virginia, they made one stop.

Now Stella takes the photos they retrieved from the lockbox out of her purse. As the suburbs on the outskirts of Portland become fields, she studies her mother's art. It's a treasure map, but also a map of murders committed long ago. Bodies found in suspicious circumstances, then forgotten in moldering files. Each star represents a tree in the forest. Lightly, with the tip of one fingernail, Stella traces the lines between the stars.

"Do you think it's all still there?"

Paula makes a sound somewhere between a laugh and a snort. "It's there all right. The real question is how we move it."

"What do you mean?" Stella looks at her sister without comprehension.

"She traded the cash they left behind for gold. Little by little, so no one would get suspicious. Gold's heavy."

Paula says this as though the weight of gold is common knowledge, but Stella has no idea how much a bar of gold weighs. Much less multiple bars buried deep in the forest.

Outside, the air is heavy with rain. Stella presses one cheek to the window and imagines her mother spinning death into gold. Amassing whatever fortune lies underground by putting both of her daughters in harm's way. For years, Stella believed *that* was the thorny knot at the center of her problematic childhood. Now she understands that she was looking at it from the wrong angle. It was the central theme, but it wasn't the knot.

It was the lesson.

Protect yourself. Protect your offspring. No one else will protect you with the same devotion. She thinks of mother animals in the wild. No wonder the human version has been defanged. The female of every species is ferocious. Focused on one thing.

Survival.

Their own, and that of their offspring.

At any cost.

Threaten either one and you put your own survival at risk.

The image of her children's decimated college savings accounts paired with Tom's patronizing responses rises to the top of Stella's brain.

A hard ball of anger swells inside her. Anger at Tom, but also anger at the way she's been complicit in her own demise. Trapped in a story where the only plot is motherhood. It made so much sense to trade her job for her children's future, but two wire transfers was all it took to transform her glittering reward into fool's gold.

Stella grinds the heels of her palms against her eye sockets. It's time to rewrite that age-old story and replace it with a brand-new genre.

Driving through Livingston feels like traveling back in time. Same trees in the parks, only bigger. The storefronts have changed, but the buildings are the same. She and Paula drive past the high school and the sprawl of strip malls on the far side of town, then enter the country of their childhood.

When Paula slows the truck to turn into the gravel driveway, Stella's palms go damp. From the road, the brambles hide the old farmhouse and its secrets. When she left, she told herself it was forever.

Yet here she is.

What if escape is allowed only once? Like a single wish granted by a genie.

Stella realizes her hands are trembling. She squeezes them into fists, disgusted at her own weakness. She used to be tougher.

"It's gonna be fine," Paula says.

Stella nods. She can feel the grim set of her mouth. The truck stops. She opens the door, and her feet hit the gravel with a crunch.

The front door to the farmhouse swings open.

"Julie?"

Her mother is framed in the doorway. Unchanged, as though the years have passed everywhere but here. Long, flowing hair. Trim body in a bohemian patchwork dress that would look ridiculous on anyone else, but her mother wears it with timeless ease.

Thoughts of witchcraft and fairy tales steal into Stella's mind. Is her mother a priestess of the dark? Did she steal youth from the men she murdered?

It's only when her mother steps into the light that Stella sees the passage of time. The way her mother's long red hair is shot through with gray. The lines on her face.

"Mom?" Stella says. Without warning, her eyes fill with tears.

Her mother crosses the distance between them. She wraps Stella in a hug that catches her off guard with its strength. This is not an old woman on the verge of surrender. This is a commander in chief welcoming home her faithful soldier.

"Let me look at you."

Her mother's gaze has the same intensity Stella remembers from childhood. Her smile reveals the familiar gap between her front teeth.

"You look good," her mother says, then she takes Stella by the hand and leads her into the house.

It's the same house Stella refuses to remember. The stairs where she once listened and watched, unobserved. The living room where men ate their last meals in front of the television.

"Hungry?" her mother asks.

Stella nods. She's more than hungry. She's ravenous.

The three of them gather around the table. Her mother brings out multiple dishes of food. It feels celebratory, like Stella's childhood vision of how things would be when Paula came home, but instead, she's the one who has returned. They eat until they can eat no more. Then they eat peach pie for dessert. It's made from home-canned peaches. Stella can taste the summer sun bottled up inside of them. She devours her first piece, then eats a second while her mother watches with an approving smile.

Here, there is no need to check her appetites.

"It's supposed to be clear tonight," her mother says, looking first at Paula, then at Stella. "I got you girls some blue bags from IKEA. They hold close to fifty pounds each. Anyone sees you out there, you tell them you're hunting mushrooms. Plenty of people still do that."

The word "IKEA" sounds incongruous in her mother's mouth, but of course her mother has access to things like the internet and Amazon Prime. Despite all appearances to the contrary, this is not an enchanted cottage. Her mother is not a witch, and yet she's also not a typical woman in her seventies.

Stella studies her mother's face. How she presides over the table with strength and independence. Her mother has an aura of self-satisfaction. The kind Stella associates with older men. Presidents of powerful nations, CEOs of Fortune 500 companies, men who command empires with a single nod. Men who draw upon the wisdom of their age and feel entitled to drink deep and unapologetically from the well of society.

"What if someone comes poking around?" Paula asks.

Her mother laughs. "You ever known me not to take care of things?"

It's a fair question. And one that makes Stella ask the same of herself. Has she taken care of things?

The answer is clear.

She has not.

Instead, she let Tom take care of things.

After their meal, they go outside where trees press in from every direction. More gray than green, as though they've been dipped in the clouds. It's no longer raining, but the air is damp. It sends a chill down Stella's spine, making her shiver.

The barn is gone, replaced by a charred foundation.

"It had to come down," her mother says, following Stella's gaze. "Anyone could have wandered inside and taken a picture. If they happened to notice the numbers on the trees, it wouldn't take more than a few minutes on the internet to realize it was a map. Of course, most people wouldn't credit me with the smarts required to concoct a plan like that, but you never know. Can't always depend on people underestimating you."

Stella nods, but she's remembering the dark shining colors of her mother's painting. The beauty of it. It makes her wonder what her mother could have created if she'd had the freedom to focus on more than survival.

In the distance, there is the sound of a car slowing down on the road. When it turns, her mother inhales sharply.

"Julie, in the shed," she says.

Stella does as she's told, running to the small shed where, in another lifetime, she stacked the wood they burned in the winter. She crouches behind a wheelbarrow and a large garbage can, like a child playing a game of hide-and-seek.

Her mother's voice carries to Stella's hiding spot. "That man has a sixth sense for when I most want to be left alone."

There is the crunch of tires on gravel.

Voices carry on the wind. Her mother's musical laugh mixes with the deep timbre of a man's voice. A car door opens and shuts.

Clearly, when her mother mentioned someone wandering into the barn and out into the forest, she had someone specific in mind.

Someone male.

Someone who poses a threat.

Add those factors together and the result is always the same: Someone is about to move on.

Thirty-Six

FALL

PAULA

Julie. Every time Mom says it, Stella flinches, but she doesn't correct her. Despite my best efforts, we've both been reclaimed as characters that Mom bends to her will.

When Schaeffer pulls up, I'm not all that surprised. That man has a nose for trouble. Why else would he have blown up his marriage and career sniffing around Mom?

"Sharon and Paula." Schaeffer smiles as he gets out of his car. "I was at Dunlap's Bakery in town and saw they had that pound cake you like so much, Sharon. Couldn't resist stopping by with dessert."

"Most people know the thing to resist is stopping by without an invitation," Mom says.

"Good thing I'm not most people." Schaeffer's smile widens into a grin.

His grin is too friendly. The way people smile when they're trying to cover something up.

"I guess you better come in," Mom says.

"Is this a bad time? Don't want to intrude if you ladies have other plans."

"Why would it be a bad time?" Mom asks.

The way she gazes at Schaeffer—eyes wide and innocent, a hint of a smile, as though she has nothing in the world to hide—is the reason he keeps coming back for more. It's impossible not to go along with her, even if you know she's lying. The tension between the way Mom's looking at him and whatever Schaeffer knows about her is the reason for the gamble that is their relationship.

I know that Mom wants Schaeffer around right now as much as she wants pigs in the house. But for a moment, even I believe her.

The three of us troop inside. Schaeffer sits down heavy in the same chair Stella occupied thirty minutes ago.

"Heard you had to go out of town, Paula?" Schaeffer says this like it's an offhand comment.

In the split second it takes me to consider a response, Mom has already replied.

"Went to see a friend. From her Hermiston days."

"You drove all the way out to Hermiston? What is that, an eight-hour drive?"

These are the kinds of questions you ask when you're trying to catch someone in a lie. I've asked similar questions myself.

"Not *to* Hermiston, nosy pants." Mom nudges him with one hip as she hands him a plate with an oversize piece of pound cake. "A girl she knew *from* Hermiston. Lives somewhere in Maryland now. Got into some trouble. Paula's a good friend. Let's leave it at that."

To his credit as a police officer, Schaeffer doesn't leave it.

"Seems like a whole lot of travel for a weekend."

"Maybe you should start parking at the end of her driveway. You know, just to make sure she's not up to anything suspicious. I could start writing letters to LPD again. It would be just like old times," Mom says.

Her words are like a bucket of cold water that extinguishes the twinkle of curiosity in Schaeffer's eyes. He shifts in his seat like he can't get comfortable.

"Two scoops or one?" Mom holds out a dish filled with her home-made strawberry preserves.

He ladles two scoops on his pound cake, then passes the preserves to me.

"No thanks," I say.

"You sure, Paula?" Mom asks. Her tone is sharp.

Schaeffer looks at me with surprise. "You don't like strawberry preserves?"

"Not in the mood." I avoid Mom's gaze.

Thankfully, the conversation shifts. Schaeffer talks about his grandkids and the sports they play and the new gourmet store that opened up on Main Street. He talks and talks and talks. Mom doesn't do one thing to hurry him along. As though Stella isn't crouched outside in that damp shed waiting for us to come back.

When he says yes to a second helping of pound cake, I wonder if I've given credit to the wrong instinct. Maybe he's just following the same scent that brought all the other boyfriends to our house.

Finally, he pushes back from the table. Pats his belly. "Guess I should be going. Early day tomorrow."

He looks around one last time, surveying the scene.

It's that last glance that makes me certain. He's not here as Mom's boyfriend. He's here as Detective Schaeffer.

Mom walks him to the door. I try not to imagine the kiss that fills the moment of silence before the door closes. It's not the intimacy that troubles me. It's the knowledge that Schaeffer is like a child playing with a loaded gun. It's only a matter of time before that gun goes off.

"I don't understand," I say when Mom comes back to the kitchen.

"What's that?"

"Why Schaeffer?"

It's not the first time I've asked that question. Usually she ignores it, but tonight she answers.

"As long as Schaeffer's around, I can't get lazy. It's good to have a challenge. It keeps you young. You should remember that, Paula."

"One mistake and he could put you in prison."

"I don't make mistakes."

I roll my eyes, and Mom steps closer.

"You think it's luck?" she asks. Her voice is fierce. "I took care of you and Julie. I'm still taking care of you. Trust me, it's not luck. It's how we survived. You think I don't know what people in this town said about me? The names they called me after Schaeffer left his wife? If you think there was even the slightest chance I'd let them define me, then you don't understand the first thing about me. It wasn't luck, Paula. It was strength."

For once, I refuse to let her silence me. "You *know* what's in Schaeffer's file, though. Why let him in so close?"

"*You* know what's in his file. *I* know what's on his mind."

"So what's on his mind right now?"

It's a question that hits too close to home for her liking. She grabs my chin. Holds my face so I can't look away.

"All you need to know is I've got a plan for Schaeffer. Same way I planned out everything else. And one other thing, Paula." Her fingers dig into my flesh. "If I offer you food, it's *always* safe to eat. I've killed for you. More than once. So you can rest assured I'd do anything to keep you alive."

She lets go of my chin, and a slow smile creeps across her face. "You keep scowling and your face is liable to freeze like that, sweetheart. Now go on. Get your sister."

I know she's telling the truth.

She *would* do anything to keep us alive. That's what scares me. Violence begets more violence. I've learned that firsthand in my years on the force.

There's nothing unique about Mom's background. Her father took out his temper on his family. Like most people, she drifted to what was familiar. Married a small-time drug dealer who got in deep with the local loan sharks. Her husband's slaps got harder and the bruises got bigger. In my years on the force, I've seen it more times than I can count.

What's unique is the part where Mom decided to fight back. Although she did more than just fight back. She waged a war.

The female species best known for murder is the black widow spider, but her murderous instincts are mostly a myth. In the insect world, the female praying mantis is the real murderer. After she mates, she devours the male. If she doesn't eat him, he'll eat her young. A bonus is that eating the male gives the female the fuel she needs to give birth and protect her young while she's still weak.

When I first read about the female praying mantis, I immediately thought of Mom.

She shouldn't have brought those men into our lives, but she did. It set us all on a collision course. If she didn't devour them, they would devour us. After they were gone, she collected what they left and saved it for us.

As I walk out to the shed to fetch Stella, worry twists inside my stomach. Mom's unpredictable in almost every way except one. Like she said, she's killed for us. Given the right set of circumstances, I'm certain she'd do it again.

PART SIX

Thirty-Seven

NIGHTTIME

JULIE

Alone, on the damp floor of the shed, Julie thinks about motherhood. She had so carefully crafted the depiction of the mother she was going to be, not realizing the value of what she was erasing.

Her mother also carefully crafted the mother she was going to be, one with sharp teeth and sharper wits.

The shed is cold, but Julie is sweating. She realizes Stella allowed herself to be declawed.

Out of habit, she reaches for her earlobe, her fingers twisting one of the diamond studs Tom gave her when she turned forty. She'd been overwhelmed by the gift until Tom bought himself a new BMW.

"I got a bonus," he told her when she asked about the cost.

"Where's my bonus?" she'd asked, with a flash of uncharacteristic anger.

"Guess you'd have to get a job if you want one of those," Tom said with a chuckle.

Stella let that comment slide, but Julie would have doubled down. And Julie is here now. The animal inside her has been uncaged. It's hungry and ready to hunt.

When Paula comes back, she feels alive in a way she forgot existed.

"Ready?" she asks.

Paula nods.

"What did he want?"

Paula makes a face. "He knew I was out of town. Hard to say what else he knows or suspects."

Julie remembers the low simmer of rage on Gwen's face. She wonders if Schaeffer is the heat source that keeps it warm.

"How many does he know about?" There is no need to explain what she's asking.

"Three," Paula says. "Dad, Kevin, and a guy named Brett Foster."

"Brett Foster." Julie lingers on each syllable. "He had it coming."

"True," says Paula.

"What's Mom's plan?" Julie asks. No need to explain this either.

Paula shrugs. When her eyes meet Julie's, there's understanding. They are complicit in their mother's story. Men who behave badly do not escape unscathed.

No, that last word makes it too soft. They don't escape. End of story.

As they walk back to the house, Julie realizes they've always used words to soften their mother's acts. Like wartime politicians discussing "collateral damage" on the ground. The people who cause that damage aren't murderers. They're heroes. Mom was fighting a different kind of war, but Julie has never been sure she was a hero.

"Girls, come on."

Together, they go over the plan. It's solid, well-crafted. No detail spared or overlooked. Julie notes that not once does their mother mention Schaeffer. She doesn't know how to interpret that omission. It's possible she doesn't want to know how to interpret it.

They load shovels on top of the IKEA bags in the back of the truck. Julie breathes in the chill night air of her childhood. As she looks up at the sky, the clouds part to reveal the moon and the constellations beyond.

"Lucky you got a clear night," Mom remarks as they climb into the truck. Then she hugs them both, long and hard.

"We've had nothing but rain this fall," Paula says as they bump along the gravel road that leads into the forest. "River is already flooding."

Julie nods, half listening. She looks up at the sky, then back down at the photograph of her mother's painting. Each star represents a number that corresponds to numbers carved into trees in the forest. One number leads to another, mimicking the shape of the constellation that used to be on the back wall of their barn. Their treasure lies under the prime numbers, marked with stones from the river.

They're headed toward the first star in the Big Dipper, Ursa Major. The first constellation their mother painted all those years ago. The bottom of Ursa Major is a star numbered 221. A prime number marking treasure. The tree that stands over the burial site is on the far northern corner of their property. Beyond that lies the river where Paula taught Julie how to balance over water running swift and deadly.

Paula switches the headlights off. "Just in case," she says.

They reach their destination and leave the truck. Paula shines her flashlight until they find the first tree. Its number is still carved clearly into its bark, as though someone (their mother) has maintained these carved mileposts throughout the years. Holding their shovels, they follow the path. When they reach the bottom of Ursa Major, they find three river rocks.

And then they dig. The only sound in the forest is that of their shovels. They move topsoil, then cut through heavy clay. They're both panting with effort by the time they hit treasure. It's signaled by the sound a shovel makes when it hits plastic.

Julie pulls a square plastic container out of the mud. It's heavier than she expected. Also, the container is familiar. In the moonlight, she recognizes its thick white base and faded green lid.

Tupperware.

"Go ahead. You open it," she says, handing it to Paula.

Paula peels off the lid and together, they peer inside. The gold, reflected in the moonlight, makes Julie gasp. She touches the bar. It feels alive in a way that makes her think of gold fever, a nonsense concept from the pages of a history book. Now, feeling the life strumming through her fingers, she understands. If there's more gold in these hills, she wants it.

"How much do you think it's worth?" she asks.

"More than she paid for it," Paula says with a smile.

Julie thinks of the way Tom substituted his judgment for hers, putting a small fortune at risk. Gold can't disappear like that. It's solid and real.

Accounts owned by only one person can't disappear like that either.

This gold represents a chance to reclaim both independence and dignity. She won't squander it. Her share of this gold will be buried again. In an offshore bank account with her name as the sole signatory, waiting for her children to need it. She's finally internalized the lessons of her own childhood.

Underneath the gold is a ziplock bag. The same kind their mother used to pack sandwiches in their childhood lunchboxes. Paula opens the bag and takes out a piece of paper folded in thirds. When she opens it, a faded photo falls out.

Julie picks up the photo while Paula trains her flashlight on the piece of paper and reads their mother's spidery cursive out loud.

Scott Turnbull. Aged thirty-two. His dad broke his arm three times before he was ten. He cried after he hit me. He knew it was wrong, but he couldn't stop himself. So I helped him out.

In the photo, their mother stands next to a man who looks familiar. Julie studies it, trying to remember. Was that Mom's boyfriend when Julie was in fifth grade or fourth? She glances at Paula to ask if she remembers Scott Turnbull and notices the color has drained from her sister's face.

"Paula, what's wrong?"

"Jesus," Paula whispers. "Why would she have written this? She's so careful about everything."

"She wants us to know what she survived."

Julie feels the truth of her words. The way they contain their own internal logic.

"It's evidence. Basically, a confession," Paula says, shaking her head.

"Well, true," Julie says, as though this is a minor point. "Do you think there are more?"

Paula's eyes widen. She puts one hand on her stomach like she's going to be sick. "If there are, we have to get rid of them. We can't let anyone find them."

Julie nods. She understands. The anyone, the only one, who would be digging for clues in these woods is Schaeffer.

"Let's keep moving," Paula says.

The second star on the map is marked by a similar pile of rocks. Another Tupperware with a ziplock bag and two gold bars. Another note that identifies the man in a faded photo and his preferred form of violence. Their mother is in this photo too. She smiles at the camera, unmistakable, unchanged.

"We can't keep these letters and photos," Paula says as they lug the two Tupperware containers back to the truck.

Julie knows Paula is right, but she already feels a pang of loss.

As they turn toward the third burial site, Julie notices lights in the distance and is startled to see a bridge that crosses the water.

"I don't remember that bridge."

"They built it about ten years ago. Put in a whole new road along the other side of the river. There's a housing development in the works too." Paula pauses, and a change comes over her face. "It's still there, you know."

Julie hears the rush of water below. "The logjam?"

"You remember?"

"Walk the Plank," Julie whispers.

Paula grabs her hand and squeezes.

The next star their mother painted leads them down the hill, closer to the water. Both of their shovels hit Tupperware at the same time. Two containers, buried next to each other in twin graves. Three gold bars in each container. Julie struggles with the weight of the container closest to her.

The ziplock in this container holds two yellowed newspaper clippings. The first one is a wedding announcement. Her parents, both of them younger than Julie or Paula are now. The second clipping is an obituary.

"This is the money she stole from the loan sharks," Paula whispers. "After Dad was gone. Do you remember? They took us up to the mountains?"

The memory has been buried, but now it emerges pristine. Julie is eight. She knows this because Dad has moved on. Paula is watching TV when Mom pulls her into the kitchen.

"There's a drawer in the barn," Mom says. "It's Dad's secret."

She nods. On her lips is a promise not to tell anyone, but her mother smiles. The real smile that shows the gap in her front teeth.

"It's part of our story, Julie. At first, you won't tell the secret. No matter what, not until I give you the signal. Then you'll know it's okay to tell it."

"What signal?" she asks.

"I'll say you and your sister are just little girls. Girls who don't know anything. People always believe that about girls."

Julie nods. She remembers the cigarette smoke. The way it makes her feel like she can't breathe. The relief of fresh air when she gets out of the car. The signal from her mother and the tears she lets fill her eyes as she tells her secret.

Buried memories and buried gold. Gwen was right about one thing. It *is* a strange feeling when things come full circle.

Paula hands the letter to Julie. "I can't read it."

With shaking hands, Julie opens it and reads her mother's words aloud.

Paul David Waits. Aged thirty-five. Married to Sharon Hughes on July 22, 1965. For a while, it was perfect. I loved him, but only one of us was going to survive our marriage. It had to be me. It's the only way I could protect both of you. I chose a story that would let you both write your own.

Paula is silent.

So is Julie.

It's the same message their mother has told them over and over throughout their lives.

It wasn't advice. It was a warning. Sharon Waits knew how much pressure the world would apply to them. She knew the cost of succumbing to that pressure and the violence of having your story stripped away.

This note is a reminder to take what they need.

Survive on their own terms.

Don't get lost in someone else's story.

Thirty-Eight

NIGHTTIME

PAULA

You ask me, Mom should have gone into the investing business. The value of gold had increased by a factor of ten since she started buying it in the early '80s. It was one thing when I thought it was just gold. I could tell myself there was no way of knowing where it came from. After we found those notes and pictures, it turned into something else altogether. The way I saw it, I had a choice. As an officer of the law, I could hand over Mom's confessions and go about my business with LPD, but that meant handing over the gold too.

My other choice was to destroy the trail of evidence Mom had left behind and become an accessory to murder.

There was a full-blown argument going on in my head. We were digging up blood money. We shouldn't profit from someone's death. But the more I shoveled, the more I realized I *couldn't* turn Mom in. Not because I wanted the gold, but because I didn't believe she should be punished. I've read about those sponges in the ocean that soak up toxins in the water. They eventually die from the poison, but during their lives, they make the water better for the other fish. That was Mom. She waited until those men showed their true nature, then soaked up their toxins. If she hadn't, they would have poisoned someone else.

It wasn't a question of if.

It was a question of when.

After I decided to destroy the evidence, I realized I'd need to find a new job. I couldn't stomach the idea of upholding laws that I'd broken for myself. Maybe I could become a private detective or something along those lines. One thing for sure, I wouldn't need to make much money. Mom had seen to that.

By the time we found Mom's confession about Dad, it was getting late.

"Should we split up?" Julie asked.

Neither of us wanted to talk about how many burial sites we'd dug up. Fewer than Ted Bundy's, but enough to put Mom on any list that tracks that sort of thing. There were two stars left, and we were both ready for this night to be over.

I nodded. "I'll take the one back up on the hill. You do the one closer to the river. Easier digging down by the water."

"Thanks," she said.

As she turned to go, I called her back. "Here," I said. "Take the other flashlight."

As I dug up the last site, my mind was on Mom and Schaeffer. A few years back, I'd asked her if she thought he'd ever move on.

"I suppose it's up to him," she said.

"No one chooses that kind of thing."

She laughed at that. "Oh, Paula, you'd be surprised how many people skip to the end to see how things turn out."

"You think they know what's at stake?" I asked.

"You think they'd believe me if I told them?" She grinned, the gap in her teeth on full display. "The problem isn't me. And it's not them either. Not exactly. It's bigger than all of us combined. They're doing what they know. It starts small and builds to something bigger. They're the storm, because that's what they learned to be. I'm the calm that comes after."

As I dug, I thought a lot about that calm.

After I hit Tupperware, I headed back to my truck to put the gold in the cab and wait for Julie. Everything was calm and quiet, like the storm had passed. I breathed the night air deep into my lungs. When I exhaled, I heard a noise.

I'd thought the storm was over, but we'd been in the eye.

The sound was a car engine too close to be coming from the bridge.

First thing I did was lock the truck. Manually, so as not to give myself away with a flash of headlights. Then I backed into the undergrowth and waited to see who was driving out here in the middle of the night.

Most likely it was teenagers looking for a quiet place to get high and have sex. Or maybe people cheating on their spouses, looking for the same. But the worst-case scenario was Schaeffer had doubled back after his visit with Mom and watched me and Julie drive into the woods.

The car that pulled up next to my truck was a white four-door. Nondescript, like a rental. I noted the plates, but then the driver stepped out and I forgot them altogether.

Gwen Thompson.

Ginny Schaeffer.

This was a worst-case scenario I hadn't considered. I was certain Mom hadn't planned for it either. Gwen shut her car door, careful to be quiet, and walked over to my truck. Jiggled the handles, then looked around the clearing like she was deciding what to do next.

"Hello," she called, cupping her hands around her mouth.

And my sister, despite being one of the smartest people I know, answered.

To be fair, Julie couldn't have known anyone else was out here. She was down by the river where the water would have covered up the sound of the car. Voices tend to sound the same when people yell. Mom had thought of everything, except for Schaeffer's younger daughter appearing in the woods without warning.

From where I was crouched in the underbrush, I could see the smile spread across Gwen's face.

That's when everything fell into place and I knew we were in trouble.

Like Megan said, Schaeffer and Gwen were always coming up with schemes. My guess was this one involved Schaeffer returning to Mom's house while Gwen tracked us down in the forest. Mom would think she was keeping Schaeffer busy, but instead, he was distracting her.

People on the force said Schaeffer was like a dog with a bone. Made sense he never really gave up on his theories about Mom. What hadn't occurred to me was that Schaeffer would rope his daughter into his theories. Or that she would be susceptible to being so easily pulled along.

"Paula?" Julie called again. "I'm almost done."

I watched as Gwen headed off in the direction of Julie's voice.

Schaeffer's a damn good cop. I'll give him that.

I started working the case like I was him. What I would have done after I left our house is watch from the road. The minute I saw us getting the truck ready, I would have known I was onto something. After the truck left, I would have signaled Gwen and gone back to Mom's house.

Stayed there long enough to make sure Gwen drove down the same gravel road without being spotted. After that, I'd have made an excuse to leave and staked myself out along that road.

Soon as I'd walked myself through it, I was pretty sure that's what he'd done.

Schaeffer knew better than to involve anyone on the police force with his plan. Instead, he'd sent his daughter to flush us out of the woods like a pair of startled birds. When we headed for home, he'd be waiting to make the kill.

This road used to be dirt and dead-end at the river. When they built the new bridge, work crews put in gravel and expanded the road so they could bring in materials. It runs all the way to the bridge now. Given that Gwen was on her way to confront Julie, who'd be digging up one of Mom's letters of confession and a Tupperware container filled with gold, heading for that bridge felt like our best shot at avoiding a night that ended with the three of us in handcuffs.

Gwen wasn't going to get cell service down by the river. Even if she spotted my truck and figured out where I was headed, she'd have to hoof it back to Schaeffer to tell him.

With any luck, Julie would see the truck going by. She'd remember the old road and put it together with what I'd told her about the new bridge. It was a little more than a mile, which meant she could catch up with me on foot. We could be long gone before Gwen got back to Schaeffer.

As soon as Gwen disappeared into the dark, I jumped in my truck. Cut down the road, toward the bridge. This time, I kept my lights on, hoping Julie would read the signal I was sending.

Then I parked my truck under the bridge to wait and worry.

Turned out, I was worrying about all the wrong things.

Thirty-Nine

NIGHTTIME

JULIE

Closer to the river, the ground *is* soft. Almost like it's been recently disturbed, but it's probably just the rain. When Julie pulls the last Tupperware out of the earth, it releases with a squelching sound. In the distance, she hears Paula.

"Almost done," she calls, then she removes the lid.

Gold. By now that's a given.

Also, another ziplock bag with a note.

The knowledge that her mother is as methodical about her burial rituals as she is about everything else makes Julie smile. Then she feels a pang of guilt. She shouldn't smile about this. It's death. Murder. Men stripped of life as though their only value is what they possess. It reminds her of the way she's been assigned value throughout her life. Then it reminds her of the way one man, in particular, assigned her value.

The man who believed his decisions about her body trumped her own.

She assigned him the same value he assigned her. The difference is her crime endures in a way that would still have consequences. The only place his crime endures is inside of her.

Julie unfolds the note.

It's addressed to her.

Somehow, this isn't a surprise. Process of elimination, or instinct? Hard to say. Doesn't matter. Even if she could say for sure, she's just a girl. Like her mother once said, people always underestimate the things girls know. Even the girls who know the things underestimate themselves.

She trains her flashlight on the paper and reads.

Julie, I'm sorry.

I was supposed to protect you. I thought I had everything under control, but it didn't work out the way I hoped. Kevin and I had a fight. He told me what he planned to do to you, then pushed me down the stairs. I don't remember much after that, but I do know he believed he had a right to take what he wanted. He didn't think we had a right to anything.

That's why I called and begged him to come get me from the hospital in the middle of the night. Do you remember when I came home and told you to go up to your room? I waited for him to pass out drunk. When I held a pillow over his face, he went real peaceful. Almost like he was grateful I'd put him out of his misery.

You ask me, he signed his own death warrant.

I know you were scared when I put you on that bus out of town, but I needed to know you were safe. You didn't do anything wrong that night. Matter of fact, you did everything right. You took your freedom and started a new life.

Some people say they'd die for their children, but I always figured it made more sense to stick around. That's not to say I wouldn't step in front of a train for you and your sister. It just means I was always able to avoid it.

No matter what anyone says about me, I was in the business of saving lives. Don't need to look farther than the lives you and Paula built to know that's true.

I love you.

Mom

A primal sound burrows out of Julie's chest.

In her hands, she holds absolution and apology mixed with a story. Permission to let go of the weight she's carried for so long, woven together with new elements.

The plastic bag that held the letter has weathered better than the others. It feels almost new. She looks at the letter again. Rereads the sentence about the train, and any doubt she had disappears.

"No," she cries, shaking her head as though denial can change what she already knows. This isn't just another story. It's the last story.

Her mother saw the oncoming train. The threat she needed to walk in front of in order to keep her children safe.

There's a noise in the underbrush.

"Paula," Julie sobs, wiping at her tears.

At first, her brain refuses to categorize the person who steps out of the shadows. It offers up a thousand alternatives. Fatigue, middle-aged eyesight, or a mistaken impression caused by the dark shadows of the forest.

The woman who steps out of the shadows wears her hair in two fat braids that make Julie think of Swatch watches and a ridiculously complicated dance routine. She's wearing expensive yoga pants and a baseball cap like she's headed to Barre. Blandly pretty, in the way that allows her to be truly invisible. It's how she slipped into Julie's life like a cancer undetected.

Ginny Schaeffer, metamorphosed into Gwen Thompson.

Ginny's eyes sweep over Julie. Take in the dirt-crusted Tupperware container and the hole at her feet. A familiar look passes over Ginny's face. Julie remembers it from eighth grade. Triumph mixed with contempt, as though Ginny has caught Julie in an act that will make her the butt of a joke told to the entire class.

"Long night?" Gwen asks.

"What are you doing here?"

"Visiting family. You?"

The conversation is oddly familiar. It's one they could have already had at a PTO meeting, at the summer pool club, while passing each other in the grocery store, or at a school fundraiser. The pull of social conventions are unbreakable, even in the nighttime forest of their childhood as they stand over a hole that contained both a confession to a murder and buried treasure.

"Whatcha got there?" Gwen asks. "Looks like some kind of evidence."

Her tone is condescending, as though she's still the most popular girl in middle school.

Julie clutches the Tupperware tight to her chest, but it's not the gold she's protecting.

It's the letter.

Gwen pulls something out of her pocket, and Julie flinches.

Instead of a gun, Gwen holds up her phone. Same pink glitter case that Julie turned over in her own hands. She buried that phone in the middle of the night. Now she imagines Gwen tracking her through the empty streets of McLean to her hiding spot under the bridge. She imagines the contemptuous expression on Gwen's face as she dug it up.

Loser.

She can almost hear Gwen say it in her head.

"My name is Gwen Thompson," Gwen says as she touches her phone. "It's November second and I'm with the suspect's daughter, Stella Parker."

"Gwen," Julie says softly, "what are you doing?"

"What the fuck do you *think* I'm doing?" Gwen moves closer. "You know what your mother did."

Julie swallows uncomfortably. It's unclear whether Gwen is talking about her father's fall from grace or all the men Mom killed.

"You helped her. You could have done the right thing and told the truth, but you didn't."

"What do you mean?" Julie asks.

"Everything's always worked out for you, hasn't it? You got away with all your lies. Perfect life with your perfect children. No one realizes you're a fake, but I do. You don't deserve any of it. I know all about your mother and how you helped her. She's a murderer, and she destroyed my father's career. Because of her, he became a punch line. Everything bad that happened to our family traces back to the two of you. Full circle. People should know the truth."

All this time, Stella thought she was invisible, but the fury in Gwen's gaze makes it clear she was seen. Gwen sees Stella's success as an affront to her own failures. What Gwen will never understand is that in a different version of the story, they could have been friends.

"Come on, Stella. Or should I say Julie?" Gwen taunts. "You could have come back, but I guess you were afraid to return to the scene of the crime, right?"

"I don't know what you're talking about," Julie says.

This is another lie, but she's buying time. Mind churning through the possibilities for escape.

"My dad taught your sister everything she knows. Then he watched her. He knew she'd be the key to finding you. No one believed his theory about your mom, but I did. I remembered the way you snuck around and lied about cheer tryouts in middle school. You're still lying. Sneaking around McLean in the middle of the night and pretending to be someone else. You're just like your mother. My dad thinks you ran away so you could avoid telling the truth about a guy named Kevin Mulroney. Ring any bells, Julie?"

It does ring a bell.

A Juliebell, to be exact.

A small sound emerges from her throat. That name calls up a version of herself that survived at all costs.

Behind Gwen, up on the road, she catches a glimpse of light. Brake lights; there, then gone. A split second. She looks down so Gwen won't follow her gaze.

Paula's leaving her behind?

That doesn't make sense. No, of course; Paula's headed toward the river. The old road that leads to the new bridge. Paula's plan is clear.

But to get to Paula, she has to escape Gwen.

Julie pulls herself together. The best defense is a good offense.

"You're crazy. Your father stalked my mother, and you stalked me. It's like you want to *be* me or something." It's the kind of taunt Ginny would have used in middle school, which is, perhaps, what makes it effective.

Gwen narrows her eyes and grabs for her arm. Julie twists away, gripping the Tupperware tight. The ancient lid cracks, splinters spreading across its top.

Gwen lunges. Hard fingers fasten around Julie's wrist. Gwen's grip is surprisingly strong.

"Okay, fine," Julie says.

She turns and offers the Tupperware and letter to Gwen. Gwen relinquishes Julie's wrist with gleaming eyes. The moment her fingers loosen, Julie turns and runs.

Oldest trick in the book.

Gwen might be stronger, but Julie hopes she's faster.

To be fair, neither of them is particularly fast. Julie runs through once familiar terrain, at her middle-age sprint. Gwen is right behind her. If Julie were younger, she'd be focused exclusively on speed. Now she's more cautious. She can't risk spraining an ankle, tearing a ligament in her knee, falling in a way that results in a severe muscle bruise while clutching the piece of exculpatory evidence that will ensure her life doesn't shatter into a thousand pieces.

The sound of Gwen's footsteps fades as Julie emerges from the underbrush onto the old path along the river. There's a split second of triumph over winning the race, but it immediately fades.

Instead of chasing her, Gwen veered around her through the underbrush. Panting, hands on hips like she's in charge, she stands between Julie and the bridge.

"What are you gonna do now? Swim the river?"

The words sound like a dare. Julie glances at the water. It's swift and dark, a smooth ribbon broken only by the logjam.

A dare is a dare.

If you don't take it, there's only one option.

You walk the plank.

Julie turns, container and letter clutched to her chest. Her foot feels for the first log. She puts her weight on it, tests its density. The first log is always the easiest because you can still turn back. The hardest part is in the middle. There, the water has softened some of the logs. Covered them with a thick coat of slippery moss.

"Julie, wait!"

Gwen's voice is high and plaintive over the rumble of the water, but Julie ignores her. The tricks of the game come back to her. Feet inch along the logs. Eyes focused on the opposite bank. Hold your weight in your stomach.

She feels for the second log with one foot. Tests it, then shifts her balance. One foot in front of the other. A slow slide. Her middle-aged stomach tense. She breathes deep, filling her lungs with air that tastes of childhood.

Carefully, she slides over the slick moss.

The water rushes below, dark and cold. It offers no second chances.

"Julie, come back," Gwen calls. "Don't be stupid."

Gwen's voice is the voice of someone whose plans have taken an unexpected turn.

Three more steps. Julie transfers her weight to another log. Another step.

Her foot slips on moss, and she has to catch herself. Regain her balance. She was rushing. She forces herself to stop. Finds her focal point on the opposite bank. Girds her center and pulls her shoulders back. Charts a new route. One step at a time. Exactly the way Paula taught her.

Then the logjam does something unexpected.

It shakes with additional weight.

Julie turns her head, even though she knows better.

Darkness swirls. The water below is an icy threat. One wrong step and it will drag her down. She feels its call, pulling her off balance. Swiftly, she lowers to a crouch. One hand on the log, the other still clutching the Tupperware and her mother's letter.

Gwen is two logs back.

Julie considers her options. She can tell Gwen to go back, but it's unlikely she'll listen to her. Besides, once you've passed the first log, it's more dangerous to turn around. The logjam is trembling, communicating the shake in Gwen's legs.

"Julie," she calls. The anger in her voice has drained away. All that's left is fear.

Ginny's balance was never that good. Slowly, Julie stands up out of her crouch.

"It's okay," she says. "You can do it. Don't look at me. Chin up. Eyes on the bank. Hold your balance in your stomach. It'll be okay."

Gwen nods, but the tremors in her body shake the entire logjam.

"One step at a time," Julie calls, swallowing her own fear.

Gwen takes a shaky step, edging out over the swiftest part of the river.

"That's right. You've got this." Her words are filled with encouragement like those of Daisy's field hockey coaches.

Gwen takes another step.

She's getting closer.

"Feel for the next log with your foot," Julie calls. "Watch out for the moss."

Gwen takes two more shaky steps. Their eyes lock. They're in the middle of the logjam. Twenty feet separate them from both banks of the river. Childhood knowledge returns to Julie. This is the most treacherous part. If she can save Gwen, maybe this will all be over. Gwen will let it go.

Gwen inches closer, suddenly moving fast.

Julie reaches out, offering her hand. "Careful. Go slow."

Gwen reaches too, but it's not Julie's hand she's reaching for. It's what she's holding.

"No. Don't," Julie whispers as the heavy Tupperware with her mother's letter is pulled from her hands. The loss throws her off balance. She teeters on the middle of the logjam. For a split second, she thinks she might fall. Then she pulls her chin up, shoulders back.

Gwen shifts away from her, turning on the log. Headed back to the bank they left behind, with evidence that will prove Sharon is a murderer and Julie kept her secret.

But that's Gwen's mistake.

In the middle of the river, moss grows thick on the logs. When you walk the plank, you have to slide your feet and move slowly. Instead of shuffling, Gwen takes three rapid steps.

Her foot slips. Gwen looks down, her fingers grabbing at air.

For a moment, time slows. In the moonlight, everything is clear. Julie takes one careful step toward Gwen, but she can't close the distance between them. The look on Gwen's face isn't terror, it's disbelief. The ancient Tupperware hits the water and sinks, but the letter is buoyed up by the breeze.

"Julie!" Gwen screams as she falls.

Julie reaches out, but she's too far away. The only thing she catches is the letter.

For a moment, she considers diving in after Gwen, but she knows that would be suicide. The night goes quiet. Deadly still. The only sound is that of rushing water.

Julie tucks the letter into the waistband of her pants. Then, carefully sliding her feet along the log, she turns back toward the opposite bank.

She walks the plank.

One foot in front of the other. She holds her balance in her stomach the way Paula taught her. As long as she's moving, she's not thinking about what happened.

Not the splash Gwen's body made when she hit the icy water.

Not the sound of Gwen's voice calling her name.

And definitely not the way Gwen struggled for her last breath as the treacherous current swept her under and down.

Forty

FALL INTO SPRING

PAULA

The first thing I felt when I spotted Julie walking across the bridge was relief. The second thing I felt was worry. She was coming from the opposite side of the river. From upstream, there's only one way to get across that river.

She walked the plank.

My stomach started churning, even though the danger already passed. It was pure foolishness to cross that logjam in the dark. As kids, we fooled ourselves into thinking we could outswim the current, but if you fall into that river, there's zero chance of survival.

She got into the truck, and a heavy silence followed her.

"You okay? Where's Gwen?"

"Let's go, Paula," she said without looking at me.

"Where's Gwen?" I asked again.

"Gwen's gone," she said.

Then she pulled a piece of paper out of the waistband of her pants. Folded in thirds like all the others. I thought I knew what it was when she handed it to me, but like all of Mom's stories, I was one step behind.

The letter brought me up to speed in a hurry. Those notes Mom buried weren't meant to be confessions. They were her way of saying goodbye. When I was done reading, I looked over at Julie. She was still staring out the window.

"What do we do now?"

Julie started talking real quiet.

"She didn't tell us everything. If we'd known, we wouldn't have left her. She needed us to play our part. She's protecting us, Paula. Schaeffer must have given her a hint about what he knows. It must have been enough for her to step in front of the train."

Tears were running down my cheeks, but I didn't bother to wipe them away.

"I understand," she continued in that same low voice. "I'd do the same for my children. Anything at all, if I thought it would keep them safe."

"Maybe we got it wrong. Maybe she's fine."

Julie's eyes went hard in a way that reminded me of Mom. "This is the end she chose. We have to do her proud, Paula."

We followed the script Mom wrote, best we could. Drove straight to my house where I'd left my cell phone. No one had called yet, but I knew that wouldn't last.

In the garage, we moved the gold into the old car I had before I saved enough money to buy my truck. We filled both bags Mom gave us with hens of the woods mushrooms, their edges like ruffled feathers. Undersides pale and meaty, like my face when I caught a glimpse of it in the rearview mirror. I put those bags in the truck's cab.

I tossed all the letters and photographs, save one, into the stove and threw in a match. As we watched them burn, my phone started buzzing. It was Schaeffer.

"Paula, where are you?" Schaeffer sounded like he'd been punched in the gut.

"At home. What's wrong?"

"I need you to get out to your mom's house. Soon as you can." Schaeffer's words were thick in a way that told me what to expect.

I told him I was on my way and ended the call.

"They've got to find her letter." Julie's eyes were glassy like she'd eaten some of Mom's poisonous peaches. "That's what she wanted. We owe it to her to get it right."

I hugged her real tight before I left. Then I got into my truck, circled the block, and pulled over to make sure no one was following me. After I was certain, I called my house phone and gave Julie the all clear.

The rest of Julie's part is something I have to imagine.

She waits in my house for the call, then backs my car out of the garage. She drives through town, careful to go the speed limit. On I-5 she heads north, passing through Portland and driving until she gets to Seattle. Once she's there, she punches the code into the front door of the Vrbo Mom booked while we were on our flight back to Oregon.

It's a place with a garage. A place Julie can be assured the contents of her car will be safe.

The next day, Julie keeps the appointments Mom scheduled with four different people in the business of buying gold.

I picture her telling them a story about divorce. "It's been . . ." She would have paused long enough to let the person sitting across from her draw their own conclusions. "Let's just say it hasn't been easy." Her smile would be brave as she blinked back the moisture in her eyes. "I'm ready to start a new chapter. This time around, I'm going to make sure I'm protected."

She has a copy of the divorce decree if they want to see it. The man across from her—in my imagination, it's always a man—nods and barely glances at the paperwork she pulls out of her fancy purse. He doesn't bother to dig too deep, because there's no reason not to believe her. The look on her face will say she survived something difficult and came out stronger. He'll classify her as a fighter, but the sweet kind.

He'll definitely want to help her by setting her up with what she needs. Something safe that won't allow her ex-husband to track the money. It's why the account in the Cayman Islands makes sense.

Two accounts, actually.

That part I don't need to imagine because I have the account she set up for me. We split what we found that night. Even steven.

As for my part of the story, I don't have to picture it, because I lived it.

By the time I got out to the farm, it was lit up like a church on Christmas. Police cars flashing their lights in the driveway. Every light in Mom's house blazing bright.

They didn't want to let me inside, but seeing as how I was on the force, they didn't have much of a choice. I went in through the back door that leads into the kitchen. It was empty. Dishes still in the sink and the pound cake Schaeffer brought us from Dunlap's on the counter. I slipped Mom's letter under the pound-cake plate and headed into the living room.

There was blood everywhere. She'd used a gun. Soon as the responding officers spotted me, they tried to get me out of that room, but I shook them off. Took a step closer so I could see her face. Most people who kill themselves with a gun aim for the head. She shot herself through the heart. Even in death, she had to do things different.

That was my last thought before I vomited all over that crime scene.

THE NEXT THING I REMEMBER is sitting outside on the grass. Someone covered me with a foil blanket and said I was in shock. I sat there shivering and telling myself I should have known from the moment I read that first note. I knew it wasn't like her to confess when she was so careful about every last detail. Another voice in my head, one that sounded a lot like Julie's, told me it wasn't my fault. Mom was an expert at contingency plans and making sure everyone played their roles.

When Schaeffer found me, he sat down next to me on the grass.

"I loved that woman," he whispered under his breath. "I know what she did. She ruined my life, but God help me, I still loved her."

I stared at the house I'd grown up in and wondered how long it would take Schaeffer to blow up our lives.

The minute Schaeffer got wind of Mom's letter, he was on his feet. He read it over the responding officer's shoulder.

"That's not what happened!" he screamed, grabbing it out of the officer's hand. "Read my goddamn report on Sharon Waits. Read the autopsy. Kevin Mulroney wasn't suffocated. Don't any of you morons know how to read?"

It was a strange sensation to watch someone else be caught in Mom's web. Spit bubbled up at the corners of Schaeffer's mouth. It took two officers to get that letter back. Two more to calm him down. I caught the moment their eyes started to avoid him. Something was starting to shift.

That something was set in stone the moment they found Gwen's body.

"Paula was out there in the woods!" Schaeffer screamed, stabbing at me with one finger. "She killed my Ginny. She's a murderer. Same as her mother."

He looked deranged, and I wasn't the only one who thought that. The officers who'd been trying to calm him down switched to containment mode. Same way they'd treat one of the homeless junkies raising a ruckus behind the bus station.

I had to discredit his accusations, and Mom had given me the tools to do it.

"He's right. I was out in the woods," I said to the officers charged with containing Schaeffer. "Take a look in the truck. I'll show you what I was doing." The words came out of my mouth real natural, the way I'd practiced with Mom.

When I held out the bags of mushrooms, Schaeffer grabbed one away from me the way a drowning man grabs at a life preserver.

"Hens of the woods," I told the other officers.

My voice was flat like there was nothing left inside me, which is how I felt. Like Mom said, the best stories always have an element of truth.

"My mom wanted to cook up a surprise for him." I gestured at Schaeffer with my head. "You got to hunt them at night. Flashlight catches the flesh different. I didn't think it was safe for a woman in her seventies to go stumbling around in the woods after dark."

My voice broke on that last sentence and the tears started up again.

"Liar." Schaeffer's face twisted into something ugly and unrecognizable. "Can't you see she's lying?"

For a moment, I felt for Schaeffer, I really did. Then I remembered my conversation with Mom. How I'd claimed no one chooses to move on and she said I'd be surprised.

As they pulled Schaeffer away, all I could think about was how his harsh grip would destroy those mushrooms. Same way he'd destroyed his family, his daughter, and whatever form of happiness he'd found with my mother. In the pursuit of good, he'd done an awful lot of harm.

And for what, a perfect record with a small-town police department?

Mom was right about something else. Even if she'd tried to warn him, told him what was at stake, he never would have believed her.

One of my friends on the force drove me home. I sat up all night thinking. Right about sunrise, I realized it was time for me to move on too. Not in the way Mom used those words, but in the way most folks do.

I needed a fresh start.

The next day there were questions from the LPD. Somehow, that investigation never did get much steam. No one had the stomach to reopen a case from two decades ago. Especially not after a troubling double suicide.

That was the theory behind Mom and Gwen's deaths. A double suicide.

It was no secret that Schaeffer's girls didn't like Mom.

I was surprised Schaeffer didn't challenge that theory. I didn't figure out why until a few days after Mom was gone. I got a letter from her, mailed the day she died. In it, she explained how Gwen had passed along compromising information about Tom that Schaeffer had been using to pressure her.

Finally, I could see the whole story.

Based on where the LPD found Gwen's car and the lack of any evidence, DNA or otherwise, on her body, the prevailing theory was that Gwen had confronted my mother. Blamed her for breaking up Schaeffer's marriage. Guilt over that accusation caused Mom to shoot herself. The stress of witnessing that incident made Gwen stumble away and drown herself in the river.

Ridiculous story, but then again, not many people have my mother's gift.

WHEN I TENDERED MY RESIGNATION to the LPD, I said there were too many ghosts in Livingston. I needed a clean slate. People seemed to understand.

I moved to Sacramento and bought a little house that doubles as my office. These days, my only title is private detective. I don't have many clients, but I've got an account in the Cayman Islands that means I don't need to do a lot of business. Leaves me plenty of time to think.

My thoughts often return to my time at LPD. What made Schaeffer fixate on my mother and the events surrounding Kevin Mulroney's death?

Was it the case itself, or was it that his prime suspect was a woman?

It doesn't escape me that Schaeffer's quest to unravel the mystery resulted in the death of two more women.

I heard through the grapevine that Schaeffer was asked to leave the force. That bit of news made me smile and think of Mom. If she'd moved him on, it would have played into his narrative. Instead, she went for the twist. Took her own life to save ours and destroy his.

Like she always said, everything she did was for us girls.

Forty-One

FALL INTO SPRING

STELLA

Stella goes home. She is not the kind of mother who abandons her young.

Her children treat her absence like a quirk. Or a midlife crisis.

"I needed to see the place where I grew up," she told them upon returning.

"But why did you leave your phone?" Daisy asked, as though that, not Stella's disappearing act, was the piece of the plot she couldn't buy.

Stella shrugged. "We didn't have phones when I was growing up. I guess I wanted to experience it the same way. Without distractions."

"The eighties were such a vibe," Colin said wistfully. "Can you imagine? No one tracking you? It must have been, like, total freedom."

"I guess," Stella said with a laugh.

That was that. Her brief disappearance forgotten, as though it never happened. Her children's curiosity about her is limited. Stella thinks about the ocean of things she will never know about her mother and doesn't judge them. Colin and Daisy have their own lives to lead, which is the goal of parenting.

Eventually, everyone flies on their own.

Tom, on the other hand, has not forgotten.

Upon Stella's return to their too-big house, Tom was disheveled. Unshaven and dressed in clothes that looked like he'd picked them up off the floor. When he saw her, tears filled his eyes.

That caught her by surprise.

"I didn't think you were coming back," he said.

"Because of Gwen?"

At the sound of Gwen's name, Tom winced. Then he launched into a story of his own. The only problem is, Stella's not convinced it's the truth. To believe it is to believe in a series of coincidences and to ignore what she saw.

According to Tom, he had a relationship with Gwen Thompson, but not a clandestine affair. It was always about money.

"Blackmail," he said.

Gwen had proof that Stella's name, birth date, and background were all forged.

"She called you a liar," Tom said, and his eyes begged Stella to dismiss that claim.

"And you believed her?"

He shook his head, then lowered his forehead to his hands. Gwen had proof. Documents and a police file about a missing girl named Julie Waits. A photo that looked vaguely like Stella. He looked up at her with tears in his eyes. "I didn't care about any of it, but there was more. Gwen had a whole dossier. We filed taxes and applied for a mortgage using your name and social security number. You can't use a fake name for financial transactions. It's a felony. We both could have gone to prison for years. I could have been disbarred."

They were in the sitting area of their bedroom. The one Stella had carefully decorated for their private moments. When Tom's pronouns turned from "we" to "I," Stella stood quickly and walked to the window overlooking the backyard.

"So you made the decision to pay her without talking to me."

"I did my own research." His voice was cold. "Gwen was right. I'm not blaming you, but those are the facts. I paid her once, out of some money I'd set aside to surprise you and the kids with a vacation. I thought she'd go away, but she didn't."

Stella kept her back to Tom so he wouldn't see the anger spreading from her eyes to her outer extremities, numbing her fingers and toes.

"Gwen came to the house. She claimed you helped your mother get away with murder. She said your mother killed your father and all these other men. I told her your mother is dead, but she wouldn't listen. She said I don't know you at all. I was going to give her some cash, just so she'd go away, but when I started up the stairs, she followed me. She was screaming, calling you trash and saying you deserved to rot in prison.

She was crazy. Dangerous. I needed her out of our house." Tom shook his head like the memory pained him. "I asked her to leave, but she said she was going to ruin our lives."

A chill of foreboding passed through Stella. She turned away from the window. "What did you do?" she asked, her voice barely a whisper.

Tom's voice turned pitiful. "She was threatening our family. I grabbed her. Not to hurt her, just to try to calm her down."

Stella moved closer. Sat back down across from Tom so she could study his body language.

"She was so loud. I needed her to stop screaming, you know? I shook her by the shoulders, just a little, but she started fighting me. She twisted away and fell down the stairs." Tom's face crumpled into tears. "I was protecting our family. You understand, right?"

"Did Gwen fall, or did you push her?"

Tom's face grew sullen. "It was an accident."

Thoughts of another staircase accident made Stella's jaw tighten, but Tom wasn't done.

"Things got worse after that. She said it was assault and threatened to involve the police. I couldn't risk it. My career, everything was at stake."

His eyes were wet and pleading as he explained his search for a risky investment. Something she wouldn't be able to question when it didn't pan out. After that, he drafted a fake contract, along with the rest of the documents in the file he brought home for Stella to read. Gwen's silence was bought by draining Colin and Daisy's college savings accounts.

Stella was silent as she considered Tom's version of events. Then she asked him to move into the guest bedroom.

The same week Stella returned from Oregon, Paula called to tell her Schaeffer knew about the money Gwen received from Tom.

"It's in a trust set up for Gwen's kids. Schaeffer's named as trustee. He won't want anyone digging too deep into how it was funded," Paula said.

It could be classified as hush money or money paid as a reparation for Tom's violence, Stella told herself. No different than the money tucked away in her Cayman Islands account.

That winter, Stella retreats to her secret room with more frequency. That's where she was when Colin called to tell her about his first college acceptance. She jumped up from her ancient desk, but moved too fast. One thigh bumped the desk, and Stella heard a thunk. The sound of something hitting the floor.

After she ended the call, she dropped to her hands and knees. Underneath the desk, she spied a familiar shape. The knife with stars carved into its handle. No one had been in her secret room. Instead, she must have accidentally pushed the knife off the desktop, causing it to become wedged between the back of the desk and the wall.

She fished it out, put it in her pocket, and went for a walk on a trail along the Potomac River. At a quiet spot where she knew she wouldn't be observed, she tossed the knife into the water and returned home feeling lighter.

Cleansed.

That night at family dinner they raised their glasses to toast Colin's future. He was uncharacteristically chatty, reminding Stella of the little boy he'd once been.

"Solid day. I'm going to college, and I got an A on my AP English essay," he said with a grin.

"You were always going to college," Stella said, but her eyes avoided Tom's.

He shrugged. "Still, it feels good to be sure."

"I want to hear about this essay you wrote," Tom said.

Colin nodded and described his study of conflict and character in *A Streetcar Named Desire*.

"My thesis was that Tennessee Williams was calling out societal misogyny by physically embodying it in Stanley. You see it in the way he manipulates Blanche and Stella. Stanley claims he's protecting them, but he's the one who benefits most from his actions."

It wasn't so strange that her teenage son should encounter this particular play. All these years later, it's still standard high school curriculum. And of course there was the echo of her name that must have registered with him. Even so, the moment felt too randomly perfect to be anything other than a message from the universe.

"Don't worry, Stella," the universe seemed to be saying. "Colin isn't Tom. No more than you are your mother. We all evolve."

The rest of the winter, she thought about Tom's tale of woe.

Like any good writer, he based some of it on the truth. His secret rendezvous with Gwen, understandably mistaken for an affair by her friends. His panic over Gwen's threats, felony charges, and a threatened police report.

In Tom's words, he *took care of it*.

What he doesn't understand is that his taking care of it denied her the opportunity to be his equal. He silenced her, then demanded her gratitude. He didn't hit her, but that doesn't mean it wasn't an attack.

The rest of Tom's violence fits the standard definition, although she'll never know what actually happened on the staircase of her too-big house.

The only other person who can answer that question is gone.

In Gwen's absence, Stella is left with remembered glimpses of what she saw. Marks on Gwen's face. Her hunched-over gait as she hobbled to the car. Not a twisted-ankle sort of walk, but a punch-to-the-ribs kind of walk. It's not the kind of nuance most people would catch, but Stella's childhood gave her a unique expertise in the variations of violence a man can enact upon a woman's body. The problem is, memory is notoriously unreliable. If only she'd had the nanny cam trained on the staircase instead of uselessly recording the emptiness of her secret room.

What does that mean for Stella?

She's parsed her options.

Divorce is an obvious one, but like all the other girlhood promises of equality, this too is hollow. Yes, she'd get half, but it's a misogynistic half.

Half of a too-big house and a too-small savings account. A half that assigns limited value to the career she gave up and the work she's done since the children were born. The value she added to their lives would be as invisible in divorce as it was throughout their marriage. The more she thinks about it, the less willing she is to accept this appraisal of her worth.

More important, she's uncomfortable sending Tom out into the world. Unleashing him upon unsuspecting women, until she better understands what happened. How far would Tom go to protect his place in the world? Did he push Gwen, or did she fall?

Details are important.

She is, after all, her mother's daughter.

ON A RAINY FRIDAY IN April, Stella is in the basement boxing up her family's unwanted items. She pulls an outgrown jacket from the bag and freezes at the sight of Daisy's Lilly Pulitzer bag lying underneath.

The bag is a reminder of the Thompsons, who moved shortly after Gwen's demise. Slowly, Stella unzips the purse. Inside, she finds a receipt from Chipotle and Daisy's middle school ID. She removes them both. Then, on a hunch, she unzips the interior pocket of the bag.

Tucked inside is a faded photo.

Cheerleaders in a pyramid.

Ginny Schaeffer is balanced at the top, her arms stretched out in a V for victory. A depiction of the way Ginny believed both their lives would play out. She was supposed to be the star. Julie was never supposed to be in the picture.

Stella studies the photo for a long time. Then she replaces it in the zipper compartment, puts the bag in one of the Goodwill boxes, and loads them into the back of her SUV. As she drives to Goodwill, she imagines long conversations between Schaeffer and his daughter. The story he told Ginny would have been about the natural order. The way things are supposed to be. A morality tale where royalty regains the throne. Monsters are not rewarded with a spot on varsity cheer, a picture-perfect life in McLean, or a quiet retirement on their rural farm. Instead, they are brought to swift and certain justice.

"Thank you so much," Stella says to the man at Goodwill who rushes out to help her unload her family's unwanted items.

He smiles. "My pleasure. And thank you."

Stella catches a glimpse of herself in the shop window. The resemblance to her mother catches her off guard. She squelches the urge to check behind her, as though her mother is lurking from beyond the grave.

As she navigates the car toward home, Stella thinks about her mother's version of happily ever after. A unique spin on an old trope, but wasn't the plan for Stella to do it better? Create a life her sister and mother couldn't even imagine?

She considers this, then at the next stoplight, she texts Lorraine. Happy hour? My house?

Lorraine responds immediately. 👍 🥂

In Stella's kitchen, Lorraine perches on a blue velvet barstool while Stella pulls the baked Brie she picked up at Trader Joe's out of the oven. The wine has already been poured.

"New dishes?" Lorraine asks, nodding at the Sur La Table bags on Stella's kitchen desk.

"New hobby," Stella says, handing Lorraine a glass of wine. "I'm going to teach myself to can. You should do it with me!"

"Absolutely not." Lorraine rolls her eyes. "I'm too old to become some Brooklyn hipster. And I'm just going to warn you right now: If you buy an Airstream, we can no longer be friends."

Stella laughs. "No Airstream, I promise."

They toast to Stella's lack of Airstream and nibble at the Brie. Their conversation is benign, but pleasant. Outside, rain pelts Stella's backyard. School is out for the day, but they are both uncharacteristically free. Their combined pack of children have gone to other people's homes.

Perhaps this is why Lorraine allows herself to have a third glass of wine.

Stella opens a second bottle. When she turns back, she catches a look on Lorraine's face. Guilt mixed with something else.

Anger.

"I need to tell you something," Lorraine says.

"What is it?" Stella sits down, refills her glass too.

"I should have told you earlier, but after everything that happened, I couldn't." Lorraine's eyes are liquid with tears.

"About Gwen?" Stella asks.

Lorraine nods. "I think about Dave and those kids all the time, you know?"

"Me too," Stella says, which is true.

"I saw her with Tom at a coffee shop. The way they were looking at each other. It was so intense, there was no doubt what was going on. I should have stayed out of it. Minded my own business, but it unleashed something inside me." Lorraine looks down and chews on her bottom lip. "I never told you this, but Paul had an affair about five years ago. I mean obviously, it's not the kind of thing I wanted anyone to know. I thought about leaving. If it weren't for the kids, I would have. We did couple's therapy. I thought things were good, but then I caught him again."

When Lorraine looks back up, her eyes are like daggers. "He's the one who wanted four fucking kids. It's not that I don't love them. It's that I gave up everything to stay home. And now . . ." She shrugs and looks out at the rain pouring down on the patio outside.

Stella nods. She completely understands.

"When I saw Tom with Gwen, I kind of went crazy. I bought a burner phone. Started sending them threatening messages. Stuff like 'I saw you.' It was ridiculous, but somehow, it made me feel better. Like I was reclaiming some small piece of my dignity. Then she died. At first, I panicked because I thought I'd be a suspect. Then I was like, 'Phew, she drowned.' Then, obviously, I felt like a total asshole."

As Lorraine speaks, Stella is recategorizing everything she thought she knew about her friend. All this time, she's been selling Lorraine short.

How many of the other mothers of suburbia has Stella reduced to fancy blonde highlights and fancier SUVs? She's been complicit in trivializing these women. Former lawyers, doctors, investment bankers, professors, accountants, advertising and marketing executives who bought into the false promise of equality only to end up in the ghetto of motherhood.

It's a realization that shakes her.

"You didn't think I had it in me, did you?" Lorraine says.

Stella shrugs, then she grins. "I suppose we all have our secrets. As Dais and Ains would say, this one confirms our ride or die status."

"Ride or die," Lorraine says, clinking her glass against Stella's.

Later, when Lorraine is gone and Stella is alone, she thinks about secrets and stories. She's an expert in both. Secrets that simmer to the surface and stories that develop over time through the smallest of details.

She's been working on reclaiming her story ever since she heard Tom's. Like her mother's painting on the back of the barn, it's a work in progress that could go in a number of ways.

It's impossible to anticipate what Tom might reveal through a careless word or gesture.

In the meantime, Stella is okay with waiting.

Watching.

Preparing multiple options.

Whatever truth is eventually revealed, Stella is no amateur. Unlike Gwen, she understands that no one is owed a happy ending. It takes work and planning. Which is why when the time comes, she'll have a perfectly crafted story of her own.

Acknowledgments

This book starts with a dedication to my father, David Copeland. What the dedication doesn't describe is how he read to me every night of my childhood for hours on end. He was a teacher, a reader, and an incredible man who inspired generations of students. He passed away in 2013, but I know he would have been so excited and proud of his daughter and the book she wrote.

Books are written alone in a room, but writers thrive with tremendous support from a vast group of people. My people include all of the following:

Christopher Schelling, my wonderful agent, who plucked me out of his slush pile. Your guidance is invaluable and your quips always (no really, always!) make me smile. Also, thank you for knowing that even when I tell you it's going to be a quick call, that actually means an hour, and for reading and re-reading and re-re-reading this book. I feel so lucky to be your client and friend!

Sarah Stein, my razor-sharp editor. From our first phone call, I could tell your vision for this book aligned perfectly with mine. Your ideas have made the book stronger, tighter, and better in every way. Also, you have an amazing eye for a handbag, so it was kind of a foregone conclusion that we'd become friends.

The entire team at HarperCollins has been the best, including David Howe, who always comes through when I email him in a panic; Katie O'Callaghan, who has so much enthusiasm for this book, evidenced by all her ideas for marketing it; Robin Bilardello, who fell in love with the story and went through multiple covers in order to get to the best cover possible; and the copy editors who caught all the tiny but crucial details that make this story better.

Chris Lotts and Greta Lindquist, my foreign rights agents. Your sales abroad give me new reasons to travel the world in search of the best bookstores.

Every book needs outside readers before it goes to the professionals. My readers are also my closest friends. Thank you to Rachel Shields for reading on an airplane, texting me in real time about every plot twist, and insisting I rewrite the original ending. I love you to pieces, and not just because we can spend all day texting each other bad jokes or that you taught me the importance of Second Breakfast. Thank you also to Sara Eddie, who not only insists on reading my work but is also my only PNW friend still awake when it's midnight on the East Coast; Liz Murray, who is my biggest cheerleader in McLean and is insistent that she get a first read on the next book; and Julia Epstein, who is quite possibly the kindest, most thoughtful person alive and who always talks me off my ledges. This list wouldn't be complete without Sarah Hardy and Erika George. Through no fault of their own, Sarah and Erika didn't get an early read of this book, but their unconditional love and support has made every step on the way to publication feel like a celebration.

Victoria Sanders, who is not my agent but took notice of the book's announcement all the same and passed it along to two of her clients, May Cobb and Karin Slaughter, who read it and wrote amazing blurbs. I'm equally thankful to Colleen McKeegan, Polly Stewart, and Jenny Milchman for their early reads and blurbs. I admire the stories written by each of these women, and feel so overwhelmed and grateful to have their support for this book.

Savannah Garth, my daughter, who did not play field hockey, but did teach me about TikTok, and Sebastian Garth, my son, who keeps me up to date on all the most recent Gen Z slang, even though I'm still pretty sure "Nay, Reggie" is not a thing. I'm the luckiest person in the world to have you both in my life. You've had a front-seat view of the ups and downs of an "artist's life," so it makes sense that you're both majoring in business. Thank you for teaching me the width and breadth of what it is to love as immensely as I love the two of you.

Jared Garth, for your years of friendship and support.

Phyllis Copeland, my mother, who is a force of nature and one of my best friends. Thank you for making me completely paranoid about home canning. I'll try not to use any more of your life warnings as future murder weapons. Also thank you for being the role model for ignoring other people's expectations and walking my own path.

And Jay Dunn, who not only read this book multiple times but spent countless hours dissecting various plots points with me. Thank you for taking on the full-time job that is me and embracing that job with unlimited love, enthusiasm, and patience. Your unwavering belief in my ability to tell a story inspires me to write better, dig deeper, create outline-adjacent documents, and write in the afternoons. Most of all, thank you for being the person who makes me feel like I've finally come home.

About the Author

JOHANNA COPELAND is a native Oregonian and former corporate attorney. Her writing has been featured in various publications, including the *Washington Post*, *xoJane*, *Stonecoast Review*, and *Literary Mama*. She currently lives in McLean, Virginia, and visits her college-age children as often as they will allow. She has one child still at home who likes frequent walks, chasing balls, and sleeping on the couch while Johanna writes.